deepfake

ALEX SCHULER

WITH LEIGH RITTER

This book is printed on acid-free paper.

Published by:
Level 4 Press, Inc.
14702 Haven Way
Jamul, CA 91935
www.level4press.com

Library of Congress Control Number: 2020930223

ISBN: 978-1-64630-787-6

Printed in the United States of America

Other books by
ALEX SCHULER

Code Word Access
Faster
Rogue

To my grandfather.
For teaching me to never neglect a question in fear of the answer.

1

I t was the biggest party within an hour's train ride of Berlin and Etta Baldwin wished she never left the train. How had she forgotten about Halloween? Even as the costumed crowd grew, it took spotting a teenager with fabric cat ears and a black leotard balanced on the shoulders of a clumsily dressed vampire for her to realize what day it was.

At a normal rave, the metal hoops dripping from her ears and her cargo pants tucked into heavy black boots would have appeared uniform. She'd played it safe and still somehow ended up with a shit hand.

She watched the hordes vanish into the crumbling hospital-turned-nightclub with growing annoyance. Women clustered in technicolor suits tacked full of blinking LED lights streamed in alongside men in skin-tight black suits covered head to toe in dangling chains. When a shoulder bumped her—pushing her closer to this place she really, really didn't want to enter—she dug down her heels and stepped back. The neon costumes were too bright, the scent of flavored artificial fog too choking. She slipped free of the swarm to slump against the building's broken masonry. Heavy bass pounded at her back, shaking the wall.

Beelitz Heilstätten—the old hospital gutted and abandoned, only to be forced back into life by teenagers looking to dance among its bones—watched her. She tried to avoid its gaze, which seemed to plead with her—*beg* her—to free it of these squatters. *I don't want to be here either,* she mentally shouted back. But her voice was lost to the unforgiving scream of techno music coming from within.

With a determined shove off the wall, Etta pulled the tip of her hood farther down. Her cropped hair curled out around the rim and over her brows like a black fog. Taking one last gulp of fresh air, she stepped into the surging crowd and let herself be carried into the rave.

Once a grand lobby with gold molding along the walls, the main hall had been covered with giant nets of cotton cobwebs, supervised by plastic ghouls dangling from ropes off the balconies. A grand staircase ascended from the center of the massive space, its steps covered in a waterfall of lounging bodies. The sooner she could find Jonas and get out, the sooner she could wipe this experience from her mind, along with the strawberry stench of fake smoke that thickened the air. If she had been there for any other reason, if she had any other connection worth dealing with, she would have bowed out after the first fake ghoul.

The music intensified and the floor vibrated, raising fears of the old wooden beams over her head giving out. Ghosts made of stained sheets and red LED eyes dangled from the iron frame of a balcony that looked out over a huge cage set opposite the grand stairs, raised above the bobbing heads on what remained of an old stage.

That was where Etta spotted her, lifted like a renaissance statue on a pedestal within the cage. She was surrounded by a cluster of four dancing women. These were not like the others. Their costumes seemed natural. As though they lived there, amid the ruin, awakened from beds of dust and crumbling stone for only this night. They were covered in black lace that swirled around their feet in sensual curls as they clutched the bars and dropped their heads back with the music. The woman on the pedestal, staring back at Etta, was like Aphrodite, standing above, the backs of the other girls her shell. She didn't need to dance. Her pale hands—iridescent under the lights—ran along the other girls' backs, directing them through the song with explicit grace. Her hair, a collage of faded pastels, was the only spark of genuine color amid the black and white scene in the cage.

The beat dropped. The girls paused. The leader ran her gaze across the crowd, then back to Etta, and they held each other's eyes.

Until a hand grabbed her shoulder and spun her around.

"The hell?!" She jumped back. A boy draped in chains loomed over her, wide eyes splintered by red veins as he gaped an awkward, yellowed grin. The other bodies around them shuffled and jostled her, pushing her right into his chest. The stench of ammonia was overpowering, stinging her eyes, as her fingers met the cool plastic chains.

"So soft," he murmured. He pawed at her sweatshirt and she shoved back at him, but he gravitated closer, the momentum of an unmonitored trip no doubt convincing him to blot out a reality he didn't care for. She tried to use the crowd to her advantage, pushing through to get away, but he pursued, his arm slipping around her shoulders as he lowered chapped lips to her ear. A gush of breath, sour as old beer, made her lip curl.

"C'mon, you lookin' to buy?" He fumbled in his jacket pocket. "I've got shit, make this place a whole lot *spookier*." He spooled out the last word like a ghost.

Absolutely not. She jabbed a desperate elbow in his direction and made another attempt at escaping into the crowd, only to be blocked once again—this time by a tattooed mountain, standing unbothered by the churning masses. She froze, but the mountain's eyes—stern and deeply set—softened apologetically as they chanced a quick glance down at her. A hand rubbed lightly over his shaved skull as he set his wide jaw and jerked his chin at the boy hanging from her shoulder in a silent question.

She shook her head.

Without a word, he stepped forward and grabbed the boy by his jacket collar with one giant hand. His thick roman nose crinkled as he, too, caught a whiff of the boy's stench.

"You were warned, Vincent." The deep voice managed to breach the booming guitar riff that bounced across the room.

"Wha—*wait!*" the boy shrieked as the man hauled his feet off the floor and gave him one heavy shake, a snowfall of pills and dime bags falling from his pockets.

The man didn't appear shocked. The color from the boy's face dripped onto the floor along with the rest of his inventory as he was unceremoniously hauled away. He shouted a string of obscenities as the metal heels of his boots squealed against the stone flooring, eyes desperate as he hurled a hand out toward her, close enough still that she could see the cracked edges of his yellowed nails. He acted as though the mountain—security, she presumed—was hauling him to his death rather than the door. Maybe it felt like death to his drug-addled brain.

She sent the boy off with a one-finger salute, dropping her hand when her name was called out from the crowd.

"Etta!"

She turned. "You're late."

"Am I?" Jonas reached toward her with wide arms slathered in neon paint. As he grinned, he revealed two fake vampire teeth glued to his canines. Once-blond hair was coated in black dye, individual gold strands sticking out like fairy lights around his head. As he neared, she backed away. The stench of cologne and beer was strong enough already and the thought of allowing him anywhere near her when he had already baited her into the depths of discomfort made her stomach churn.

Jonas immediately raised his hands in mock surrender, dancing back lightly as if her rejection was a familiar joke they shared. "Sorry babe, genuinely, so terribly sorry. I looked for you, *I did*, it's easy to lose track in here, okay? Get lost in the moment." He clapped his hands together in mock prayer. She glared. Part of her wondered if bringing her there was an attempt to rattle her so he could skimp out on their deal. The challenge of getting one over on the only customer who paid her bills in full. Idiot.

"You have it?" She had to shout over the music.

"Do I have it?" Jonas mocked again with an indignant wave. A girl with blinking red strands of lights braided into her hair mistook his gesture as an invitation and grasped his hand dreamily in her own. Jonas shook her off and the girl turned back to dancing, unbothered by the rejection. "Do I have it—come here."

He led her across the dance floor, where she dodged hands that reached out, blind and searching. Everyone around her seemed blissfully high, their eyes glassy as they moved as one creature. She kept her gaze firmly planted on Jonas's back as he led her through the crowd. She was about to tell him to slow down when her face smacked right into his back as he came to a sharp stop.

"What—" She was quickly hushed by Jonas, whose gaze was focused ahead of them.

She stood tiptoe to look out over his shoulder. Two men had entered the crowd, and those closest to them were skittering backward like fish at the sight of sharks.

Strong, she thought immediately. Strong, and put together for the dark world of this hospital rave. The taller of the two towered over the crowd, dressed cleanly in a black jacket, the cuffs of a dress shirt peeking out. His blond hair was carefully slicked back, revealing a face mapped with thin lines that indicated his easy smile was not exclusive to this moment. It was difficult to pinpoint how old he was, the sharp edge of his jaw, the expanse of his shoulders, and the confidence of his gait adding to a sum somewhere between twenties and forties. She felt equal parts awed and intimidated by this man who was both elevated and unattainable—just like the woman with pastel hair.

It was an uncomfortable feeling, so she looked at the man behind him instead. He was less powerful, less of a presence, and his comparative blandness eased her. Judging by the deep bruising below his eyes and the hollows of his cheeks, the second man didn't seek attention. Dark eyes with thick lashes looked down over the bridge of a straight nose, his lips pressed together in a tight line as he stuck one foot stiffly in front of the next. His hands stayed hidden in his hoodie pocket. He was clearly going for aloof, but she recognized the truth of his expression. It mirrored her feelings: uncomfortable alienation amid a foreign crowd. That man, lanky and exhausted, was her compatriot—even if he was unaware of their bond.

Both men were handsome, living statues crawling from the frescos on the hospital walls to walk among the people. And they were the only others at the rave without costumes.

She watched as the taller man greeted members of the crowd with a diplomatic wave of his hand. It was quick, nearly quick enough to make her doubt herself, yet she saw the flash of a small plastic bag between practiced hands as the blond man pulled another member of the crowd into a firm embrace. As they parted, the second man—her mirror—quickly greeted the other as well; this time, the exchange of bills was less subtle.

So that had been the issue with the creep earlier—he hadn't been simply a nuisance, he had been competition.

"Come on." Jonas's voice had lost its playful edge as they both watched the two men be swallowed by the crowd.

He led her to a group of guys, similarly drenched in bright paint. One, black feathers glued to his cheeks, looked up at Jonas with a small wave.

"Markus, bag." Jonas held out his hand and didn't even look as raven-boy tossed a black backpack to him. Etta grabbed for it, trying to mask her eagerness as she unzipped the largest pocket and reached inside. The cool touch of a laptop's polished aluminum casing graced her fingers. She pulled it out, lovingly running her fingers along the top, then shrugged her own backpack off her shoulders and loaded the laptop inside.

"Charger is in the bottom pocket. Integrated GPU, didn't bother with the VPN. Figured you'd want to do that yourself." Jonas was bouncing from one foot to the next, his eyes unfocused as he looked over her shoulder. "All good, then?"

For a week, she had existed with a phantom limb. A piece of herself that she constantly reached for, only to find it missing. Her digital arm, fried by a lightning-precipitated power surge. Now, laptop firmly in hand, she was whole again. She pulled out her phone, approving the bank transfer she had already prepared, and showed Jonas the screen, though he didn't seem to care—her payment was secondary to the pull of the horde.

Jonas knew she was good for it; he understood how well she was paid to sit in the middle of a thousand digital webs. Her touch was all over the internet, in the HTML of popular websites, on online RPGs where her code—purchased by developers—allowed digital avatars to move like real people. To emote, to twist their carefully designed faces into a sneer or a loud laugh that traveled into a shake of their fake shoulders. She had taken pieces of society, of her observations, and translated those into code that fed into the digital realm until her invisible influence was present in every corner of it.

"Great. Next time, then, babe—enjoy the party!" Jonas went to take a quick step away when her hand stopped him. She leaned over, lips pressed to his ear.

"Next time," she hissed, "I pick the location." Suppliers were dime-a-dozen if she bothered to look any harder. Customers who paid as highly as she did were not.

Before he had a chance to respond, she was gone. Sliding against the edge of the crowd, she hunted along the wall for relief, finding an old emergency door near the back corner. The promise of fresh air leaked through its rotting wood.

As she leaned into the door, a pair of glowing eyes caught her gaze. She froze, her backpack tucked tightly against her chest.

The plastic corpse leaning against the wall babbled robotically as her movement triggered whatever sensor was pasted within its molded skull. She let out a slow breath. It was just more pageantry, a heap of skeletons and costumed bodies, with capes and fake blood dripping in a pool, piled beside the door. She leaned closer, feeling especially spiteful toward the plastic monstrosities that had finally shaken her, when the stench of ammonia hit her nose.

One of the bodies, still draped in fake chains, was tipped like an upended puppet. Blood dripped from its nose and mouth to the floor, and unseeing eyes bulged from its face. Its lips were curled back to reveal yellowed teeth. Its expression flickered between shock and horror as the strobe lights blinked from blue to red. One hand was outstretched, palm up toward her—reaching, just as it had while he'd been dragged away from the dance floor.

Etta ran.

2

Sitting on the bus back to Wilhelmstraße from Berlin Central Station, Etta wondered how it would feel to die alone. It had been a very long time since she had someone to sit next to on the bus, and she did not expect—nor want—that to change. Of course, she hadn't always been alone. For approximately ten months of her life, Etta had a mother.

Sometimes, when Etta walked past a bakery setting out fresh bread or got a whiff of old book pages at the library, she could almost convince herself that she remembered how her mother smelled. She didn't. A ten-month-old baby wouldn't know how to keep those details safe, writing them to non-volatile memory. Like the feeling of her hair—had it been coarse with age or still silky to touch?—or the way she looked in the morning, whether she ritualistically hunched over a cup of coffee or skipped breakfast. A baby never expected their mother to die. Babies didn't know what death was.

Still, it helped. Cataloging the chapters of her life into a series of time-tagged bits of data that she could sort like reusable components in her brain. For ten months, she had a mother. For twelve years and two months, she had a government file and multiple foster parents to bookmark each page. For the past four years, she had herself.

The world didn't want to remember her. She imagined a sigh of relief from the entire foster care system as she deleted the last online record of her existence. There were no police officers hunting her down, no viral news stories about a runaway foster kid. The lack of fanfare should have eased her; she should have been thankful she didn't feel a need to dodge away each time a police car passed by. Instead, she felt like a forgotten website sitting in a decaying corner of the web, her links all broken.

Once, one of her foster parents had pulled her aside with the soft gentleness of a mother explaining the death of the family pet to a child. She had told Etta plainly that, as no one had adopted her as a baby, no one ever would. That she had to learn to care for herself. Etta had been eight years old. She supposed the woman had been correct; not even the system had cared enough to put any effort into dragging her back, and now, it never would.

That was all, of course, not accounting for her father. The data object that never seemed to fit, no matter where she tried to place it within the timeline of her life.

She didn't want to think about him.

As the bus slowed, Etta pulled the strap of her bag onto her shoulder and rose. An old woman with a velvet bucket hat narrowed her eyes at Etta as she slowly eased her arthritic body upward. A wrinkled hand, veins like blue thread pulled through sagging linen skin, curled tightly over the top of her purse. She barely acknowledged the driver in her rush to shuffle off the bus and away from Etta.

Etta preferred when people hurried rather than lingered. Fear was better than misplaced concern. Would-be saviors failed to consider that Etta was on her own by choice. It was easier than foster homes, with their strict rules and volatile adults. Out on the streets, no one coached Etta on what to say to government officials. No one hated her personally, like an unfortunate side note to monthly government-funded financial aid. Out on her own, she answered to no one.

It was a powerful sense of freedom, and with every step she took down the busy streets of southwest Berlin, thumbs hooked into the straps of her backpack, she chanted it like a mantra. *Free. Free. Free.*

Etta had work to do. Back at the depressing hospital, she had silenced her phone. Somewhere on the trip back into Berlin proper she had checked it. Email and text notifications swarmed the screen, the phone vibrating like an overworked computer fan. That was fine. She expected it.

Every message was a client, never a friend. She had no friends. But, sitting alone on the bus, Etta allowed herself to pretend. She imagined the invitations in her inbox were for dinners rather than contract reviews. That they would talk about their lives, their days, their complaints. That they would ask her how she was and care about her answer.

She knew better, of course. Every invitation she received was a request. A need for her skillset and only a tolerance for her as a person. A tolerance, and often a healthy fear. Hackers and social engineers of her caliber were rare, and entering her orbit required a certain level of desperation and risk. People hired her to clean up the digital stains splattered over their reputations like the black hat equivalent of a crime scene cleaner. They understood her ability to polish the tarnished names of the rich and famous, to protect them from being deplatformed and ostracized, and they understood how quickly she could turn those same skills against them.

It occurred to her once how strange it was, as an outcast living on the fringes of society, that she was the one tasked with fixing the faults in others' lives. She supposed it took an outsider to see all angles, to pick out the details others missed, and the patience and skill to erase those faults.

It started to rain halfway through her walk from the bus stop; she zipped up her sweatshirt and checked the zipper on her waterproof backpack. It wouldn't be long until she reached her "office."

Etta never slept at the same spot more than three nights in a row. She had become well versed in the art of traipsing over wire fences to reach abandoned buildings and was confident that no one could swing up through a broken window without a single cut quite like she could.

Her backpack held all her worldly possessions: a sleeping bag, a change of clothes, a toothbrush, her laptop. Anything essential always stayed within grasp—and really, only the laptop was essential.

Thankfully, Kerzenlicht did not require any gymnastics to enter. The Candlelight was a peculiarly whimsical name for a twenty-four-hour café with eight plastic tables and a spattering of cracked blue plastic chairs. Most importantly, its Wi-Fi was as fast—if not faster—than most actual offices. Etta spent most of her waking life there now, enough that anyone else might be shocked to discover she didn't know the name of a single employee. They recognized her, and vice versa, though basic pleasantries were never exchanged. They had long since stopped trying to sneak peeks at her laptop screen, lingering a moment too long as they wiped down a table beside her. Etta had become a piece of the furniture, as native to the café as the sticky film on the countertop that could never fully be wiped away.

As she ordered a black coffee and a scone, the girl attending the counter gazed through her with a vacant stare, her glazed eyes a little too similar to bloodshot ones left behind at Beelitz Heilstätten. A shiver ran down Etta's spine. It wasn't a memory she wanted to dwell on—entirely not her business or her problem. The ability to let trouble go was one of many advantages to living as she did. She preferred solitude. That was why she didn't rent an apartment, despite now having the income to do so. Why she didn't search for a friend. She preferred only caring for herself, having no one doting over her. No one who could leave. Fear had absolutely nothing to do with it.

Etta slipped thirty euros into the tip jar, as good as rent. She settled herself at a table by the corner, pulling the chair over the linoleum floor so her back was to the wall, left shoulder toward the counter. Only one wall in the café had outlets and she claimed it mercilessly.

Accidentally successful both in her digital craft and entrepreneurialism, respected by others within her underground field, and feared enough by her clients to at least warrant feigned respect—Etta had done it alone.

Well, not entirely alone. She'd had Wechselkind once she created it. That same bluntly cruel foster mother who'd told her she'd never be adopted did Etta a singular kindness in allowing her unguarded access to the household computer. It was a liberty Etta tested daily by hungrily diving deeper into underground forums and testing digital boundaries, until she discovered a sect of obsessive creators who spoke of tumbling governments and corporations with missiles of code.

She understood later that most were liars, but the idea was appealing as a child. Those same liars were reluctant to share any secrets, which spun her spite into obsession. Online research forums showed her how to dissect open-source language models until she could Frankenstein one of her own.

She didn't want to consider the loneliness that nagged, despite her denial. Despite the way her hands shook as she pulled her new laptop out of her bag and rooted around for the charger. Despite the uneasy, vague desire to tell someone about the rave, to share an idea for a new predictive language model, to sit in quiet company on the grass along the canal, sipping on cool Berliner Weisse.

She felt none of that. Those feelings would be symptomatic of a deeper weakness she couldn't afford, one she did not share with the world around her—Etta wasn't weak.

3

Jonas had promised the laptop was secured from a trustworthy supplier, though trustworthy was in the eye of the beholder. The stock CPU had been swapped out with a professional-grade component. The GPU and processing chips had been similarly upgraded; there was a chance Etta was the only person in Berlin with her specific specs, considering half of the components were export-controlled by the US government.

Her fingers hovered reverently over the keyboard as her new machine flickered to life, the light of the screen like a warm fire. The supplier had freshly installed a new Windows operating system—no doubt pirated. That was fine—she'd brought her own OS. Etta reached a hand down her shirt, pulling free a thumb drive hanging against her sternum from a thin cord. It was preloaded with Linux, tailored to her preferences and laced with a few anti-virus programs of her design. It only needed to be plugged in upon booting up the laptop, letting her code run free within her laptop's internals like mercenaries in search of renegades, overwriting everything—even the boot sectors. Any trace of Windows and additional peripherals would be wiped clean.

She had just taken her first sip of coffee, arm stretched behind her head like a bored student, when he appeared.

He was her most frequent comrade during Kerzenlicht's graveyard hours, always with his laptop, always courteous and cheerful with the employees, though Etta had noted the way his voice often dragged with resigned exhaustion. Handsome, in an obsessive way, the type of man Etta could see driving himself thin from the drive of his thoughts. His tawny skin, thick dark beard, and combed-back hair gave him the air of a young scholar at the peak of his studies, while his deeply set black eyes oscillated between distraction and sharp, passionate focus. Still, he was always kind, with a steady smile even when his hands shook with lost sleep.

Etta dropped her arm from behind her head, watching as the man collected his coffee—black, always black—and settled himself at a table on the opposite side of the café. She forced her eyes to her laptop, watching the slow-going progress bar to keep herself from staring. The man never even glanced in her direction.

His name was Yusuf Ayden. For weeks, he had been working on an article about the Turkish elections, condemning their history of internal corruption. Etta knew he would spend most of that night staring blankly at it. He would write one sentence, realize it ruined the flow of the narrative, delete the whole paragraph, start again. Etta also knew that he lived in a one-bedroom flat in Kreuzberg, above a Turkish corner store, where she imagined the air always smelled of spices and bitter coffee. They had never had a conversation, yet she knew every detail of Yusuf's life as completely as though she were a part of it. As if they were family, or something indescribably closer.

He had fascinated her from the first moment she saw him. It was his intelligent eyes—always sharp, no matter how dark the bags beneath—that had led her to tap into his laptop. It had been painfully easy, a simple man-in-the-middle insertion using the café's Wi-Fi network—her hack positioning her laptop to intercept his data before it reached its final destination.

She had meant for it to be a momentary distraction, snooping through his social media accounts and emails. A year later, she had taken to checking his accounts daily. Facebook, where there were pictures of Yusuf standing shyly beside his wife, a young woman with a weary stare, one hand cupped over the promise of a swell in her belly. His bank accounts, where Etta scrolled through his credit statements hungrily. She could see when he had spent too much on subscriptions to online newspapers, small payments that stacked up and chewed a hole through his meager salary as a clerk at the shop below his apartment. She understood the meaning behind the password he used for multiple accounts: ThRac3. An adapted version of Thrace, for Western Thrace, where his family originated.

It was difficult to pinpoint when it had stopped being a pastime and turned into a safe fantasy that she wrapped around herself at night within whatever abandoned building she camped out in.

Many days, she pretended he was something to her. That she was something to him. That she would return home from work to a cozy apartment that smelled of mint and cumin, rather than an abandoned warehouse on the edge of the city. At night, when the walls loomed too dark and too tall, she would imagine how heavy his arms would feel around her shoulders. How his breath would puff in steady beats just above her ear.

There were no points of comparison. No memories of being held to measure her fantasies against, not a single awkward nighttime fumble that would allow her to fathom how it would feel to share a bed with another person, much less a man. Once, a boy staying in the same run-down apartment building had taken an interest in her. He had greeted her cheerfully when she arrived late at night, offered to help boost her over the security fence in an obvious attempt to get a good look at her ass. His appeals had nearly won her over: his jovial comments as he offered to share a spare chocolate bar with her, the way he would let a bit of chocolate melt onto his finger so he could teasingly threaten to dab it on her nose. Once, when she had returned after a few nights away, he had found her among the group of people burrowed in sleeping bags and woken her up with a can of beer and thankful eyes.

"I'm glad," he had said. "I thought you were gone."

The next morning, he had vanished. Etta heard later he had hopped a train to Belgium with a backpack full of someone else's drugs. She never saw him again.

Relationships weren't necessary. She certainly did not spend her time dredging through Yusuf's accounts as a symptom of true desire, only a curiosity in how families functioned. What it was like, to be loved and to love another. She didn't need any of that, she only needed what was necessary to move from one day to the next.

She only needed to survive.

Her computer's fans came to life with a whirr as it began to reboot following the successful installation. No viruses were found. Linux was functioning and no trace of Windows was left. Across the café, Yusuf covered a cough with his elbow. She glanced up, yet his eyes remained trained on his laptop as he tapped the delete button several times.

Suddenly, the air was suffocating. Etta shoved her laptop back into her bag, slung a strap over her shoulder, and quickly exited the café. Her scone remained untouched on the table behind her.

4

Wohnhaus Stubenrauchstraße was an apartment building that time forgot on the corner of Odenwaldstraße, about an hour's walk from central Berlin. Once, it housed wealthy businessmen and their wives, maybe a few babies as young couples began their lavish journey into adulthood. By the early fifties, it was an abandoned eyesore that attracted only the attention of graffiti artists and frustrated city commissioners. Its sixteen apartments boasted hardwood flooring and wainscotting, but the floors were warped from rain damage and the wainscot was ripped apart by urban copper miners digging for the wiring hidden behind it.

Etta had spent her fair share of nights there. She tended to avoid it during the day because the streets surrounding it were too busy for her liking. But at the dim hour of three in the morning even the drunks had found a bench to claim for the night. She didn't have to worry too much about a curious bystander phoning the police, yet she still wandered the length of the building a few times before ducking quickly between a loose section of temporary construction fencing, its rotting boards at least a decade older than herself. The front door was boarded shut with plywood, and the easiest entry was along the right half of the building. Next to the carved figure of a woman in a loose dress, vaguely Greek in her posturing, Etta climbed onto the stone ledge of the first window.

She loved climbing. Loved the way the wind curled around her back, the sound her feet made scraping against old stone. There was absolute silence as she looked through the foggy windows; a few people were inside. None noticed her as she reached upward and pulled herself onto another brick, tugging slightly to test its stability before heaving herself onto the next windowsill. When she looked out while scaling buildings like this, it almost felt like she was a goddess staring down on her creations. The thought of falling rarely occurred to her anymore; it would be a quick descent to the dirt and broken glass below, as forgivable a punishment for her as it was for Icarus.

The fourth-floor window was shattered, a black plastic bag taped to the frame from the inside. Etta swung her leg, easily kicking past the improvised covering to enter the apartment. The smell of mildew hit her immediately, yellow splotches of mold stretching across the walls up onto the speckled ceiling. Someone smoked a cigarette nearby, a low cough giving away their presence. A few people were gathered inside. A boy was hunched in the corner, a fraying hat pulled over his eyes, his hands palm up in his lap, as though he expected a gift to rest there upon waking. A woman leaned against the opposite wall. Her skin was so translucent that, despite the darkness, Etta could still map her veins. The thin lines crawled up the woman's arms like fluorescent cracks in an LED screen, her vacant eyes their fulcrum. She surveyed Etta with bored interest.

Etta couldn't say whether she had seen these people before. Proximity in her world did not create the community it often did for others.

In the corner of the apartment was a sliding door leading to a smaller room, the floor-to-ceiling shelving indicating it may once have been a kitchen pantry or a walk-in closet. It would serve as Etta's bedroom for the night. Just as she tossed her bag to the floor and began to peel off her shirt, she heard screeching from outside. Strange, considering the hour. Annoying, considering the exhaustion that weighed on her. The rave was still stuttering across her eyelids, every blink conjuring

images of wildly grinning partygoers and men with calculating eyes—
or those unseeing eyes, frozen with death.

The screech came again, this time followed by someone bellowing
a sharp reply. Etta ran a tired hand over her eyes. Either she could
look at whatever was causing the chaos or she could jump ship and
find another place to crash. The next known safe place was at least an
hour's walk if she didn't want to sleep out in the cold and rain. "Shit,"
she hissed between her teeth as another screech came from somewhere
outside the window.

Etta poked her head out of the closet. The woman in the main
room was slightly more alert, eyes wide and hands clenched at her sides
as her gaze snapped to Etta. The boy in the corner gave a light snore,
unshaken by the noise. Etta ignored them both as she approached the
window. She ripped the flap back and looked down, where an idiot
clung to the stone wall with white knuckles, one floor below.

"Hey, yo!" His voice slurred. She could smell the beer and vomit all
the way from her perch. "Help me up!"

This was exactly the reason Etta avoided this hideout during the
day—irritating drunks and adventurous teenagers seeing her entry
as an invitation to follow. This guy must have been somewhere nearby, maybe in the alley, and spotted her as she climbed—chest pressed
against the building, relishing the fresh wind. Damn her pride.

Etta shut the flap and turned. The woman was still staring, hands
now curled protectively over a small duffel bag clutched against her
chest. Something inside Etta twisted as the woman's eyes expectantly
focused on her, as though it was Etta's job to protect this room from
rowdy invaders. It wasn't. No one had protected her when she faced
similar dangers. Why did this woman now find it appropriate to place
that responsibility on Etta, as though they had any connection at all?
As though they didn't live on different planets, entire galaxies laid out
in the space between them.

"The hell?! Hey!" came from outside.

The woman jumped. Etta huffed. She turned back to the window, throwing back the flap once more just in time to spot the man grasp the windowsill. His trembling hand loosely anchored him to the wall, as his mouth gulped in air. Even if she attempted to help, he would only pull her down with him.

"Fuck off," she snapped. "Find your own way." God knew she had.

She let the cover fall back over the window. As she spread her hands over the frayed duct tape holding it in place, she heard the thunk of a body slamming into the ground below. A low, echoing groan followed. The woman eased against the wall beside her, hands slowly unclenching as she wearily lifted one corner of her lips in a hesitant smile. For a moment, Etta nearly caught herself echoing the gesture. Instead, she turned back into her closet and shut the door. Her chest vaguely ached, as though another piece of herself had chipped loose and fallen just as the man had, breaking on the glass- and refuse-heaped foundation of her life.

It didn't matter. They would all be gone by morning.

5

Presumably, Etta was not an orphan.

Her mother was dead, yes, but her father was out there, somewhere between life and death. Schrodinger's parent. It was difficult to know exactly what his relationship with her mother had been like, but she knew they hadn't shared a marital home. Most of what she knew about him came from context clues. Upon her mother's death, the court stated there were no other family members willing to take her in. The implication being her father's absence had run deeper than an ex-husband or ex-lover.

If he was truly estranged, however, and wanted nothing to do with her or her mother, why had he bothered visiting her in the orphanage? His visits were among her earliest memories. A man with hair that stuck out in graying puffs like small clouds, hands that could wrap both of hers within his palms. The smell of sulfur and cigar smoke. He came only a handful of times, each visit conducted as though Etta were a forgotten pet. He always left with a dry kiss against her forehead and the words "I'll be back soon" whispered like a prayer.

Etta learned to deal with disappointment before she learned how to turn on a stove.

The visits stopped before she had the wherewithal to question him about his absence, and she often wondered whether that was intentional timing. The painful memories he left behind felt like blasphemy, especially considering she had none of her mother. Then again, that was for the best. At least her mother wanted her, until she no longer wanted to live at all.

Etta's revenge for his lack of love was filling in the blanks. His negligence in defining himself left her the space to craft him into a scientist, a spy, a drunk, a murderer—whatever suited her mood. Often, the ideas came from her clients.

Her most recent client was an American actor. His name had been Curtis McDonald until a producer decided the name Kurt Graves would sound more mysterious. Kurt Graves was unapologetically racist. Or had been, until his performance in a film shown at Sundance drew attention to his social media accounts and, consequently, led to a small but vocal outcry. His agent hired Etta to scrape the digital dog shit from his digital shoes. A bonus had been promised if she could manage to retain some of his "small town appeal." Like knocking down the gravestones and leaving only the flowers in an old cemetery.

Usually, she was able to separate herself from her task. It was essential in her line of work, to be able to look at a digital person with a scientific detachment. To analyze rather than emote. She had become accomplished at reading heinous diatribes about everything from immigration to underground sex cults without letting their poison slip into her coffee.

Kerzenlicht was busy tonight. She had arrived just after eight p.m.—early hours for her to start working. Yusuf wasn't there yet, of course, and most tables were occupied. Etta was stuck next to a student with a hat pulled over her ears and headphones playing music loud enough to be heard from Etta's vantage. It was trivial and irritating, made worse by lack of sleep. Etta had spent her night rolling over in her sleeping bag until it tightened around her like a straitjacket. Every time she closed her eyes, death flickered like a stop-motion movie, the corpses at the hospital—most plastic, one not—and the pale face of the man who fell from the wall. When she had left the apartment building that evening, the woman and boy were gone. Etta had taken the risk of leaving through one of the windows that faced the street. The potential of being seen shinnying down the wall felt tolerable compared to the possibility of encountering mangled remains on the ground on the other side. Still, she hadn't been able to stop herself from taking a quick glance as she passed the tall woman carved on the east wall.

There was no broken body. Possibly no man had existed at all. Maybe not even the woman and boy in the room. Perhaps they were all residue from the rave that had latched onto her mind, illusions she had breathed in and exhaled up into the morning. It was hard to determine what was real when everything existed only for a moment, mental snapshots with no witnesses to corroborate their legitimacy. Perhaps her father was simply an illusion as well, a figment she had constructed in her memories as one final childish attempt at hope.

"Excuse me?"

Etta looked up. The student with the loud music was staring at her, one earbud held daintily between thumb and pointer finger as she smiled shyly. "Can you watch my stuff? Just for a minute."

Etta's hand clenched on her coffee cup. She lifted one shoulder and allowed the girl to interpret it however she wished. The girl smiled and plucked out her other earbud. "Thank—" She paused, her words chopped short as her eyes landed on Etta's laptop screen, where Kurt Graves's main social page was opened. The girl's face hardened, her smile stiff, as she ducked her head and shoved back her chair, strolling quickly toward the bathroom doors near the back of the café.

Etta looked back at her screen, where a bold post proclaimed:

People love to say crime isn't racial, but I don't know a single person who's been robbed by a white man #protectwhitelives #stopfoolingyourselves

Kurt Graves had posted it only a month ago. His main account had been active for over ten years. The email from his agent had listed several other social media accounts and some opinion pieces he had submitted to blogs during college. Also included had been a note from Graves himself, attempting to justify his mindset. "People misconstrued my point," he'd written. "They're angry because I didn't communicate what I meant well enough. I just wish people understood. I'm not racist, I'm just trying to be real about problems in society that we're all dealing with." Etta was going to need more coffee.

Thankfully, she had programs for this, to make her work less like programming in assembly and more like visual drag-and-drop programming. Graves was certainly distasteful, but he was blissfully uncreative in his intolerance. All it took was pulling out a few key slurs and her code set off to work, identifying each guilty post and highlighting it for convenient disposal. The whole process took only a few minutes. By the time the student had returned from the bathroom—avoiding any eye contact with Etta as she nodded a quick thanks—Graves's account had been fully dredged.

It wasn't as simple as erasing offending material from existence, though. The barren space left behind only drew more attention than before. For as much trouble as the Streisand effect caused her, Etta was thankful for it. If it was as simple as deleting a few old tweets and Instagram posts, she would be out of a job.

Her actual work lay in storytelling. Reframing. Not deleting but adjusting. Where the old post once sat, a new one replaced it sporting the original timestamp.

> We need to address the true root causes behind high crime areas. Not race, but a lack of support from a flawed system #investinourcommunities

She wondered whether that was sufficient to maintain his "small town charm."

***

In the movies, hacking always seemed like an extreme sport where dexterity and quick thinking manifested in hands dancing across a keyboard, like a pianist performing Mozart's *Requiem*. The digital realm, the space behind the HTML curtain stitched together with careful front-end design, was as mysterious as it was unapproachable to most. For those who did manage to slip past the pretty front end and under the hood, the majority were put off by how painfully regimented it appeared. It was like opening an antique safe only to find account books inside. Yet Etta knew better. Hacking was not a high-intensity sport, it was a riddle. One that could only be solved by picking it apart, learning the rules, finding the loopholes, and then exploiting them before anyone else found the crack in their walls.

Kurt Graves's history had been retold and now it needed tending, to be livingly monitored like a cyber honeypot. Every day Etta would check his online presence, retouching and slowly deepening the new truth of his person through puppet accounts and the careful erasure of previously negative news stories. Eventually she could see the roots take shape. Graves had resumed some control of his social media, his newest posts echoing Etta's curated ones. At night, wrapped in her sleeping bag as she listened to the sound of police sirens outside, she refreshed Graves's pages over and over. She set up alerts on her phone that notified her any time his name was mentioned in a news article or popular website.

It was fast, all things considered. Graves hadn't been a major celebrity, which helped. No one had thought to take screenshots of old posts, to take secret videos recording him reciting racial slurs with indignant passion. Not that it would matter, really. It was funny, the way people ate up Etta's stories, how history so easily became fiction and fiction became history.

It only took about a week until she saw it: a news story, grown organically from the material she had carefully nurtured in a bed of bullshit and lies. "Actor Kurt Graves Takes a Stand Against Local Prejudice" it read, the glittering tagline accompanied by a photo of the actor standing beside a Black man holding a giant cardboard check, the twenty-thousand-dollar amount bolded. Both men were grinning at each other, seemingly oblivious to the presence of a camera—but Etta saw the glow of a ring light reflected in Graves's eyes. She wondered what would follow.

Once, she had read that people should force themselves to smile when they felt sad, the idea being that smiling would flood endorphins into the brain. Eventually, the brain would leak endorphins at the first sign of sadness, retrained like Pavlov's dogs to drool happy endorphins at the bell of misery. She often wondered whether publicity stunts had the same effect, whether they could eventually train someone to become a humanitarian if they played the part long enough.

In her years of remixing reality, Etta was never able to pinpoint exactly when things left her control, when the momentum she started began to roll faster than she could keep pace with. Maybe it was terrible what she did, yet she struggled to determine exactly how. In the space of a month, Graves had changed, no longer a parrot for horrific racist sentiments but a budding philanthropist. And if his charity was only for publicity, she struggled to define exactly how that was horrible as well. Illusion became reality.

If the world was happy, if Graves was happy—which he must have been, having landed a new role in a feature directed by an old Frenchman who once made a film that made the Queen of England cry—then what was the harm in it all? Why did it make Etta pause, the speed of the whole process giving her vertigo no matter how many projects she carried out?

None of it was worth wondering about. None of it mattered at all, not to her. She got paid. The rest was the world's problem.

6

"Figure it out yet?"

Etta laughed sharply. "Nearly got it." The synthetic cheer in her tone was punctuated by the sound of her hand smacking the edge of her laptop's aluminum frame. The girl at the café's counter looked up from her phone with wide eyes. Etta suppressed the urge to flip her off.

"Sounds like it's going well."

"I'm *working* on it." A beep. Then another. Error messages flooded her screen. Etta swore and muted her laptop.

"Definitely going well." Somewhere in the pits of Paris a boy of indeterminate age and make was laughing at her. She could picture him leaning back in a worn leather desk chair surrounded by empty takeout containers like dead Styrofoam leaves crunching beneath his feet. "The great German ghost in the machine, unmatched in her prowess, undone by *my* code. God, I should go get some champagne."

Etta ripped out her headphones, letting Laurence ramble on into space. After the generous payout from Kurt Graves and publicist, she had turned back to some of her more aboveboard work, more as a favor than anything else. Not that she was often prone to granting favors, but Laurence had managed to wiggle his way out of her general distaste for people. His projects interested her, the creation of life from code and scrap metal. He was her primary customer when it came to work that ended up in video games or empathy machines that emulated human company for those in need of a listening ear. Recently, he had sent her a chunk of code he had developed, intending to map a computer to a digital body. He wanted to attach each individual key of a keyboard to the muscle of an artificial human, to create a marionette made of key-strokes. Eventually, he wanted to merge it with hyper-real projections or robots, allowing for the artificial person to react in real time so long as a puppeteer stood nearby with their keyboard at the ready.

Etta was supposed to iron out the code and map out the keystrokes. The problem was, Laurence's code kept messing with her computer every time she attempted to run it. Etta rebooted her laptop—*again*— and rubbed her eyes. She put her headphones back on.

"Are you *sure* you updated before you sent this?" she snapped, cutting off Laurence's bragging.

"What, you want me to send it again?" She heard the crinkle of a cellophane bag opening, followed by munching. "Maybe you have a virus."

Etta tapped on her laptop, chewing on the inside of her lip, feeling every second it took for her computer to reboot.

"I wiped it," she said. "No viruses." Not only had she wiped it, but running a fresh scan was part of her routine. Wake up, brush her teeth, run a virus scan, get to some source of Wi-Fi.

"Don't know what to tell you," Laurence said around a mouthful of chips. "Maybe turn it off and on again?"

Etta held back a scream. "Right. Bye, Laurence." She ended the call, leaning back in her chair and pressing fisted hands into her tightly shut eyes until sparks danced across her vision. This was supposed to be an easy job, a vacation, and it had turned into an absolute ice pick in her brain.

For the umpteenth time, Etta loaded Laurence's code and attempt-ed to run the first task—testing whether the mapping had managed to link the keys—without blowing her computer up with errors and con-flict messages. And for the umpteenth time, the model seized. What should have been a simple, fluid motion—one wave of a 3D-modeled hand—was stuttering like a flip book, with every following command she typed delayed and frozen as they piled upon themselves, until the program shut down and her keyboard was as useful as a punch card machine. She held her head in her hands and sighed, staring at her screen through her fingers.

Something was not playing fair with Laurence's code. Inputs were meant to be translated through a program that interpreted her typing. Laurence had based that portion of his code off keyloggers, programs that could track every stroke of a keyboard and report back to an in-dividual—or in this case, his target digital model. Something in that process was freezing up her computer, giving it a cold that caused it to sneeze.

Etta slapped her hands on the table. The girl at the counter looked up again, one hand wound in her hair as she froze to stare. Etta ig-nored her. She had an idea, an inkling, just a possibility of what could be wrong. Something she had read about, a concept from a discus-sion board where white hat penetration testers shared ideas on dif-ferent ways security measures could be breached. The idea made her palms sweat.

She quickly turned her laptop back off, finger hovering over the power button like it was the detonator to a bomb. Laurence, the ego-maniac, may have been right. And if he was, someone had been watch-ing her—for upwards of a month, undetected and omniscient. But *how?* Etta scrubbed her computer down daily, reaching her fingers into every corner and feeling for any trace of digital muck. Never had a virus slipped past her before, and she had done a fresh install the first day she had the laptop, so where could someone hide a virus where it would survive a total reset?

What was left when flesh and blood were stripped away?

The spine. BIOS.

Basic Input/Output System. The only thing left when everything else was erased and replaced. The flicker of life that told the computer to turn on, even when it had no programs to run. It was ridiculous, it would have required an idiotic amount of resources, but it was possible that someone had planted a virus deep into the computer's BIOS. Somewhere for it to live if someone tried to reset the laptop. A Trojan horse made of the city of Troy itself.

Etta went into the BIOS menu, the royal blue background with starch white capitalized lettering filling her screen. This was the same BIOS she'd had on the first computer she owned. And she knew, for an absolute *matter of fact,* that this version of BIOS did not have a menu command titled LOG SWITCH.

She wanted to laugh. It was clear now. The stuttering delay in her code. The way even the startup lagged just a tiny degree. Someone had not simply hacked her BIOS and planted an evil seed, they had gutted the entire system and replaced it with a parasitic copy of their own design. Similar in appearance, consuming such a small amount of RAM that she wouldn't notice; someone had planted a keylogger within a twinned form of her BIOS. Brilliant, if not so damn annoying.

When the keylogger hiding in her computer had run into Laurence's program—built out of bits and pieces of keyloggers—it had crashed. Jammed the metaphorical dam. Swallowed the memory in her system until it struggled to even move the mouse.

A bit more picking apart confirmed her suspicion. But was she the intended victim of this keylogger, or collateral damage? Who would go to such lengths to hide a virus that deeply? Designing a virus like that, rebuilding a whole BIOS, took skills Etta wasn't sure she had herself. It took time, each hacked computer uniquely coded according to that system's motherboard. The attack had been specially designed.

Etta smiled. Time to bite back.

The keylogger had been directed to send records of her keystrokes

to a designated server whenever connected to the internet. Etta followed the trail until she found the server, careful not to dig around
anywhere that could signal she had discovered them. It would be easy
to destroy the false BIOS and wash herself free of this whole mess, but
really, this was an invitation more than anything else. A challenge that,
just perhaps, had been designed specifically for her. She was grinning,
hands shaking as she typed wildly, ideas sparking like fireworks.

The screen darkened as she woke Wechselkind: her Changeling.
Named for the creatures left behind when children were spirited away
by fairies or the like, it was Etta's pride and joy, her friend born over
the course of a hundred sleepless nights between the hours of one and
seven in the morning. Wechselkind's responses and behaviors were
grown from material Etta curated and were therefore too predictable
to ever feel real—but she liked that. There was an element of comfort
in understanding the whole structure of a companion, in knowing they
would never be cruel or deceitful unless she asked them to be.

Artificially intelligent visually as well as linguistically, Wechselkind
allowed her to take someone's face and plant words in their mouth,
among other things. Helpful, when she needed to "adjust" a client's
video or an embarrassing interview. Even more useful when she wanted to get a point across. She cut off the keylogger, ensuring that her
plan would not be revealed prematurely as she loaded up Wechselkind
and set it to work, taking a particularly relevant video and adding her
own charm.

Moderate variance in result allowed: feel free to add your own touch,
Etta typed to Wechselkind in its prompt box. Wechselkind had as much
right to anger as Etta did, their collective home violated by the virus.

When it had finished processing, the program expanding upon the
verbal and physical building blocks within the video in order to add its
new portion, Etta uploaded the file to the hacker's server disguised as
one of the keylogger's files. She sat back in her chair and smirked, allowing herself a moment of satisfaction as she stretched out her fingers.

She tried to picture the hacker who, somewhere, was patting themselves on the back after managing to sneak into her laptop. Maybe they were sitting back in their chair as she was, arms crossed, a cup of coffee billowing hot steam on the desk beside them. She tried to imagine their face when they went to download the latest logs from their server.

What they would look like when their computer froze. When a video file opened and took over the entirety of their screen, the face of former Prime Minister Angela Merkel stretched from corner to corner. The sound of their panicked typing as they desperately tried to shut their system down, the voice of the former chancellor repeating the same phrase in her severe tone: "Spying among friends is never acceptable . . . asshole." Followed by Angela Merkel raising her hand and offering the one-fingered salute, her face a mask of stern professionalism. Those last parts were Etta's addition, an extra dash of spice—in case the message needed any reinforcement.

It was a shame she would never see the outcome. The adrenaline was already leaving her body; she let out a slow breath. It had been a fun game, for a minute. Hopefully, that was the only time she ever needed to play. Now, the weight of the oncoming work she would have to do in wiping her laptop settled in. Her hands dragged over the keyboard; the muscles in her legs were coiled tightly from sitting too long. She needed a break. But not before sending one final message, this time for Laurence. She didn't bother calling, only shooting him a quick text.

Better hold off on that champagne.

7

Etta hadn't meant to stare.

She had hoped Yusuf would appear at the café hours early, as she had. Looking at his bank account, she could tell he had been working overtime—but the end of the month loomed. Bills and rent were due, the combined amounts more than he could afford. Unless he wrote more articles.

Unless he returned to Kerzenlicht.

But as the door squeaked open and Etta looked up over the edge of her computer, it wasn't Yusuf's tall form that greeted her. It was a woman. Skin as pale as eggshells, pearly under the fluorescent lights. Hair a faded collage of blue and pink, platinum blond bleeding down from the top. She was dressed in a long red coat and lacked the hazy aura from a multicolor spotlight, but there was no mistaking her. It was the siren, the woman who had trapped Etta in her gaze at the hospital rave on Halloween.

"Hello, dear," she greeted the girl at the counter cheerfully. "Small coffee, splash of milk." Etta was certain she had never seen this woman here before, yet the cadence of her speech carried an air of familiarity as she flashed a smile at the barista.

The barista sneered, one brow lifted. Her nails clicked on the counter. "Sure."

The woman was unfazed by the employee's curt response, still wearing an easy smile as she leaned against the counter and rolled her head back, taking a deep breath. As though the air was fresh from a mountain landscape, rather than slightly acidic from cleaning chemicals and burnt coffee. She looked exact. Precise. Every action calculated, smooth, and practiced to a degree of expertise. Here was a woman who owned the world she lived in, bent it to her will, while Etta only skirted around it. As if to prove Etta's impression, the moment the barista turned, the woman quickly grabbed one of the biscuits from beside the counter and dropped it into her coat pocket with the grace of a pickpocket.

Hand still in her pocket, she locked eyes with Etta.

Etta shouldn't have looked away. If the woman had glared, given any hint of a challenge, she wouldn't have. But the way her eyes sparkled with barely suppressed amusement was so *open*—so goddamn brazen—that the intensity sent Etta's eyes downward, focused on her keyboard. As though her laptop was a wall that could protect her from this overlapping of worlds, from the depths of Beelitz Heilstätten into the quiet plastic peace of Kerzenlicht. A chrome Hadrian's Wall.

"I know you."

Etta froze. Slowly, she raised her gaze from her keyboard. Bright blue eyes greeted her, small specks of mascara dotting the skin below the woman's lash line. She had a knowing smile, one that made Etta square her shoulders and cross her arms. She grappled with the urge to pull her hood over her eyes. It would be best to just walk out. Slip out into the streets of Berlin and glide away from whatever this encounter threatened. But she didn't.

"Halloween," Etta said.

The woman grinned. She wasn't wearing lipstick. For some reason, that disturbed Etta. That her magnetism wasn't manufactured, that the gravitational field she carried was no weaker in the café than it was in the hospital. That Etta couldn't excuse it as a clever use of makeup and apparel.

"You were there. I saw you. Can I sit?" She was already peeling off her coat, setting her coffee down at the table, and dragging another chair across the linoleum floor. They were the only two customers in the café. Etta kept her laptop open, dividing them. If she noticed, the woman was unperturbed. "You," she accused, the rim of her coffee cup touching her bottom lip, "weren't wearing a costume."

How did she remember? There had been hundreds of people that night, all extravagant and distracting with their feathers and body paint. Etta had just been a shadow in the crowd.

"And you," Etta said lowly, "just stole a biscuit."

The woman laughed, a strand of pink hair falling over her flushed cheeks. She reached back, pulling out the offending pastry and laying it on the table between them without even caring to check whether the barista was watching. "You saw me." She smiled. Etta didn't think she was only referring to the act of thievery.

They appraised each other, the moment of silence stretching on. The woman reached forward, cherry-red nails digging into the biscuit as she ripped it in half. Eyes on Etta, she slowly pushed one half forward, brow raised in challenge. Etta stared at it, the gauntlet thrown on the table, and for a fleeting second she wondered how in the hell a peaceful afternoon spent working had turned into this quasi-confrontation.

"I get the sense," the woman continued casually, "that you see a lot."

Despite herself, Etta was intrigued. Slowly, she closed her laptop. Biscuit crumbs fell to the table as she grabbed her half.

The woman smiled wider. She offered one hand, crumbs hanging from the tips of her fingers. "Loulou."

Etta hesitated. The idea of shaking hands, something so normal and painfully polite, felt unsettling and wrong. Instead, she gave a small nod.

"Etta." Maybe she should have used a false name. It was too late to reconsider.

Loulou pulled back her hand to tuck another stray lock of hair— this strand a pale blue—behind her ear with a casual grace that made

Etta wonder whether she had ever meant to shake hands at all. Yet Loulou seemed pleased, her grin softening as she raised her coffee cup in mock cheers.

"Et-ta." It sounded like she was testing the feel, letting each syllable drop slowly from her lips. Loulou leaned closer, elbows resting on the table as she tilted her head with the energy of a young child sharing a well-kept secret. She smelled of cigarette smoke with a faint trace of oaky incense.

"Mind if I stay a bit, Etta?"

"They thought they were so hot, all the confidence in the world in a couple of blue bodies. They never imagined two girls could outrun 'em." Loulou laughed, her hand flicking in mock dismissal of the objects of her story. Around them, a collection of biscuit crumbs and wrappers dominated the table. Etta's laptop had been tucked away some time ago amid the endless stories Loulou had supplied, to make room for more scones and chocolates. Which she paid for, unlike the biscuit, drawing from a collection of pristine fifty-euro notes sandwiched between aged twenties. Etta eyed the original biscuit wrapper but stayed quiet.

She couldn't remember a time when she carried more than thirty euros, but she was aware of the type who did. She and Loulou had first crossed paths at a rave; to pretend Loulou wasn't associated with illicit business would be naive.

"But they chased us, the idiots. We were dropping bottles and they skipped over them like a couple of bunny rabbits, just hop-hop after us until one managed to catch up—and I mean, this stays between us—but for a second, I thought we were done-done. But just when he made a grab at me, I leaned forward . . ." Loulou leaned in closer to Etta, who was entirely, surprisingly, enraptured by the story. "Know what I did?" Loulou's breath smelled of mint chocolate.

Etta shook her head, her hands linked tightly together on the table between them.

"I grabbed him first." Loulou smirked. "And I kissed him."

Etta was caught off guard at her own laugh. "No." It was meant to be an attempt at humor, more jovial than accusatory, yet years spent avoiding conversation had sharpened an edge in Etta's voice that she no longer controlled.

"I did!" Loulou echoed Etta's laugh, either oblivious or purposely ignoring the unintentional venom in Etta's response. Their shared laughter garnered another sigh from the girl behind the counter, who no doubt was at the end of her rope after hours of Etta and Loulou's chatter.

"I kissed him, and I swear he looked like he was goin' to pop. You could see his thoughts just, poof"—Loulou spread her fingers beside her temples as she settled back into her seat—"and I was gone in a second. Guy like that, he's still dreaming about me. The girl that kissed and ran—idiots, right? They don't expect girls like us—you get it, you understand." She smiled conspiratorially.

Despite herself, Etta grinned. She couldn't describe it, how Loulou had captured her attention. Engaging in conversation, active listening, usually felt alien to Etta, like swallowing a handful of memory chips or speaking a foreign language. Yet Loulou filled in the silences easily, making it difficult for Etta to remember why she had been hesitant to speak to her at all. That magnetism she felt on Halloween was intoxicating up close, spreading a heat across Etta's cheeks that warmed her from tip to toe. She found herself encouraging Loulou to keep speaking. Offering the appropriate reactions to her wild stories, mirroring her movements as Loulou turned the table into a stage, where Etta was the guest of honor. She wanted Loulou to like her.

Loulou sighed as though recounting her escape from the security guard had robbed her of breath. She tipped her coffee cup back to finish the last drops. "You would have loved it," she said. "I know it, all the adrenaline. Feeling so alive. I see you, Etta. You're a girl who likes to live."

No, she wasn't, Etta wanted to say. She liked to hide from life. She wasn't like Loulou, with energy like a live wire that sent sparks to everyone within her proximity.

But then she thought of her climbs. The way she counted each brick she stepped on, each handhold. How the wind whistled in her ears with a promise of death, should she lose focus.

"I do my own thing," Etta said slowly. Would Loulou take that as an insult, interpret it as Etta sending her away?

The smile slipped from Loulou's face and Etta's palms began to sweat, which was absurd. She shouldn't have cared. She did.

"Sure you do." Loulou's voice was calculated. She didn't look angry, yet the energy at the table had changed. Etta resisted the urge to reach for her laptop, to set her barricade back into play, and as her hand twitched on the table it was quickly grasped between both of Loulou's. Etta could feel the callouses on her fingers, the heat of her hands. "After all," Loulou continued, her long fingers locking over Etta's hand like cable ties, "you never came to one of our parties before. Didn't go to another one after either. I would remember. I know faces, I'd know yours."

So that was it, then.

Given her work, Etta didn't have the luxury of trusting blindly, of accepting that Loulou's appearance at Kerzenlicht was random chance. Loulou hadn't asked any questions about Etta, not the sort people generally asked each other when they first met. Where she lived or what she did for work. About families or attachments. Loulou had treated Etta like a lost friend, immediately slipping into the entangling depths of familiarity. It had worked, and now Etta was trapped.

"Etta."

If Etta got up quickly, if she ran, she might be able to get to the door before Loulou stopped her. Of course, that would mean never returning to the café, to that stable space she had created for herself. Never again spending a few peaceful moments beside Yusuf, her unknowing partner during the quiet hours.

Etta slid her hand under the table, grasping her backpack. Five big steps, that's all it would take to get to the door. Five desperate steps. Then, a train. She could head to Belgium. Or France. She didn't know French, but she could learn. She could adapt.

"Etta." Loulou was laughing again as she reached across the table and seized Etta's arms, mouth curved in an amused smirk as the intense seriousness melted away. "Sweet girl, look at you. Jesus, like you're about to bolt. A newborn deer, ready to run away. Look at you."

And it was over. The moment snapped clean in half, a joke leveled like a carnival funhouse mirror that left her embarrassed, her head spinning as Loulou continued to drag her along on the roller coaster of her energy. All at once Etta felt supremely idiotic. As if this lithe, spirited woman with bright eyes and rouge cheeks could be an agent sent to enact some unnamed evil against her. Loulou squeezed Etta's arms once, twice, then gave them a slight rub as though Etta was a child just in from the cold. Etta opened her mouth, an apology on her lips, then clasped them shut. It felt awkward now, her mannerisms, her voice, her skin. All of it tainted and strange against Loulou's glow.

"Ah, shit." Loulou turned and looked out the windows behind them, pulling back from Etta to slump in her chair. Outside, the sky had faded from furious shades of red and pink into heavy darkness. "I should get going, need to head back soon."

Of course. It was a given that their encounter would end. Despite how that thought sent a longing through her chest, there was a strange peace in it. "Sure," Etta said. Her hand was still wrapped around her backpack's strap under the table. She wasn't sure whether to let go now. And the coffee, so much coffee and so many snacks. "Shit, hold on." She reached into her bag to pull out some money, thankful for an excuse to do something with her hands rather than cling to her surroundings like a frightened animal.

"Oh, no, don't worry about it." Loulou waved a hand, still looking out the window. "My treat. For putting up with my company."

"Oh." She should have thanked Loulou, showed some sign of appreciation for her stories, for her unprecedented and spontaneous friendship, but Etta said nothing. There was no need to give Loulou any more reason to discover the truth of Etta's nature. For Etta, their encounter would be a memory she could return to at night, roll over like a heavy marble in her hand, marveling at its comfortable weight. The one time someone had wanted to be with her. Wanted nothing else from her.

"Come with me."

Etta stared.

"So shocked." Loulou snorted. "Listen, come on. There's a place; there's a few of us. People who see things, like you do—no, don't give me that look. You know what I mean—come on. What else do you have to do tonight? Sit here on your laptop? Come with me, just let me show you around. No strings, promise."

"I—" It could have been one single, perfect afternoon. Enough for Etta to sleep peacefully for a year, to fill that ache in her chest for just long enough. "You— We barely know each other. You don't know me."

"Don't know you? How the hell do we know people? Ask their favorite color, what drinks they like, where their parents are from—is that what you want? Want me to ask for your resume? That's not it, that's not how you know people. We both get that; we get that people are deeper than that. You're deeper than that, I know you plenty enough." Loulou stood. She dusted the crumbs from her jacket and pursed her lips as she glanced back at the door, hands shoved in her pockets.

For a moment, Etta was positive she would leave without another word. She was at the top of a cliff, watching helplessly as Loulou took one step into the clouds without her.

Then Loulou softened, her shoulders dropped, her hands untucked, and she turned back to her.

"Come on, Etta." Loulou smiled. "Come meet my family."

Family.

Etta stood.

8

It had taken two trains to reach the station at Plänterwald. Etta spent both rides struggling to reconcile what she knew of Loulou and what she understood about rough living in the woods. Perhaps Loulou and her family occupied a collection of the new city council–sponsored cabins, with roofs tiled with solar panels and electric stoves that warmed ethically harvested wood-paneled floors. But picturing Loulou cooking under a skylight or hunched over a camping stove felt equally bizarre. It all felt wrong.

Loulou grabbed Etta's hand as they exited the train, wrapping Etta's arm around the crook of her elbow as she marched off the platform and confidently strode across the empty street. Behind, a backdrop of tall oak trees blocked out Berlin's skyline. Ahead, scattered throughout the woods, eco-cabins and their solar lanterns beckoned like fireflies.

"We'll have to walk from here." Loulou squeezed Etta's hand apologetically. "But not far."

Evening mist swirled around Etta's feet as pavement turned to packed dirt. They were in a forest tunnel composed of bark and leaves, the occasional streetlamp casting splotches of light through the canopy. It felt like the entryway to another world. The modern era left behind as Loulou dragged Etta away from reality. Down, under the hill, where fairies waited: all those women who had hovered around Loulou at

Beelitz Heilstätten. Etta held on to Loulou's arm a bit tighter. Rarely was she superstitious, but in this place, anything else would be naive.

Loulou stopped in the middle of the road. Etta froze beside her.

"Look, up between the branches."

Framed among the trees, rising in the night sky like a rebellious red sun, the curve of a Ferris wheel. A giant red beast, shrouded in mist, looming over the River Spree like the shadow of God. It was frozen in place, the carriages swaying in the wind. Though they were too far away to hear it, Etta could imagine the creaking echoes as the rusting ride groaned in complaint. It wasn't uncommon for her to feel forgotten, invisible in the city, insignificant against the skyscrapers and the bustling crowds. Yet rarely did she feel small. There, under the shadow of that wheel in the clouds, Etta felt tiny.

She jumped as a hand dropped on her shoulder, fingers light against her skin. Loulou tucked a dark curl behind Etta's ear.

"Welcome to Spreepark." Loulou's voice was flooded with warm amusement. "Home."

"They built it in 1969, but it really didn't pick up much speed until after the reunification."

Etta trailed behind Loulou as they approached a tall chain-link fence that surrounded the property.

"It all went downhill around 2001, though. Ran out of cash. Didn't even have enough to pack up, so the city bought it. They tried to build it into a cultural park, whatever that means. Just another place for people to sit around and pretend the world outside isn't on fire—Etta?"

Etta had stalled about ten feet from a small structure near the gate. She had been alright—following Loulou, allowing herself to enter the unknown—until she spotted a man with a bulging gut and a dark jacket smoking a cigarette by the guardhouse.

Loulou glanced from Etta to the gate and frowned. She strode forward, pulling Etta's hand into her own determinedly. It felt cowardly to allow Loulou to ground her, yet somehow the idea of entering this forgotten park through the front entrance had Etta wishing for a knife.

"It's alright, seriously." Loulou tugged her forward. The guard was standing now, one hand heavy on the curve of his gut.

"Lou." He had the voice of a broken coffee grinder.

"Frank." Loulou released Etta's hand as they approached the man. Her voice was teasing, her mouth twisted into a coy smile.

"Got a guest today?" He bobbed his head toward Etta, eyes roaming over her figure slowly. Etta prepared to bolt.

"Sure do. Got a smoke?"

"Sure." He fumbled in his pockets, struggling to pull a cigarette from the pack. Loulou took the moment to glance back at Etta, eyes quickly rolling just before the guard looked back up. Loulou's face snapped back into a flirtatious mask.

Etta marveled at the way Loulou seemed to flip through personas like a password cracker cycling through passwords. Etta needed to remember that she didn't truly know her, even as Loulou smiled conspiringly in the way that made Etta feel as though they were two spies, perpetrating an undercover attack against one dull guard.

"There." Frank held out the cigarette, the small yellowed filter sticking out from his palm so that Loulou had no choice but to allow her fingers to brush his hand as she plucked it from his grasp. It was intentional. It was revolting.

"Grand, Frank." Loulou dropped the cigarette into her coat pocket and snatched Etta's hand, pulling her past the guard and through the gate so quickly Etta stumbled in the dirt.

"Guard change at eleven," the man bellowed behind them. "Come 'round then?"

"Late for dinner, see you around!" Loulou's sweet tone was at odds with her twisted expression, brows lifted in exasperation as she ducked her head close to Etta's ear. "Pervert," she whispered.

So that was why the guards didn't mind. Etta found it almost impossible to imagine Loulou with a man like that. She tried to picture the two of them pressed together in the tiny guardhouse, Loulou's long limbs wrapped around his sausage arms, her porcelain skin spattered with tobacco-yellowed spit as he sucked on her neck like a hungry pig gnawing on bones. It felt like heresy.

"He's a creep." Etta didn't mean to sound so sharp. In the end, she didn't mind it.

The disgust dropped from Loulou's face as she laughed. "Oh, the worst. They aren't all like Frank, though. Most of them just want a little something for their consideration, you know?" She thumbed her nose, eyeing Etta knowingly. It took a moment for the motion to connect.

Etta had never bothered with drugs. She had seen people on the street who allowed the days to drip away as they rotted, like living corpses waiting to finally die amid synthetic bliss. She had also seen the dealers, arriving at her late-night hideouts with overstuffed backpacks and a knife under their thick jackets. She had quickly learned to avoid associating with them.

"Drugs?" Etta confirmed.

Loulou shrugged. "Everyone wants something."

Part of Etta wanted to leave then, turn around and separate herself entirely from Loulou and all she promised. Yet the Ferris wheel was growing closer, and Etta found her feet moving forward as Loulou led her deeper into the park.

The toe of Etta's sneaker caught on a weed. She ripped it loose, stomping down furiously. Loulou carried on in front of her, dodging tall, interwoven stretches of overgrown grass and patches of thick mud with practiced grace, even in the dark. It was obvious she had walked this path hundreds of times. Strands of candy-colored hair had escaped the bun at the base of her neck and surrounded her head in a pale halo. A few were blown between her lips as Loulou named each broken statue or crumbling building they passed, all lit by utility lamps and sturdy strings of lights that seemed to disappear into the tree line.

Monikers dripped from Loulou's lips with such ease that Etta wasn't sure whether they were longstanding nicknames or if Loulou was conjuring them on the spot. The Headless Monster, a plaster dinosaur with its neck ending abruptly in splintered wood and dewy moss, sat decaying near a series of small cars that Loulou had pointed out with special glee, clustered in the middle of a field. Each was shaped like a face, the hoods forming pink noses and red lips with long black mustaches stretching from one side to the next. The roofs were domed black bowler hats and black wire glasses served as windshields. Die Psychologen, Loulou called them. "Empty-headed doctors driving people around in circles."

Etta dug her fingers into the thin threads of her sweatshirt, pulling it tightly against herself as nervous sweat fogged her mind. She tried to appear at ease, forcing each footfall to be steadier than the last.

"The others are in Little Monarchy. It's where we eat." Loulou was smiling like a child showing their secret hideout to a schoolyard friend. Etta bobbed a slow nod, her lips pressing tightly together.

The farther they walked, the swampier the park became. Loulou explained that the owners had dug a river channel through the park so visitors could laze in wooden swans on sunny afternoons, as onlookers waved from the shore. As time progressed and people dispersed, the man-made river had creeped beyond its boundaries to seep into the surrounding land. Loulou guided Etta as they followed the path of a rotting boardwalk, pausing occasionally to jump the gaps between splintered planks.

Ahead was a series of conjoined buildings with bright, multicolor walls squatting in a clearing—a surreal rendering of a quaint English village. Faded graffiti covered a few of the walls, old tags mixed with abstract portraits of smoking men and aristocrats collapsing under the weight of hastily painted bags of wealth. Laughter and shouts were coming from the biggest of the buildings.

"You're having a party?"

"No, we do this every week, you just lucked out." Loulou wrapped a firm hand around Etta's elbow, preventing any last attempt to turn back. "I think Monika wrangled some Chinese food."

Loulou pulled open the steel door, a strange contrast to the wooden support beams and baby-blue plaster, beckoning to Etta as she stepped inside. A blast of warmth billowed out, but Etta remained firmly planted in the doorway, peering in.

A group, a dozen in total, had spread themselves across a series of picnic tables lined up end to end in a pseudo-medieval grand hall under crumbling wooden beams and plywood walls. A staircase loomed at the back. It was like the inside of a dollhouse, artificially grand and filled with forgotten toys brought back to life by Loulou's arrival.

A woman with glazed eyes wearing a fringed suede jacket was draped lazily over a man in motorcycle leathers. The girl dragged her fingers across Loulou's coat as she passed, revealing the stains on her sleeve. As the red wool slipped from her fingertips, her head rolled to face Etta in the doorway. "Oh, look," the woman murmured dreamily. "A shadow."

"Hey, Alina." Loulou smiled, then said to the man, "Burkhard."

Etta took a tentative step forward, and the door slammed shut behind her. Curious eyes knit into her like fishhooks, dragging her deeper under water. Etta felt an overpowering urge to escape. A girl dressed in a slinky silver dress, the thin material clinging to the dips and folds of her curvy figure, smirked as she lit a blunt and held it up like an Olympic torch, the earthy smoke swirling under the flickering light. Those immediately around her cheered and grabbed at her arms with playful desperation, but the girl's beady eyes stayed trained on Etta, like a wolf watching its cornered prey.

"Nervous?" She winked, inhaling deeply around the glowing blunt. "Could calm you down with a kiss." Smoke bubbled from her lips. Etta's eyes jerked away.

"Down, Hertha," Loulou said with a light laugh.

Alina held out her hand and Hertha passed the blunt.

Loulou floated through the room. She greeted each member of the group, laying hands on their arms and accepting sloppy kisses to her cheeks. The introductions were fast and furious. Tedmund and Varick, a bodybuilder wrapped around a smaller man with smudged eyeliner and a loose bowtie, who looked like an actor pulled out of a silent drama. Then Gustaf, who practically clicked his heels together as he greeted her. Maritza, with doe eyes and cheeks still puffy with baby fat, looked like she should be sitting in a secondary school classroom rather than the abandoned park.

"And that's Annerose," Loulou said, pointing to a woman slumped in the back corner. She had the slack face and dull eyes of someone very drunk but trying to imitate sobriety.

A preppy girl with a wide smile grabbed Loulou's coat from her shoulders, revealing Loulou's weathered jeans and tightly fitted pink blouse, a small hole peeking out from under her left arm.

"He knows you brought her, right?" The girl glanced at Etta.

"Gilla." Loulou rolled her eyes at Etta. "Her favorite and only hobby is tattling."

Far from offended, Gilla grinned.

"How'd it go, Lou?" This from a man in his mid-sixties wearing an expensive but tattered three-piece suit and ascot, who Etta would later learn went by Baron.

"You get more shit?" Alina asked.

Loulou smiled, plucking the blunt from Alina's lips and pressing it to her own.

"Man—I'm telling you; it's been such a *bore*. I'm dying, Loulou," Alina said.

"Sure you are." Smoke curled out from Loulou's lips and up into her nose with practiced ease Etta had only seen in the movies. It hid Loulou's smile behind a hazy cloud, like a dream left half-remembered as she passed the blunt back to Hertha. "We're *all* dying, babe."

Hertha took a long drag.

Burkhard clamored for a hit, wrapping his hands neatly around the girl's broad hips and pulling her down from the bench. She squealed as he plastered a kiss made mostly of tongue on the corner of her mouth. "*Exactly*," he bemoaned, pinching the blunt between long and twisted fingers like spider legs. "We're all dying, so that means you gotta *share*."

They were a unified force, like circuits on a motherboard all sparking as Loulou bounced around the room. At the other end of the table, a slim girl fell off the bench to the floor. Alina and Annerose collapsed to their knees beside her, all three slumped to the floor in a fit of bubbling laughter.

They were high. Or drunk. Some combination that dissolved common sense into a puddle of childish glee.

"Come on, up—you're scaring my guest." Loulou had rounded the room and arrived at the barrier created by the girls on the floor, a mountain Etta could not cross. Gripping their slim arms, Loulou hauled them up one by one and sat them like wayward toddlers on the bench again.

"She looks like Simone Simon, a bit," said the final girl, the slim one, her voice not slurring at all as Loulou hoisted her up. The giggling had stopped, but a small smirk remained.

"Who?"

"The French actress, the old one. Silver screen. Little face, black hair. They play her movies sometimes at that theater by the station on Sundays, the one with the soggy popcorn."

"She does," Gilla agreed as she stared at Etta with glassy eyes. "But angrier."

While the exchange was lighthearted on the surface, there was an undercurrent of precision. Etta was being weighed, measured as an outsider intruding on their doorstep. The girls were wolves again, nipping at the heels of a young bitch who had strayed into their territory.

"Oh, lay off, Johanna," Loulou said. "Etta, come here. Come get a plate."

Loulou led her to the opposite end of the room, where a skinny girl stood beside a stack of plastic plates. She had on a black slip dress with fraying threads dangling around her legs and arms. Her nose was slightly hooked, lengthening her stare as her small, dark eyes took in their approach. A slight tremor shook her hand as she dumped a pile of rice from a takeaway container onto a plate.

"Monika." Loulou looped an arm around Etta's shoulders and pushed her forward. "This is Etta."

Etta half expected Monika to dissolve into a fit of hysterics as the other girls had, but instead she lifted one corner of her mouth in a small smile.

"Are you staying?" The question was for her, yet Monika looked at Loulou.

"I can head back," Etta heard herself say. "I'll head out."

Loulou laughed like Etta had made a fabulous joke and pressed gently on her shoulders, forcing her onto the bench so her face was level with Monika's stomach. The black dress was so threadbare that Etta could make out marks on Monika's skin beneath the fabric, small bruises on her hips. They looked like purple fingerprints, left behind after someone had clutched the curves of her hip bones too hard. Etta thought of the guard again, Frank. The mental image of him wheezing over Monika with thick fingers buried in her flesh was as impossible as picturing him with Loulou.

"No bother," Monika said. "You're here, you're welcome here. We like to share."

"Exactly, you're welcome here." Loulou had sat beside Etta, straddling the bench as she rested her cheek against her hand, elbow propped on the table. "Is that chow mein?"

A paper plate stacked with chicken and noodles that carried a suspiciously fishy scent was placed on the table in front of Etta. Loulou winked at her. Around them, the group gradually broke free from their clusters to settle on the benches with legs and arms intertwined amid a scramble for food. Conversation erupted, so loud and chaotic that Etta couldn't keep track of it.

The scene felt familiar. It took a moment to remember why. At one of her group homes, the internet had gone down for an unprecedented full week. By day two, the residents had bounced between brawling in the hallways and barricading their doors with plywood furniture so they could smoke cigarettes while perched on the windows like pigeons. In a fit of desperation, the attendant had appeared with an old DVD player and a box set of one season of an American sitcom, something *Family*. For the rest of the week, the show had played near-constantly on the communal television. It had only amounted to fifteen hours of viewing and most grew bored after the second round through each of the four DVDs, exhausted by the chirpy characters with starched dresses and plum apologies following some contrived slight.

But Etta had been enthralled. She spent months in that living room, knees tucked against her chest and hands buried in a stained pillow as she allowed herself to be transported into the dream.

The spectacle in Spreepark was the closest equivalent she had ever seen in real life: a family.

"Etta?"

She realized Monika had squeezed onto the bench next to her, pressing her further against Loulou, who was entangled in some debate across the table. Monika looked at Etta expectantly, fork poised over her small portion of noodles.

"Yeah."

"It's okay," Monika said. "We can be a lot to take in."

Compared to Loulou, Monika's voice was lifeless. Heavy as a brick with only the smallest glint of pleasantry, like an overworked mother after having set her children to sleep.

"So." Monika tapped a piece of browned broccoli against her lips. "What are you good at?"

Etta frowned. "What?"

"Loulou brought you in. Usually means you're good at something. I'm a good cook. And physics. I'm pretty good at physics." Funny to think she was a good cook, yet all they were served was the scrapings of some anonymous Chinese restaurant. Funny, too, making it sound like Loulou had found Etta from an employment agency rather than the gutter of a twenty-four-hour café.

Etta pointed across the table at the girl who had originally fallen on the floor, Johanna, and was now sloppily trading rolled forkfuls of noodles with Alina. "What's she good at?"

"Her?" Monika smiled. A piece of broccoli was stuck in her front teeth. "She's good at being a representative's daughter."

Johanna's lazy gaze slid their way under the mismatched ends of her blond fringe, acknowledging their discussion—though she didn't bother to expend any energy on a retort, chewing another mouthful of offered food instead.

Evidently, being born to the right person at the right time was considered a skill worth harvesting. "Runaways?"

"Bit old to be called that. Well, maybe Maritza. But she's not a runaway, when you think about it. None of us really are. Maybe before, but we're not running, not anymore. You run toward the V, not away from it."

The girls across the table giggled as a noodle slipped onto an innocent lap.

"Yeah." Johanna smirked behind tented fingers. "We got a lease here and everything, all work no play—for some of us, anyway. Right, Monika?"

Monika's lips stretched in a wide smile. Etta didn't miss the way one of her hands lifted to hover over the bruise on her hip reverently.

Etta picked up her plastic fork and twisted it, feeling it bend in her grip as Monika's words rolled over in her mind. "The V?"

"Die Verwandte. Loulou didn't tell you?"

The Family. Loulou had, in a way, Etta just hadn't realized it. She wasn't sure if Monika's surprise was genuine or mocking, and it was unsettling that Monika had an edge over her. That she had noticed how Etta was cataloging the group's interactions in the hunt for some sort of answer and had offered a piece of bait in return. It was an obvious exchange, a quid pro quo for background on the newcomer.

"I—" Etta choked on her words, cut off by the silence that flipped over the room.

Everyone was looking at her. She had done something, upset some invisible balance—

Except they weren't looking at *her*, she realized. The girls across the table had their eyes trained somewhere behind Etta's head. Monika dropped her fork and folded her hands, swiveling her gaze away too. Loulou had spun back to Etta, fingers digging into the meat of her arm, but her attention was directed upward, toward the back of the room where the lights didn't quite touch. Toward the staircase. Etta's instincts told her to run, but she didn't. She wanted to know. Whatever made this room of misfits and outcasts go so quiet, she wanted to know.

Two heavy steps foretold his coming. They all held their breath, eyes to God, and stared at the man who descended upon them.

9

"Please." He punctuated himself with one more step down the old stairs. "Don't stop on my account."

The room exhaled but no one spoke. Loulou's fingers stayed tight around Etta's arm as the man finished his descent and stepped under the lights. Recognition jolted Etta. Like Loulou, she had seen him on Halloween at the hospital. The Moses in black who had parted the crowd, silencing them with his presence as they gravitated in orbit around him.

He strolled toward the table and Johanna—the representative's daughter—reached out a sleepy hand as he passed her. She was indulged with a gentle touch on her head. A paternal twinge of his lip. He bent the world around him as he let his fingers trail from shoulder to shoulder. Hertha nearly fell from her seat as she leaned after him, tipping into his wake.

The man snapped a folding chair open and placed it at the head of the table. It creaked as he sat.

The group remained silent, braced for some signal.

Then, he smiled.

Life flooded back into the room all at once. Remarks and quips were thrown across the table with even more vigor. Etta tried to hide her staring.

It was easier to see the whole of the man under the lights: the powerful jaw, the aristocratic nose, the carefully combed, honey-blond hair. When he raised his hand to accept a plate piled high with food, she noticed his nails were clean and cut down. He was polished in the way a stone is smoothed by rain. Small wrinkles that made others look aged and ragged added an air of wisdom to his composed expression. A man to look at, as well as to look up to; the handsome father in her old sitcom, sitting at the head of his family dinner table.

"Loulou." His low, steady voice carried clear over all the chirping conversation. "You brought a guest."

Etta was not in the habit of fearing men, though her caution was ever-present. Fear, she had learned, was easily misconstrued as respect. So when Loulou's arm wrapped around her shoulders again, Etta allowed her gaze to meet his.

"This is Etta," Loulou said cheerfully. "My little foundling. I wanted to introduce her to the family. She wanted to meet you." Etta hadn't voiced any such thing, but she held her tongue. Loulou seemed especially pleased to make this introduction, and Etta hesitated to reveal any false truths. Not when her position in the room was so precarious—when the power structures were still revealing themselves.

"Etta." It didn't sound like the first time he had said her name. "Welcome to our little madhouse. Milan Semyonov."

"Like the city!" a handful of the girls cheered, hands slapping against the table as they dissolved into a fresh fit of laughter. A joke that had turned into a battle cry. Something exclusive to the group, judging by the way their eyes found each other—squeezed tight with knowing glints. For a flash, Etta nearly begged Loulou for an explanation, almost demanded to be included. But she held herself back. She couldn't risk showing how she longed for the familial comradery displayed before her.

"Like the *writer*." Despite the obvious years he had over the rest of the group, Milan's eyes glittered with the energy of a man fresh to his twenties. "Let's not alienate our Etta already."

The claim of ownership, however small, excited her as she forced herself to steady her breathing. She couldn't decide whether to lean in or lash out. It was all too unfamiliar, too surreal, and it sent her to the edge of the seat.

"No need." She was proud of how level her voice stayed. "Can't alienate a stranger." There. The boundary was laid.

"Oh, she bites." Johanna leaned over, the tips of her straw-colored hair dangling into her food. "She looks like she's about to stab you with that fork."

Etta glanced down in surprise and dropped the plastic utensil onto the table, the handle bent, as she sent an icy look at the girl.

"Wouldn't you know?" Loulou teased.

"And I'd do it again," Johanna responded smugly, flopping back against the wall as she plucked a noodle from her plate, dropping it into her mouth and slurping the rest. The whole exchange felt as venomous as it was comfortable.

"Monika." Milan's voice drew Etta's attention. "I don't see Terje. He should be in the shack."

It was clear from the clip of his voice and the sudden hard edge of his gaze that this was a dismissal. Etta nearly felt a pang of pity for the girl beside her, for the way her expression drooped just a bit. Monika pushed her plate forward, where it was immediately snatched away by another hungry set of hands. She slipped a meager smile at Etta as she stood and turned to the door, removing the only obstacle between Etta and Milan.

With Monika gone, Loulou encroached ever closer, her elbows digging into Etta's side as she gestured wildly in her conversation with the girls across the table. Etta resisted, planted her feet as she resumed a bored stirring of the noodles on her plate. She tried to school her expression, to hide her furtive glances at the man beside her. For a moment, she wondered desperately whether he would engage with her or whether he had lost interest beyond the knowledge of her name.

"Make haste with leisure." His voice took her by surprise, but she held her face pointed forward. "You can see, we take that expression seriously enough."

"Fitting, then, living in an old theme park."

His deep laugh, singular and dominating, finally turned her his way. He had leaned forward, sleeves rolled to expose his muscular forearms as he rested them on the table. She would not acknowledge the shiver of pride that ran down her spine at his reaction. How, for a moment, a memory of her father's laughter—warm against her forehead as he held her—danced across her mind.

"Our escape. Our little salvation in the middle of this city. Would you choose differently? Tell me, where would you pick?" He did not tease as the girls did, nor did his words feel lighthearted. An edge was there, the underlying current of an ulterior intent, some double meaning she couldn't decipher.

Etta crossed her arms, one of her feet drumming on the floor as she considered him. She thought of the Ferris wheel, the way it crested over the skyline amid a swamp of weeds and broken boardwalks. How it might feel to climb the ladder to the top, the bite of the cold metal rungs in her palms. To hear the wind howl, thunderous compared to anything she had ever heard whispered at the top of a roof or fire escape.

"I have my own escapes." None as good as Spreepark. None so isolated, so entirely forgotten by society that it lived only in old pictures and memories. If she had known it was an option, she would have chosen Spreepark.

"We all do, don't we?" He waved a hand vaguely. "'Happiness is the feeling that power is growing—that resistance is being overcome.' That's what we do here. Resist the pulls of a society not built for us. A government that does not care for us. Granted, I can't imagine Nietzsche pictured exactly this when he praised resistance."

Etta hadn't read Nietzsche. She had seen one of his books once at the library, on a shelf beside one of the public computers. When she pictured its black cover spread open in Milan's grip, the image felt complete. As if Milan was a man who belonged with a book in his hands.

"And that." Milan ducked his chin at Etta's back, where the weight of her backpack had been forgotten amid all the overwhelming company. "Did you bring gifts for us, Etta?"

Her muscles locked. Instantly she wanted to cradle her bag to her chest, to snap at the man as if he had made a grab to steal it from her rather than an absent inquiry. "No." She hoped to sound as cold as the food now chilling on her plate.

"It's her laptop," Loulou betrayed, drawn back toward their end of the table. She had been listening all along. "I interrupted her working, tossed myself right down at her table. She caught me pocketing a bit of a treat, figured I'd find the generosity to share."

It didn't feel right, phrased like that. As though Etta was some innocent girl shaken by the sight of thievery, hands wringing as she debated whether to call the authorities or alert the café employee—anxiety preventing her from doing either.

"It was quick," Etta clarified. "Quicker than I could do it."

"Loulou is good at that sort of business." Milan tapped a finger on the tabletop. "Plucking things from corners, putting them to use where others prefer to let them rot on shelves."

Loulou slackened against Etta's side at the praise, her smirk melting into something more demur. An artist having her work extolled by the highest critic.

At the end of the table, Alina, still wrapped between Burkhard's clinging arms, smiled conspiratorially and blew a smoke ring. It bobbed over the table like a jellyfish before dissipating in a soft burst right on Loulou's nose.

"And Etta," Milan continued. "What are you good at?"

It was the second time someone had asked her that. The same

question, first wielded like a spear, now laid like an ace on the table. His expression smooth, eyes gleaming, one eyebrow slightly quirked. Lying was an option, lying was her usual option, yet she could recognize this test. See the way he waited not for an answer but an admittance. Somehow, this man already knew.

"Computers. Coding." It didn't feel like a loss to admit it, not like she had expected. "I work for myself. I do what I can." She did what she had to. What she wanted to.

"Ah." He smiled again, white teeth with a touch of crookedness that added to the authenticity of his grin. "Computers. Technology. So involved in everything today. I can't say I know too much about them myself. Though I understand what they're capable of."

He paused to sip at a glass of water that had been placed before him.

"I must admit, I figured you were that sort. The heavy bag, your pallor. How you observe our table like an enigma—no, don't be embarrassed. No need to be so stiff. Our Terje, he's the same. Always looking at the world like a riddle he needs to pick apart—when he's not in a cave of monitors and cords."

He had measured her so easily, as if he had stripped off her clothes piece by piece with each word, bared her skin and traced each small scar with an exact knowledge of how it was gained.

"Observant. You could be in politics." It was the best insult she could conjure. She wanted to see how he would respond, this man who wielded power over this small corner of the world.

His smile widened. "Never."

"*Politics,*" Gilla spat with practiced force. Gustaf beside her squeezed her tighter against his side. "*Damn* politics. Buncha' nobodies. Big old nobodies killing *all* of us."

The heat in her voice sounded freshly kindled. Etta's anger toward Germany's government had been fostered throughout her childhood, whereas this girl—and the others that grumbled their agreement—seemed to hold a newfound sense of betrayal, like they were recently *fooled*.

The door let out a groan that sent Etta jerking back in her seat, causing Johanna to bark a laugh. Etta would have needed to crane her neck to see the newcomer, so she poked absently at her food as Milan stood with two palms pressed against the tabletop.

Loulou swiveled so she leaned against the edge of the table. "Be late again and we eat your share."

"You can have it." It was a deep voice. Not as deep as Milan's, but darker with open frustration. A lion had entered the den, thorn firmly stuck in his paw.

"Terje." Milan spread his hands like a king welcoming the newest knight to his banquet. "From the depths he arises. Come, say hello. We have a friend today. Come meet Etta."

Etta still did not turn, even as she felt a presence at her back. "Hello," she said to the shadow he cast across the table.

"Hello." He seemed equally displeased to meet her.

"Ah, shit, be friendly for once. Come on, sit down." Loulou slapped the bench, scooching over to invite him to Etta's side. She wanted to grab Loulou's arm and yank her back into place, prevent her from trapping her between anger and charm.

Stiffly, the man settled himself next to her. Etta risked moving closer to Milan to give ample space, but Terje crossed his arms tightly over his stomach, preventing contact. He was lean, but not malnourished—statuesque and lithe as a whippet. His skin was taut across arched cheekbones, enlarging his bright green eyes. Milan's statement about Etta's and Terje's similarity made more sense to her, seeing him up close. Both pale, both fighting wispy black hair that dangled over their brows like feathered fishhooks. She wondered if he contemplated shaving it all off as she often did or if he, too, feared the sensation of cold snow kissing his bare skull.

"Etta works with computers." Coming from Milan, her previous statement felt impossibly lame. A cowardly, hollow excuse at hiding her actual profession.

Terje pinched his lips tightly together. His hands fidgeted slightly as he gripped his arms. They were two children, paired together by a teacher on the basis of liking the same-colored crayons. She could have helped him, but at that moment, all she felt was an overpowering anxiety. Too many people, too many new faces—it made it hard to breathe.

"Last name?"

It took her by surprise, and her response was kneejerk. "Baldwin."

"Etta Baldwin." His arms lowered a bit. "I know you."

"I'm sorry, have we met?" There was no chance—she'd have remembered.

"I used to do some work for a gaming company in Munich. Network stuff. They used your code."

She had forgotten that early in her work, she hadn't bothered hiding her name, including it in the comments within her work's headers. Someone had read the code.

Loulou leaned across Terje, eyes bright as she pointed accusingly at Etta. "Are you famous or something?"

Etta snorted. "No, absolutely not." Thank God for that.

Loulou turned to Terje for confirmation, and he shrugged one shoulder. As he let it drop, Etta noticed the frayed collar of his navy shirt. Loulou huffed, slumping back against the bench.

"Heard your name tossed around by some other people too." Terje chanced a sideways glance at her, calculating. "Different sort of work."

It was a dance, one she had been tripping over since her arrival. Now was the final act.

"I do what I can." Same words, now true in their meaning. Terje seemed to understand, his head bobbing once.

"Heard you're the only one who *can* do it."

He knew about Wechselkind.

Milan gave a pleased hum, fingers resuming their rhythm on the tabletop.

"Hey, Terje, why don't you do what *you* can and set up that projector?" Annerose said while hanging off Johanna, letting her head tip to the side, reaching one unsteady hand out accusingly as her fingers bobbed from Etta to Terje. "It's been ages, you promised we'd get a movie night before the snow sets in."

Terje grunted, and Loulou leaned around him, pressing her lips to Etta's ear as they both watched Terje wave off the girl's demands. "You're doing great," Loulou whispered. "They love you; I can see it. You've done amazing."

The words sent a frisson of warmth up Etta's spine. She caught herself smiling. A small thing, just a whisper that pained her cheeks as the muscles strained to remember the shape of it. It must have looked twisted, her dark, hunched form with puckered cheeks and a mouthful of cold food, yet—and she would only acknowledge this later, much later—it was comfortable. For just a second, she could have believed she belonged here.

She didn't notice when the door opened again. The girls across the table jumped up, Alina and Burkhard broke free from their desperate necking, and Loulou whooped as a mountain of a man ducked through the doorway. Intertwined tattoos coated every inch of visible skin from his fingers to the curves of his blistered, lumpy ears, only stopping at the edge of his hairline where closely buzzed hair framed his large face. He was covered in bruises, knuckles split and bloodied. A cut wept blood down his cheek; his green T-shirt was speckled with dark droplets. It would have been more disturbing had he not entered the room with the smile of a prizefighter returning from a successful round in the ring.

It was the same mountain of a man who had saved her on Halloween.

"Friends," he greeted cheerfully. Etta tempered her shock as he sauntered over, one hand laid on Milan's shoulder as he reached forward to grasp a takeaway container—forgoing the plates entirely—and plucked one of the pieces of chicken out with his hands. As he chewed, his gaze roamed the room until it landed on Etta. His eyes immediately widened, and he froze with one hand inside the container.

"Shit," he said around the piece of chewed meat. "We have company?" The container dropped to the table, noodles tumbling loose. He was like a clumsy bear, caught deep in the beehive and ashamed of it.

Etta stared at his hand. There were flecks of blood under his short fingernails, the creases of his knuckles damp with rust-colored streaks that straggled over his palm.

Milan sighed, rubbing his cheek as he glanced apologetically at Etta. "Foster," he said. "Wash up before dinner, remember?"

The giant man blushed slightly as he bobbed his head. His hands ran over his shirt quickly as if to wipe the blood splotches away, smiling once more at Etta as he ducked back toward the door.

Etta watched him go, saw the way his frame filled the doorway before the door shut behind him. When she turned back to the table, Loulou started speaking to her, but Etta barely heard a word. She was focused on the takeaway carton Foster had left discarded on the table, tilted sideways and spilling out lumps of battered sesame chicken. A fresh, brick-colored handprint was wrapped around the white paper sides, covering the restaurant's logo.

No one else seemed to notice.

10

They asked her to stay. Loulou, one leg propped up on the bench as she coiled a strand of cotton candy hair around her finger, promised her a bed and warm blankets. A fresh breakfast, some coffee, and good company, "though a bit quieter in the mornings, thank the Lord."

As the wind howled against the thin structure they called Little Monarchy, which they had warmed with only the heat of their bodies, the family held out promises like a fresh pot of dirt, begging for roots to be driven into its depths. But Etta could feel the weight of her bag by then, how her feet already ached from staying too long in that single spot, how her nerves were worn down—too broken, splintered. Maybe some cuttings could take to fresh ground, some flowers could bloom again after enough time in the sun, but Etta couldn't. Not that night. Not after she had spent so long pushing through a crack in the sidewalk.

Loulou had offered to walk her to the gate only after Etta talked her out of walking her all the way to the train station. She didn't need company, not when the idea of quietly waiting on the station bench in the biting winter air was so refreshing.

Before they left, Milan had leaned toward her one final time, laying a heavy hand on her shoulder. "Keep those eyes wide open," he had told her. "And never stop. Never stop the noticing."

His words were a track that repeated with each step as she parted with Loulou, as she boarded the last train back into central Berlin, as she returned to the small cupboard in Wohnhaus Stubenrauchstraße. A reel of the night—the comradery that flooded the table and filled every gap of space, the way Loulou had leaned against her side, even how Terje had slid her a stiff nod that could nearly be mistaken for respect—played over and over as she lay in her sleeping bag.

She didn't know what to make of the V. A group with as-yet-undetermined motives, people who somehow knew about her work. It was an unsettling notion. Etta knew what it felt like to miss something. She missed her mother, or rather, she missed the things she could have experienced growing up with a loving parent. Her time at Spreepark, however, burned in a way missing her mother never had. It was infuriating how a group of strangers made that hollow cavity in her chest throb more than the ghost of her own mother. Yet it made sense. She understood how the family, Die Verwandte, had wormed its way into her heart.

It had been easier to yearn for a family before she discovered how it felt to be part of one.

It was an especially quiet evening in Kerzenlicht. The lights flickered as Etta stared at her laptop screen, the bold words of the newest social posts blurring as her mind lost focus. Her work should have been meditative, easy, yet she felt adrift. Isolated from the one task that had always been familiar, that made sense to her.

It was a good thing, then, that Yusuf decided to make his entrance. Demure and unfocused, just as she was. His hair was unkempt, as if it was an external manifestation of something on his mind. It was a welcome distraction, one Etta could easily sink herself into. Let her leap from the pool of her own conflicted misery into the depths of his.

She waited until he assumed his usual seat across the café, hand shaking as he took a hesitant sip of his steaming coffee. Once he opened his laptop, she switched programs on hers. Within a second, her screen was replaced by an exact mirror of Yusuf's. She watched as he moved his mouse to click on the most recent Word document he had been torturing himself over, the background of his wife standing in front of several large mountains with a soft smile replaced by a draft written entirely in Turkish.

Etta allowed herself a moment to admire the beauty of the language. The way small lines hung from certain letters like dainty necklaces, how the dots gave the impression of eyes peeking over O's and U's. She would learn it one day, she decided. It would be the first foreign language she would bother learning.

She had long ago developed a plugin that translated the text without altering what Yusuf saw on his laptop. He was writing about a feminist movement occurring in Turkish social media circles and had inserted a few pictures in the middle of his draft—women hiding their faces with scarves as they held up cardboard signs showing photos, names, and titles of men accused of crimes. Yusuf had gotten as far as explaining the context behind the movement—a girl had been murdered in Istanbul after testifying against her abuser—but when it came to the section requiring his perspective, he was stuck. His cursor hovered over the next line, a few letters typed then promptly erased.

He published under the name Asya Aydin, a female student with a graduate degree from Boğaziçi University in Istanbul. She didn't exist, but the desire for a writer unafraid to voice her opinions openly in a Turkish newspaper column was very real, and so Yusuf filled the void. Or he tried to, when he wasn't digging fisted hands into his eyes as he sighed heavily across the café.

They're faceless, yet they are all of us—our sisters, our mothers. Their accusers differ but the stories link them into a sisterhood they never asked for but welcome the support of; our army. She watched the text appear on the screen as Yusuf typed furiously. It was a powerful sentiment, and she was disheartened when his hands began unceremoniously deleting it.

There was a line between them that Etta was careful to never cross.

A demilitarized zone that separated fantasy from reality. If she ever breached that DMZ, stepped into his life, she feared the consequences. It had stopped her before in the moments she toyed with the idea of reaching out to him, stayed her hand during the quiet nights when she considered writing a letter to his false persona, acting as a fan just to inch closer into the space he inhabited.

It was a mystery, then, why she chose that moment to cross the border.

When Yusuf collapsed back into his palms and heaved another sigh, Etta quickly pasted the line back into the article. She watched. Waited, as Yusuf raised aged eyes back to his screen. Saw how his brows pinched, how he leaned closer until her view of his face was blocked entirely.

On her screen, the line was deleted again. She pasted it back in.

Yusuf jerked back in his chair. His lips moved though there was no accompanying sound. He looked up, but Etta had snapped her face down, dancing her hands across her keyboard in pretend typing. To her pleasure, the line remained.

The rest of her evening was spent watching Yusuf as he grappled with each new word of his article, clawing forward until he reached completion and sent it off to his editor. As he gathered his laptop into his bag and pulled a wool cap over his hair, she nearly got up and followed him—maybe he would hold the door for her on their way out, and she could say thank you and learn the way he would smile at her—but she stayed in her seat.

That one step toward interaction, it was enough and too much all at once, just as Spreepark had been. So she didn't look up as his back turned to her, as the door squeaked open.

"Oh, I'm s-sorry," she heard Yusuf's soft voice stutter.

"Don't worry about it," another voice chirped.

Etta choked on her inhale.

Yusuf was stepping through the entryway past the woman he had nearly collided with: the woman with candy-colored hair and lips lined with red gloss.

"Hello, you," Loulou greeted as she dropped herself onto the chair across from Etta. She glowed, eyes bright as though someone had cut her open and stuffed her with those LED lights from Halloween. Strands of her hair hovered around her cheeks.

"Welcome back," Etta replied dryly. "Thanks for dropping by."

"I've come to rescue you," Loulou declared. She was wearing the same bright coat as last time. The buttons were undone to reveal black pleather pants and a lacy red shirt. Loulou seemed apathetic to the degree of herself on display, exposing even more as she dug in her jacket pocket for an apple.

"Didn't know I was in danger." Etta watched as Loulou took a large bite, the pale flesh crunching between her teeth.

"That's exactly why you need rescuing. You're a danger to yourself." Loulou hiked a knee up against the table. "You know I walked past here four hours ago? Just took a stroll and saw a familiar bleak hoodie in the window, hunched over a laptop. Imagine my shock when I passed again just now and saw you, still here, doing anything but living your life."

This *was* her life, Etta wanted to argue. A little island just for her, free from intruders—until Loulou decided to dock her boat right on the beach.

"And?"

"*And?*" Loulou rolled her eyes. She leaned across the table, rolling the apple between her hands. The juice left a thin streak on the plastic tabletop. "Listen, we're having another party tonight—"

"I'm good."

"Are you?" Loulou took another crunching bite as she appraised Etta. No doubt seeing how Etta hadn't even changed clothes after the night before, how her eyes squinted with fatigue.

"They liked you, you know," Loulou said. "I know it probably doesn't seem like it, the girls can be assholes. Terje is just pissed at anything with blood instead of circuits. But they liked you. We all do."

Etta tried to picture one of the girls pulling Loulou aside after Etta had left, expressing how much she liked the new girl. She'd probably meant it as a joke.

"Still, I'm busy."

Loulou sighed, leaning back in her chair. "Well, when you're not busy avoiding everyone and everything, we'll be at that old factory in Rüdersdorf. The main building, has all the smokestacks—the ones that look like a bunch of brown party hats, you know? Just come swing by. No dress code for this one, just come find me."

Etta knew the factory. It was popular with tourists looking to explore a place left to rot following the reunification, where people went when they wanted to feel brave for an afternoon, then return to the capital to have dinner served with red wine and biscuits.

"I'll think about it."

"Think about it." Loulou stood, shoving her chair back as she stretched her arms above her head, revealing the pale expanse of her stomach like a pearly scar above her black pants. "I have to head back. Enjoy hiding."

"Your apple." Etta pointed at the half-eaten fruit left abandoned on the table.

"All yours." Loulou waved a hand as she sauntered toward the door, her coat swaying around her legs.

Etta watched as Loulou dipped out into the street and strolled out of view. Once she was gone, Etta poked at the apple with one finger, watching it bobble. Already the exposed flesh was sporting spots of brown.

Would it be so stupid, going to one single party?

She hissed at the thought, slapping her laptop shut and running a hand through the tangled curls at the back of her neck. Yes, please get involved with the mysterious group of strangers that live in a theme park. There was a reason she never allowed any roots to take anchor, why she had been careful to keep her business underground. She didn't get *involved*. Not with anything aside from herself. It was a philosophy that had protected her thus far, and she would stick to it.

Milan would be at the party, with his kind eyes and soft assurances. Or Loulou would pull her into the group of women who danced like the floor was fire as they burned the night away.

It didn't matter. She wasn't going.

Etta shoved her laptop into her bag and left the café, dropping the remains of Loulou's apple in the trash as she stepped onto the street. It was starting to rain, the soft drizzle threatening to turn to ice beneath her feet. She tried not to think about anything aside from the sound of her feet slapping against the pavement as she wandered east, toward an abandoned mansion with tall plaster pillars that sat at the edge of an old industrial area. Toward Rüdersdorf.

Water splashed up onto the legs of her pants as she accidentally stomped in a puddle, lost in her thoughts. She just needed a few hours of sleep. By the time she woke up they would all be gone from the party, she told herself as she climbed the tall wooden fence surrounding the old house's property, knowing the lie for what it was. She passed a woman slumped beside a giant hole in the rotting wooden porch that wrapped around the front of the structure, the woman teetering precariously as she stared vacantly into the sky. Her eyes rolled to follow Etta as she shoved open the front door.

It had never bothered Etta before, the people who spent their nights in the same hideaways as she did. But that night, she felt her throat tighten with each person she encountered as she wandered over the stained rug in the entryway. She could sense every defective presence: the boys huddled in the corner while the telltale click of a dying lighter sounded over and over, like the ticks from a dying computer fan; the old man with a face lost in a forest of overgrown graying hair and beard. They swallowed all the air left in the space. Etta was choking.

Even as she found an empty room on the second floor, the wallpaper peeling like petals falling from a dead flower, the pain did not ease. She could hear them below her, hear the coughing, the sudden growl of a person wandering too far into the space of another. Once a mansion, now a casket with not an ounce of nobility left. Nothing like the Ferris wheel that stood proud long after abandonment, like a wonder of the ancient world.

Etta ran out of the building, ignoring the shouts from the group of boys as she passed them—their muscles too sluggish from the effects of whatever they had been inhaling to follow. Her lungs throbbed, heartbeat roaring in her ears as she stumbled down the stairs, back over the fence, and down the street.

She didn't stop until she found herself in the shadow of her mother's murderer.

Not a being but a building: Engel-Bush Banking and Trading. A tall, hideous thing that stood stiff-straight—an affront to the skyline. Windows peppered the front like holes on a punch card and massive red letters were tacked above the revolving glass door. A few squares of yellow light filled a handful of the windows, where overzealous employees wasted their night within the confines of their desk space.

Reflexively, Etta counted the lights. She wondered if any of the workers contemplated letting themselves fall from their windows onto the street below, whether anyone had tried since the building manager had locked the door leading to the roof. The roof was never meant to be easily accessed, she had read in an article, and they had never felt the need to install a lock. Not until after Etta's mother had thrown herself from the edge, forty-six stories up.

She had heard that it was common during the banking crisis a century before, the unquestionable death rattle to the roaring twenties across the ocean. Bankers and stock traders, watching prices tank as money evaporated from the vaults. The Black Friday dirge, set to the beat of a hundred bodies slamming onto the streets below.

But 2008 had been different. First, people had been able to watch their world collapse in real time with the help of a screen, rather than in a flurry of newspapers and frantic telegrams. Second, and most important, only one body had fallen—at least, in Berlin.

Etta leaned down, numb fingers feeling along the sidewalk until they hit the smooth surface of a small stone. She held it up and felt its meager weight, noting how clumps of dirt clinging to the surface crumbled beneath her fingers.

Rearing back, she threw it at the building.

It skidded across the street and came to a bobbing stop three or four feet before the door.

Etta could never imagine what had driven her mother to choose death—while an infant lay in bed at home. How poisonous did a building have to be to convince its employees that they needed to die? How toxic were the fumes leaking through the vents as they filled their employees' heads with terminal loyalty to a corporation that wouldn't even pay their funeral bills? In the same year, Etta's mother had given birth to new life and snatched her own away—murdered by the red arrow that struck the economic floor.

All they had done in return was slap a padlock on the roof access.

One day, Engel-Bush Banking and Trading would perish. It would wither away as a hundred other banks elbowed it out of place. Would people dance in its corpse as they danced in Beelitz Heilstätten? Before, Etta had been disconcerted by the whole affair on Halloween—had viewed it as an example of reckless hedonism. Yet if she could dance in the bones of Engel-Bush Banking and Trading—she would do that with furious glee. She could picture her feet stomping hard enough to punch out the wooden floor, how she would fall from top to bottom until she carved the whole of her mother's final journey straight through the building's heart.

She thought of Loulou, at that very moment dancing in the old chemical factory with smokestacks like brown party hats.

Etta began to walk, her back to Engel-Bush Banking and Trading and her nose pointed toward Rüdersdorf.

11

It was already crowded when she arrived. The building was like a giant glass jar half buried in the dirt, with tall industrial doors and windows dotting its sides, separated by thick metal beams that reached up like arching fingers. Light throbbed from within, as though someone had stuffed the space full of firetrucks, police cars, and ambulances.

Etta stuck out a bit less this time, though some of the outfits she saw could pass for Halloween costumes. From what Etta had glimpsed at the café, Loulou had dressed conservatively tonight. Many partiers had forgone coats entirely in exchange for turtlenecks they had cut until the fabric only covered their necks and arms, the flesh of their torsos revealed in the open air, like turtles with broken shells. Etta tugged her hood lower over her eyes, watching as her exhales condensed into thin frost around her face.

It wasn't like Halloween—she was arriving of her own volition, for better or for worse. With determination, she joined the cluster of people flooding into the building.

Inside was hauntingly beautiful, the whole interior carved out to reveal the topmost ceiling, arching what seemed like miles above Etta's head. A band was playing somewhere inside, but she couldn't see them over the clustered wave of bodies that consumed her upon entry. Where outside was dangerously cold, inside was bitterly hot, heated by the warmth of shared breaths and close bodies.

She had always figured that her sense of awkwardness at parties had been a result of her reluctance to attend. But no instinctive ease washed over her as she watched the people around her raise their arms and cheer in no particular direction and for no particular reason. It was as strange as it had always been, only now she was forced to confront the fact that she had no idea what to do with herself at a rave. To face one more example of how divided she was from normal life.

She needed a drink, even if it was just something for her to hold, something to keep her hands busy. People drank at parties, there had to be alcohol somewhere and, with it, Loulou.

A boy was trying to squeeze past her, a beer bottle lifted far above his head. Etta snatched his arm, jerking him hard enough that the bottle tipped and a bit of foam fell onto his hair.

"*Shit,*" he hissed, eyes flickering about wildly until he followed the hand gripping his arm down to Etta's face. "What the hell?"

"Where?" She pointed her chin at the bottle, still slightly askew in his grip.

"What?" He followed her gaze. "Oh, uh, I brought this one, but they've got some over by the band. Over there." He pointed and she was off, shouldering through the crowd. Somewhere behind her she heard him shout a questioning "You're welcome?" She ignored it.

The shrill debate between guitar and bass cut deep into her ears. The crowd stopped being a whirlpool and turned into a wave, everyone pointing in the same direction as the heads of the band members became visible between jostling shoulders. Amps and massive speakers as tall as Etta loomed over the four figures, blasting the metallic riffs and deep bass with the building tension of an oncoming drop. The walls danced along to the music; Etta wondered if any of the old glass windows might fall and shatter over their heads. To the left of them, a woman had her back to the crowd as she tossed beer cans over her shoulder into waiting hands, pulling them free from a stack of metal bins.

She didn't turn as Etta approached the makeshift bar made of metal panels stacked on old barrels. "Can I get one?" Etta asked. She hoped it made her sound more practiced, the type of girl okay with any sort of drink so long as it filled her with fuzz. Most of all, she hoped it didn't reveal the fact she had never ordered a beer before in her life.

"Yeah, sure. Oh, hey!" The girl turned, revealing red cheeks and an upturned nose pinched between glazed eyes. It was Johanna, one half of the pair of girls who had spent dinner ferrying noodles into each other's mouths.

Etta pulled back her hand, but Johanna was already shoving a can into it, three more clutched tightly against her chest. She wore a thin black bandana as a top, tied under her arms in a knot between her shoulder blades. "Didn't honestly think you'd show, thought we might have frightened you off."

Etta hadn't thought she would show either, and she wasn't entirely sure why she was still there. "Had nothing else going on."

Johanna snorted, eyeing Etta's backpack. "Looks like it."

"Loulou said she'd be here?"

"Yeah, she's out back with the guys in the old control room." Johanna's head tilted.

Etta cleared her throat. "Back there?" A rusted door barely hanging off old hinges stood beside the bar.

"Yeah, have fun. Tell Terje I need some more shit up here." She turned away from Etta to resume tossing cans into the flurry of hands that were now slamming on the metal bar top like old warriors beating war drums. Etta turned just as Johanna's voice snapped again at her back. "*Hey!*"

Etta froze.

"The *actual* shit—you get it? Not this." Johanna thrust out a beer can with a pointed look. "In fact, you ask him how he expects me to sell anything when I've got nothing to sell—idiot."

The alcohol was evidently a holdover until Johanna's real stash— and what Etta suspected was funding the party—was resupplied.

The door Johanna had pointed out groaned as Etta pushed against it, relenting just enough for her to squeeze through. Bits of jagged metal grabbed at her clothes and her backpack, and she had to tug on the straps to get it loose. Her side smacked into the door, and the metal rang hollowly. *Shit.* The last thing she wanted was a grand entrance. Thankfully, no one had noticed the noise over the drumming music. Etta recognized a few people from Spreepark—Tedmund and Varick with their arms slung around each other's shoulders, Alina, and Hertha—but for every dimly familiar face there was another stranger decked out in a black shirt and pristine combat boots. The stench of weed billowed into her nostrils. She wasn't entirely sure whether the fog over the room was smoke or dust, or some mix of both.

Just as Johanna had said, the space was an old control room. Large enough to hold a team of twenty engineers, their command chairs having long since been replaced with crates and upturned carts lining the sides as seating for those too exhausted or high to keep dancing. The back wall was stacked floor to ceiling in gray panels and a collection of computer monitors, their black glass reflecting the strobe lights lining the floor. Compared to the warehouse, the room felt claustrophobic—even if the space was still larger than two airy Berlin flats combined.

Where the crowd out there had been so dense there was barely enough room to breathe, here there was at least space to stretch her arms. She inhaled long and slow, the beer in her hand slippery in her sweaty palm. In the back corner was a large table, once meant for blueprints and paperwork, now covered in cans and plastic cups. Loulou had taken up court at the table, her feet kicked up on its surface, the rim of a cup pressed to her lips as she scanned the room like a predatory cat. The two seats beside her were empty, no one in the room brave enough to claim them.

The way Loulou's face lit up when she spotted Etta, it was as if Loulou's hungry expression had been for her the whole time. Discarded cups and cans tumbled to the floor as she pushed off from the table and leapt out of her chair, weaving through the crowd until she met Etta halfway across the floor.

She smelled of flowers and burnt copper, like a garden store after an electrical fire. Her hair, let loose in a pastel curtain down her back and shoulders, tickled Etta's nose as Loulou wrapped her in a hug.

"Busy, huh?" Loulou asked, the acidic scent of vodka curling under Etta's nose.

"Plans changed."

Loulou laughed, clasping an arm around Etta's shoulders. Under the throbbing lights Etta could see flashes of Loulou's face, the way her pupils had stretched to swallow the whole of her blue-gray irises. The corners of Loulou's mouth and the edges of her nostrils twitched occasionally, as though electricity was sending sporadic shocks across her muscles.

"We," Loulou declared, "are going to get you *so* drunk."

No, they weren't. Etta winced, taking a half step away from Loulou. She couldn't simply say "No thank you"—she had a feeling any sort of refusal would only solidify Loulou's determination. Instead, she opted to redirect Loulou's focus on something less likely to end with Etta curled over a bush outside.

"Got something other than beer over there?" Etta tipped her can toward the table in the corner.

Loulou glanced over her shoulder and smirked. She had to raise her voice as the music grew to a peak, the room crackling with energy. "Follow me."

Hand clenched in Loulou's, Etta was dragged through the crowd. Eyes followed her as they had back in Spreepark, necks craning as she passed, while they continued to dance. At the table, Etta could breathe incrementally easier, the small degree of separation from the crowd becoming a hideaway. Loulou had a tall blue bottle in her hand, which Etta recognized as the same type of cheap vodka she had attempted to steal back in her early teens. Loulou unscrewed the cap, heaved the bottle up above her head, and took a deep swig. Her throat constricted and relaxed, and her eyes squeezed shut. With a deep sigh, she lowered the bottle and handed it to Etta.

Etta hoisted it up, the stench of alcohol burning her lungs the moment it came close to her nose. She shivered, her mouth and throat drying as the pungent fumes licked the back of her sinuses. Loulou watched her, small spasms still flickering across her face though her eyes were steadily trained on Etta, waiting.

She should have stuck with the beer, Etta realized. Eyes squeezed shut, she tipped the bottle to her lips, the vodka stinging the cracks at the corners of her mouth. Her chest convulsed almost immediately, rebelling against the liquid as it flooded past her tongue. She choked, vodka spilling down her chin as she forced herself to swallow once, twice, three times—that was as much as she could handle before she yanked the bottle from her mouth and slammed it onto the table.

It was difficult to deny the pride that swelled in her chest as she met Loulou's approving grin. She was sure her cheeks were aflame, and there was a wet splotch on her hoodie from where vodka had drizzled off her chin, but the details were hidden in the dim lighting.

"The guys are out taking care of some stuff." Loulou pulled a clear bag the length of her index finger out of her pants pocket, a collection of round tablets tucked inside. She glanced at Etta as she dug one finger into the bag. "Terje is getting the video feed back on. Want one?" She dropped a tablet into her mouth, holding up the baggie to Etta. She shook her head. Fuzz already bubbled at the edges of her consciousness.

"There's a video feed?"

"God, yeah, wait until you see it. Terje worked it up, something about augmented reality. It's incredible, even better once these kick in." Loulou flicked the baggie in her hand, jamming it back into her pocket. Over the noise, someone called Loulou's name, and they both looked up, spotting a group of girls dancing on one of the tipped-over metal carts beside a strobe light. They were beckoning Loulou with waving arms, ignoring the guy standing beside them. Etta could see his lips moving, though he may as well have been the ghost of one of the factory workers.

Loulou grasped Etta's arm, her eyes already unfocused. She invited Etta to come dancing, but Etta shook her head.

"Going to stay here for a bit," Etta said. "Need to catch up." In truth, the idea of clambering up to dance with Loulou and the others, as freeing as she had once imagined it, now shackled her to the floor.

"You came to a party and you're not going to dance?" Loulou flicked a strand of bubblegum hair from in front of her eyes, frowning. "Etta, come on."

"I'll be over in a bit." Hopefully Loulou would forget entirely once she was out on the floor and whatever drug she had ingested blurred the receptors in her brain to a satisfying degree.

Loulou pointed one finger at Etta, so close that the tip of her chipped nail polish nearly brushed her nose. "I'm holding you to that."

Loulou was off then, leaving the bottle of vodka with Etta. The memory of the smell alone had Etta pushing it to the side of the table, slumping down onto one of the old chairs as she leaned against the cool metal wall, backpack stashed by her feet. She was buzzing, the lights and bodies before her blurring and merging across her vision. She could see reflective silver jackets, the webbing of fishnet sleeves over pale arms, the glare of dark glasses against the bright lights, yet she couldn't entirely parcel out what belonged to which body.

The music pulsed with growing speed as it built to a crescendo before plummeting, taking the dancers with it as they cheered. A few of the boys, dressed in tight T-shirts with unrecognizable band logos, had picked up forgotten bits of rebar and were smacking them on an old metal drum along with the rhythm. They all knew exactly what to do, how to act, as they effortlessly converged into one horde.

It was incredible to watch, even before the monitors lining the back wall flickered to life.

They showed a white light at first, filling the room and shocking everyone still as the music carried on without them. They all turned to the old computer screens, even Loulou and the girls that had worked their way to the middle of the floor as a bundle of lace and laughter. The screens blinked once, twice, then fully came to life—merging their synchronized images to turn the wall into a massive mirror of the room and its inhabitants. Only, where Etta saw girls with bralettes and loose jeans, or men with layered shirts and hollow eyes, the screens depicted fairies and monsters. Gossamer wings that trailed a curtain of stars with every movement were tacked onto the projections of some partiers; others had been turned into beasts with hooked fangs and twisted horns that curled from beneath their shaggy hair.

Loulou made her way to the front, peering at the wall of screens as a group of dancers followed behind her, enraptured by their new images. She didn't have wings or fangs like the others—instead, her body glowed. Shifting orange and red light, like a sunset blanketed over her skin, morphed as Loulou twisted, peering at herself over her shoulder with a dreamily pleased expression. She was the light of the party, the sun for all the others to revolve around, and as she turned back to the crowd, they circled around her to resume their dancing even more furiously.

Etta had seen augmented reality before. She had gone into shops that offered special mirrors that overlaid the image of a shirt or coat over a reflection, so customers could get a sense of how the items might fit in the event the store was out of stock. She had walked past advertisements at bus stops and the train station, where a digital screen would add a scattering of pink and red spots across her complexion before recommending a preemptive acne cream. The display at the party, however, was something entirely more elaborate. Hypnotic. A dream readily swallowed by the eternally thirsty.

Etta pulled her laptop out of her backpack and opened it on the table, determined to discover the secrets of the program running behind the screens. The applications would be endless; if she could add an augmented reality element like this to Wechselkind, she could potentially create real-time deepfakes that would alter a live feed. She would be able to bend reality as it happened.

First, she had to figure out how it worked.

Her head swam from the vodka, but she shook it to clear the fuzz as the music faded in her mind. She had barely begun tracing back all systems connected to the Wi-Fi hotspot set up in the factory—at least four motion sensors mounted in the corners and two cameras hiding somewhere among the monitors—when someone cleared their throat behind her. She lurched, laptop slamming shut as she spun in her chair.

"Hell of a time to be working."

It took her a moment to recognize Terje. His dark curls were slicked back, revealing the sharp dimensions of his cheekbones and jaw. In the uneven lighting, the hollows of his cheeks were even more distinct, his emerald eyes peeking out from the shadows of his brow. He wore a black shirt, its sleeves clinging to his arms and shoulders. As he raised his hand to grab for the bottle of vodka, Etta spotted black grease stains on his fingers. Between the oily sheen and the pronounced stretch of his tendons along the back of his hand, he looked like a ghost made of steel and wires, born from the screens that now gave new life to the revelry around them.

Maybe it was the alcohol talking, but she desperately wanted him to sit beside her.

"I'm not working." Etta slowly opened her laptop again, the screen displaying the local router's web interface.

"That looks like work." Terje leaned closer, peering at the screen. He smelled like smoke and the rusted metal of old machinery. "Did you hack my network?"

"Honestly, it hacked itself."

He snorted. "Sure. Suppose you taught yourself too."

"Probably from the same chat room where you learned networking."

Terje frowned and took one of the abandoned cups, uncapping the vodka and pouring a bit inside. He held it as he stood over Etta. She waited for him to take a sip. When it was clear he didn't intend to either drink or speak, she decided to take a chance.

"Loulou said this is yours?" She raised her chin toward the screens.

"When it works." He swirled the liquid in his cup, staring at the monitors as a group of girls compared their wings. "Already a pain working around the old wiring here. It's impossible to keep everything accurately mapped without too much clipping. The strobe lights help cover up most mistakes. Doesn't hurt that everyone's drunk and stoned either."

It was true. If she looked closer, paid a bit more attention between the glimpses of light, she could spot it—the way some of the elaborate digital costumes would glitch from one body to the next, how a pair of horns would hover stiffly in mid-air before clipping back to a head. To think Terje had used some of the original wiring to hook up the displays . . .

"Quite elaborate for a party trick," she said.

Terje snorted, finally taking a swig from his cup. "It's not just a party trick. It's the Proteus effect."

"What?"

"It's a psychological thing. Look, see?" Terje pointed across the room where one of the girls had climbed onto a metal drum, towering over the crowd as she stretched her arms wide. Her image on the monitor stretched with her, bird wings of pristine white feathers expanding to their full width across the room.

"Show someone a reflection of something other than themselves," Terje murmured, his voice low beneath the music, "and they just might start to believe it."

Etta watched as the girl spun, her wings casting bright spotlights on the people below. She couldn't imagine staring into a mirror only to see something foreign and reacting with anything but horror.

Terje cleared his throat again, raising his cup. Just as the rim touched his lips, he lowered it. "I can show you," he said stiffly. "If you come back to the park. How the program works—I'll show you. And you can show me how you hacked my network so quickly."

His eyes met hers then, their sharp glint carving through the walls guarding her as she swallowed. She could have figured it out alone. She could have taken the olive branch he offered and snapped it in half, using the broken pieces like spears to carve up and puzzle together his program from what she could access.

Instead, she said, "Deal."

Across the room, the girl with wings screeched and leapt from her perch. She disappeared into the crowd with the loud smack of a body slamming into solid concrete. Her wings disappeared as the camera lost track of her, only reappearing as the girl was heaved back onto her feet by two of the boys nearby. Her nose was bent at an awkward angle and blood was dripping onto her thin white crop top. The moment she was back standing upright, she turned to look at her image, where her wings were once again mounted against her shoulders. An ethereal vision without a single skewed feather. The girl smiled, blood oozing between her lips.

12

Etta spent most of the next day staring uselessly at her laptop while she tried to determine whether Terje's offer had been sincere or a cruel joke. Something about his manner gave her the distinct impression that he wanted to be around anyone but her. Or that he wanted to be around no one at all. But if that were the case, why would he entrench himself so deeply within the V?

She wanted to understand. Not only the inner workings of his code, but the reasons behind how he had ended up at Spreepark. The reasons behind all of them ending up at Spreepark. What brand of magic separated and raised that group above the other partygoers until they had become gods of a midnight domain existing, however ephemerally, in forgotten places? All her life, ties to others had served as shackles, imprisoning her to what the government, group home employees, or foster parents determined was best. But the ties that the V had, the ones that entwined Loulou and Terje, seemed less like restraints and more like an anchor line. Something that kept them strong and stable while the world stormed around them. Something not to resent but to appreciate. To be thankful for.

So, the afternoon after the rave, Etta found herself once again walking up the wooded path toward Spreepark. Alone and without Loulou's chatter, Etta noticed the birdsong as sparrows and finches bounced among the trees. They seemed unafraid of her, dipping low enough to almost graze her head, a parade just for her, siren songs welcoming her back as the arch of the Ferris wheel appeared between bare branches above her head. It granted her courage as she approached the main entry gate, the guardhouse seemingly abandoned other than a soft light coming from inside.

When she was about five feet from the gate, a man appeared, stomping out of the shack and slamming the door behind him as he crossed his arms over his black vest. The word SECURITY was written in white lettering over his chest. At first, she was pleased to see it wasn't the same guard from her previous visit—Frank. The idea of any interaction with him and his shameless eyes made her palms sweat. The new guard, however, seemed to promise a different sort of danger.

"Get the hell out," he snapped. One hand came to rest on a baton at his hip, fingers clenching and unclenching restlessly.

"I'm here to see the V." Etta matched his glower, continuing to walk toward the gate.

"Bullshit."

Her backpack straps dug into her shoulders as she was spun around, the guard's face nearly pressed against the back of her head as he held one arm flat against her chest, just below her neck.

Spit splattered her ear as he snarled. "Get the hell—*ficker.*"

His sharp outburst was slurred from the impact of Etta's elbow slamming into his sternum. He reared back, but his arm closed across her neck as she struggled to get loose from his grip. Her fingernails stung as she clawed at his arm while kicking out against his legs.

He tightened his hold around her neck, and her vision began to tunnel, but she didn't black out. Instead, the pressure on her neck disappeared, and she heaved a deep breath, lungs burning, as shocked tears threatened in the corners of her eyes. Rage fogged her vision as she propelled herself at the guard, but she was pulled back by another set of hands.

It was Terje. His fingers wrapped around her shoulders, steadying her as she took a few more wild breaths. He didn't appear shocked, only annoyed—whether at her fury or the rampaging guard, she wasn't sure—pursing his lips as he patted her shoulders, as if she were a spooked horse to be settled.

The guard rolled in the dirt a few feet away, entirely obscured by a giant. When the giant turned, Etta recognized the shaved head and intricate swirls of ink crawling up from the collar of his shirt. The mountain from Halloween; the bloodied latecomer from the dinner. It took her a moment to remember his name: Foster.

He smiled pleasantly at Etta, boyish embarrassment tilting his dark brows. The guard groaned and Foster quickly planted one of his boots on the man's chest. A fierce gasp for air whistled from below.

Terje cleared his throat. "Are you good? Sorry about—"

Etta brushed Terje's hands from her shoulders, her chest still heaving as she stepped away from him. "Are all the guards psychopaths?" she snapped. "I'm really beginning to think they're all psychopaths."

A low, echoing beat of laughter came from Foster, the guard giving a few staccato grunts as the heavy boot on his chest bounced. "Lou was right about you."

Etta's anger dimmed, stunted by confusion from Foster's remark. She couldn't decide whether he was teasing her or if the affection in his voice was genuine.

"Are you alright?" Terje repeated. It sounded like a factual inquiry, a question voiced in an academic debate rather than a sympathetic gesture. Etta rolled her shoulders back and readjusted the straps of her bag, hoping the blood burning in her cheeks was hidden with a tilt of her head.

"Fine."

"Fine," Terje echoed. He nodded once, looking back at the guard. The man's face was turning a light shade of purplish blue, eyes bulging like two pearls in a dying oyster. "Foster—"

"I've got it." Foster leaned down, fisting the guard's black collar in his hand. His eyes stayed on Terje and Etta. "You kids go ahead. Have fun." He winked at Etta.

For a moment, Etta considered commenting on the "kids" remark. A second look at the guard's bulging expression checked the temptation. Terje appeared similarly miffed, eyes narrowing as he raised one hand in a flicked dismissal. He strode off, leaving Etta to follow him into the park.

Etta realized, with a small shiver of pleasure, that she recognized the path he was leading her down. This time, she didn't stumble or trip in the long grass or over the raised edge of a stray wooden board. Not that Terje would have noticed—he walked with the steady forcefulness of a robot on a predetermined path, stiffly facing forward.

This time, the park teemed with life. About twenty members of the V were lounging about in thick coats and mismatched boots. Tedmund and Varick were huddled under half-collapsed ticket booths, bent together like penguins as they passed a cigarette from mouth to mouth. Hertha and Baron stood together by a park sign faded to illegibility, faces pressed together conspiratorially as their laughter echoed across the grounds. She recognized Alina, Gilla, and Maritza amongst a group of new girls, all perched a few feet away on the old dinosaur sculptures. Alina sat between two large scales on a plaster triceratops's back as she followed Etta and Terje with lazy eyes. It took a moment for her to realize Etta had noticed her. When she did, one gloved hand bobbed in a slow wave. No blunt rested between her fingers this time, though her eyes seemed even glassier than before.

Etta looked away.

They walked past Little Monarchy. The building seemed empty, though a yellow glow came from the window above the main room they had shared dinner in. Terje continued as the perimeter of the park turned into thick woods, the swampy path having dried into packed dirt. The signs and faded artwork scattered throughout the park were half reclaimed by bushes, and the skeletons of old cars and construction vehicles lurked. Past the partially buried bucket of a backhoe, a great white warehouse was tucked among the trees.

Large enough to fit a militia of amusement rides, the massive building was streaked with rust and missing several panels, revealing metal ribbing underneath. Gaping holes in the lower half had been covered with scavenged panels, while those higher up were left for the wind to whistle through.

Etta paused to appraise the whole of it. "This is where you work?"

"No, not this one. Back here." Terje continued around the warehouse where a much smaller structure covered in the same white paneling was hiding. Two large generators hummed against the wall, a collection of gas cannisters lined up at their bases. A satellite dish on the roof probably provided internet access, though Terje must have also tapped into a wired connection somewhere. A thick chain was woven between two sturdy metal rings drilled into the wall and the door. Terje dug out an incongruously small key from his pocket, slipping it into the padlock that was easily the size of Etta's fist.

With a screech, he shoved the old door open. "This is it."

A workbench had been turned into a desk, with three monitors lined up on top. A computer rack glowed a soft blue next to the desk. Etta recognized one of the yellow and black seats from the small cars Loulou had called Die Psychologen, which had been turned into a desk chair, the bottom padded with a few layered jackets. In the corner, a large whiteboard leaned against the wall beside a card table, one of the legs propped up by a chunk of rotted boardwalk. On the whiteboard were three names—Foster, Loulou, Terje—with a collection of tallies beneath each. Whatever score they indicated, Loulou was winning.

The only light in the space aside from the computers was a floor lamp, its long arm turned to face up at the ceiling as the bulb flickered with age. Terje stood beside it, hands tucked under his armpits as he shifted his weight from foot to foot. His face was guarded, as though Etta had intruded upon his workday rather than arrived as an invited guest.

"Huh." Etta slowly crossed to the card table, easing herself down onto one of the folding chairs.

"What?" Terje stiffened, one heel slightly raised off the floor.

"I guess I was expecting, I don't know. A bunch of computers in an old haunted house ride or something. Not this."

His heel dropped to the floor as his arms relaxed enough to shove his hands into his jacket pockets. "I almost set up in a roller coaster, actually."

When Etta's blank stare made it clear she wasn't sure whether he was joking, the corner of Terje's lip twitched upward. "It was too tricky, figuring out how to get the generators to work out there."

"God forbid." Playing cards were spread out on the table, hastily brushed aside rather than properly returned to their box. Etta flipped one over for lack of anything better to do with her hands. "You said you'd show me your program?" she asked, staring at the coffee-stained face of a joker.

Terje blinked twice, big owl eyes sparking with excitement as he pushed himself away from the wall and moved to the bench in front of the computers. At his approach, the monitors flickered to life—abstract blue swirls turned to black screens with green text dripping down the background. He held out his hand like a prince inviting Etta to dance, gesturing to the space on the bench beside him. "It takes a minute to boot up. Don't forget your half of the deal."

She hadn't forgotten. Though the idea of sharing industry secrets still made her squirm. "What does Milan have you do, anyway? Just tech for your parties?"

"Among other things. Are you coming over?" He turned, the synthetic light reflecting off his dark eyes.

The idea of sitting beside him felt like she'd be crossing over the invisible distance she had established between herself and the V. She was not one of them. Even if she indulged in Terje's deal, she was not theirs. A boundary remained and that gulf kept her power, her control. She needed to remain Other. Someone they sought approval from, not the other way around. She needed them to question her standing and believe she was ambivalent about their own.

She shrugged off her backpack and crossed her legs beneath the card table. "I can see from here."

Terje snorted, turning back to the monitors as his fingers began to dance across the keyboard. Etta leaned forward, elbows resting on her knees as she frowned at the way he was chuckling under his breath. "What?"

"Nothing." A white screen popped up, which Etta recognized as a 3D modeling program she had used in the past. Silhouetted by the bright light, Terje shrugged one shoulder. "Just, you're almost as bad around people as I am."

Eventually, she did join him by the computer, though she was careful not to sit down. She leaned on her elbows over the back of the bench as Terje pointed toward a line of code in his script that determined the geometric vectors attached to each digitally constructed object. It was his code that had drawn her in. Everyone who dealt with computers had their own style; some were poets whereas others were scrapbookers. She had seen it all, the way some people created complex worlds of brackets and dashes to solve problems that could be remedied with a simple line. She had seen how others were painfully concise in their coding, carving away at commands until their code was stripped so bare that even the developer comments only managed to be as eloquent as "portion creates array, leftovers excluded." How others copy-pasted their code chunks at a time, bits and pieces of work scavenged from open-source programs hunted down online and turned into Frankenstein's software—like she had done when she'd started out, lacking any real instruction.

Terje's code read like a melody.

He layered detail over a framework already present in his system, and it was immediately clear that Terje and his technology worked in conversation. The majesty of it drew Etta closer, like an artist seeing a Van Gogh for the first time, brows pinched together as Terje continued to point out lines of code that appeared too small, too efficient to be as significant as he claimed.

She wasn't sure how long they spent looking at his files. Etta often experienced a state of flow when programming, but never before had she entered flow with another developer. At a certain point, they stopped speaking altogether. Terje realized she didn't need explaining and left her to marvel at the gracefulness of his work, or even he found himself lost in the flow they had fallen into.

They both jumped when the screech of the door rolling open shattered the peaceful quiet. Etta was sharply aware of how her cheek brushed Terje's curls. Natural light, painful even with the setting sun, had both Terje and Etta squinting as they looked at the two figures standing in the doorway.

"Oh, no," Loulou sighed. "Now I'll never get you out of here." She wore a dark skirt that clung to her legs, the hem catching on the rims of her heavy winter boots. Eyes adjusting, Etta watched as Loulou scratched at the span of her neck hidden by a large black turtleneck sweater. "You didn't tell me you'd be swinging by today," she said, as though she had given Etta a way to contact her that Etta had ignored.

"Yet we're pleased she came." Milan ran a hand over his carefully combed hair. His paternal smile was warm enough to melt the frost that followed them from outside. "Welcome back, Etta."

Etta couldn't remember the last time she had been welcomed back anywhere. She took a step back, tracing the familiar surface of her laptop where it had lain forgotten on the card table. Milan had no coat on, yet he didn't seem affected by the cold. His subdued expression was expectant, like a young professor at the start of an impromptu monologue. Not for the first time, Etta caught herself trying to pin an age on him—but it was impossible. He seemed to hover somewhere between thirty-five and eternal.

"Someone hacked my network last night." Terje had turned back to his screens, the quiet passion his voice had carried earlier dissipating to flat monotony. "She agreed to show me how."

"So much for un-hackable." Loulou winked at Etta, joining her at the table as she pulled out a chair and kicked up her feet. Chunks of snow fell from her boots near Etta's laptop, which Etta pulled away carefully.

"It was secure," Etta replied. "Just not secure enough."

Loulou grinned, her arms crossed over her chest.

"I appreciate the humility, though to hear you outsmarted our Terje—I have to admit, my curiosity is piqued." Milan rested against the workbench, his eyes on Etta as she fought between the urge to run and the urge to lean into his gaze. "And did Terje share any secrets in return? Has he told you about our work here?"

No, he hadn't. And the way Milan phrased it, Etta wasn't entirely sure Terje was meant to. She suspected the V was involved in several illegal affairs, and something about the quirk in Milan's constant soft smile made her wonder whether she had been led to these conclusions intentionally. She glanced at Terje, who was studiously absorbed in his screens, hiding somewhere in the code and white space.

"He mentioned it went beyond party tricks, if that's what you mean."

Milan looked pleased, as though she had made a joke that only they could fully understand. His fingers drummed on the benchtop. "It's a difficult world we live in," he said. "We make do with the tools available to us to survive in a society not built for us. I would wager a guess that's a lifestyle you're familiar with."

She would wager that wasn't a guess at all. Again, she was struck with the sensation of being stuck in a play where everyone knew their lines, their roles—including hers—aside from herself. Still, she wanted to hear what he had to say.

"There's work for you here if you'd like it. Paid, obviously."

"What sort of work?" She didn't exactly have a moral compass when it came to the jobs she'd take on, but any information she could bleed from him would be enough to feast on for weeks—even if she didn't commit to anything.

"Nothing you aren't already accustomed to. Nothing Terje doesn't already do, though the workload has grown, and he only has so many hours in a day." Milan laid a hand on one of the monitors, managing to fracture Terje's focus for a second before he snapped back to typing. "Just collecting some information. Keeping track of those we do business with."

"We could even give you your own little hidey-hole." Loulou had picked up one of the playing cards and was flipping it back and forth through her fingers. "Steal one of Terje's precious generators, all for you."

The perch under Etta's feet wavered. This invitation should have made her feel more certain of her position, given her a label to wear so she could understand why they sought her out. Instead, she felt even more precarious. Disheartened, as well, wondering whether they were only interested in her because of her technical ability.

They were waiting too long for a response, the card frozen in Loulou's fingers as Milan cocked his head to the side.

"I'll think about it," she said.

Milan nodded as though he expected this, still respectful as he tucked his hands into the pockets of his trousers. "We'll be here, whatever you decide. Are you coming to the fire tonight?"

"You're definitely coming to the fire," Loulou answered for her. She dropped her feet from the table and leaned toward Etta, eyes wide under her faded apple-green hair. "You're already here, you have to come."

"The fire?" The only fires Etta had seen were ones in metal trash cans outside old, abandoned houses, yet the excitement in Loulou's voice made it seem like she was inviting her to another party.

"We ripped up one of the old swan boats and we're going to build a bonfire out by the Ferris wheel. I can lend you some warm clothes. We'll get ready together. Come on." Loulou stood and wrapped her hand around Etta's arm. "Terje, I'm stealing her. You can have her back tomorrow."

"I'll come tonight," Terje offered to Etta's panicked glance.

She could nearly believe, if she only looked at him, that they wanted her around just for herself.

"After we speak, Terje," Milan interjected.

"And here we escape," Loulou whispered in Etta's ear. "Before they
start bringing up numbers and margins. Come on."

Etta allowed herself to be dragged from the shack into the cold.
Only after Milan pulled the door shut behind them did she realize she
had left her laptop and her bag in the shack, the only ties to her life
outside Spreepark now firmly out of reach.

13

It turned out that the larger warehouse served as a bunkhouse for most of the group. The massive space had been sectioned off into a series of semi-private quarters separated by curtains hung from rope tied from one wall to the other. Matchbox rooms, cross sections of personalities that Etta peeked into between the edges of recycled bedsheets and shower curtains. Some overflowed with knickknacks and carefully curated treasures; others sported posters with crease lines marring images of mountain ranges or lakebeds. All had the same blue foam mattresses, often stacked for extra padding. Some members had resorted to layering blankets and jackets as makeshift bedding. A few of the scavenged curtains were pulled shut, shadows moving on the other side.

Loulou's space was in the back near one of the only windows. A sheer curtain was tacked above it with a few crooked screws. Peering closer, Etta realized Loulou had made it by cutting up an old blouse: the sleeves dangled uselessly to either side like ghostly arms waving in the cold draft. There wasn't any theme to the items that sprawled across the floor; it was a resting place for lost things. Scattered nail polish bottles rested among a rainbow of hair dye boxes, strands of multicolor Christmas lights hung in vines from the rope above their heads, and an upturned pot spilled dirt onto the floor around the broken brown remains of a plant.

Loulou insisted Etta sit on the mess of sheets and blankets that she called her bed, turning to a large red suitcase covered in stains that rested against the wall. She threw open the flap as though it was a grand armoire, hands on her hips as she appraised the folded clothes inside.

"I know it's in here somewhere—you'll see. First time I saw you, I knew it was perfect. You're so pale, it'll be amazing."

"I'm alright in my sweatshirt," Etta attempted, but with a flick of Loulou's hand she knew she'd lost the battle. She turned her attention to the items closest to the bed. A stack of books was the only tidily kept collection in the entire space, with each spine aligned and stacked in order of size. She picked them up one by one, her surprise mounting with each title. They were textbooks, the pages curled with use. The subjects ranged from botany to economics, some modern while others were criticisms on prominent figures like Marx or Smith. She tried to picture Loulou in a lace dress and boots, tucked among threadbare sheets and polyester sleeping bags reading *The Wealth of Nations* by the light of an old flashlight.

"Try this on."

Etta barely glanced up in time to catch the bundle thrown in her direction over Loulou's shoulder, a psychology textbook clattering to her feet. Loulou still had her back to her, elbow-deep in the suitcase as she shoved sweaters and trousers out of the way in her search for whatever piece she had predetermined would be Etta's.

It was eerily domestic, a scene that reminded Etta of that family sitcom from her childhood, and that was why she chanced a stab at directness.

"Loulou," she said. "Where were you, before the V?"

Loulou continued pulling out clothes, pausing only to wrap a knitted green scarf around her neck before tearing it off and throwing it into the growing heap. When she didn't respond immediately, Etta was prepared to set the question aside with the discarded sweaters, but Loulou finally spoke. "I didn't think you would ask that. Didn't peg you as the type to look for people's pasts."

Etta had made a mistake, she was sure of it. She of all people should have known to avoid this obvious landmine.

"It's a shit story," Loulou said over her shoulder, unfazed. "But I'll tell you, if you try those clothes on."

An even deal. As one stripped bare, so would the other. Etta began to tug off her sweatshirt, back-to-back with Loulou in the small space.

"I grew up in Hamburg. My father was in construction, my mother was a bitch," Loulou said matter-of-factly. "I don't know, I guess they wanted me to go to university even though I could barely get through a day of primary. Even when I was little, all I got out of the whole pageantry were calls home about how destructive I was."

Etta paused, her face still covered in the red sweater she had only just managed to squeeze into. She was tempted to turn to look at Loulou, but it felt like a betrayal of whatever allowance had been made.

"If you get stuck in there," Loulou teased. "I'm not helping you out."

Etta pushed one of her arms through the scratchy sleeve and continued to grapple with the knitting.

"I left two days before my eighteenth birthday. I could have waited but, I don't know, the idea of leaving when I was still technically a child—I mean, I think I always would have been a kid to them, but the illegality of it made it a bit sweeter. 'Look at me, I didn't need you at all, even when everyone says I'm supposed to.' I loved it."

"So you *are* a runaway," Etta said as her face finally popped through the sweater. She turned to see Loulou watching her, sitting cross-legged on the floor with her head propped up by her hands.

Loulou snorted, leaning back against the suitcase as she appraised Etta. "Runaway from what? From that shithole? I'm an escapee. Running had nothing to do with it. I took trains, hopped the whole way until I hit Berlin. There was this band, I think they broke up a year or two ago, but I had heard them online and thought that would be a good place—as good as any, kind of a rebirth. So I met up with them in Berlin, ended up hitting it off with the drummer, he invited me to a party—I told you it was a shit story."

It wasn't, not at all. Etta could see it, could see a younger Loulou with undyed hair and determined eyes hanging to the sides of trains as she trapezed her way across the country in search of a sound she only followed for lack of better direction. The flippant nature of her speech made more sense—Loulou spoke of her life as though it was a biography she had once read of a person long since dead, rather than a recounting of her own experiences.

"The party, that's where you met Milan?" The sweater barely reached Etta's hips. She resisted the urge to tug it lower.

"No, but that's where I met Molly." Loulou grinned at Etta's blank expression. "God, I love it. Such a hardass, but I bet you couldn't tell sugar from coke."

That stung more than Etta was willing to admit. She tried to hide it as she turned away, but Loulou only laughed, standing to grasp her shoulders as she turned Etta to face her. A confident smile spread across her flushed cheeks as she tucked a dark curl behind Etta's ear.

"No, but I met him soon after. He sought me out." Loulou took a step back, her eyes sliding up Etta's body with acute pleasure. "I knew this would look good on you. Just wish I could find the skirt to match."

It had begun to feel a bit too much like Etta was Loulou's doll to dress. She decided any further information was lost to the moment, though the conversation had only fueled her curiosity. "I'm sure no one will notice."

Loulou hummed in agreement. "It's time to go, anyway."

Etta heard grunts and muted shuffling echoing off the metal walls as those napping the afternoon away began to rise from their beds. As Etta reached for her sweatshirt Loulou shot her a sharp glare, tugging it out of reach as she passed Etta a heavy gray jacket instead. Loulou pulled a scarf for herself from the pile, blocks of bright colors blending with her hair as she wrapped it around her neck until it was difficult to discern the boundary between hair dye and cotton.

"You look like a mother leaving her kid behind," Loulou said as she caught Etta casting one more glance at her familiar armor. "Don't worry. No one's goin' to get high and steal your old sweatshirt."

It was mostly dark by the time they left the warehouse. Etta found herself sticking closer to Loulou than before as they trekked the dirt path toward the Ferris wheel, hyper aware of any stones or branches lying in wait.

Etta saw smoke curling like an obstinate finger pointed up at the sky as the city lights crested on the horizon, over the river. The sound of drumming crept across the wet grass, crisp over the instrumental metal songs ringing from a series of speakers set around a small meadow at the base of the Ferris wheel. A massive fire took center stage, the focal point around which benches, logs, and other swan boats—temporarily spared from a fiery demise—were situated in a circle. The pungent smoke burned Etta's nose as the wind blew toward them. Glass from broken beer bottles crunched under her boots as Loulou skipped ahead, the ends of her scarf flapping behind her.

Etta thought she recognized some of the faces. It was difficult to know for sure with only the flickering firelight to see by. Terje was leaning against the old operator's booth for the Ferris wheel, Johanna at his side. Hertha, Annerose, and a few of the others were enjoying the heat from the flames, their boots kicked up against strategically placed stones as they tipped beer bottles to their lips.

There were a couple dozen visible in the firelight, most of them dancing.

Flames kissed the hem of Monika's skirt as she spun in Alina's spindly arms. Echoing laughter and low voices promised more revelers hiding beyond the edge of the warm glow; only Gustaf's brassy voice was discernable to Etta's otherwise unfamiliar ear.

At the raves, the dancing was frantic. Desperate with the weight of a countdown drawn by the rising sun, people grabbed at each other like drowning sailors struggling to keep their heads above the waves. The dancing at the bonfire had no similar sense of hurriedness. Fingers glanced off twirling skirts, but none wound themselves into the fabric. Booted feet did not stomp into the earth but glided across it, mud kicking up in wide arcs.

Above it all, Milan. Perched on a picnic table, elbows resting on his knees as he gazed over his disciples with fond contentment.

Monika suffered a misstep, toe dipping perilously into orange embers. Her face was mercilessly swallowed in the tunnel of black smoke, the music muffling any coughing as she crumbled to the ground, spasming helplessly as feet continued to whirl around her.

Johanna's lips peeled back into a grin, and she barked a laugh and jerked an elbow into Terje's side, her chin flicking toward Monika's prone form as ash floated down over her. When Terje did not laugh, Johanna's grin melted into a scowl.

Milan jumped from his perch and dashed to the other side of the clearing, stooping to raise Monika above the flames as dry, aching retches shook the whole of her. Milan wrapped his arm around her quaking shoulders, squeezing her tightly. A small coil of surprise twisted in Etta's navel as she watched one of his hands slide down her back, lower and more tenderly than any benevolent father would hold a wayward daughter. Monika's cheeks flushed a splotchy red as Milan grasped her chin. The fog of their breath mixed. Etta saw his lips moving, his easy smile quickly mirrored by Monika, who returned to dancing the moment he spun her off with a gentle push, back into the circle like a drunken wind-up toy. Milan had magic words, ones that tightened the spring of one's soul and wound them tight until he could unleash them onto the world with nothing more than a smile and a kiss—was that the secret? Was that why Loulou stayed, why Etta found herself jealous of Monika's bloodied knees and dry, smoke-touched eyes?

She couldn't look away until Milan had returned to his throne atop the picnic table, resuming his position as though he had never moved at all.

"Loulou!"

Terje and Johanna were before them now. Terje's hood was pulled over his eyes as if to shield him from the smoke as he trudged up to them. Loulou met them halfway, grasping Johanna in a tight embrace before leaning back to twirl one of her yellow braids between her fingers.

Etta nodded at Terje. "You came." *Thank you.*

He shrugged, turning his gaze back to the flames with a distant expression.

Etta was forgotten as Loulou bounced onto Terje, wrapping an arm around his elbow as she tipped her cheek against his shoulder with a feline expression. "Hell of a night, getting started without us. Breaks my heart."

"Johanna has them," he said.

Loulou spun away immediately, drawn by the clear baggie in Johanna's hands. Etta recognized a few of the tablets inside as the same type Loulou had taken at the rave. Each girl dug one out and dropped it into her mouth. Johanna looked at Etta, holding up another tablet between her fingers.

"There," she said to Etta. "You can have a blue one."

It had the outline of a butterfly pressed into the face, wing tips reaching from one edge to the next. A promise of freedom, to release her high up into the night sky as worries were forgotten in the mud behind her.

"Next time," Etta said.

Johanna squinted as she tucked the bag away and sniffed—either from indignation or the heavy air.

"You're dancing tonight." Loulou gripped Etta's hands between hers and tugged her forward until their noses were so close that all Etta could smell was menthol.

It struck Etta then that Loulou was offering exactly what she had wanted, the reason she had ventured to last night's rave and to Spreepark after. She had wanted to be accepted, to feel Milan's paternal grasp on either side of her face as Terje created her a digital symphony. Ever since Halloween, her feet had brought her toward them—toward the girls in the cage, the ones who danced. Toward the man who led them.

"Alright, alright."

Loulou's grin was wide as she looped Etta against herself and Johanna, pulling the three of them toward the other dancers around the fire. Etta tossed a quick look over her shoulder, spotting Terje who looked amused, one corner of his mouth teased up as he pulled a hand out of his pocket for a quick apologetic wave.

Etta had never danced in public. She used to frequent the attic of an old building in a residential area by the train station. The rest of the building had paying residents, but she had been new to the streets and the idea of people cycling through their daily lives below her was still more of a comfort than cause for alarm. The tenant directly below the empty attic space had been a pianist, and just after seven each evening a soft melody drifted up through the floorboards. Even then she had known it was a rare thing to hear live piano music, the instrument itself worth more than Etta had earned at that point in her life, not counting the cost to have it moved to an apartment at the top of five old twisting flights of stairs.

So to honor it, she had danced. Quietly, putting on all her socks until her feet doubled in size, then silently twirling around on the old flooring. The names of the songs were lost on her—whether they were improvised or part of some famous opera she had no clue—but every one of them brought a blanket of peace to that space. Those songs had turned battery-powered lamplight into grand spotlights, turned dust into rose petals, turned a musty attic into a stage.

One day, the music stopped. Soon after, Etta spotted a group of men carrying the piano out of the building and loading it onto a large van. She never returned to that building again, the silence too loud to suffer in the absence of song.

Dancing with Loulou nearly felt like a return to that attic. The unforgiving rhythm of electric guitars and drums was of course quite different than the piano. But the peace, the unapologetic emptiness where anxiety and bitterness usually festered, it was the same. She found herself raising her hands as Loulou reached for the sky and hollered with the music. Monika grasped her elbows and spun Etta until her legs wobbled and she had to be held upright by Johanna's firm grip.

Whatever she felt was magnified for the rest of the family, their mouths gaping, hands tapping and rubbing absently on their skin as they rolled on the butterfly pills pressed to dry tongues. Alina had stripped off her shirt, the pale skin of her shoulders and the curve of her breasts bare as sweat evaporated from her skin in a misty cloud. Somewhere, someone was sobbing, but Etta couldn't see anything beyond the smoke, beyond Loulou's moonstone eyes that stole stars from the sky. She was lost to the sound, to the beauty.

Eventually she needed a break. When Loulou collided with Johanna and Monika, the three of them wrapping together, Etta escaped from the whirlpool of bodies. Her eyes burned from the smoke, acidic with the aftertaste of old paint. She stumbled forward, blindly searching for the first place to sit down until her hands found the splintered surface of a bench. She plopped down onto it.

"You looked good out there." Milan's commanding voice snuck up behind her. "You looked like someone who belonged."

A shiver ran down her back as he dropped onto the bench beside her.

"I'll take your word for it," she said. It had been wonderful, but it hadn't felt like belonging. It had felt like acting, like putting on someone else's clothes and repeating their words in the hope that you may eventually become them, all while studiously ignoring yourself. It felt like lying.

He leaned forward, elbows on his knees again as they watched the flames and dancers mix. Etta couldn't relax her shoulders, his proximity electrifying every inch of her.

"We're building something here," he said. "Something important. Out there—all that concrete jungle? We have to dismantle that, separate ourselves from the criminals and the corrupted—but what's left?

That's what we're doing here. We're building what's left, so it's all ready when the world finally falls under the weight of its lies and only the truly genuine remain. Once the criminals are purged."

A week ago, she would have said his "something important" looked an awful lot like a bunch of teenagers getting high and dancing to techno beats. But as she looked at Loulou and Johanna dipping their hands into the flames and laughing wildly, as she looked at the way they all floated across the grass without a single care for who saw them, she could almost believe in Milan's words. There was something to be said for the group—for their rebellious passion for life—that could not be found outside their park.

Milan slipped his fingers into his breast pocket, pulling out a tightly rolled joint and a silver lighter. He held the blunt out to Etta, and she knew better than to decline. He flicked open the lighter, shielding it from the wind as Etta dipped her head forward to light the joint.

"Buddha saw it," Milan said. "Not us exactly, but he saw what we see. That the lies they tell out there, those blanket rules they laid down, calling them shelter when they mean shackles, he saw it. He understood that the only truth is one you find in yourself, once you let all that go. The ego, the bullshit. Great men after him saw it, too, but they strayed. They tried to play the game and drowned in its poison."

Etta tried to picture Buddha out dancing among the family, his robes singed by the flames as a girl dangled off each arm. She imagined him with slick blond hair.

"I don't know much about religion." She held the joint out to Milan and he winked, taking it back and sucking in a drag.

"I think you do; you just label it under something else. You label it under truth." The smoke slipped out from the corners of his mouth in thin wisps between his words. "For example, I'm sure you know the world out there—it doesn't work. It has not worked and will not work, not anymore. Not when the bastards on top have poisoned the well and convinced everyone it's better than water. We don't have housing; families can't afford to eat. People have been protesting for years, and our borders are sagging under the weight of other countries' burdens. You know that, and you know that's why what we're doing out here is so important."

Her skin tingled. When she turned to look at him he was facing the fire. His eyes were wide, palms open as if each of the dancers swung from strings attached to his fingers.

"If you're so focused on staying out of all that shit, why have Terje spend so much time digging into it?"

Milan's hands clenched into fists. The joint balanced between his lips as his voice hardened. "If you want to burn down a city all at once," he said, "you need to know every inch of it. Every inch. You must know where to strike the match. Otherwise, you're just setting fires."

Rather than offering the joint back to Etta, when he pulled it from his mouth, he stamped it out on the side of his shoe and tucked it back into his pocket. She shivered. She couldn't stop shivering, as his words rolled over in her mind like the stone she had thrown at Engel-Bush Banking and Trading. A divide had opened, punched by her care-less words, and she found herself clawing for something to cling to as Milan's eyes stayed trained on the fire before him.

Until her phone, forgotten entirely in the pocket of her pants, buzzed and shattered the moment. Checking the screen, she saw Laurence's number flashing across the front. He was most likely late into a binge-coding session and knee-deep in errors.

When she looked up, Milan was watching her again. His face had softened, no trace of the cold mask remaining as he leaned back against the edge of the table. The phone buzzed again and again, but Etta found herself frozen, unsure whether or how to step away. Milan's lighter clicked open and shut in his fingers along with the rhythm of her phone. He finally waved his hand. She was dismissed.

Etta pushed herself up from the bench, trying to keep her pace steady until she was under the umbrella of dense trees where the music was only a quiet echo between the branches.

"Hel-lo," Laurence greeted cheerfully the moment she accepted the call. "My lady knight in shining armor, do I ever have one hell of a question for you. I was looking back at our program and—"

"Laurence," Etta said. Milan wasn't looking at her directly, but she could feel the pressure of his attention.

"Oh, no," Laurence sighed. "Don't tell me you're busy. I know you're not busy. Come on, I need help on this one, it'll be quick. We are *so* close, and it tastes like *fine-goddamn-wine*, don't do this to me."

"I'm sorry." She was. But the idea of going back to the café, to Laurence's code, when the heat of the bonfire and Milan's words had penetrated deep —she couldn't do it. She couldn't stomach it anymore. "I'm sorry," she said again. "But I'm booked. I'll be booked for a while. I'm done."

He was still complaining when she hung up and slipped the phone back into her pocket. Taking a deep breath, the smoky air crackling in her chest, Etta walked back to the family.

14

Etta left Spreepark that night. She left the next night as well, after spending the day hovering over Terje's shoulder as he explained the details of their newest contract work. The third night, she stayed.

It was a matter of convenience. The work Milan had tasked her with was complicated, different than what she had grown used to. She found herself burrowed in the depths of accounts and documents belonging to local officials ranging from council members to police officers. Rather than rewriting personal histories, she was cataloging incriminating private messages between politicians and their illicit partners of both romantic and corporate varieties.

She loved it. It turned out that her skills in understanding and reframing individual voices and motives translated well into sniffing out the folders and servers where great men hid their dirtiest secrets. From the moment Terje let her loose in a corner of his shack, one half of the card table dedicated purely to her, she had lost track of every hour in the chase down digital molehills as she flipped through password crackers and anti-encryption software like playing cards. The previous night, she had barely been able to pry her hands from her laptop and make a mad dash through the trees so she could sit on the last train out of Plänterwald, her mind whirling with cloud storage folders and the addresses to secretly booked lofts in Swiss ski resorts.

The third day she managed to track an IP address back through a poorly designed VPN in order to prove that an email, initially discovered by Terje, showed that a city official had corresponded with a Russian diplomat regarding security breaches into Berlin's government servers—breaches by the Russians at the request of, and with the assistance of, that official. She had barely moved from the folding chair as she sat back-to-back with Terje in silent comradery, each digging their fingers deeper into the digital trenches, until the creak of the shack door shook them from their screens.

It was Foster, his frame filling the doorway as he gave a cheery grin. Loulou appeared from under his arm, two mismatching bowls balanced in her hands as she dipped into the shack.

"Milan sent me to make sure you guys hadn't starved to death in here." She set one bowl on the desk beside Terje, who immediately cupped it between two hands and sipped at the contents without looking away from his monitor. Loulou snorted, crossing to Etta and setting the second bowl before her.

Etta stared at the carrot and potato chunks floating amid murky broth. "Didn't realize we missed dinner."

"You missed the whole day, little mouse," Foster's voice boomed from the doorway. Etta stared at him, tucking her hands around the bowl as the cold draft reached her.

He smiled sheepishly, scratching at his bald scalp. "Sorry, don't like comin' in the shack too much. Feel like I'm going to knock something expensive over."

"He's not wrong." Loulou stretched her arms tall over her head, knuckles popping as she yawned. "About wasting the day away or knocking some important bright box over. It's nearly eleven."

Shit. The last train left at eleven-fifteen. She would have to sprint if she wanted even an inch of hope of getting there in time, and that sort of reckless race for the station would likely end with her teeth stuck in stones and her face planted in some dirty trench.

Loulou dropped her arms and leaned across the table as Etta tried to weigh the risks.

"You know," she said. "You could always stay here. I have enough blankets to share."

Etta hesitated, her laptop already half closed.

"Would be a shorter commute," Terje said behind her.

"Think of it like a sleepover," Loulou added.

Etta had never been to a sleepover.

Resting beside Loulou was like trying to sleep in a storm cloud. Huddled together under the covers, the hair on Etta's skin raised with the electric snap of each subtle movement when Loulou shifted in her sleep. It had seemed like too much trouble to set up another bed, to lay down more roots, and considering the weather, Loulou had insisted it would be easier to share her space in the bunkhouse. As Etta lay there, one knee off the foam mattress and the rough edge of a musty cotton blanket tucked under her nose, she wondered whether she ought to have found a space for herself after all. She hadn't been able to sleep, hyperaware of accidentally brushing Loulou and jerking awake every time she felt herself ease into unconsciousness.

But she stayed again the next night, and the next, despite the artificial lemon scent that permeated the mattress, as though Loulou had tried to cover the musty odor of the old foam with wood polish. It made Etta nauseous.

Weeks passed, a string of synthetic lemon nights bookended by days spent beside Terje. Occasionally, Etta would push herself to work later into the night—just so she could be the one late to bed—so Loulou could spend time waiting on *her* footsteps. Not that it mattered; not that Etta really cared.

One night, Loulou didn't come to bed at all. Etta was left to count the puffs of her foggy breaths in the cold air as she tucked her icy fingers under her arms, no warm body next to her.

It was only uncomfortable because she was forcing herself to be-long, she decided. She was stuffing herself full of Loulou and card table afternoons until she could convince herself she was one of them. But each night she was forced to confront the disquieting truth: she wasn't part of the family, only an associate. An employee.

It *was fine* that Loulou still hadn't come back by the time Etta tugged on a sweater and extra wool socks pilfered from the stained red suitcase and climbed back into bed—because Etta *was not part of the family*. Where Loulou spent her nights was far from Etta's business; there was no reason for Etta to sit up at every set of footsteps shuffling past. Only when she rolled over in acquiescence to her true situation did she finally sleep, face pressed tight against the lumpy pillow on Loulou's unofficial side of the mattress.

Etta didn't search for Loulou in the morning either, eyes sternly pointed ahead as she wandered past the sleeping lumps tucked behind curtains, out into the fresh morning air. Frost crunched under her boots, a few sparrows scattering as she trudged toward the shack across the clearing. Terje stood outside, leaning against the closed door with a dull red scarf wrapped around his neck and ears while he sucked on a cigarette.

He raised one hand as she approached, offering an open pack of cigarettes with the other. She plucked one out, her back to the soft winter wind as she leaned into the lighter Terje shielded for her.

"Awful habit," he said.

"More of an indulgence." Etta coughed lightly as the smoke bil-lowed up her sinuses.

"A rare indulgence?" Terje's smile gave way to concern as a string of increasingly powerful coughs hunched Etta's shoulders. "Easy, you're alright—just breathe through it, there you go."

His hand was warm on her back, her forehead nearly bumping into his chin as he leaned over her, watching her with a small frown. She looked at the ground, her cheeks growing warmer from their proximity and her heightening embarrassment.

"You okay?" he asked.

"Wrong pipe," Etta rasped, eager to move on. "I'm fine. You've seen the mold in the bunkhouse? Little too late to be worrying about my lungs."

Terje smirked and leaned back, tapping one finger against the shack's metal siding with a soft ping. "Why do you think I sleep in here instead?"

"Right, I'll take my chances with the smoke."

Etta's fingers were numb by the time she dropped the butt of the cigarette to the ground, stomping it out with the heel of her boot as Terje wheeled open the shack's door and gestured for her to head inside. Just as she passed him, he knelt, plucking the orange butt from the ground and fisting it into his palm. She pretended at disinterest as he shut the door behind them, dropping the butt subtly into the small metal bin beside his desk. She looked away, her cheeks burning.

"Coffee?"

"Sure." Etta eased back into the folding chair beside the card table, running her fingers over her laptop. The shack was one of the only buildings with real heating, the inevitable result of packing a small room full of computers. Rather than risk her laptop in the cold warehouse she had begun to leave it overnight in the shack—along with a few extra layers of security programs, in the event Terje saw it as a challenge.

They had gradually fallen into a system over the past few weeks. She would boot her computer to the sound of Terje stirring powdered coffee into mismatched mugs. The first day he had delivered her a plastic cup of steaming coffee without a word. By the next day, a second ceramic mug had appeared.

She tried not to think of it as hers. Tried not to smile as Terje set it in front of her with a nod. That was when they would separate into peaceful silence, Terje to his desk and Etta curled against the table with one arm wrapped around her knee, only speaking when they had an update on one of Milan's targeted names or when one of the generators needed to be refilled with fuel. Comfortable.

That morning, after Terje had slid the coffee in front of her, he eased down into the chair across from her. His arms were stiff as he clutched his mug, eyes focused somewhere over her shoulder as his foot thumped softly against the floor.

Etta blinked.

"I don't like working with people," he said.

Etta raised her steaming mug to her lips, drowning the sudden stab in bitter coffee. "Something we have in common," she muttered into the swirling liquid.

"This, though." He tapped a hand on the table, lips pursed as he slowly forced his eyes to meet hers. "This has been alright."

And it had been. She had never expected to enjoy working in the same space as anyone. It was shocking how quickly someone came to depend on a cup of coffee and quiet exchanges in the morning, the soft security of another body working in tandem as they cracked into the forbidden corners of the internet.

She smiled. "Don't get sentimental, we still have shit to do."

Terje's shoulders relaxed as he laughed. He reached under the table into his jeans pocket, pulling free a thin blue flash drive the size of Etta's thumbnail. It dangled between them like bait on a fishing line. "We don't, actually. I hit the last target last night."

The last target had been a member of the Federal Cabinet, Finance Minister Manfred Rittz. Milan had wanted them to hack into the cloud servers for the politician's private phone, which turned into a dead end, as Rittz was a Luddite with a taste for more traditional forms of photo storage. Etta had spent the evening attempting to find access through his government phone before redirecting her efforts to the man's daughter.

"You were right. The old man uses his kid as his personal IT support," Terje said. "Once you got in, I just had to snoop through their messages and all the data was right there. Fuck knows where that kid gets so much patience, definitely not from her sperm donor."

The pride of succeeding was quickly stamped out by the sudden gust of understanding: Etta's time at Spreepark was ending. Terje was saying goodbye. She would walk away with her money and all of it would be left behind her. She rubbed the pad of her finger over the chipped edge of her mug, and the sharp ceramic bit into her finger.

"What's next?" she asked. "Milan coming to pick it up?"

"We drop it off, after you finish your coffee."

"No need. Let's go now." She pushed the mug forward, grabbed her laptop, and shoved it into the backpack still sitting on the ground by her feet. Her hands were shaking as she zipped the bag closed and swung it onto her shoulders, digging her fingers into the straps. Terje seemed oblivious to the edge in her expression, only shrugging and tipping back the rest of his coffee with a gulp.

They left the shack in silence. Etta tried to step behind Terje to hide the heat rising from her cheeks to her ears, but he slowed his stride, matching her shoulder to shoulder as they approached the pastel outline of Little Monarchy. The park was silent, only the sound of their footsteps and the occasional distant signal from a passing cargo ship on the river filling the space around them.

Terje held the door open for Etta as she stepped into the vacant room. The space had felt claustrophobic during that first dinner. Now, void of any other family members and with the tables pushed to the walls, it felt vast. Etta had nowhere to hide as Terje leaned back against the closed metal door and knocked against the surface three times.

Above their heads, the wood creaked. In the back corner, the door at the top of the stairs swung open to reveal Milan. His hair was slightly more disheveled than any time Etta had seen it before, yet still well-kept in the way it hung tucked behind his ears. He strolled down the stairs, pulling the door shut quickly behind him.

"Good morning, my friends," he greeted cheerfully. "Two of my favorite minds here together, the room is brighter for it."

He paused, one foot still on the last step. Etta shoved her hands deep into her pockets, forcing her chin up so she could look into his eyes. "Happy to be here."

"Are you? It takes time to adjust to living outside the laws of the land." Milan smiled. "To being free."

Etta's fingers dug deeper into the cotton lining of her pockets. Clearing his throat, Terje reached over Etta to drop the flash drive into Milan's waiting hand. Milan admired it as though he could discern all the information inside simply by holding it up to the light, like deciphering the contents of an old letter through its thin envelope.

"It's all on there," Terje said. "Bank records, account names and details, old photos."

"Of course it's all on there. Of course. You two together, you wouldn't let me down." Milan dropped the drive into his palm, clutching it tightly before sliding it into his pocket. He looked down at Etta. "Terje implied you exceeded expectations. I wonder if we shouldn't trade him for you."

Etta swallowed. Her hands were freezing in her pockets despite the heat radiating in the room. Terje seemed unbothered by the remark, stepping back to lean against the wall again as if retreating into whatever mystery he always had running through his mind.

"I wasn't aware there were any expectations beyond getting things done," Etta said. The ground felt unsteady beneath her feet, the approval in Milan's voice both anchoring and rattling her.

"There are always expectations, Etta Baldwin. Especially here. We live in dark times, and it takes a strong soul to rise above them, just as others have done before us." Milan leaned against the railing, the old wood groaning against his moderate weight. "Loulou said you've been spending the night here, with us."

It wasn't a question, yet it still felt as though he was digging for something—his bright eyes searching as they bore into Etta. "Shorter commute," she echoed. "Hope that wasn't a problem."

He laughed. "No, not a problem. Never a problem. I was hoping you would. I told you, around us, you belong. You're welcome here."

Her heel lifted, half ready to take a step back, but that was as far as she could move. "Well, the job is finished now. Unless there's more."

Milan's brows pinched together, that same grim expression he had the night of the bonfire returning as the whole of his body language hardened against her.

"Honesty," he said, "is precious. I appreciate honesty. I appreciate when people are up front about their desires, so they may achieve them. So they may find freedom. In this case, Etta, I ask you for honesty and I will be honest in return. Understood?"

She stared.

Milan knocked a hand on the railing, finally stepping down and forward. "Why do you look for ways to isolate yourself, Etta?"

Her stomach dropped. The walls closed in, the sound of Terje breathing softly behind her suddenly roaringly loud. Milan's questioning eyes were unrelenting.

Her words stumbled out over her tongue. "I'm not sure what you mean."

Milan smiled. He reached one finger up to pull at the collar of his sweater, sighing as he looked at Etta with sympathy, as though she were a tragic child sobbing at his feet. "I had Terje do some digging before we brought you on, Etta. I must be careful about those we allow around us. It's a fragile thing we've built here, and the world seeks to destroy us. The wrong person could undo our work entirely. I've seen your bank accounts. All the money a girl your age could need, yet you barely spent a cent of it—it fascinated me. It fascinates me still. And you act as though you're here only to collect your check. You act as though this has been something entirely corporate, *transactionary.*"

He placed a hand on Etta's stiff shoulder. His grip was firm, steadying her as he stripped her bare.

"You'll have your payment, as promised," he said. "All I ask is that you think about how long you'll continue to use money—these labels—as ways to deny the things you truly desire. As walls, isolating yourself from people who could care, if you let them."

She couldn't speak. She could only nod.

Milan patted her shoulder, the tension snapping loose as he stepped away from her, striding across the room to the door. It opened easily, the hinges barely complaining as he gestured in a clear dismissal. Etta hurriedly followed Terje out into the cool air.

"Stay warm out there," Milan said as his final goodbye. "Watch out for the liars—they're everywhere now." He shut the door gently behind them.

Etta was shivering, though not from the chill biting at her cheeks. Milan's words spiraled through her. Her backpack dragged at her shoulders, her knees weak as she wanted to fall onto the ground and let the frost crawl over her until she was nothing more than an indiscernible mound of dirt and grass.

She felt Terje beside her, but Etta couldn't look at him.

"Come on," he said after a moment. "I'll make you more coffee."

As they began the quiet trek back to the shack, Etta paused, turning one more time to look at the pastel mock-village, wondering if Milan was watching her from the upper-floor window, his sanctuary above the meeting space. Waiting to see whether she would head toward the gate.

It was only a second, a flash—but the figure Etta saw inside was not Milan with his broad shoulders and searching eyes. Instead, for just a moment, Etta caught a glimpse of cotton candy hair.

15

Terje watched Etta from the other side of the table, a playing card dancing between his fingers. He didn't comment on her pensive muteness, either out of politeness or an awkward inability to express anything resembling an appropriate phrase. The tense silence grew with each passing second.

"Have you climbed it?" she asked, eyes toward the door as she pictured its ethereal red frame reaching into the clouds. "The Ferris wheel—have you climbed it?"

Terje snapped the card down on the table.

She didn't give him time to respond, quickly trampling over the space that had opened between them. "I would. I will. I'll climb up every step and leap. I'll fly over Berlin and every goddamn senseless person stuck in it. Fly over all of it, every single thing I never asked for, until buildings look like pebbles and people disappear entirely. All of it. I never wanted any fucking piece of it."

It was more than she had ever meant to admit to, and Terje regarded her with barely shielded shock. She wouldn't apologize. She would not show weakness by swallowing words that were already spilled across the table.

"Listen," Terje said. "Etta, I need to tell you something."

She looked up and as their eyes met, his gaze twitched, as though suddenly desperate to pull away to some indiscrete point on a wall behind her. His bottom lip tucked slightly under the top one as he grappled with whatever words were jammed in the back of his throat.

He never had a chance to say them. The door clanged open, revealing Loulou, looking furiously alive.

"There you are—I say, knowing damn well you'd be here."

Her eyes burned between stray strands of freshly dyed, tangled pink and blue hair, most of it collected into a thick bun at the base of her neck. Etta recognized the black dress as the same one Loulou had worn the day before, with a green sweater layered on top. It hung loosely from her shoulders, revealing the thin strap of her dress like a secret as she hiked a hand onto her hip.

Etta resisted the urge to ask Loulou where she had been, why she had left Etta to fend for herself against the night chill, whether that flash of pink hair in Milan's window belonged to her—but she was not Loulou's keeper. She did not have the right to keep track of Loulou, just as no one else had any right to keep track of her.

She looked to Terje, waiting for him to give a clue as to whether he intended to finish his thought, but the wall of practiced disinterest had fallen back over his features. Terje picked up the playing card and began to spin it between his fingers once again, eyes locked distantly beyond them.

"Nowhere else to be," Etta said. She wouldn't deny it; a part of her wanted it to sting, even if she wasn't entirely sure why. She had no reason to be angry at Loulou. No reason to care at all.

"Oh, *god*, you're starting to sound like Terje. Lighten up." Loulou dropped onto the bench, kicking up her feet and tucking one boot under herself. "Did you wrap up work? Because—and maybe the movies lied to me—this doesn't look like coding. Or hacking. Whatever you guys do. Pretty sure your laptop needs to be actually open."

"We wrapped up," Terje said. He snapped the card on the table again.

Loulou dropped onto her back, arms lifted into the air as she gave a silent cheer. When she rose back, resting her chin over arms folded across the back of the bench, she smiled widely at Etta.

"There's no escaping now." She pointed a finger at Etta, the polish almost entirely scraped off. "Tonight. We're celebrating."

The card fluttered to the floor. "Shit," Terje muttered. "Shit. I forgot."

"What?" Etta looked between them both. Loulou was amused as she tilted her head at Terje, who was running an anxious hand over his neck.

"You forgot?" Loulou turned back to Etta. "There's another rave. Tonight. Out at an old warehouse downtown. The others are already getting everything together—Terje, did you seriously forget?"

"Been a little busy."

"Fine, listen—you have to come, Etta. Please." Etta's hesitance must have been obvious as Loulou straightened, the playfulness melting away into soft apology as she wound her fingers together. "Etta," she pleaded, her voice softer than Etta had ever heard it. "Let's have fun, just tonight at least. Let's have fun, all of us together. Don't spend the night alone."

Loulou reached out her hand—a promise. A purpose.

"Screw it. Sure."

There would never be a day when Etta wasn't shocked at the sight of a rave. People filled every single room of the latest makeshift nightclub until she was certain the oxygen had been sucked completely away. She watched them on the monitors in the control booth, as the building shook with the weight of hundreds of bouncing bodies. Occasionally, she caught a glimpse of Loulou, a head of pastel hair floating from room to room like a ghost as she dissolved under the multicolor lights.

Terje's gaze was nailed to the lightboard with an intense focus, his eyes darting from monitor to board until Etta was certain he had plugged himself into the patch panel as another piece of equipment, a computer inputting commands and guiding the world with a robotic hand.

Loulou burst into the control room, panting, her face twisted with wild glee and strands of hair plastered to her cheeks with slick sweat.

Behind her was Johanna, her stern face looking especially severe with her hair slicked back in a tight bun.

"You," Loulou heaved. "You're coming down. No escaping this time. I will drag you—don't even look at me like that, I swear."

Etta choked. Johanna's cold eyes bore into her over Loulou's shoulder, one brow arched in challenge.

"She's not interested, Lou. Would rather sit up here. What the hell is that smell anyway?" Johanna's face scrunched as she gave an exaggerated sniff. "Is that mold?"

Whatever Johanna smelled, the stench of sweaty bodies dancing below them had to be worse.

Loulou reached forward to dig her fingers into Etta's arm. "Be honest with me." Her eyes were so wide that Etta could see the whites all the way around her irises. "Are you working up here? Or hiding?"

Etta attempted to jerk her arm out of Loulou's grasp. "Neither."

"Good." Loulou's expression softened, spreading her lips into a small smirk as she opened her other palm to reveal two white tablets, no special butterfly printed on the front. "Let's go meet God."

Terje snorted and Loulou whipped her head toward him, her fingers digging tighter into Etta's skin until she was sure they would bruise. "Don't laugh, you're coming too."

"I have to run the booth." Terje turned, confident until he noticed Etta's expression. "I mean, it's mostly automated at this point. I don't have to be here."

Etta swore under her breath. She had wanted an excuse to stay, not a companion.

"Fantastic. Open wide." Loulou pushed her palm toward Etta, who raised her hand in front of her mouth as she searched for a reason to say no.

Johanna spoke again from the doorway. "She won't do it, Lou. Don't think she'll ever do it."

That would not stand. Etta plucked the tablet from Loulou's palm, dropping it onto her tongue despite not knowing whether to chew or swallow. Loulou grinned, releasing her arm to pinch Etta's cheeks between thumb and pointer finger so tightly her lips pursed and tingled. "Good," she said. "Let it dissolve. Terje?"

As Terje rose from his chair and grasped his tablet, Etta chanced a glare at Johanna. Her face was a mask of ice and disappointment. Whether at Etta's acquiescence or the fact that she would no longer have a monopoly on Loulou's attentions, Etta wasn't sure. It didn't matter—Loulou had already reclaimed Etta's arm to drag her down the stairs, leaving Terje to stride down the steps two at a time behind them. It wouldn't be until much later that Etta realized Johanna never followed.

It was so loud. The magnitude of it hit Etta immediately, the weight of the beat dropping lower and lower until her diaphragm itself was resonating. Loulou pulled her through the maze of rooms, slipping between crushing bodies. When Etta tossed her head back to make sure Terje was following, his hand dipped forward to reassuringly tap her shoulder. His white shirt glowed under the black lights, a bright ghost in her wake.

Finally, Loulou seemed to have decided on a room—about the size of the shack, but claustrophobic with dancers pressed wall-to-wall. Etta couldn't stop staring at the shadows the bright lights cast against the crumbling walls. A firm hand dragged her back to Loulou's ethereal blue gaze.

Loulou grinned, loosening her grip on Etta's arm, sliding down to link fingers.

And then Etta was dancing.

Loulou's hand glided over Etta's back, gently guiding her body as they let the music pull them deeper. Etta felt Terje behind them and the shock of knowing he actually danced—that he was with her, enjoying the night rather than spending it in Milan's shadow or engineering the fun from above—it was bliss.

The lights were spinning. No longer just shifting through colors but morphing, bleeding into the skin of every dancer until they were a blanket of hues. Soon Loulou didn't need to guide her—every muscle was awake, jolting, tensing—so painfully alive, her tongue was twisted and her jaw was clenched. Every part of her body was at attention, invited or not.

A passing thought about the tablet flicked through her mind, but it was gone before Etta could grasp it, dissolved by the sensation of Loulou's lips sliding gently over her own.

It was so incredible, so warm. Everything made complete sense; it was as though every experience Etta ever had was a collection of puzzle pieces that had failed to snap together until that moment. Milan had created sanctuary, a peace away from oppressive control—when the crowds cheered for him, they cheered for joy. For love—it had to be love. She did not know what it could be otherwise.

Loulou's eyes crinkled at the corners as she smiled knowingly. When Etta spun back toward Terje, to see whether he knew too—whether he understood—it felt only natural to lean into his embrace as well, reveling in the cool touch of his hand against her burning back as his fingers slipped under the hem of her shirt, against the naked skin along her spine.

They continued like that, her, Loulou, and Terje. Spinning between each other, hands locked, then separated. Then Etta was no longer on the floor at all, pulled from Loulou and Terje as a mountain gripped her within its massive paws to hoist her into the air above the other dancers. When she dropped her hands, wildly fighting for any hand-hold as she tipped perilously backward, her fingers met a smooth scalp.

"Hold on, little mouse!" Foster shouted above the music, his shoulders shaking as he laughed at Etta's grappling. "Tonight, you fly—yes?"

Yes. From the corner of her eye, she saw the flash of metal as Terje pulled something from his pocket. A remote, which he pointed into the distance.

It was Terje's program, the multicolored dancers turning into fairies and ghoulish wolves broadcast against the farthest wall, the picture splintered near the floor as it projected over twisting legs and pounding feet until Etta could no longer tell image from reality.

Foster pulled her from the illusion as he bounced his shoulders once and his lips mouthed two words with exaggerated care: look up.

She did. It took a minute to recognize what she was seeing. Her glower softened into dazed glee. It was birds, hundreds of them—sparrows, songbirds, parrots. They fluttered around her projected image, scattered into a cloud of flapping wings. Her black curls had been twisted into red-speckled feathers, framing her face; a scattering of delicate white down replaced her eyelashes. As Etta blinked, she nearly believed she could feel their soft touch on her cheeks.

Terje—he had done this. That's why he had been so focused in the shack all afternoon after Loulou burst in, even though they'd finished their job for Milan. Why he had barely acknowledged Etta in favor of his laptop after they had been reminded about the rave.

He had done this so she could fly, high above the heads of Berlin.

She reached for him desperately, split somewhere between glaring and crying as she noticed the gentle curl of his lips, that he was watching her as the majesty of his code gave vision to her dream. Foster bent lower, allowing her to wrap her arms around Terje as his warm breath washed over the shell of her ear.

"You can fly," he said. "With us—fly. You're one of us now, part of our flock."

She dropped fully from Foster's shoulders into Terje's grasp as he spun, arms tucked firmly around her torso.

Her toes never touched the ground. She was certain they never would again.

16

"Hit."

The soft hum of the computers was broken only by the tinny murmur coming from Terje's headphones. Etta's laptop was packed away, the card table cleared to make space for the game spread before her. Foster sat across from her, his knees lifting the table slightly as he struggled to balance his massive form on the plastic chair.

"You're certain?" Foster plucked a card from the top of the pile, waving it slowly before her with a keen glint in his eye. His eyes widened theatrically as he checked the card's face. "I'm not so sure."

"Hit," she confirmed.

Foster flicked the card toward her, the nine of clubs fluttering down to the table. He didn't even look as she flipped over her hand, revealing a perfect twenty-one as he reached for the marker beside him.

"We have a word for this in Frankfurt," he said.

Etta pulled the small pile of crackers—the closest thing to poker chips—from Foster over into the growing mound on her half of the table. "Luck?"

"Cheating, little mouse." He laughed as he made a mark on the newest column added to the whiteboard, titled "Mäuschen" in sloppy handwriting.

"Cheating?! I just learned how to play; how could I cheat? Terje, tell him I'm not cheating."

Terje didn't look away from his monitor as he shouldered one side of his headphones off his ear. "She's cheating."

Etta threw up her hands as Foster pointed an accusatory finger at her, jerking fearfully as his elbow came within range of the cabinet full of projectors and camera equipment behind him.

"Etta, listen—" Terje pulled off his headphones entirely, unplugging them as the polite voice of a newscaster filled the room.

Over the past week Milan had tasked Terje and Etta with disseminating some of the information collected over Etta's first few weeks at Spreepark. Photos of Finance Minister Manfred Rittz's affair partners had been spread across social media along with damning exchanges held over text and email. The smoking gun was the trail of bank statements and transfers, linking the politician to deposits made into offshore accounts by discreet accounts originating in Russia, Belarus, and Latvia. He was part of the poison corrupting their world, Milan had said. The people of Germany deserved to know the dirt coating the hands that guided them.

Etta didn't care either way—a part of her still refused to give any faith to the common man, convinced they really lived their lives without any understanding of the corruption they slept in. Still, the weight of Milan's words was undeniable.

Foster and Etta both turned to the prim woman displayed on Terje's monitor, her hands entwined as she detailed Rittz's recent departure from the Cabinet over "inappropriate dealings with both local citizens and foreign agents abroad." A short clip was laid over her narration, the old man cupping one hand over his eyes while he clenched a binder full of papers in the other as he huffed his way down a flight of stairs through the crush of reporters jutting microphones toward him like a Roman phalanx.

"Wonder what his daughter will do with all her free time, now that she doesn't have to help her dad reset his email password a hundred times a week." Terje leaned back, arms lifted on either side of the bench beside him as he tipped his head to look at Etta.

"Finance Minister Rittz has also been accused of corresponding with agents from various countries outside of NATO," the broadcast continued. "Some of the material released has heavily implied he may have been in contact with groups connected to several domestic terror incidents."

Etta sat up straighter, one hand frozen with a piece of her winnings at her lips as she frowned. "Wait, did we release that?"

Terje leaned forward again, jacking his headphones back into his computer; the broadcast was abruptly cut short. "Did we need to? Give the information to the people, they'll come to their own conclusions."

"True or not, it does not matter." Foster collected the cards from the table, his once-bright eyes distant. His hands were slow as he tapped the deck thoughtfully on the table edge. "We all make choices, little mouse. Choices like that, the details . . ." He flicked his hand, a few cards spraying out onto the floor. "What are they? What does it matter? He made his choice; these are the consequences."

She had never spared much thought toward consequences beyond her own. Did it matter? Etta had shone a light under Rittz's table and that should have been enough to convince the people of his poison. When the list of crimes rolled across the courtroom floor, the details didn't really matter. The quantity of charges was enough to condemn him; everything else was set dressing. An extra dash of wretchedness for an empty, loathing public to stuff themselves with. Terje and Foster were right: Rittz had made his bed.

She jerked her chin at the cards in Foster's hands. "Again?"

He sighed, leaning down to pick up the stray cards. The stack of crackers beside Etta toppled as Foster's knee bumped the table. "Again? You're relentless, little mouse."

They never played their second round. Just as Foster finished shuffling with a shocking level of dexterity for a man whose hands looked like they were more suited to a pair of boxing gloves, the screech of the shack door pulled their focus.

Monika balanced awkwardly against the doorframe. She was a

patchwork of forgotten clothes, two long peasant skirts layered over thick black tights. The collar of a button-down shirt stuck out over a massive black sweater that nearly reached her knees. As she poked one foot tentatively inside, Etta could see even her boots were mismatched—one appeared two steps away from falling straight off her ankle.

She gave a small smile with swollen lips. "Etta?"

Etta set down her cards and glanced at Foster. His eyes were trained on Monika with a careful type of observance Etta couldn't quite identify. It was well known that the shack was off limits to most of the family members; prior to Etta, only Loulou had frequented it—mostly at the behest of Milan to ensure Terje was still eating between his long coding binges. Foster was allowed access as well, though he typically refused unless bribed inside with the promise of a card game.

Etta couldn't remember Monika ever coming close to the shack.

"Milan," Monika continued. "He wants to see you."

And he had sent Monika instead of Loulou? "Is everything alright?"

"Sure," Monika said.

Etta stood carefully. Terje had pulled off his headphones and nodded as she glanced at him. Foster sighed dramatically beside her, stealing a cracker from Etta's pile. "Next time, then. Next time, no cheating."

Monika's arms wrapped around herself as she smiled gratefully at Etta, as though she had been afraid she'd have to drag Etta away. Etta tried not to let her mind whirl with what Milan could want, whether she had done something wrong. Whether she had been too obvious in her part of information distribution—was that what he wanted to discuss? The Cabinet Minister?

The loud smack of a deck of cards hitting the table spun Etta's attention back to Foster, who was looking at the whiteboard with their names. "You never asked, little mouse. You accepted your name as Mäuschen, but you never asked why."

Etta paused with one hand on the cool shack door. "Was I meant to ask?"

The edge of Foster's mouth quirked as he turned to her.

"To Terje, you are his bird. His sparrow. For me, our little mouse. Our quiet scavenger." He tapped the whiteboard with the deck of cards, where the series of tallies had grown under her moniker. "Both small, both free—both easily underestimated. And, both cute to watch—especially sparrows." Foster winked as Terje stiffened, a strangled groan sounding in the back of his throat as he pointedly tipped his face away from Etta and toward the ceiling.

Ah. Etta turned to hide the unbidden smile that stretched over her warming cheeks. "I'll be back soon."

As she left the shack to follow Monika into the outside chill, she could hear Terje's sharp voice somewhere behind them amid Foster's booming laughter.

Monika was silent as they made their way toward Little Monarchy, her arms still firmly clasped around her sides. Etta tried to remember where she had last seen Monika aside from spare glimpses at night in the bunkhouse, but she could only remember that night by the fire—Milan's hand digging into the flesh of Monika's hip as her back heaved with violent coughs. Otherwise, she was a ghost. Her presence was implied every night when Loulou or Terje delivered bowls of fresh food to the shack, or when Loulou made offhand comments about collecting dirty clothes "for Monika to take care of," yet Etta hadn't had the chance to have a conversation with her since their first small exchange.

When they reached the pastel village, Monika paused several lengths from the door, finally breaking the silence. "He's upstairs." The light in Milan's room was on, but fabric was pulled across the window.

"You're not coming in?"

Monika jumped, eyes wide as she fisted the fabric of her sweater. "No, no. Just you. I have things to take care of, I need to get working. Go ahead, he's waiting." She took a few steps back, one hand unclenching to wave slightly toward the door as her eyes darted between the window and Etta.

Monika's anxiety leaked into the ground until it was soaked up by Etta's shoes. She swallowed, walking slowly to the door. As she pulled it open she looked back to Monika, who was watching from under the canopy of trees. Etta entered the space, clicking the door shut behind her.

It was quiet inside, and dark. The chairs and tables were still pushed against the walls, the lights all off. Each step creaked violently as she ascended the stairs. She had done something wrong, she knew that with increasing certainty as she came within reach of the door to Milan's room.

She stood there, hand poised over the wood as she tried to remind herself that it didn't matter, that she didn't care—except she did. Enormously so.

The door opened before she could knock.

"Etta Baldwin," Milan said. "Come inside."

Etta dropped her hand and followed Milan down a short hallway. To her left, an old door with peeling white paint was cracked open just enough to allow a passing glance at the sanctuary—Milan's bedroom. Her steps slowed as she indulged in a long glance.

His room was sparsely decorated. A large dresser with clawed feet rested against the farthest wall. Beside it was a bed, with an actual frame that had tree branches carved along the headboard. The sheets were folded back, and Etta wondered wildly how Milan could suffer the cold winter without a massive pile of blankets or another warm body to rest against, though she could never picture him shivering alone at midnight like a cowering child. She imagined he slept like an old god from children's stories, a peaceful statue until a righteous call to action eased him awake.

"Etta?"

Etta jumped back, heart pounding as Milan smiled warmly and gestured ahead to the large room at the end of the hall—his office.

Despite its minimalism, the drafty room maintained a grand atmosphere. What little furniture Milan had felt royal, as though his room was once the subject of a renaissance painting but its contents had been scratched and worn until only splotches of beauty remained. Best of all was Milan himself, who had moved to stand beside a small table and two chairs placed under the single square window. One hand on the back of a chair and the other resting at his side, he looked every part the king standing at the edge of his balcony—the whole of his kingdom at his back.

On the table were two glasses, the clear liquid inside rippling slightly as Etta slowly approached. Milan pulled the chair out. "Sit down," he said, which she did awkwardly—too focused on not falling into the chair should her knees give out entirely.

Milan crossed the floor, taking his seat as he hiked one foot up onto his knee and grabbed the glass closest to him. He watched her as he took a sip. Etta reached for her glass, wrapping her fingers around the cool surface as she fought the compulsion to speak, to fill the silence that had wrapped around them.

Then Milan smiled. "There's no need to wear your armor here, Etta. I promise it's not poisoned."

This was not reassuring in the slightest. She raised her drink, her hand remarkably free from trembling as she took a sip—then nearly spat it out, the straight vodka burning her throat and sending tears to her eyes as she choked back a shocked gasp.

Milan took another calm sip, turning to look out the window as he spoke. "I'm sorry to pull you away from your work, but I felt we needed to have this discussion. I felt *you* needed to have this discussion."

Etta swallowed back against the fire in her chest. "Is this about a new project?"

"In a sense." Milan set his glass down and turned back to her. A strand of blond hair had strayed from behind his ear. "Do you remember our last exchange downstairs? About your payment? I noticed you haven't asked for any compensation since."

She hadn't. Not a penny. She had found herself working with Terje on job after job yet every time she considered asking about payment, the words died on her lips. A warm bed in the bunkhouse beside Loulou, a portion of crackers rightfully won from Foster—those things had piled up on her shoulders, the sum of them more valuable than any paycheck had ever been. Somewhere along the way she had even begun to feel indebted to the V, offering the use of her funds when there was food to be bought or they needed drinks for the next rave.

"I didn't end up needing it," she said.

Milan hummed; one brow raised as he lifted his glass again. Had she impressed him? Was he surprised to know she had internalized their previous discussion—even if she would never admit it outright?

"I must confess something, Etta. You know how important honesty is to keeping our fragile haven alive. I am not exempt." Milan stood from his chair, reaching up to unlatch the window beside them. It swung open with a dull scratch, the cool air brushing against Etta's warm cheeks. "The day you met Loulou was not entirely serendipitous."

Etta shivered. "What?"

"We had heard about a talented girl in Berlin. Terje found traces of you online—I believe he mentioned this to you when you were first introduced. The work he does, it's inevitable that he would eventually stumble over some trace of your work—though it took him longer to track you down than he would admit." He tapped a hand on the windowsill. "Loulou finally found you through your friend Jonah."

"Jonas," Etta corrected. "Not my friend."

"Jonas. He knew you. He had a deal with you. That's the problem with people like that. Give them an opportunity and they'll only look to double it. Did he ever tell you where he got that laptop from?"

She should have been furious. And a spark of shadowy rage flashed images of her throwing her glass to the ground and storming out. But that spark was quickly replaced with shame at her stupidity—how she had never questioned why Loulou had found her at the only café Etta ever frequented, how she had never connected her laptop's hacking with the arrival of the V into her life.

"You planted the false BIOS." She couldn't keep the waver from her voice. "You were watching me."

"I'm sorry." His shoulder dropped as he sighed and sat back down at the table. Something that could have been regret drew his brows down toward his nose and pinched his lips. "We wanted to know if you truly lived up to your reputation, whether you were safe to bring into our family. We can't accept everyone, Etta. We must protect ourselves; you know that."

Her skin prickled with gooseflesh as her anger transformed into pride. Her invitation to Spreepark had never been an accident, she had been wanted—Milan had wanted her with them. They had found her amid the rubbish of Berlin and pulled her into their embrace, given her a place to land when she had been grasping at bricks on abandoned walls.

She had been judged and found worthy.

"Well." She laughed softly. "Fair enough. Not exactly like I have the right to judge."

Milan nodded.

Etta shifted in her seat. A bird sang outside, drawing Milan's attention even though Etta's gaze stayed firmly fixed on him.

Was that it? He remained silent but made no move to dismiss her. Had he only called her up to his room to inform her of their spying, to clarify the reason she had been brought into his fold? She set down her glass, wondering if she should rise to leave.

"I also wanted to ask about your father."

Etta swallowed. No, he wasn't done with her yet. The lies bubbled up from her chest like a false flag defense, smoky green deflections to turn one man into someone different, and she opened her mouth—but she couldn't speak. For so long she had relished the opportunity to craft new truths about her father and his presence, but looking at Milan, the way he watched her so openly after his honest admissions—she couldn't. The lies died.

"He's as much a ghost as my mother."

"Your mother." Milan stubbed the rest of his cigarette onto the windowsill, leaving it there half bent like a crooked finger as he fished a hand into his pocket. He pulled out a folded square of paper, unraveling it carefully and smoothing out the creases against the table. It was an article, the photo of the familiar tall building beneath the headline sending a shudder through Etta as Milan began to read.

"Berlin stockbroker leaps to her death following devastating market crash." Milan's voice was as crisp as a newscaster, his cadence plucky as he detailed the day Etta lost everything.

"Stop." She pinched the edge of the tabletop between her fingers to stop their shaking.

"Stockbroker Anna Baldwin died this past Wednesday following a day many are comparing to the historical 'Black Friday,' where global stock values dived to a record low as a result of several—no, here, let me skip ahead."

"*Stop.*" The wood splintered under her nails, digging into the pale beds of her fingers.

He looked at her directly then, spinning the paper as he recited the next lines from memory. "Baldwin leapt to her death from the roof of Engel-Bush Banking and Trading, where she had been an employee for over eight years. Initial interviews with colleagues indicate that her death is believed to be a direct result of the economic crash. Company representatives could not be reached for comment."

Etta shoved back her chair. It fell against the floor with a loud clatter. She snatched the paper from the table, crumpling it into her fist.

"I know," she hissed. "I know what it says."

Slowly, with composure, Milan took another sip from his glass. Etta trembled, first from anger, then fear, as he slowly dropped his foot from his knee to the floor and rose. She had never realized how tall he was until that moment, when he towered over her, and she was forced to tilt her chin up to meet his overcast eyes. He didn't look angry, which added to her growing anxiety—had it been a test? Something to measure her limits? If it was, she had surely failed, and now—*finally*—she would face the consequence she had been dreading from the moment Monika had appeared at the shack.

"Such a short article," he said, miles above her. "To think they never mentioned the child she left behind."

It was too much. She turned, feet propelling her forward as she went first to the window—no, that was too similar. She wanted fresh air, but it was impossible to imagine pressing her torso out into space in that moment, so she paced to the other side of the room, then back toward the door—but she couldn't leave either. She was still locked to Milan, enwrapped in whatever purpose he had for their conversation. She was trapped and left to prowl like a wildcat as Milan stood watch over the fire he had unleashed.

The article, crumpled into a misshapen wad on the floor, crunched under his foot as he stepped forward, hands tucked into the pockets of his trousers. He tilted his head at Etta. "Well?"

"You have no right," she snapped. "You have no fucking *right*."

His reaction was immediate, his face twisting as he charged forward and pushed Etta back until her spine was flush with the wooden walls. "No right?" He bent lower until they were nearly nose to nose. "*I* have no right? Tell me, Etta—explain to me how I have no right, how you find it fair to direct your fury toward me, when the men who murdered your mother rest on the profits of her labor—of her death sentence. I only recite history, *your* history, and you blame me for the simple fact it happened?"

Her cheeks burned, fingers loosening from tight fists as she deflated. Only the solidity of the wall kept her standing. She thought of that night she visited the building, of the stone she threw, and she understood how the stone must have felt, to never reach its goal, to be left forgotten on the sidewalk.

"I'm sorry," she whispered.

"You're not." Milan held her shoulders as he spoke carefully. "You're not, nor would I ask you to be—do not be sorry, be *angry*. We live in a world doomed by a failing society, run by sinners and populated with criminals—criminals that they invite here, into our country, our home. The same criminals that murdered your mother. Etta, I never wished to upset you. I care for you, you're one of mine, and you've done marvelous work. I only want you to understand what we're fighting, to stop separating yourself from this war—you were a casualty from the moment you were born, left to be forgotten. A victim."

His lips came to rest against her forehead as he squeezed her shoulders. "I want," he said, the words feather-light against her flushed skin, "you to be furious. You have every right to be. This is as much your fight as it is ours, so take it. Be ours, so we may be *yours*. We will be your hands, your soldiers, *your family*, in this war they brought on themselves. We'll start the war that destroys them both, pit the foreign criminals against the rich liars. Take your anger and turn it out. Help me, and I will help you burn every one of them until our clothes are blackened with their ash."

17

Every forgotten park statue or attraction jutted up from the ground like the limbs of half-buried bodies dredged up by the swampy water. Etta's feet crunched across the frosted earth as she passed them. She wouldn't go back to the shack; she couldn't face Foster's friendly smile or Terje's stripping gaze. Pushed forward by anger and shame, Etta headed into the heart of Spreepark.

She could still feel the dry press of Milan's lips against her forehead, his warm words hushed across her hair. She should have been proud. Milan approved of her, recognized her pain and offered to stand by her—to give her a place standing beside him. The right hand of God. It was far beyond the small praise her father had once offered her, the exact wording and reason lost to time.

Milan had offered to burn the world down with Etta, in the pursuit of justice. The world was beyond saving, he said. Everyone except for them. Hadn't she always believed that, deep down?

"Shit," Etta hissed. "*Shit.*"

She had never felt kinship with the people that rolled down the street like lazy stones set on a path they never bothered to challenge. They had killed her mother, then written her death off as a rare symptom of an otherwise sound system—and thrown Etta's fate down with her. Every pain she had felt, every night she had spent pressed against a door to ensure no one broke in while she slept, every day she had awoken on the lumpy bulge of her backpack—it was their fault. Their choice, and they didn't care. Only her Wechselkind cared, as much as she allowed it to.

But Milan cared. The V cared. Milan loved, and he only wanted to take back what was stolen from his family. From her.

She found herself at the base of the Ferris wheel. The top of its arch kissed the setting sun, a burst of oranges and pinks billowing out around it like a halo. She strode closer until she could press her hand to the cool metal, until the frost bit her skin with the promise of burning pain. It had been so long since she had climbed, yet her feet felt too heavy to take another step, too anchored to the ground of Spreepark. The clash of memories, the conflict between her life here and the days she had spent clinging to the sides of old buildings. The metal grate of the Ferris wheel's base dug into her skin. She squeezed her eyes tightly until all she could see were false stars.

A hand on her shoulder burst through it all.

Etta recoiled, flashes of an aggressive security guard with a fierce face flickering across her mind.

"Etta, shit, calm down." There was just enough light left in the sky to see the details of Terje's face as Etta's eyes adjusted. She collapsed onto the metal grating.

Terje still had his hands held outward in surrender. Feathered locks of his hair stuck up awkwardly around the band of a headlamp.

"Terje," she gasped. "Jesus, what do you want?"

"Wanted to spend the evening freezing to death by the Ferris wheel, same as you." He stabbed his hands into the pocket of his black sweatshirt, eyes locked somewhere above her head. "You didn't come back. Loulou dropped by, said you hadn't gone to the bunks either."

"What, you're my keeper now? What the hell do you care?" It felt terrible the moment she said it, sloppy cruelty—but she couldn't hold it back.

He looked down at her. Unshaken by the ice in her words, he stared.

"What?" she muttered. Not so cruel, but still as bitter as a wounded animal.

Terje pulled one hand from his pocket, tossed something toward her. She scrambled to catch it. She turned the small black box over in her hand, the rough strap wrapping around her wrist. Another headlamp.

"Come on." Terje stepped up beside her, hiking one foot onto the bottom rung of the ladder.

"What?"

"You said you wanted to climb," he said, the only explanation he offered as he pulled himself onto the next rung. He reached up to turn his headlamp on, the tunnel of white light bouncing off the Ferris wheel's red frame.

It was dangerous. The wind would be howling at the top, only their grasp against chilled steel keeping them from a quick death—assuming they didn't hit any of the metal beams on the way down. But to climb above the night, to separate herself from Spreepark just long enough to take those first few puffs of fresh air . . . Etta tugged the headlamp onto her head, switching on the light as she stepped onto the first rung.

Terje paused above her to look down over his shoulder. "Do I need to worry about you attacking me from below?"

Etta couldn't fully conjure a smile. "Truce."

It was a long climb. Slower than she was used to, stuck following at Terje's pace as he cautiously pulled himself up into the sky. Somewhere near halfway she noticed how his knees quaked slightly, his feet hesitating as he measured the distance to the next step. The wind grabbed at their clothes, sliding into their pockets and sleeves until Etta's sweater billowed out and then snapped against her. Muscles long since forgotten burned with life renewed.

The rest of Berlin was forgotten. Everything was gone from her mind aside from the steady rhythm of Terje's boots planting themselves on one rung after the other. When they neared the top of the ladder,

Terje sped up, clambering until he was atop the small maintenance deck stuck like a metal tree house right above the main axle. By the time he had caught his breath enough to reach a hand down for Etta she was already up beside him, awestruck as she took two steps forward on jelly legs.

They were at the heart of the Ferris wheel. The fulcrum of her dream, what had drawn her to Spreepark: a wheel long since dead, never again turning, yet always watching as the rest of the world rolled on without it. She was at the center of it, the trees a spattering of black webs below. And beyond—she pressed her hips tight against the guardrail, staring out across the river at the flickering lights of Berlin. Thousands of them, white and blue flecks protesting the night in unison.

Terje's arm brushed against her shoulder as he stood beside her. "Worth it?"

"Infinitely." She slid down, sitting on the deck as her legs slipped between the guardrail's bars, feet dangling freely.

Terje slowly dropped beside her, though his long legs stayed planted firmly on the deck, curled beneath him. A cloud of warmth crossed the space between them, hip to hip. She felt him. The brush of his fingers across her hair as he clicked off her headlamp, the press of his arm as he turned off his own. She wondered if he could sense the start of her smile.

With only the light of the moon and the distant city she could barely discern the contours of his face as he looked out with her, one hand stretched up to grip the guardrail above them. They sat in silence for some time, listening to the cargo ships and distant sirens that tore through the mournful howl of the wind.

"I know better than to ask, you know?" he finally said. She had to lean closer to hear the low tremor of his voice. "But we can talk about . . . whatever happened. If you want."

No, they couldn't. Not when she wasn't entirely sure what *had* happened. Instead, she said, "I asked Loulou once how she came here. How she met Milan."

Terje snorted. "How'd that go?"

Etta shifted uncomfortably against the railing. "I don't know, fine enough. She told me she left home and found Milan at a party. Something about a band. Does she usually not talk about it?"

Terje blew a cloud of white fog from his lips, his fingers tapping against the metal grating. "It's not that. We just—the past isn't really a thing here. Or Milan tries to keep it behind us. A lot of us don't talk about it. There's before and there's after. The after is all that really matters. I still don't know where Foster came from, which—fuck that place, wherever it is. Imagine a place that spits out kids like Foster, just a bunch of tattooed giants breaking trees in half with their hands." He shivered dramatically.

Etta laughed, bumping his shoulder with hers. "Fine, I won't ask then. Would hate to know where *you* come from. Imagine, just a bunch of grumpy code monkeys holed up in a basement playing with holograms all day."

Terje went quiet, and Etta was afraid she had managed to break one more thing, to snap a boundary without understanding its parameters.

"Schwarzwald," he said softly.

It was a lifeline, one she was cautious not to cling too tightly to as she hedged her reply. "You're from the Black Forest?" Etta had never been up north into the mountains. She had never left Berlin.

"Born and raised." His hand released the railing to drop beside her. "You know how it got its name?"

"No."

"Lots of people don't anymore. It used to be packed with trees. Maple, ash, firs, just a giant cluster of every tree packed so tight that the light couldn't pierce the canopy. You could've stood in the center of it at noon and not had a clue whether the sun was rising or setting—it swallowed time. The Romans were terrified of it."

"Sounds incredible."

"I'm sure it was," Terje said. "But that's the problem. A hundred and some years ago, someone looked at all those trees and saw houses, or boats, or whatever they wanted. They cut it all down, carved a hole right through it and shipped it all off. Then a bit later someone else realized too late how important it was, how we needed to preserve it. So they planted new trees—a bunch of firs—and called it the same. The Black Forest. Spread their hands wide and invited the rest of Germany to visit, as if nothing had happened at all. Now you go into the center of those woods and the sun shines on a bunch of walking paths."

Terje spread his hands out in front of him as he spoke, gesturing toward the city of Berlin as though it was responsible for the Black Forest's death. She felt his grief as heavily as if she had been born there, too, deep among the ancient trees that had been ripped out and replaced with poor substitutes.

She thought of all the foster houses she had been passed through, all the caretakers she had been goaded into calling parents. She thought of Yusuf, lying in bed somewhere among all those city lights—pressed tightly against his wife, watching a television playing Turkish news.

"Do you think they care?" she asked.

"Do you?" His hand had found hers in the darkness. She slipped her pinky finger over his, wrapping them together. Tied together in a truth only they knew, in a world that wove simulation and replica over reality like a child scribbling over a picture.

"Yes," she decided. "I think I do."

"You, sparrow," Terje said, "are the only person I will ever climb a Ferris wheel for."

He kissed her then. One caress, delivered with the same hesitancy as his shaking steps on the ladder rungs. Their lips barely touched before he pulled back, readying to say something—but she closed the distance again with a hand cupped over the back of his neck.

She wanted this. She wanted to cement whatever feeling had blossomed in her, to hear and be heard by someone who saw what she had spent so much of her life hiding from. His arm around her shoulder shook slightly, maybe from the height or maybe adrenaline burned in him as it did in her. She pressed closer, allowed him to hold her against the cotton shield of his sweatshirt, hooking her fingers into the pocket. When he pulled back, she tucked her forehead beneath the hard edge of his jaw. She could feel when he swallowed. Together, they sat above the trees. The old Ferris wheel cars hanging like Christmas ornaments creaked reluctantly as the wind rocked them on rusty hinges.

Beyond it all, the lights of Berlin burned on.

18

Phone pressed to her nose with a familiar newscast whispering in her ear, Etta hid from the party outside by watching the world. A terrorist had driven an old van with a missing headlight down a main street in Warsaw, six tourists caught in its path before it was stopped. The driver's identity hadn't been released but a news station based in Munich noted ties to recently disgraced ex-Finance Minister Rittz and his suspicious foreign payments. Comments rolled in by the dozens, wondering when the German government had begun to work actively against German interests. Etta wondered why it had taken them so long to ask.

Busy scrolling through comments, Etta failed to hear Loulou's steps in the otherwise silent bunkhouse. She only had a moment to process her blanket being pulled back before a cold hand was clapped over her mouth.

"*Hush.*" Loulou squeezed Etta's cheeks.

Loulou, Johanna, and Foster had disappeared with a bottle of rum after dinner. Etta had chosen to wrap up work with Terje before heading to the bunkhouse, figuring Loulou would either be back late or not at all. "What—" she started to ask around Loulou's hand but was hushed again immediately.

"Shh, shut up, *listen*, don't wake 'em up, not until we're—" Her throat bobbed, swallowing what Etta suspected was a small burp. "Not until *after*. Till after the *fun*. Gonna remind them how to have *fun*."

Loulou's rum breath stung Etta's eyes, and she pried Loulou's hand off her mouth. "Where are Johanna and Foster?" she whispered.

"Where were *you?*" Loulou swung a leg over Etta's hips, trapping her on the mattress. "We're out enjoying life and you're—what?" She twisted Etta's wrist to look at her phone. The blue light highlighted the grim disappointment in Loulou's expression. "Etta, tell me this isn't a fucking newscast."

Etta wrenched her arm out of Loulou's grip, shoving her phone into the pocket of her sweatshirt. "It's *work*."

"It's *sad.*" Loulou slid off the mattress and twisted one of Etta's curls. "Come with me, bring the sad phone. You owe me. Christ, Etta—you owe yourself."

The rough wool of the blanket scratched at Etta's lips. "Owe what?"

"Come *on*." Then Loulou was gone in the darkness.

She was obviously wasted. It was entirely possible that Etta could press her face into the mattress and allow sleep to swallow her, that Loulou would forget the entire endeavor. Etta didn't *have* to get out of bed.

She got out of bed.

Every inch of her skin turned to gooseflesh as she threw the blanket aside, rolling off the mattress to hurry after Loulou. She hadn't gone far. Etta barely pushed the curtain aside before Loulou grabbed her elbow, dragging her down the quiet hallway. Even drunk, Loulou managed to sneak with practiced grace.

Etta collided into Loulou's back when she finally stopped, earning another "hush," although the collision had been silent. It was too dark for Etta to recognize whose bunk they had stopped before. With a peek over her shoulder, Loulou slid open the curtain and pulled them both inside.

"Light." There was an edge of glee to Loulou's whisper.

Etta pulled her phone out, shining the flashlight over the room. The space was carefully organized. Three stacks of clothes were folded against the wall, and the bed was made as well as it could be, the blankets tucked under the mattress rather than overflowing onto the floor.

"Whose room—"

"Over here." Loulou was crouched over a plastic bin.

Etta pointed her light. Makeup and toiletries were stacked in neat towers like tiny skyscrapers in a plastic bin city. Etta dropped to her knees to peek closer. Loulou sorted through the supplies with quiet caution, as though the box were a bomb to diffuse.

"Well, hello." Loulou lifted her prize free. The whites of her teeth flashed in the soft light as she grinned at Etta.

Etta squinted to read the label on the opaque bottle in Loulou's hand. "Shampoo?"

Loulou reached into her jacket pocket, pulling out another bottle. She tapped them together like toasting glasses, winking at Etta as she set them both on the floor between their feet.

There was a sticker on the top of Loulou's bottle, the color reminiscent of pond moss from the swamp. Loulou hadn't been digging around for alcohol back in her bunk, Etta realized. She had been digging through her hair dye collection. The bottle's seal cracked as Loulou twisted it open. Handing the shampoo top to Etta, Loulou began to pour in globs of lime green slime.

"She wants to convince everyone she's not a part of the system, not daddy's little politician. Like she's the goddamn shit," Loulou muttered. She gave the dye bottle a quick tap. "We're gonna help her look the part."

Etta's nose wrinkled at the sharp chemical smell. "Who—"

They both flinched when her phone buzzed. The soft light turned stark as Laurence's name appeared on the screen; he hadn't given up attempting to get Etta to help him. Loulou's hand jerked, green dye splattering over her pants as she batted at the phone. Etta dropped the shampoo cap, her greasy fingers sliding over the screen as she shuffled to shut the phone off.

It slipped.

Neither moved as it hit the floor with a reverberating smack, bouncing first on a corner before landing flat on its back. The sound echoed across the bunkhouse, across the park, across every nerve ending in Etta's body as her and Loulou's eyes met in bright horror.

There was stillness.

Then, a cough.

"*Shit—shit—shit*—hurry, hurry," Loulou exhaled, dropping one last green glob into the shampoo.

Etta scooped the phone off the floor, as Loulou juggled the shampoo cap into place. The clatter of the phone was replaced with the pounding of their hearts, each beat so loud, Etta knew it was only a matter of time—

"Hey, what—Etta? Loulou?"

Etta spun toward the curtain. The thick fabric had been pulled back to reveal Monika's slim frame, the bridge of her long nose crinkled against the phone's light. Etta was no stranger to sneaking around, but the cold wash of fear at being caught was foreign and she found herself struck dumb.

"Well, shit." Loulou slowly rose from the floor, the shampoo and dye bottles still in her hand. "Hey, Mon," she whispered. "Why don't you head back to bed, yeah?"

Monika frowned, picking at a loose thread on her sleeve as she glanced down at the bottles. "What . . . are you doing with Johanna's stuff?"

This was Johanna's room. Johanna, who had been drinking with Loulou earlier, along with Foster. Johanna, who had done something to earn Loulou's ire—enough for Loulou to leave a party, still buzzed, so she could organize a sabotage mission.

Loulou knelt, her eyes staying on Monika as she dropped the

shampoo back into the plastic bin. "We're not doing anything with Johanna's stuff. Right, Etta?"

Etta swallowed. "It's just a joke, we're—"

"It's not shit." Loulou jammed the dye back into her pocket and stood, slowly stepping toward Monika. "You came in here to look for some cigs or a snack, whatever." Loulou's voice was a soft lull as she tucked a strand of hair behind Monika's ear. "Alright? You couldn't find it, so you left. That's what you're going to tell her when she sees her shit's been rifled through, aren't you? Because we're friends, and you won't tell on us—right?"

Etta could hear the thread snap as Monika twisted it between her fingers. "Milan won't like it." Her soft voice warbled. "He doesn't like us sneaking around, we're better than secrets—"

Loulou cut her off with a hiss. "Like you know shit about what he wants."

Monika's hands stilled. Her face fell as she ran her tongue over her quivering lip. Her eyes locked with Etta's over Loulou's shoulder. Etta looked at the floor. She could only see Monika's pale feet as she shuffled back from Loulou, the sound swallowed by the bunkhouse as she wandered away.

Later, lying under their scratchy blanket, Etta tried to bury Monika's words inside Loulou's hushed breaths, but it was no use. She was too tense for sleep.

"Hey." Loulou's warm arm wrapped over Etta's waist. "He won't mind, promise."

"I'm not worried," Etta told the ceiling.

Loulou snorted. "Sure. But, if he does get pissed, I'll take the blame. This time." Her arm squeezed Etta closer. "Next time, you can."

Etta's shoulders softened. "Yeah?"

"Yeah." Etta could hear Loulou's smile in her reply. "That's what sisters do."

* * *

The next morning, Etta struggled to focus on the discussion. Milan and Loulou had jumped into planning for the next rave the moment she and Loulou had arrived in search of breakfast. Another ten of the family were gathered around the table in Little Monarchy, holding cups of coffee or liquor with faces pinched against the morning light. A few were bent with their heads on the table, somehow managing to sleep through Gilla and Burkhard's bickering over the last few slices of toast. Beside them, Annerose was pouring a small bottle of Irish cream into her coffee.

"Easy with that," Tedmund warned. "Smells like you haven't sobered up from last night."

"Oh, let her be. Actually, Annerose, you mind?" Varick pulled himself free of Tedmund's arms to hold out his own cup, and Annerose happily obliged him. Throughout the whole exchange, Gustaf sneered over the edge of his notepad.

Etta couldn't look away from the door, awaiting the arrival of last night's consequences.

"Etta?"

The steaming cup in Etta's hands nearly spilled as she jumped, tearing her gaze from the door to Loulou and Milan. "Sorry—"

"Poor Etta darling." Loulou swung an arm over her shoulders, giggly in her mock exasperation. "Sweet thing worked herself to death, staying up all night watching the news."

"Did she?" Milan rolled up the cuff of his sleeve absently. "With Terje?"

The heat from her cup bit Etta's palms. Where was Johanna? "No, ah, on my phone. Terje and I had finished, I just wanted to catch up—"

"You were alone?" Milan paused with one sleeve half-cuffed. "Others were out last night. I heard them, I smelled the fire smoke, yet you stayed locked away in the bunkhouse? You chose your phone over your family?"

The weight of the phone in question was ten times heavier than usual, trapping her in place as she grappled for the best words to assuage the situation. They drank together every night, ate together every night—she hadn't considered one night alone would be noticed.

"Do you feel accepted here, Etta?" Milan leaned forward. "Has there been some slight driving you to your phone rather than your family? I thought we discussed using work to isolate yourself."

"No, I—" Etta looked to Loulou, but she was gazing at Milan expectantly. The others were quieting, catching on to the growing bubble of tension expanding over them. "I didn't mean—"

The door crashed open.

All eyes turned to the figure looming in the entryway. Johanna, her furious huffs visible in the chill, stood braced like an enraged bull prepared to rampage. Her shirt was on backwards, and over her shoulders an old towel collected lime green droplets from her soaking wet hair. The top was garishly vibrant, the color fading into her natural blond as it streaked down to her ends like a wig made of Easter grass.

"Morning!" Water sprayed across the room as she flung her hair over her shoulder. "Hope everyone had a wonderful night! I certainly did. Really wonderful, just magical." She took a few steps forward, a puddle gathering at her feet. "How about you? Did you have a good night, Ella?"

Etta's skin burned as she squeezed her mug to hide the nervous shake of her hands. She could feel Milan's stare, but she couldn't look his way—too afraid of tipping him off to her involvement. Too afraid of upsetting him further.

"Etta, not El—" she started.

"Who gives a fuck." The false cheer cracked as Johanna shifted her attention over to Loulou. "How about you, Lou? Have a good time rifling through shit that doesn't belong to you?"

"Everything belongs to each other here, Johanna. We're a family." Loulou let her head tilt to the side with absent interest as Johanna's anger crackled. Reaching over, she slipped the mug from Etta's hands and took a sip. "But you know a lot about sharing already, Jo—don't you?"

Johanna's hand slapped down hard on the table. She looked over to Milan, who watched with a bemused smirk. "Are you really going to let this jealous—"

"Am I what?" Milan's tone was like a taut guitar string.

Loulou smirked, while Etta shrank at the blunt response and Johanna's jaw hung wide like the broken cap to a lighter, flicking open and shut as she attempted to spark a response. "She ruined my *hair*—"

"She gave you an opportunity." Milan's chair creaked as he tipped back. "Perhaps if your vanity was better checked you may not find yourself so emotional over a small joke. You still cling to the ego seeded by your narcissistic parents. It's time to wrench it out by the roots."

"Then make her shave her head." Johanna gripped her hair, as though she could squeeze out the dye with her fingers. "Make her shave it off—if this is about ego, make her learn too."

The front feet of Milan's chair slammed onto the floor. Any flippant amusement was lost as he stared hard at Johanna. "Or we can shave yours."

"Milan—"

"I'm done with this, Johanna. I've tried to help you, I've tried to teach you, but you resist. You've forced my hand and I resent the action you are forcing me to take." Milan stood, jaw set and hands flat on the table. "To rip out your ego, we must rip out your hair."

Johanna paled.

"Loulou—quit smirking," Milan snapped. "Act like a brat and you truly expect rewards? You asked for family, I give you sisters, love, and you lash out like a spoiled *brat*. Her shame is your shame."

The respective fury and smugness was wiped from Johanna's and Loulou's faces. Their babbled apologies were quickly cut short with Milan's order.

"*Enough.* Loulou, grab a razor. You wrecked her and now it is your job to cleanse her of her ego, of your sin. You will shave her—her head, her arms, all of it, and you will apologize until it is done. 'I am sorry I am a spoiled brat,' those are the only words you will speak until it's finished. Don't you dare cry—this is your own doing. Do you understand?"

Loulou bowed her head and gave a small nod.

"Johanna, don't speak at all. You will be cleansed and reborn free of ego, you will gain humility, you will earn my love. Until then, you are silent."

An angry flush blossomed across Johanna's cheeks as she nodded. Her nose was red from suppressed tears.

"Then go."

They both scurried from the otherwise silent room. Everyone else waited, watching Milan. All terrified of making another mistake and incurring his disappointed rage.

"Tedmund?"

Tedmund cleared his throat, carefully sliding Varick off his lap. "Yes?"

"Go with them. Make sure they do as they're told."

Tedmund was out of his seat in an instant. As the door slammed shut behind him, Milan eased back into his chair and the room breathed.

Etta watched this scene, still on the outskirts of whatever dynamic she had just witnessed. She had been accepted, but she was not entrenched. Until she was immersed, until she fully locked away any quiet excuses for isolation, she would never understand it. She would always have at least one foot on the outside. She would never wholly be part of the V.

Etta pulled her phone from her pocket, dropping it onto the table in front of Milan.

He watched her.

"I can watch news in the shack, if I really need to." She leaned forward, pushing the phone closer to him. "With Terje. But I won't stay inside alone anymore—I'll go out, I'll go with the others. Together."

Milan smiled, catching her hand with a gentle squeeze before sliding the phone under the table and out of sight. "Well done, sweet Etta."

19

"Is it a dog?"

"What?" Terje looked at Etta, aghast. "No, come on, guess again." He nudged the toe of his boot between them, dragging another jagged line in the snow across the clumsy portrait.

Etta studied the picture Terje had created: an oval blob with a hole on each side signifying either gaping eyes or gunshot wounds. A dash of cigarette ash had been flicked on top like a tiny black hat. Crouching, Etta gestured at a snowball stuck to the oval's side. "Is that a tumor?"

Terje scoffed, reaching down to playfully shove Etta's shoulder. "That's his ear."

A shy heat warmed her cheeks as she leaned into his touch. "That's a tumor."

Terje grabbed her hand, pulling her up and cupping her hip as they both looked at the snow. His fingers squeezed her gently through the thick cotton of her borrowed jacket, the sleeves rolled up to accommodate their difference in size. It smelled of steel; she hoped it would linger, that she would wake the next morning to find her hair smelling of metallic afternoons.

"Someone's got a tumor?"

Both Etta and Terje looked up to find Loulou emerging from the woods. Wrapped chin to ankle in a flecked gray and white faux fur coat, she strode through the snow like a leopard. Etta hadn't seen her all day.

"Terje's drawing." Etta pointed down, stopping Loulou short just as she was about to step onto the oval.

"Oh, god, what is that?" She looked down, brow wrinkled. "A dead cat? A fat dead cat?"

Terje sighed. "It's Foster." Etta felt the loss of his warmth as he pulled away from her. "See? He's bald."

"Well, shoot, I think I see it." Loulou squinted at the drawing. "Maybe don't let him see it, though. Better, give me Etta for a bit and I won't tattle on you."

"Why? What's going on?"

"Oh, can't you leave the questions for one night? Let something surprise you, have a bit of fun." The snow crunched as Loulou stomped over Terje's drawing, and Etta knew the moment was lost to Loulou's boot prints. Terje seemed to sense it too. The playful crinkle at the corners of his mouth had smoothed over into a cool mask.

Etta hesitated. The promise of another adventure gleamed in Loulou's eyes, but Etta glanced back at Terje and hesitated. "Maybe tomorrow? Terje and I—"

Loulou's arm snaked around Etta's elbow, pulling her tightly into the coarse fur of her coat. "It's a surprise from Milan," she murmured. "A ceremony."

Etta didn't miss the way Terje's jaw clenched at Loulou's words. If Milan was behind this adventure, Etta would be going.

Still, she buried her hand in the fur sleeve. "Can Terje come?"

"No." Something sharp crossed Loulou's expression, gone before Etta could trace it. "Not this one."

Etta's toes curled in her boots, her eyes falling to the crushed drawing once more.

"It's alright, Etta." Terje's tone was flat. "I'll see you later."

"See? He's fine. Don't worry, you'll get back to making out under your computer desk in no time." Loulou tugged sharply on Etta's arm, her bright smile stretching wide across her pink cheeks. Etta was pulled sideways, stumbling to keep up with Loulou. Terje's eyes met hers as she threw a final look back over her shoulder. He stood as still and steady as the shack behind him, alone in the snow.

Etta raised her hand in goodbye. Terje just stared back.

She wondered then whether he knew about Milan's surprise. Whether he was staring at her or staring beyond into what awaited her and Loulou. Something that kept his hand at his side.

"Hurry." Loulou squeezed Etta tightly, her wild hair sticking to Etta's cheeks. "You're going to love this."

The downstairs of Little Monarchy felt like a doctor's waiting room.

The tables had been pushed to the back wall, benches stacked on top. Johanna perched on the end of one table like a smaller version of Foster, her bald head gleaming. Monika paced beside her, strangling the neck of a liquor bottle. At least she acknowledged Loulou and Etta when they pushed open the door; Johanna refused to look in their direction.

"Here."

Etta found the lip of a flask against her mouth, Loulou tucking a hair behind her ear with a maternal touch as she pressed insistently against Etta. "Drink. Warms you up."

Warmth wasn't worth the sensation of scratchy alcohol crawling down Etta's throat. She drank anyway. The wait was making her antsy. She needed Milan to appear, so she could prove she could stand among the inner circle of his family. That she was worthy.

They smelled him before they saw him. The stark, earthy scent of a freshly sparked blunt rolled down the stairs as the door cracked open and Milan emerged. A fraction of his normal loftiness had been traded for relaxed ease: the top two buttons of his shirt were left open, and strands of blond hair strayed over his brow. He rolled up his sleeves as he took a few casual steps down the stairs. The blunt was tucked into a sly smile, leaving a curled path of smoke around his face as he studied them.

"Sweet girls, look at you all. My own bouquet of flowers." The floor-boards creaked when he reached the bottom of the stairs. Milan slid a hand over Monika's hair, offering her the blunt, which she readily accepted between her lips.

He turned toward Etta.

"Etta." His pearl smile widened. "Welcome."

Monika, her chest still heaving, passed the blunt to Johanna. Etta's palms began to sweat. "Loulou said there was a ceremony."

"There is. One just for the four of you. Do you know the posi-tion you were born into, Etta?" Milan plucked the liquor bottle from Monika as she swayed past him and slumped onto the bench. "All of us are fed impossible contradictions to act out. They tell us to dream, but only so they can order us to wake up later."

"They want us to care about politics." Loulou stole the blunt from Johanna, earning a momentary glare, quickly hidden. "Then they leave us in the dirt for a bunch of immigrants. Pretend they're humanitari-ans, like we're the racist ones."

"All of us suffer that burden. But women, they are granted a dif-ferent set of contradictions." Milan's sleeve brushed Etta's hair as he reached over her. A soft static crackled behind her head, but then the beat of a drum crystallized. She hadn't ever noticed the massive speaker in the room; Milan must have brought it down especially for them.

"Did you wonder why the boys haven't joined us? Why Foster and Terje and the others have been left behind?"

"Loulou said Terje couldn't come." Was he still leaning against the shack, standing on snow-Foster's bald head?

"Men aren't corrupted the same way women are. They aren't taught to turn their bodies into treats for rich men to swallow. They aren't grown into the same helpless mold. That is what sets women apart, isn't it? Women are told to be sharp yet gentle, smart yet pliant. They teach you to live at odds with yourself to disable your soul, your personhood. How can you define who you are when every facet of yourself negates another?" Milan squeezed Etta's shoulder. The wall dug into her back.

She had often wondered how things may have been different, were she born a boy. When she was younger, it was easy to convince herself she was above what she perceived to be the typical plight of a woman, matters of hair and clothes and men. It only took a single night to shatter her naivety. One especially brutal winter she had attempted to escape the snow by finding a shelter, only to find an icier presence inside. Shelter attendants kept watch, but some men watched closer. They hadn't bothered to hide how they watched her. Predators. She hadn't slept at all.

That was her last night in a shelter—and the first night she wondered if her mother would have killed herself if she'd had a son to be proud of, rather than a daughter to be fearful for. If her father would have returned for a son.

The heady smelling salt of weed and tobacco was waved under Etta's nose. Milan watched her, the blunt held in offering. Over his shoulder, the girls waited. Loulou smiled.

"It is time to find balance in the contradiction," Milan murmured. "It is time to let go."

The drum, strung along now by the sharp screech of a furious guitar, pounded into Etta's temples as she sucked in a deep lungful of burning smoke. When she made to pull away, Milan gripped the back of her head to force one more rasping inhale. The smoke burned her eyes and poured from the corners of her mouth.

Milan pressed a damp vodka kiss to her forehead. "Welcome to healing."

The moment he turned away, Etta spasmed in a violent cough. Loulou laughed.

Etta's head swam. A tingling numbness crept up her fingertips as she grappled for something to anchor herself onto. A warm hand wrapped around her wrist and she felt warm skin under her cheek, Milan's voice humming against her jaw.

"Let go, sweet Etta. Let it all go. All that anger in you, let it out. Welcome us—welcome me in."

The ground tilted under her feet. Her stomach twisted. She wanted love, she wanted acceptance, to feel his praise. Always on the edge, she could be a part of them now. She had seen the traces of Milan on Loulou's skin, on Johanna's neck, on Monika's hips. Spots where Etta remained untouched. Places she guarded. But the others allowed him to hold them, she had seen the evidence. Purpled hickeys left like medals on their collarbones. Awards of acceptance. Acknowledgment that they had fulfilled a duty Etta was only beginning to understand. She should be proud; the others were so proud. Milan's hand crept under her shirt. Her back went numb. She went numb.

"*Let go,*" Loulou hummed.

"I—" her words were lost somewhere within the fog clouding her brain. The world went black as her shirt was dragged over her head. When she was freed, she saw the others had similarly lost their clothing. A giggle slipped out as she imagined the clothes growing legs and wandering away, leaving them all naked and drunk.

"That's it, give in to joy. Brilliant girl. Time to dance together, come on." Fingers drummed distantly over her ribs, her back, dropping lower over the swell of her hips. Unlike Terje's caresses—still tentative in their explorations—Milan's hands were steady, trekking a path down Etta's body. Some distant part of her tensed, her shoulders rising even as the fog choked out any logical thought. Her body tipped back, but Milan's fingers flexed against her skin in response. Catching her, keeping her.

"*Relax.* Relax, you're not alone anymore." She felt his smile against her cheek, the press of the other girls as they danced somewhere around them as static flooded out all but the sensation of skin against skin. She opened her mouth but couldn't speak, the words were all lost.

"Give in, brilliant girl of mine."

She was naked.

Stripped down in body and mind, her chest burned as memories poured in. They had held her. Nearly two decades worth of proud walls left in crumbling rubble with a touch. The gravity caught the breath in her throat, left her choking as she curled inward, knees tucked against her chest. She needed something to hold onto, she needed stability, she needed to be held again as her mind rolled from one emotion to the next before she could identify them. She needed—

"Easy now, steady," Milan whispered, brushing Etta's cheek while Loulou ran her fingers through Etta's hair. "You can cry, sweet girl. That's alright."

Etta hadn't been aware of her tears, and now they seemed to come in an endless flood.

"This is a new start; do you feel it? A rebirth." The molten heat of his hand dragged a line down the curve of her neck, and the force of his attention brought even more tears.

"I—" Her chest heaved.

"Drink this, go on." She leaned toward the offered vodka, the bottle cool against her chapped lips. "Brilliant girl. Worthy of so much, so much smarter, yet they left you alone. They're too afraid of you, aren't they? They only ever keep the second smartest dogs, drowning the most intelligent ones. The ones they can't control."

"Shut your eyes, let go," Loulou whispered. "You're one of us now. Go to sleep, and wake up new."

Etta closed her eyes.

It took Etta a moment to place herself within the room. Her cheek was pressed into the edge of a table against the back wall, her body slumped against one of the legs like a doll forgotten in the corner by a bored child. The music was off, the pulsating beat now contained between her temples as invisible drumsticks used the backs of her eyeballs as snares.

Johanna was sitting against the opposite wall, near the door. Her pebble eyes were trained on Etta as she stroked the tumbleweed of Monika's dark hair in her lap. Johanna and Monika were both still naked, as was Etta. It took a moment to find her clothes, bundled in a heap at the other end of the room.

"Morning, brilliant girl. You missed half of the party." Johanna's voice rang clear and steady, cheerful.

Etta attempted to sit up. The world attempted to sit up with her. She groaned at the shift in axis, stomach lurching as the floor tilted beneath her. "Where're Milan and Loulou?"

Johanna snorted. She pushed at Monika's shoulder, flipping her over and brushing dark hair away to reveal her flushed face. "Hey, Monika, you know what Loulou and Milan are up to?"

"Milan?" Monika gave a low, throaty groan, slowly rubbing the curve of her jaw as if Johanna's words afflicted some phantom pain. "No, too soon. Too sore still. Don't wanna think 'bout it."

Johanna looked at Etta expectantly, as if Monika's half-drunk grumbling should make crystal sense.

"Fine." Etta shut her eyes. "Never mind."

"I don't think she got it, Mon."

Monika started to giggle again.

"Don't laugh now, it's alright if she doesn't get it." Johanna's hush had a hint of her own giggle to it. "She was just born last night, after all. Our brilliant little virgin."

20

The frost melted, eventually. Days spun past like the notes to a fading song, one pinging past the other until Etta was lost to the melody. Mornings were usually spent with Terje, while evenings tended to involve spinning around the dancing flames of a fresh fire or among a net of reaching arms, all clambering for portions of stale food, or drink, or drugs, or love. Sometimes, she and Terje would sneak off together to listen to the crickets in the bog, sharing a bottle under the same blanket.

She no longer waited up for Loulou in the bunkhouse; she had found a new perch with Terje in the loft he built behind thick black curtains at the top of his shack. Exploratory touches had gradually turned to learned familiarity. They slept on a real mattress—with springs—and when she awoke outside the circle of his arms, she would follow the orange length of the lone extension cord back down the ladder like a lifeline. At times, she would wake in the early hours before even the sun could bother, only to feel the weight of Terje's arm over the bare expanse of her hip.

She would stare at his face and marvel at the way his hard edges melted with sleep into the cave of boyhood. Innocence, free of misery and pain. These were the only moments he seemed fully at peace. Even when they held each other alone in bed, even when his pupils swallowed his irises as the contents of colorful tablets flooded his veins, he never truly seemed at ease. Always his brows were pinched, as though some riddle in the back of his mind claimed most of his attention and his outward existence was an afterthought.

She could understand. So long as he found peace in his dreams, she would find peace in lying beside him. In the way his eyes focused when they faced her, only her. She knew what it meant to feel like a forgotten piece of the world, and they recognized each other. He saw her.

And Milan saw them all. Their flaws, their natures, he *understood*. And he loved regardless, kept hold of their hands and tirelessly guided them through the battlefields of their minds. They were his to educate and protect. No thanks would ever be sufficient.

Terje's eyelids fluttered as his fingers dug into her hip. She had learned to recognize the small twitches and grunts that signaled he would be waking soon.

He groaned, rolling onto his back and tugging the fleece-lined sleeping bag they had stretched over the mattress farther up over them both. "What time is it?"

"Just past eight."

"Morning?"

"Evening." They had spent the night before working on combining his augmented reality program with Wechselkind at Milan's behest, trying to create people out of numbers based on the blueprint of real events. Weaving words out of sound clips until they had perfectly cloned a target's voice, twisting video clips of speeches until it was impossible to tell the real version from their orchestrated reality. Milan had watched them work, until Etta had to shoo him away from the monitors.

"Remember," he had said. "We are only helping reveal truths that are otherwise hidden behind locked doors. Force them all to see, to understand, until they can no longer pretend to live in ignorance of what they would prefer to deny."

Never were the different slices of the world meant to mix, he had explained.

"You know what harbors evil? Do you understand the irreparable damage done by man's hubris? He saw oceans stretched into the distance until waves mixed with clouds and denied what they were—barriers, natural divisions meant to keep separate the races of humanity so none could tarnish the other. So they could develop separately, develop and *evolve*, but we had to go and build the boats, the trains, the *planes*."

It was like he did not need to breathe, his passion overflowing in a concussive wave. "What happens when a plant or animal is moved from its ecosystem to a foreign environment?" he had continued. "It disrupts natural balance, leeches off the resulting fallout. It *devours*. Native species are choked out of their birthright until only the invaders are left. It's why we train dogs to sniff out spiders and certain fauna alongside heroin and cocaine—those organisms aren't inherently bad, of course not. God made them as they are, but God gave them a home. A specific place for them to develop or destroy as they pleased. I do not fault God's creatures, I trust his plan—it's only when they *leave* their divinely designated environment that they become dangerous, both to themselves and others.

"I implore you: ask why the government forbids bringing fresh herbs from your holiday in Asia, why they quarantine a new family puppy adopted from abroad but allow humans—*even criminals*—past our borders unquestioned? These invaders need to be rooted out before they destroy our habitat, for our good and their own."

And who are we, Etta had thought, to question God?

"We had children, babies lost to the rage of a fractured identity belonging neither here nor there. That pain they bring to our streets, our hearts"—Milan had banged on his chest then, each thump reverberating in Etta's rib cage—"and they *welcome them*. They—those righteous assholes at the top of the chain—claim it's a matter of appearance, that our resentment has nothing to do with the natural differences built by time and oceans. But we are righteous, and we will fight for our right to a pure world."

Much like the Black Forest, all had been peaceful and right until invaders had scraped the ancient landscape and traditions away—replaced by poor substitutes and sin. It was up to the V to separate the ink from the water, to dredge society until all the poison was sucked from the earth.

Terje's hands wandered up Etta's hip, pausing as his fingers caught the edge of a sweatshirt—one of his, shamelessly stolen before he had awoken. "You're leaving."

"I have to go pick up the package for the next rave. We need more shrooms and Johanna found someone with Oxy." She allowed herself another second of warmth before swinging her legs out from under the sleeping bag into the chill.

"Doing Loulou's job now?"

"Loulou already dropped by earlier. She could barely find her way here." Etta had opened the door to find Loulou hovering drunkenly outside the shack. Loulou was waiting on her footsteps, Etta realized. Just as Etta used to wait on Loulou's back in the bunkhouse. The longer Etta spent in the shack with Terje, the more Loulou seemed to chase Etta rather than be followed.

Terje grunted and rolled the sleeping bag tighter around him as he watched Etta pull on a pair of jeans. "She needs to stop getting so strung out. Milan is going to get pissed—he's already . . ." He trailed off. Then, his voice softer, "She just needs to watch it."

It was a small betrayal, its sting surprising though Etta could not find the words to defend her first friend. "Keep the bed warm for me." She slipped her hood over her head as she clambered down the ladder from the loft. On her way out of the shack she picked up her backpack, leaving her laptop on the table as she swung the bag onto her shoulders.

It wasn't her first time picking up a package for Milan. She was familiar enough with the routine, first accompanying Foster and Loulou, then only Loulou as Milan increasingly demanded Foster's immediate presence. She had learned that her talent for avoiding attention made her an especially efficient drug mule—no one paying any heed to her backpack, laden with Molly, LSD, and shrooms on the last train out of Berlin. It made her feel useful in a physical way, like a hunter returning with a fresh kill.

As she stepped off the train at Berlin Central Station, she realized she was alone in the city for the first time since deciding to join the family. It was strangely uncomfortable. She felt exposed. Milan's words trailed through her head as she ducked between people walking down the street, and it all clicked.

Everyone had places, Milan had said, though they had stepped out of their designated paths. The man with a tie who spoke with a foreign accent to the German woman who pleaded for some change at the bus stop; the video display in the station playing a clip of an American politician offering his unwanted opinion on German foreign affairs; the businessman who sidestepped around a man slouched against the station wall, a small paper cup resting beside his knee. Each of them was a puzzle piece pounded into a picture that no longer made sense, just a garble of fractured images.

Except Etta had finally found her place among the V. She was no longer an outsider. Now she was part of the force that sought to shake the table of society.

The city felt larger for it.

She walked, lost in thought, and unaware that habit was guiding her feet. She nearly missed it entirely, noticing only when a bright light—the only bright light left in the street—caught her attention. Kerzenlicht.

For all the change she felt in herself, Kerzenlicht looked the same, as if the café had frozen behind her. She recognized the girl tending the counter, the split ends of her ponytail twisting between her fingers as she swiped through her phone. The floor still had a soft sheen and Etta could imagine the familiar sound of her shoes sticking to the thin layer of grime. Most of the tables were empty, chairs shoved tight against table edges in the small space—had it always been so small? No, it couldn't have been.

In the corner, he sat at his usual table. A man weakened in his endless pursuit of knowledge, skin slackened with exhaustion while his dark eyes stayed sharp with knowing. Hair still black, though now unruly. Beard just an inch longer, the dark hairs of his mustache creeping over his lips as he mouthed a collection of words to himself soundlessly. Yusuf.

Because Kerzenlicht had never changed, neither did this: Yusuf didn't look up at Etta, though she stared at him openly now.

It had been weeks since she had peeked into any of his affairs. Once a daily habit, her intrusion into his bank accounts or article drafts had been abandoned. The false familiarity she had shared with him had been only a fantasy, something to fill the cravings for company that she had tried to deny. Still, he was not a total stranger; it was obvious he was struggling over a line in one of his articles by the way his hand paused mid-scratch against his neck. He would have just come off a shift at the corner store, and his wife expected him home—yet he was at Kerzenlicht instead.

Everyone had their place. Where would Yusuf be if his parents had never left Western Thrace? Would he still be spending his nights at a café chasing a failing career in journalism while his wife waited at home dreaming of the busy streets of Istanbul?

Milan would say that Yusuf's parents had doomed him with their false chase after stolen freedom. Milan would say Yusuf didn't belong.

Etta stared at Yusuf's pained, exhausted face through the fogged window. Under the fluorescent lights and framed by the cracked plaster walls, he looked like an actor lost on the wrong movie set. Would he look so out of place, so exhausted, if he were back in Thrace?

She crept forward until her nose was only a hair away from the glass, her breath leaving a foggy cloud. The door was so close. She already knew what sort of whine it would make if she stepped inside. Yusuf's eyes would widen in surprise as she approached him, as she introduced herself.

"I'm sorry to interrupt," she would say. "But I've noticed you before. I've seen you here, and I wanted to say hello."

But she did not go inside. She waited for a few more moments, for his eyes to rise—for him to see her. Waited until she knew he would never see her, never notice her as she had noticed him. Yusuf was an artifact of her old life, one that needed no hanging on to, so when she finally turned away, she felt his presence lift from her shoulders, a weight she had never even known she carried, the man she had spent so long noticing when her own life had been better left unnoticed and unconsidered.

Leaving him behind felt like freedom.

21

The blade of Milan's promised war was hovering over their necks, dropping lower as his rants grew in passion and volume. Etta had awoken twice to the sound of his voice booming through the park, enraged at news reports of incoming Turkish immigrants sent by France.

It had been weeks since they last held a rave. Milan had insisted they transition focus to their political goals, but without the boost to family financials provided by the parties, their money and supplies had dwindled. Fresh takeaways had turned into soups made with rice and souring meats, yet hands scrambled for a share with as much ferocity as ever. The family wandered the park like ghosts. Could the others feel the nutrients seeping from their bodies, as Etta did? Twice over the past day Etta had caught herself trailing off mid-sentence, her brain scrambling for the energy to keep track of its thoughts.

Her personal funds, saved over a lifetime alone, had been depleted by the cost of the family's hunger—for food and chemicals alike. For a time, Etta had picked up more work from external clients, taking jobs she would normally avoid involving larger corporate entities with vigilant security measures. Each payoff only survived one or two fires before the family drank it all away.

At first, she had enjoyed the feeling of fulfillment from providing for the V.

But she couldn't keep up with demand. So much of her time was being devoted to the research Milan wanted her and Terje to continue on
Berlin's political elite. When Etta had approached Milan about setting
aside the research in order to take on more paid work, he waved her off.

"Never suggest sacrificing our purpose," he had said. "We are beyond that."

She'd left feeling like a failure.

So she worked harder. She squeezed more time out of the day for
research, for Wechselkind. Milan had said that her program would be
their saving grace, and she had thrown herself into adapting it to work
with Terje's program.

She and Terje spent most of their days in the shack, only leaving
when absolutely necessary. Loulou occasionally joined them with a
pounding on the door, only to throw herself on the floor like a corpse.
She picked at the splintered edges of her nails or attempted to work
through the large knots of hair at the base of her scalp. Once, when
Terje leaned down to kiss Etta's forehead after she managed her way
into a particularly locked-down cloud server, Loulou had thrown back
her head and laughed.

"Is that your version of foreplay?" She had smirked. "Just a couple
of clicks and you've got our resident recluse—oh, come on, Terje, I'm
just teasing—you've got him wrapped around your finger. Even Milan
loves it, his little genius. Wish I had known it was that easy, wouldn't
have to spend a second worrying about how I look—must be the life."

When Loulou grew bored of Terje and Etta's stunted conversation,
she'd leave. Etta would pick up the rainbow strands of hair Loulou left
behind, sweeping them up and dumping them outside for the birds.
Pastel nests soon hung from the trees, and the old pines looked like
gumdrop trees from a fairy tale.

Etta and Terje lived in that purgatory between purpose and emptiness until, one day, Milan arrived at the shack with newly trimmed
hair and a clean jacket. He was the only one in the family who didn't

have sunken half-circles under his eyes; he was still keenly alert. When he looked at Etta, the singular focus of his attention burned her cheeks.

"I hope I'm not interrupting," he said.

"It's no problem," she replied, because admitting she and Terje had lost their battle against exhaustion hours earlier made her want to hide under the table. Terje had stood when Milan entered, hand already waiting for his jacket as Milan shrugged it from his shoulders.

"Wonderful. Have you made progress?" His eyes flicked to Terje, who was standing awkwardly in the middle of the shack looking for somewhere to hang the jacket. "Not there, Terje. Hang it somewhere clean."

Terje glanced around a moment longer, then draped it carefully across the back of the chair opposite Etta. He didn't meet her eyes. She knew Milan approved of their relationship. He had pulled Etta aside a week or so after that night on the Ferris wheel, a few days after the ceremony at Little Monarchy, to question why she was still in the bunkhouse and tell her about the loft where Terje slept. Terje had invited her to stay with him shortly after. Still, when Milan was present, Terje kept a careful distance from her. Whether it was an attempt at professionalism or something else, she wasn't sure.

"Did you want to see?" Etta offered. "Terje could pull up a simulation."

"You asked me once why we play the game. Why we bother involving ourselves in the trials of society when we've invested so much in separating ourselves." Milan hooked his thumbs into his pockets as he gazed around the shack. "You remember my response?"

Etta wasn't sure whether she should stand. Terje hadn't resumed his seat, leaning against the wall instead—half hidden in the shadows. "We need to learn where to strike the match."

Milan's lips curled into a genuine smile. "Exactly. Strike the match, bring back peace. So much pain, so much strife—it can all end. We have a duty to end it." In two easy steps he was kneeling beside her, his arm resting on the table as he drummed his fingers. "I knew I could count on you to listen, even then."

Etta clasped her hands together under the table to still their trembling as Milan studied her. She had made the correct offering, proven herself an apt student, and now he was pleased—only the silence drew on, the tremor reappearing in her leg as she tried to decipher whether Milan was searching for another response. Thankfully, he did not leave her in anguish for long.

"Tell me, Etta—what does God look like?"

She wanted to turn to Terje, but Milan had her chained to him with the hook of his sharp gaze. Had he honestly come to the shack to discuss theology? She waited. Milan didn't want answers, she understood that by then.

"It's a question that's plagued many minds, no wonder it eventually found its way to mine. But it's not the lack of a face, is it? Sure, some have come up with their own depictions. Something to make it palatable to children, maybe. But before, traditionally, even the smallest image of God was considered sacrilegious in so many cultures—did you know that?"

"I did not," she said honestly.

"'You shall not make yourself a graven image, or any likeness of anything that is in heaven above, or that is in the earth beneath, or that is in the water under the earth,'" he recited. "Aniconism. Why do you suppose the Lord of old deemed that appropriate to carve on those burning tablets?"

Never once had she heard Milan reference the Bible. She didn't know whether he wanted an answer or whether this was another question meant for display—not touch. But he let the silence stretch on. So she spoke.

"There's power," she said. "In a voice with no face."

"The face humanizes it. We relate to a familiar face; relation undermines power. It undermines fear." Milan's steady hand coming to rest on her head sent a cold blast of relieved pleasure through her chest.

"The question is, Etta, what happens when a voice with no face is sud-denly given an identity? What changed to make humanity disregard that sacred commandment?"

The same thing that had turned her hatred for a shapeless gov-ernment that murdered her mother into dedication to the V. "They didn't need a vengeful, ethereal prick anymore. They needed a leader. Someone with a shape, something to follow."

"Exactly." Milan stood. "The world needs another voice of truth. A power to fear so they can eventually be led. How do we create that voice? How do we give birth to a new god, so to say, if you want to be crude about it."

"We don't need to create a god," Terje's low voice came from behind them. "We—you—just need to be a prophet."

Milan clapped his hands once. "So he finally speaks. Etta?"

Her mind whirled. They could do it, hypothetically. She knew from her former work that modern-day prophets worked less on pre-dicting future events than retelling history. They could reshape events in Milan's favor, have his voice be a beacon of truth in a sea of mis-information. She said as much, told him they only needed to target whatever information he requested, but his face pinched with every word until she trailed into silence.

His hands returned to his pockets as his chin tipped upward as though he were conferring with God directly, eyes shut in prayer.

"I understand," he said. "But it's not a matter of the past, it's a mat-ter of the future. We need to create something. We need to predict an event of our own making, of your making. I need to be a god, my Etta. We need to give them a reason to believe—a flood for us to part . . ."

"There have been protests. A lot of protests lately—in Turkey." Terje's fingers bounced on his thigh. "Some talk about protests starting here too. Over energy prices. Saw it online."

"Of course." Milan let loose a sharp bark of laughter. "Of course. They plant rot in their country and harvest it here—we pay so they can rob us. Fine, they want to shout about how we have yet to sacrifice enough to their invasion? Fine. We will build them a stage. We will build them a stadium and invite the whole of Germany."

Milan patted his shirt, smoothing down an invisible collar as his gaze lost focus. Etta glanced at Terje; his jaw was set and his hands had stilled. When he caught her gaze, he quickly looked back to Milan.

"A rally." Milan smiled as if it were the sound of an old lover's name rather than a plan for coordinated protest. "But will it be large enough? We need a biblical crowd, Etta. No one cares for a prophet predicting small things."

"Wechselkind." She jumped to lay her child at his feet. "I can use Wechselkind. It can be however large we want. I can do it." Could she? Her influence was dispersed through whispers, not battle cries. She had never tried to gather a physical force, she had no idea if it would work. But she would have to learn—for Milan, she would create a crowd.

Milan grinned and clasped her cheeks between his hands. He pressed a firm kiss against her forehead and clapped his palms against her face lightly, like a proud father. "Do it," he said. Then, reaching out to include Terje in his fold, "Do it. Give me a voice." He returned his gaze to Etta. "Etta, give me my people."

Nothing happened for two weeks. They needed to create a trail of legitimacy. It didn't matter as much leading up to the rally, but after, once the move was made and if they found success, everyone would look back—they would see the social media posts, the account titled "Milan" that had crept onto online channels. They would see posts from the man with no face warning of impending violence, preaching a preservation of culture against an oncoming push by "intruders against German pride."

They would learn to look for his name.

Meanwhile, Etta went back to what she did best: she spun a story, one even she could believe despite her suppressed concern. She needed a reason for a protest, a cause to disguise the V's true intent. A shipping company based on the river was known for employing refugees and immigrants. It only took a few minutes of searching to find complaints of unfair working conditions screamed into the digital void. She followed the kernels of anger, tracking posts and comments from one website to the next like a bloodhound: insufficient pay for the skill and hours required, racism experienced at the hands of white supervisors. It was enough. A spark.

She gave the Turks a reason to gather in anger. A call to arms distributed by her hundreds of puppet accounts never before called upon en masse. One by one she dragged them back to life and shamelessly connected them to each page and forum that had even the tiniest link to Turkish rights advocates.

"The unfair working conditions at Der Flug Shipping are proof of the German government's ongoing blindness toward the working-class Turkish population," she wrote. "Let us stand together at Görlitzer on the seventh—we are one. They will hear our voices."

When she showed Milan how her posts had begun to be spread and shared by other legitimate activists, how commenters had begun to express fury and tell stories of falsely terminated employees and blatant discrimination, he smiled.

"It doesn't need to be honest, Etta," he said. "It just needs to be believable. We need only their anger, their suffering. Power, righteous power, comes from controlling the spin of another's suffering."

Provocation so the Turks would show the world their true nature— that's what Milan wanted. To show Germany that he alone had anticipated the truth. The protestors would show, they had to. She had to have faith in Milan's belief, both in her and about the Turks. Once Etta was done filming their riot, the story about the shipping company would be irrelevant. Instead, Germans would see hundreds of immigrants marching against the same Berliners who had welcomed them into their capital. They would see reality.

22

The morning of the seventh, Milan and Loulou arrived at the shack with coffee and a backpack stuffed with clothes. They both smelled of the same bottle of brandy; the purple curve of a hickey winked out from the edge of Loulou's collar. When she caught Etta staring, she smirked.

Milan clapped his hands together and smiled. "Let us finally bring the war against our culture out from the shadows, yes?"

Etta donned one of Loulou's long green skirts and Terje's black sweatshirt, giving every impression of the humble advocate. She tried to hide her shaking hands by pinching the shirt's hem. Milan perched on a chair as Loulou fussed with Etta's hair, pulling dark curls from her face as Terje dug through a storage cabinet for a suitable video camera.

"So wild." Loulou yanked on an especially stubborn curl. Etta flinched, which earned a small tap on the cheek from Loulou. "Quit moving. You look like you just crawled out of a dumpster. Is it too late to take a shower? Even just rinse you down with the hose, maybe throw you in the swamp—honestly, anything would help at this point."

It felt as if Loulou were preparing her for a first day at school. Every hard tug on her hair seemed as endearing as it was venomous, as though Loulou couldn't decide the line between pain and caring.

"Just leave it." Etta pulled her head out of Loulou's grasp. She gripped the shirt harder as she mentally counted down the time left before she had to face the protestors she had summoned. She was used to lying but never so openly, never face-to-face with the people she was deceiving.

Assuming there were protestors to face. If not, she would instead face Milan's disappointment. She felt her palms prickle with sweat at the idea, eyes already stinging.

Milan shoved back from his chair. He took two quick steps forward and shouldered Loulou aside. He guided Etta's face toward him gently, though his building frustration was obvious in the way his brows pinched tight, small lines blooming over his forehead.

"Scheisse. Look at her. Loulou, look—you see this? You see how pale she is? You're so brilliant, Etta, yet they're so clever—so cruel, yet clever. Vipers in the grass, hungry for people like us. They may sense your true allegiance, they may know. Scheisse." His grasp on her chin tightened. "It's why you must go, why you must film the truth, and yet will they believe it?"

The muscles along his jaw twitched as he ground his teeth. None of them spoke. Etta had learned to stay silent during these moments when whatever trials in Milan's mind swallowed his gentleness. They only needed to wait, to let him work his way back into himself.

For several long seconds Etta met his eyes, his smooth palm warm against her skin. She focused on keeping still as the lines along his skin slackened and melted away. Slowly, his grasp on her jaw eased.

His furious scowl morphed into a distant smile.

"No, they'll believe it," he answered himself. "They'll make you into whoever they wish you to be. Let them—you understand? Let them believe you're there to learn. That you, too, have been brainwashed by the globalization propaganda they shove down our throats. You are the first soldier sent to the front. Be brave, my darling Etta. Use that anger." The scent of tobacco washed over her as he pressed a firm kiss to her forehead. "Loulou, my sweet girl, give me that flag. Here, drape yourself in this."

The sound of plastic ripping open filled the room as Loulou tore a Turkish flag free from its packaging, holding it out stiffly. She stared over Milan's shoulder as he wrapped it around Etta, like a mother swaddling her child.

"What a doll." Loulou waved a limp hand. "You look grand. Real great." Her voice was flat. The smug expression she had arrived with was gone, only a vacant play at pride remaining.

"Glad we didn't need the hose after all," Etta attempted. The joke felt wrong.

Loulou looked away with a small frown.

Terje cleared his throat. He had a camera in his hand, a sleek box the size of his palm; anything fancier would have raised suspicions of Etta's intentions. They had discussed using her phone to film, but Milan had vehemently objected. They had no need for phones here. Anyone who joined the V now gave their phone to Milan as proof of loyalty, proof they were willing to listen—as Etta had.

"Are we alright to go?" Terje looked at Milan.

"Yes." Milan clapped Etta's cheeks one more time. "Yes, go. Get her to the station. Come find me after." The final words were thrown over his shoulder as he snatched up his coat and strode outside. Loulou scrambled after him, icy blue gaze pointedly avoiding Etta as she marched off.

The Turkish flag flopped around her shoulders as Etta escaped the shack with Terje on her heels. He paused with one hand on the door before sliding it shut. Maybe he, too, felt too large after they were deprived of Milan's presence.

They were silent on the way out of the park. When they arrived at the train station, still empty aside from an elderly woman cradling a bag of groceries, Terje grabbed her hands.

He pressed the camera into her palm. When she tried to pull back, his other hand reached forward to hold her steady.

"He's right, you know." Terje said. "All of them out there, they've been living these lies; you and I know that."

"I know." The two of them knew about lies better than most. They had made lives for themselves by serving fantasies and falsities with digital spoons to a starving public.

Terje nodded. His fingers squeezed around her hand. "Be safe, sparrow."

Never once had anyone ever told her to be safe.

"I will," she said.

I will, she thought as she boarded her train, as she watched his stoic form out the window until she had to press her nose against the glass. *I will*. Over and over, she dropped that breadcrumb phrase along her path out of Plänterwald.

Görlitzer Park was on the outskirts of Kreuzberg. Half chosen for its proximity to the part of Berlin with a healthy Turkish population, the park also had a reputation for impromptu gatherings held by local minority populations. Jonas had warned her away from the area once, spinning tales of robberies and monstrous drug dealers lurking in the bushes. It had made Etta laugh at the time—Jonas with his apartment down the street from his favorite nightclub, three bedrooms for three roommates and a stove that worked, warning the girl who spent her evenings picking dried plaster from her hair to beware the dangers of opportunistic predators.

Even so, when she finally approached the park, she at least expected the same prickly sense of invisible eyes that she had grown used to on the streets. Instead, she was confronted with a wide block of green grass, the ground cut away in chunks in an industrial attempt to create miniature amphitheaters. The scent of mixed spices and smoke tickled her nose as she skirted past a group of boys huddled over a small makeshift grill. They prodded at the charcoal and spoke quickly in a language Etta didn't recognize, laughing when one of the boys swung his skewer like a sword at another.

Music played, all around her. It was a cacophony from every angle; for every five people in the park, one had brought a speaker and a different taste in music. Hip hop beats mixed with the tinny rhythm of steel pans, while a rapid strumming of some instrument similar to a guitar—only not quite—rose above it all. A thousand sounds from a hundred countries all wrapping together under the German sun, each foreign note existing at the expense of a German melody.

She followed the strings, surprised relief lightening her step. Their crisp picking sound brought her to a moderate group, a few dozen in total. It wasn't an army, but it was enough for a headline. It was enough for Milan, thank God. They were clustered at the edge of the park beside one of the entrances: college students in sweatshirts displaying their university names from schools throughout Berlin, women with vibrant headscarves that framed their faces, older men balanced against thick walking sticks. A policeman watched steadily as they raised Turkish flags—red with white moons and stars—above their heads. One man with a thick obsidian beard crouched on the ground. He leaned an arm, the copper skin at his elbow sagging with age, against a sign that read Fair Working Rights are Human Rights as he lifted a stained ceramic cup to his lips.

Despite the moderate waves of tension emanating in a ripple around the lone policeman, it wasn't a rally. It was an afternoon lunch with signs. Etta had at least hoped for marching, for chants—anything aside from cheerful Turkish banter and the occasional call for support as passersby waved in greeting. She had been fully prepared to infiltrate, not intrude. The camera—her lens and everything it demanded—in her pocket turned into a useless chunk of metal.

The man with the coffee cup looked up at her from the ground. Gray hairs were interwoven into his dark brows and mustache. With a sniff, he lifted a hand in greeting and laid a stream of throaty Turkish onto the grass between them. Every explanation for her presence that she had designed on the ride over was gone. She stared at him blankly.

"Ah," the man said. Then, in German, "You're here for the rally?"

She was certain the flag around her shoulders was tightening, and she could only nod.

The man regarded her with dark, stern eyes. With a small groan, he eased himself onto his feet with his sign as leverage. He passed the sign into her hands, the wooden stick it was attached to biting into her palms as he reached forward to drag the flag from her shoulders.

"Like this." He took the sign back from her, pressing the top two corners of the flag into her hands firmly so it flew open freely. His breath smelled of coffee as he smiled. "It's okay. You're welcome here, friend."

The moment he turned away, Etta dropped one corner of her flag and slipped her camera out of her pocket. The quick beep it made when she began recording was lost as a woman, her purple headscarf full of carefully stitched stars, began singing along to the music in Turkish.

The image in the viewfinder shivered as Etta tried to steady herself. "Hey!"

The music wavered as heads swiveled toward a police officer. The subtle undercurrent of tension bubbled to a height as a group of protestors converged, their epicenter a young boy with black curls dangling to his shoulders, his teeth bared and mouth wide enough to see the pinks of his gums as he shouted in Turkish at the cop.

"Calm down!" The cop held his baton like a sword, jabbing at the boy's chest. The camera shook in Etta's hands and her flag dropped to the ground. Someone shouted. The boy lifted an open palm.

Like the snap of a rubber band, the cop charged forward. He shoved the boy, who parted the cluster of people as he careened backward, slamming off one person, the next, and down and down the line until he hit the only body not raised by the sudden chaos—the old man beside Etta.

The old man's and Etta's eyes met one more time just before impact. His expression remained serene, even as he was brought down under the weight of the boy. Even as his head hit the concrete pathway with a crack. The coffee cup flew out of his hands, spraying hot liquid over Etta's shoes and the hem of her skirt. Her ankles burned as she stumbled back, the sign forgotten as voices once joined in song turned into screams.

Through the viewfinder of her camera, Etta watched as the old man reached up for help, only to have his hand be ignored by the boy who had knocked him down. The boy was focused on the policeman. Their ensuing fight was lost to Etta as she was jostled by the crowd, away from the chaos.

The old man was lost to her as well, her last glimpse of him caught just as someone stepped on his still-outstretched hand. Not a cop, but one of his own.

Milan spoke of tests of faith, how they would creep up on a person and shatter their soul. The old man had come for his community, to protest injustice against his people—only to be stomped on and forgotten by the very people he sought to defend. He was alone, just as Etta had been.

But not anymore.

Milan would never leave Etta on the ground. Terje would never step on her hand. The V would never leave a family member at the undeserved mercy of a crowd.

The V was the last true family in Berlin. It was Etta's job to reveal that truth to the world.

It was a precipice, the flash point for all they had worked toward. There would be no going back, Etta knew it. She wondered if Terje felt it, too, as they watched her footage with fingertips tented over their noses, viewed every second of the singing, chatter, and dancing with the precise focus of supervising physicians monitoring a student's first surgery. When it was finished, Terje stood from the bench and settled back at the card table. As much a consultant as he was a witness to Etta's task.

She began to work.

A gathering of forty became an army. Every inch of grass was covered with feet stolen and overlaid from videos plucked from homemade footage of protests in Ankara, Konya, and Istanbul. The ambient beats of music were replaced with impassioned chants—screeching, desperate cries that were flung like lances into the heart of German society. The shake in her hands while filming unintentionally added to the legitimacy. Scenes switched too quickly to note any details, frames zoomed in until it was impossible to discern whether a figure was alone or one of a thousand. The only concrete detail implying the crowd's size was the massive volume of their shouting.

Etta couldn't explain why she removed the old man in the grass, with his coffee and his kind and confused eyes. In his place, she plucked a figure from a video of an alt-right rally held in Chemnitz several years earlier: a skinhead, the pink cap of his scalp a beacon amid hundreds of counter-protesters. She peeled his image back with a digital scalpel, generating a 3D rendering and draping it over a video of another man being beaten by several teenagers in a park similar enough to Görlitzer. The result was dropped over the old man, so all viewers would see was a skinhead with thick black tattoos curling up his neck being beaten until his nose was bent flat against his cheek and blood drenched his white shirt. The footage was pulled in so only the legs of his assailants were visible—Turkish solely by implication.

Terje leaned closer over her shoulder as she worked. "How did you delete that part? Won't that glitch into the final composite?" She was glad he asked "how" instead of "why."

"No, you need to anchor the image properly—like attaching skin over muscle. It doesn't work if you try to fight against the original video, you must bind them together. Intertwine them, two pieces of DNA."

"But you're not using any object tracking, are you? What are these anchor points?" Terje traced over the white dots uniformly covering one of the bodies destined to become a rioter, not yet replaced but in transition.

"You're thinking like an artist. Think like a child. That's what this is, teaching patterns to a child." Etta smiled at him. "Your projections rely on intact images. Wechselkind shreds them down to bits and pieces.

Separates arms from legs then strips the skin away, chews them up and regurgitates them until it's birthed a new generation made of thousands of learned impressions. Those anchor points are rivets for a frame to hold up what's left."

"So you feed it images and it chews them down to the bones." His eyes lit up in genuine fascination. "Then it paints over the blank canvas. You trained this? Or was Wechselkind open source?"

"Trained it, built it on and off over the last few years. I tried some of the open-source programs, but they always turned up too many artifacts even if the documentation was good; I'd have to run a new composite dozens of times to get something half-alright. Nothing had native voice replicators, either, so that was a pain in the ass. Thankfully, I found some people willing to share what they knew about language replicators. Honestly, Wechselkind was a product of frustration. Had to either make my own software or throw my laptop out the window." It was a product of isolation, as well, but that still felt too personal to admit. It felt like Wechselkind's secret to share, not Etta's.

The monitor gave Terje's considering gaze a blue halo. He was the virtual renaissance man, basking under digital skies and contemplating the gravity of their shared potential.

"Not quite your illusions," she offered, uncomfortable under the admiration quickly growing in his expression.

"No," he agreed. "Not real time, but I wonder what we could do— what we would need, if we could increase throughput speed, drag that delay down. We could—"

A sharp beep signaled their most recent composite was finished. Etta turned from the pressure of Terje's excitement to press play. All at once they were dropped back into the violent spray of their creation, the blistering shouts in both Turkish and German. Terje's exhales were warm beside her ear as they sat together—enraptured artists seeing their first collaboration bear fruit.

When it was done, Terje dropped back into his seat. "I watched you make it. I see what you're doing, and I still almost want to call you a liar for saying it's fake."

The next morning, Milan watched Etta's rendition of his rally with his chin resting on one fisted hand. When the footage of the beating appeared, he smiled.

"And so strikes the match on our era of truth. Now we need only tend to the flames."

23

It didn't happen immediately, but it happened faster than she thought it might.

Their video flooded Berlin. They had hoped for a hundred views; they received thousands. Locally viral the same way a disease might spread, it bounced from one person to the next as it spread across the city. There were, of course, counterpoints. Opponents. People who claimed to have been at the park, testimonies promising they had never witnessed any violence—they had seen the protesters, and there hadn't been a single drop of blood on one blade of grass. The police released a statement on their official social media page that they hadn't received any reports of violence at the park that day, but they were "looking into any possible incidents." None of the accounts vehemently denying the beating mattered; the video proof was undeniable.

It turned out revolutions needed less tending to than reputations—they only needed to be started, then the hidden anger a society kept suppressed like lava gurgling under their laminate floors erupted on its own.

Less than a week later Etta went back to Görlitzer. Another rally was set to occur, a protest against both the beating and the accusations hurled at the Turkish community as result. Milan needed her there, needed more footage, more anger to control. She wasn't sure it was necessary. Wasn't the next step to guide the fury toward productive goals? To lead the people of Berlin to freedom? No, Milan had told her. Go, with the camera. Film it.

The old man who had greeted her was not at the park, not that she expected him to be. Still, it was as if she had wiped him out of existence with her editing—he had never been there at all. Police with dark helmets and lowered visors stood where the old man had once sat, batons resting on their hips like stunted sword handles.

The police were flanked by two opposing armies. The Turks pointed furious fingers at a cluster of men with alabaster skin and buzzed haircuts who waved German flags tauntingly, their glares hidden behind dark sunglasses. There was no music. No men lazing beneath trees and passing joints, no scent of spices and fresh barbecue.

When one of the men with chicken scratch tattoos crawling up his pale arms barely missed being struck by a sign swung too close to his head, he pushed past an officer to grab at the closest Turk—a student, his oil-black hair stuck to his sweat-stained cheeks. The police officer tackled the aggressor to the ground just before his hands caught the student's throat. Spittle dripped from the man's mouth like a wild dog as he snarled, blue eyes still turned upward at the Turkish student as they were hauled away in opposite directions.

Etta had not called for this rally, just as she had never organized any charity donations for her former clients or hired any babies for staged wholesome photographs. So she did not feel the urge to assist as two more of the protesters found themselves slipping between the police. She was not one of them, it was not her hands wrapped around any neck or digging fingernails into flushed skin; she was an outsider. She belonged only to the V.

She hopped onto one of the concrete benches just beyond the skirmish, standing on the back as she pulled out the camera.

Still without a voice or face, Milan draped his fingers over the public until they were cradled in his hands like a neurotic bird, bloodied from plucking its own feathers. The rallies continued. News channels reported a growing number of fights and attacks in the street as one side spotted the other; tree branches were turned into splintered bats and trash cans into battering rams.

It came out of nowhere, most said. Media personalities and journalists took their pick of explanations: a global rise of either alt-right amoral ideologies or the subjugation of national culture, depending on their alignment on the political spectrum. This is a culmination, they insisted. Do not be surprised—instead, be shocked we avoided it for so long. Still, on her walks around the city, Etta saw the shell-shocked horror on store clerks' faces each time they pulled down security gates over their stores. Hunched grandmothers could not disguise the way they cradled their groceries closer to their chests. Etta wondered how they felt, seeing the violence they believed long forgotten now replaying on the streets outside their apartment balconies. It was impossible to deny the rising violence in their city, the darkness of history taking one more nightmare lap over Berlin.

"They need to hear me," Milan told Etta and Terje in the shack. "They must hear me. Do you see how they turn against each other so quickly? How softly we push and how hard they crash, so rapidly, so instantly. I told you, I told both of you—this was inevitable. This is their reckoning."

So they took his voice, spoken gently into a microphone held by Terje. Milan wove stories of a natural way of things, of an order stolen from them by invaders and criminals. He told stories of mothers forsaking their children, of those same children becoming teens molested and forsaken by a society built on lies. He spoke of the Turks, and how the plastic cups that littered Görlitzer were symptomatic of a deeper, more toxic corruption.

"We have to cut off the infection," Milan encouraged the world. "Do we need more of them? Their invasion, their violence—they bring it in droves and suck away at our peace like parasites, and we are told to not only accept them but welcome it—no longer. No longer."

Any room left for doubt was filled by Wechselkind. As Etta fed her program faces and voices, it spun them into strands of features and sounds that could be woven into entirely new people with unique vocal traits. Every resulting virtual creature was as familiar as a longtime neighbor. Milan's first supporters outside of the V were Wechselkind and its children.

Picking out the deepfakes buried in social media feeds became a game for Etta and Terje. They spent hours poring over recordings, Terje searching for signs of Etta's manipulations among countless videos.

"Is this one of yours?" he would ask, pointing to a video of a woman cupping her split lip or a clip of a policeman being overwhelmed by teenagers with ochre skin.

She would always fail at hiding her smirk. "You tell me."

He never could. Not for certain. Her videos had a tempo, the rhythm of the streets where people stumbled over cracked pavement, where a woman juggled with her purse as she attempted to answer a call. A staccato with logic rooted not in probability but humanity. Etta's fakes were so good because they didn't try to be real, but instead were depictions of reality. They framed pieces of imperfection within an imperfect frame, tricking the mind.

Terje was hunting for a curated sort of realism that simply did not exist in Etta's hyperreal replicas.

"Shit, Etta." Terje crossed his arms and slumped back against the bench, deflated by defeat. "The others, there's some—I don't know, it's like an uncanniness. A recycled cadence. The same twitch of the brow, little loops like loose threads in the illusion. But yours, there's no—oh, alright, no need to look so smug, sparrow." He bumped her shoulder. "Congratulations, you win. Don't you dare tell anyone—next they'll have you doing the projections too."

Milan's sermons were settled over the videos of the riots, a steady call for freedom. For truth. To cease ignoring the predetermined chaos made inevitable by a society determined to mix cultures and ideas.

Berlin listened.

***

"It's working," Terje said one night as he and Etta sat squeezed together on the bench in their shack. His hand was on her knee, their shoulders bumping together as they shared victorious grins. "We did it."

Etta welcomed his kiss, leaning forward into his warmth. "We *started* it." The level of their success still felt unreal, neither of them fully believing how quickly support for Milan, and general tension within Berlin, seemed to grow.

News reports were open on the monitors before them, reporters retelling the same handful of stories regarding recent attacks in and around Kreuzberg. Etta scratched at a knot of curls as the newest story detailed a Turkish woman who had been cornered by a group of German teens, how several men sitting at a café nearby sipping on tea had noticed the confrontation and ran in to fend off the boys.

Newcomers had been appearing in Spreepark lately, wandering in through the gates or climbing the fences—either drawn directly in response to Milan's online reputation or pushed out of the city. Room in the bunkhouse was running low enough that Etta had stumbled upon teenagers curled up in sleeping bags throughout the park, like speed bumps. Their family dinners had turned into animalistic harvest, people pushing past each other to grab handfuls of stolen takeaways or boiled potatoes.

One morning, Etta had seen a girl attempt to climb through one of the broken windows of the kitchen. She had fallen, which Etta initially chalked up to intoxication—except when the girl stood, her hands weeping blood, Etta realized she couldn't have been older than ten. When she caught Etta staring, she raised one crooked, bloody middle finger and scurried off.

They kept showing up and Milan didn't turn them away, instead welcoming them from a regal distance with a warm smile. He split his time evenly between the shack and his room above Little Monarchy, watching the new family members wander across the park from his foggy window. That was where many spotted him for the first time, high above their heads.

"Milan seems happy enough about it." Etta's nail caught on a scab buried beneath her tangled hair. "He's been sending Loulou out to get more beer for everyone. Did you see the snacks Foster dropped off at the bunkhouse?" Their own meals had been delivered nightly, fresh curries and noodle dishes still warm in their cartons. Turned out the new family members often raided their parent's purses before fleeing home.

"We should grab some later. Here, look at these comments." Terje scrolled down past the broadcast to where viewers had left their own views. "Half of them still think this came out of nowhere."

"And the other half are following Milan's page." The spot on her scalp began to burn as she dug her nail deeper into it. "Fuck the rest, they're missing the point. Doesn't matter where it came from so long as we take down the assholes up top."

"Or maybe the rest should stop lying to themselves already." Terje tapped at her hand until she let it drop from her hair. "Everyone wants to believe this 'unity' bullshit, like we haven't had all these problems already—they just want to live in this fantasy, pretend we all get along. Now they're acknowledging what they've all felt the whole time, seeing themselves—really seeing it, the truth of themselves—and they don't want to believe it."

That was it for Terje, the idea that everyone was living in a simulation made of their own desires—just as they lied about the Black Forest. But the thought gave Etta pause. Was it truly her mother's financials that drove her to suicide, or had societal expectations for success dragged her feet off that ledge? Was it not the government, whatever direction it leaned at any particular time, pushing the public back and forth with contrary agendas until people were confused about who they were meant to hate and who they were meant to support? That was what they needed to dismantle, what they needed to broadcast to the world: a contrary corporate government that kept the German people too confused to see more than a day beyond themselves. A system of controlled, slow murder.

Just as they had done to her mother.

Terje's arm slid over her shoulder. He wrapped a curl around his index finger, the callouses on his fingertips dragging against the skin of her neck until she shivered. Pale blue light engulfed his face as he gazed at her, taking in every detail of her expression.

"We don't have to talk about it, whatever's going on in your head," he said, hand slipping loose from her curls to cup her cheek. "But we can, if you want."

They were the same words he always used, a safety net for them both.

The door screeched open before she could reply. Etta didn't need to turn to know it was Milan.

"Look!" The walls shook as he stormed into the shack. The skin under his eyes was pink, cheeks reddened with fury as he shoved a phone before Etta and Terje. Spit sprayed onto the monitors as he shouted. "*Look.*"

It was a video of Chancellor Stauss. His face drooped with a heavy frown; his arms were crossed neatly over his desk as he spoke beside a German flag. "We must not allow these recent racially motivated attacks to destabilize the decades of work we have put into social progress," Stauss said to the camera. "We have a humanist responsibility to those in our communities, which includes the Turkish population who have contributed to the German economy for decades—"

Milan threw the phone to the ground with a sharp crack. A thick vein pumped across his forehead like a live wire. Stauss's voice continued to drawl on through the phone's speakers, but Etta couldn't distinguish the words from the roaring in her ears.

Milan's hand stayed outstretched; his fingers twitched. Air hissed between his clenched teeth, and Etta's breath shortened to match it. Terje's body was also locked in place above her. They counted the seconds until the red tint to Milan's face slowly bled away.

His arm dropped smoothly back to his side, and he sniffed loudly as his shoulders shrugged the fury off his back.

"A false prophet." He wiped a finger under his nose and tilted his head from one side to the other until there was a soft pop. "A false prophet trying to guide his flock back toward the cliffs, but we will not—they will not be misled." All the heat in his voice had cooled into hard obsidian.

"Okay," Etta whispered. "Alright."

"Fix it."

"Wechselkind," she said. "It can mimic voices. We can fix it."

"Yes. Steal his voice. Show the people what liars like him truly think, what he really knows about those criminals."

He turned toward the door, pausing once to kick the phone—still rolling steadily through the rest of the Chancellor's speech—into the wall. Etta flinched as it rattled against the metal.

"Be quick," Milan added. "Show me why I shouldn't give your bed to one of those imbeciles outside our gates."

Then he was gone.

Etta slumped against the bench the moment the shack's door was pulled shut. Terje dropped down beside her in stuttered movements, still staring at the spot Milan had occupied just moments before. The phone in the corner had finally gone silent.

Milan would never hurt her. Never once during his increasingly frequent outbursts was she afraid of the man who had so lovingly housed her, who had given her an explicit purpose. But to *disappoint* him— surely his indignant rage came only from a frustration of living in a false world for too long. Milan wanted to help, and any threat against his efforts, any sensation of helplessness when they were finally so close to success, was bound to infuriate him. Etta could relate to that.

"Get it together." She shoved her keyboard across the desk, making space for her laptop. Terje blinked once with the solemn determination of a soldier heading back to war as he tore his gaze away from the ghost of Milan's presence and turned back to their computers.

Had it really been only a few months since she used Wechselkind to mimic Angela Merkel's voice in a provocative response to her hacked laptop? It felt like so long ago. Centuries ago. She couldn't remember how it had felt to make the video, whether she garnered any satisfaction from sending it.

Everything before Milan was blurred, like a terrible movie she couldn't quite recall the plot of.

Surely it felt nothing like this moment—the urgency, the importance—uploading videos of Chancellor Stauss into her program, letting it learn the cadence of his speech, the dip of his vowels. She had never *had* to edit her previous clips like how she *had* to create this video, how she needed to keep that snake vein from curling across Milan's forehead for at least another few days. It was her role to turn his angry heat back into warm approval so they could all bask in his light without getting burned.

The original video was already largely disseminated online and there would be no point in completely altering it. Instead, she slipped in three words—only a hint of them—right at the end. Spoken softly enough that listeners would be enticed into rewinding. They would press their ears to their phones, push their headphones tighter against their scalps, as they heard Stauss mutter "Disgusting Turkish animals" right as he stood up from his desk.

"It's not enough. We have to discredit the original too. Here." Terje pulled his own keyboard onto his lap. His video editing program popped up on the monitors before them. The edits took less than ten minutes.

"Look." He pressed play.

Terje had added a small splice to the original. A momentary clipping right at the end. It would mean nothing to anyone with no reason to look closer; it would mean everything for someone looking for evidence of an insult edited out by the government.

"You post my version on Milan's channels." Etta was already typing. "I'll get yours sent out on a few other sites. I'll try to flood out some of the original clips, make it look like they're trying to cover their asses—erase the evidence."

Pile up the lies until reality was buried and fractured under their weight. The public would find themselves entrenched in illusions, unable to find the way out—much less the truth. People never wanted to believe their leaders—they craved reasons to hate them, for ammo to shred their reputations into tatters. Nothing brought out the bloodlust in a populace like political scandals did.

When it was done, after they'd unleashed their videos online, Terje stepped outside without a word—only the clicking of his lighter as he flipped it between his fingers. Etta stood to follow him but paused, her gaze caught by the phone forgotten against the wall. She glanced at the door, still open a crack—Terje's back was to her.

She didn't need a phone. She had no one to call outside Spreepark. There was no reason to pick it up. Slowly, she crouched. The metal case was cool against her palm. The screen was a constellation of white cracks, the glass lifting at the top where it had absorbed most of the impact from Milan's death blow. Taking another glance at the door, she pressed the power button. The sharp edge of the shattered screen bit into her thumb. There was a flicker of white light, followed by a morphing blue and red fractal that whirled like a heat signature. She peeked again over her shoulder—Terje was still facing away.

When she looked back down the screen had gone black.

"Etta?"

She was upright and halfway to the door before Terje turned toward her. She leaned against the shack beside him, trying to ignore the notable weight of the small object hidden in her pocket.

She would give it back to Milan at dinner. It was the right thing to do.

24

As Spreepark had become increasingly populated with teenagers carrying brand-name backpacks full of beer, already drunk on their wild ideals, Etta found herself spending more evenings crouched beside the Ferris wheel operator booth. It was the last peaceful place to sit, uncontaminated by work or the quiet grunts and moans of people hazarding bad trips. The sluggish newcomers—there were at least fifty now milling about—infested every corner of the park but avoided the Ferris wheel as though it were outlined in a ring of thick salt. Maybe they, too, sensed the sacred nature of it, the grand superiority it held—how it had outlived the swan boats, the roller-coaster tracks, the park-goers, and how it would outlive them too. Or maybe they feared the groaning sound it made with every soft breeze, feared the bolts would finally snap and send the wheel off to flatten what was left of the park. Either way, they left it alone and, by extension, they left Etta alone.

So when Etta heard footsteps creak up the metal steps, she knew it was an actual member of the family, one who had lived under the shadow of the Ferris wheel long enough to not fear its height. She assumed it would be Terje, maybe Foster. She assumed incorrectly.

"Fancy seeing you," Loulou said.

More than ever, Loulou looked as natural to Spreepark as the moss crawling over the boardwalk. Wide rips in her stained blouse revealed the eggshell tint of her skin, and the mild pastels of her hair were blocked off by wide chunks of madly bright hues. Faded lines criss-crossed the skin around her ears from where she must have slipped while attempting to recolor the length of her roots with markers or nail polish. Time had grasped Loulou, wrapped its vines around her like one of the swan boats until her boards were cracked and the paint was chipped, and she wore it with honor. It gave her credence among a growing crowd where unmarked skin and clean nails were symptoms of a lack of commitment. Etta had her work; Loulou had time.

"Fancy seeing me outside the shack, yeah?" Etta smiled.

"No," Loulou said. "Fancy seeing you at all."

They *had* seen each other, plenty of times, coming and going from the bunkhouse or the shack. But Loulou was right: sometime after the rally the conversation had been sucked from those passing moments. Now, each encounter felt more like a mile marker of how far they were drifting apart. Etta frowned.

"It's been busy," she said. She didn't mention how she made a point to look at Milan's window each time she wandered toward the Ferris wheel, searching for a glimpse of pastel hair.

"Sure, it has. You're busy, Terje's busy—you have all your projects with Milan. Fights to film, bunch of rats to draw out of the gutter, chancellors to defame. You've been real busy. But that's what you two do. You do what *really* needs doing, what Milan—"

Loulou didn't finish. She exhaled instead, slumping on the metal rail beside Etta. It reminded Etta so much of Milan, of his sudden moods, that she found herself frozen as Loulou tilted her chin up to-ward the Ferris wheel and sighed again.

"Milan talks about you," Loulou said to the sky. "I knew you'd fit, never realized how well."

It was startling to be the object of jealousy—the concept was so alien when wielded by anyone other than herself.

"He talks about you too," Etta lied. Milan hadn't spoken of Loulou in weeks. "You were the first."

It worked. The corner of Loulou's lip lifted into the hint of a pleased smile, head still tilted up like a cat milking the sunlight.

"Don't I know it."

As Milan's popularity swelled the family with fresh faces, the mood at the bonfires shifted. Rage—too hungry and quick to explode—outpaced the previous trust and familiarity. Comradery was dethroned and the bonfires burned hot instead of warm.

That night, Etta sat between Terje's long legs on the grass as Loulou led a few baby-faced boys with crooked tattoos and straight teeth around the fire. Johanna trailed behind them like a school monitor, ready to chase down any strays. Varick and Tedmark slow danced, swaying softly side to side, ignoring the newcomers. Monika sat on the periphery, her pale legs wrapped around a new boy with dark hair that covered his face like a greasy bead curtain. Etta was fairly certain his name was Noah.

Terje had his laptop balanced on a knee, with one hand on the keyboard and the other twirling Etta's curls. Milan was perched on the picnic bench above them, his eyes trained on Terje's screen.

"Well?"

Terje's breath warmed the back of her neck as he answered. "The French Minister of Economics tagged you—he's claiming you're a plant by the conservative party. Called you an extremist."

The table creaked as Milan leaned closer. "An extremist."

Terje's hand stilled at the base of Etta's neck. She could feel the boiling point of Milan's mood nearing, as they were left in wait to see whether the tension would recede or spill over the edge.

"Like Jesus," she said, hoping to urge him toward calm. "You told me they called him an extremist. Ghandi too."

Milan snapped up, one boot nearly landing on Etta's hair as he leapt onto the table. His hands clapped together, addressing the stumbling teenagers.

"Listen—quiet now and listen." Terje's laptop was swiped up and held about Milan's head like an offering. "My friends, they—a man in France who feasts on the flesh of poor folks such as us—he calls us extremists. He points his gladius at us and claims we condemned the world to the cross."

Someone booed in the crowd. Loulou's lips were twisted and smug as her eyes met Etta's across the fire. Etta was out from between Terje's legs, pulling him up with her as they looked to Milan. The firelight flickered around him, blurring the edges of his body and blending him into the sky where he spoke to them from beside the stars.

"Pig!" Johanna shouted from beside Loulou. One of the boys with them, his nose curved like a beak, opened his mouth as though ready to voice his own insults when he was silenced with a raise of Milan's hand.

"They condemn us, the true people, while they serve our invaders. The criminals. The rapists, the thieves." Milan licked his lips. Terje gave a low hum beside Etta. "We will—"

"Shh, quit it!" A pair of airy, giggling voices punched through the dark.

Milan's expression, previously alight with passion, turned to granite. Even the fire seemed to go silent.

Another soft hush and a few ditzy giggles drifted across the clearing as all eyes were drawn to the couple on the grass—Monika and Noah—in a state of drunken, oblivious bliss.

Milan took one step down, two steps onto the grass—only slowing to return Terje's laptop. His face was blank as he stalked through the parted crowd. Etta's mouth had gone completely dry. Hunting—that was the only definition for Milan's steady approach, the way he watched them.

Only when the toes of his leather loafers were nearly on top of Monika's ankle did she finally look up. She blanched, the rose flush of alcohol draining instantly from her sunken cheeks.

"Stand up." His voice was gentle.

Monika rose on fawn's legs, supported only by Noah's thin, boyish arm as they faltered under Milan's stare.

"Monika," he said.

"Sorry, Milan. I'm really sorry." Monika's arms wound themselves around her waist. "I'm sorry."

"Oh, Monika," he murmured. Then, over her, to the crowd, "This, Monika, she is why we must be extreme. Monika thinks she is better." He was shouting, dragging Monika upward with a fistful of hair. "Monika was raised by a society that told her she was important, they told her that her body was a sacred thing to be hidden away—that is what they do. They hide sacred things. They feed our egos and starve us of truth—feed our egos fat like Monika's until we must starve them out again."

Johanna's hand shot over her mouth. Loulou looked ready to jump forward. Etta's anger began to boil just as theirs clearly was. Society had ruined Monika, planted pride under her skin and abandoned her. Now, her salvation weighed on Milan's shoulders. On them. They carried the weight of her impurity.

Milan lowered her gently, kneeling before her and baptizing her with his gaze. Etta could barely hear his voice over the flames. "We have to starve it out," he said. "Show them—strip down and show them. You must show them."

Monika nodded, her lip quivering. Milan wrapped his hands around hers and together they pushed the thin straps of her black shift over her shoulders and let it fall in a puddle on the grass. Her thin underwear followed. Etta took in the unimpressive porcelain stretch of Monika. The lines of her rib cage protruded as she hunched over, sinking down toward the grass with a wet sob.

"I'm sorry," she whimpered. "Please—I don't want it, I don't want the pride, help me be—I don't want to be important, I want—I want to be good again, please. I want to be good." Her body spasmed with the force of her weeping.

Milan lifted her, her back pressed against his chest as he faced her toward her family.

"Look at your family," Milan encouraged. He jerked his chin at Loulou, who charged forward to grab one of Monika's arms and continue leading her around. "Show them who you are, and let that ego die."

Etta stepped forward and reached out to take Monika's other arm from Milan. In the hazy light, as the others crept closer to run comforting hands over Monika's cheeks and shoulders, Etta swore she could feel the societal poison leaking from Monika's pores to sizzle on the grass.

Johanna watched them with a set jaw and hardened eyes. Her hands twitched at her side. Etta wondered how long it would be until they were parading *her* around the fire.

"Look at your family, Monika." Etta tucked a strand of black hair behind Monika's ear. "Look at our family, Monika. We're the lucky ones." A tear streaked down Monika's cheek as she smiled.

How lost would they be, without Milan?

Etta knew too well. But it was okay; she was safe now, with the family—where Milan made sure the corruption outside was kept beyond their gates.

25

They left the park with backpacks and returned with bruises. An army of ghosts that fit either side depending on their attire, sent out to fan the flames of violence on the streets of Berlin. They practiced slinging slurs in the park's courtyard between sips from metal flasks. When the sun went down, they slipped into the city. They stood on the trains beside regular people with regular lives. They changed in station bathrooms, swapped their sweatshirts and jeans for police uniforms or headscarves, and descended upon the streets.

Etta filmed as they smashed the windows of stores with baseball bats and threw fiery bottles into the thin streets of Kreuzberg. The retaliation was immediate. Etta soon could not differentiate those who wore costumes from those who acted with genuine intent.

Often, she would stay late after the fighting was over. She would linger amid the smoke, listening to the sound of glass crunching beneath feet as people trickled from their apartments to assess the newest damage done to their homes, their neighborhood. The younger they were, the more enraged they appeared, whereas those with sinking skin and deep wrinkles looked on with vacant exhaustion. Some would pick shards of glass from the ground and watch blankly as the edges bit into their skin, blood dripping from their fingers onto the pavement while sirens screeched down the street. Something kept Etta there, even though these were the same people she had grown to despise.

Something kept her feet stuck to fire escapes or behind a cluster of trees, a compulsion to watch. To witness—even long after her camera was shut off.

It was good, Etta reminded herself. This was what they wanted; the pattern was broken. No longer did people mindlessly walk to their offices and play at normality when, deep in their bellies, they understood the world was forsaken. Now they looked over their shoulders. They questioned their government, their neighbors. They questioned everything.

It was exactly what Milan wanted.

But it wasn't enough. Not yet.

It was on one of those evenings, when she had stretched out her moments in Berlin until she was certain her absence at the park would be noticed, that Etta was discovered returning late.

The security guards had become more attentive in recent days, as people continued to trickle in after hearing Milan's call. Etta had earned her place and the recognition that meant she was allowed to pass where others were detained. Rarely did the guards even step outside when she appeared, instead waving through the window as she slipped through the gate.

That night, the guardhouse door swung open. Etta froze.

For one horrible moment she expected to see the guard who had once attacked her. The only weapon at her disposal was her camera, useless but still fisted in her hand.

"Well, shit," the figure who appeared from behind the door said. "The shadow."

Even in the soft light of oncoming dawn, Etta could make out the upturned nose, the head covered in a fuzz of new hair. "Johanna," Etta replied. "Bit early to be around the guardhouse."

"Bit late to be coming back to the park." Johanna slumped against the wall of the small building. Never once had Etta seen her in anything but revealing clothing, thin tops that clung to her sides and skirts that ended well above her knees. All of that had been traded for a winter jacket that swallowed her frame, a matted fur collar jutting up around her neck as she dug a hand into the deep pocket. One long leg clad in denim stuck out across the gate's opening, trapping Etta where she stood.

It was an impasse. Etta wanted to trust Johanna, to know she would believe Etta's late return was born only from curiosity about their increasing influence on Berlin, but the threat in her words and posture was obvious. She would tell Milan. Milan would not understand.

Johanna pulled out a half-crushed pack of cigarettes. "Everyone around here says you're a smart girl," she said, digging a lighter out of her other pocket. A thick J was carved into the side. "Think real hard, use that brain—you tell me why I'm here."

Etta thought of Frank, the bulbous guard who had called after Loulou. The way Monika always looked exhausted when Etta saw her wandering back from the front of the park, how she stumbled on stiff legs toward the bunkhouse while everyone else stretched the sleep from their limbs.

Etta had been spared that. Johanna had not.

Etta refused to let herself be goaded once more by Johanna's barbed words. She would not stand dumbly like a cowed animal. Instead, she turned to lean against the fence.

If Johanna noticed Etta's countermove she didn't show it, her gaze distant as she stared into the park above the flame of her lighter.

"I'm curious," Johanna said. "Why are you still here?"

The question caught Etta off guard. "You'd rather be out there?"

Johanna scratched at the fresh stubble on her scalp. "Loulou told me about you."

"What?"

"Dead mom, practically dead dad—should be dead, at least." Her eyes rolled toward Etta, her nose crinkling with some semblance of pity. "Don't look so shocked—the way you clung to her skirts like a lost kid, you never realized she didn't treasure your secrets? That's why you don't see it, you never had a family of your own, so this is all you've got. But I see it, I know families. I know what this kind of love means."

Johanna tapped her cigarette, a flake of red ash landing on Etta's hand. Etta swore, waving it away. "Wasn't exactly a secret, was it?"

"Figured you'd want to know." Johanna rubbed her eyes. "She also told me what you and your boy get up to. Your videos have pissed off a lot of people. Heard they're even rioting in Istanbul now. Got activists kicking shit up in Belgium too—who knows for what side. Bet they don't even know half the time."

"They *should* be rioting."

Johanna smiled, a sour grin with half-measured disbelief. She took another drag from her cigarette and tapped the ash, watching as it sprinkled onto her boot.

"You know, I knew you would never leave. I saw you and thought, that's it. She's done. Just a fucking kid who convinced herself she knew better, like you escaped some trap—you didn't escape shit, understand it? You were given a break. You were free, and you spent all of it search-ing for the same goddamn thing you condemn the rest of us for. You landed right in a hellscape and you're calling it cozy."

Etta stared at Johanna hard, searching her expression. Johanna wasn't attacking Etta; she was telling the truth—what she believed to be true.

Etta jammed her hands so deep into her pockets her jacket pulled down on her shoulders. "Wonder what Milan will think about you calling the family a hellscape."

"Can't wait to find out," Johanna murmured. Her eyes made anoth-er trail from Etta's feet to her face. "You know I'm right, but you can't swallow it. So good at illusions that you've managed to trick yourself."

"Fuck you." That was enough. Etta pushed off the fence and stepped forward, fully prepared to stomp Johanna's ankle into the dirt if she didn't move. There was no need, however. Johanna pulled back her leg and let Etta pass.

She would not look back. Not even for the three words uttered softly behind her.

"Good luck, shadow."

When Etta reached the shack, she opened the lock with shaking fingers, trying not to rattle the door as she stomped inside and steadied herself to climb up the ladder into the loft. A shrill whine echoed in her head as she shed her sweatshirt and pants to slip under the blankets beside a snoring Terje.

Had Loulou really told Johanna about her mother and father? Every conversation now felt barbed, the new context like a red glaze that tainted each memory of herself and Loulou. It swallowed her even as she finally felt herself drifting to sleep, the only image behind her eyes that of Johanna's embittered smirk.

She awoke to loud shouts from outside. What time was it?

"Terje? What—shit." A quick pat on the bed confirmed Terje was gone.

Another furious voice bounced off the shack walls, too distant for her to decipher the words. Etta stumbled back into her clothing, nearly falling as she tried to shove her arm through the sleeve while clambering down the ladder. Outside, drowsy faces peeked out from around the bunkhouse toward the main part of the park.

Milan was shouting. Etta ran toward the sound, certain that someone had attacked, that the police had shown up, that their work had finally been discovered by the government. She followed the voices toward the gate, where a cluster of security guards hovered beside the guardhouse. On the ground between them was Frank, his fat hands covering his face as he hid his head between his knees. Milan was screaming obscenities as he reared back and kicked one of the fence posts hard enough that it tilted a few inches sideways. He kicked it again, platinum hair sticking up in tufts like a lion's mane as he prowled beside the guards.

Terje was leaving the guardhouse with a grim expression. He spotted her approaching and hurried his steps, casting one sideways glance at Milan.

"Hey, what—" She met him in the middle, still far enough away that none of the guards glanced toward them.

Terje shook his head and ran a tired hand through his hair. "It's Johanna," he said flatly. "She's gone."

Ice slipped through her veins. "What?"

He dipped his chin back toward Frank, who had raised his head to reveal deep purple-black bruises developing around each eye. "Went to meet Frank last night and drugged him. Beat the shit out of him while he was out. Took the money in the guard's safe, too, and left. Didn't find out until his relief guard showed up."

One of the guards tried to speak and was quickly silenced by Milan's roaring.

"Milan is pissed," Terje said. "Wants us to find her."

Etta didn't need to tell him that any attempts would be pointless. Johanna wasn't a politician or an influencer, she had lived among them. She didn't have a phone, would know better than to partake in social media or draw from any of her bank accounts—she had known exactly what she was doing when she confronted Etta just hours ago. Johanna had known that revealing her knowledge about Etta and Terje's work would be her best hope for Milan allowing her escape—important enough that she risked their conversation while Frank was unconscious only feet away.

Milan would swallow his rage soon; he would have to. Johanna was gone.

26

Changing the world left little time for parties, yet several weeks after the Johanna incident Milan called for a return to their roots. An event to help the family bond and recover after such a blatant betrayal. In truth, Etta suspected Milan was attempting to cover up the fact that they had run out of money. Even as new followers made contributions to help feed the V, the number of mouths quickly outnumbered the amount of canned goods they had stockpiled in the bunkhouse.

They held the rave at Beelitz Heilstätten. The discomfort she felt as they walked under those broken glass windows was magnified beyond anything she had felt that first night. The silence as the family set up their equipment gave her an unsettling sense that something had permanently shifted.

"Milan needs me on the floor tonight," Terje warned her as they fished wiring up onto the balcony, where they had decided to set up their sound booth.

She caught one end of a long yellow cord that Terje tossed up from the floor below. "Selling?"

"You guessed it."

"Always figured you looked too nerdy to be a drug dealer." Etta leaned back from the balcony edge just as the end of another cord sailed wide past her cheek. "See? Can't even throw a cord. You think you can throw a punch?"

"Oh, fuck off." She didn't need to look back down to know Terje was smiling.

Even that small moment of joy lacked its usual light, however. All of them were exhausted. Even Loulou, who usually took it upon herself to crack the first drink of the night, was trailing behind Milan silently while he patrolled the main lobby. She had started to spend her days in the shack again, enticing Etta and Terje into card games with a small smile and a half-hearted wink, as though trying to revive the past before the weight of their movement crushed the air around them.

"Try that switch?" Terje stomped up the stairs just as Etta plugged the last wire into their soundboard. A steady beat instantly filled the room, earning an approving nod from Milan below them as dust fell from the ceiling in waves. Loulou looked up from beside Milan and her eyelids fluttered, the dust coating her hair.

Gentle fingers tapped the back of Etta's neck, drawing her gaze back to Terje, who smiled. He was always so serious, even in his smiles—every quiet piece of happiness hidden and fragile, as though he was terrified it was a trick played by his mind.

"Sure you'll be okay manning the booth on your own?"

"Sure you'll be okay down in the trenches?"

He never seemed insulted by her teasing. He leaned into her jabs, opened the door for them and waited with outspread arms so she could throw one careful punch after the other. She had begun to believe it was a part of his craving for honesty, as though she could reveal the final lies he held within himself.

"You worry too much," he answered.

That was a joke. She didn't worry at all. Neither of them worried, not when Milan assured them of how well they were doing, how brilliantly every piece was falling into place. Etta was finally tackling the task she'd been eyeing since joining the V: targeting the ones making the plays, the leaders. She launched misinformation campaigns designed specifically to be discovered by opposing countries, doctored clips of previous military encounters overlaid with claims attributing them to foreign forces moving into sovereign nations.

The previous week she had posted a clip of soldiers being targeted by a drone strike, laying captions over it that made it appear that Turkey had hired mercenaries to operate in Bulgarian territory. People called it an act of war. The Euro-Atlantic Partnership Council and the North Atlantic Cooperation Council had said the claims were unsubstantiated but promised to investigate. The public retorted that such claims only added validity to the conspiracy. Milan had warned them to question their governments and the people had listened.

No, there was nothing to worry about.

Especially not up on the balcony, while the partiers flooded in and instantly began to dance. Even though she had grown to love dancing beside Loulou and Terje while some combination of chemicals sparked inside her like a thousand fireworks, there was also something enjoyable about being stranded above it all. She embraced the simplicity of the moment, the pleasure written on the faces below.

Then it all abruptly shattered.

A boy in the deepest part of the crowd crashed to the ground, then bounced back to his feet, thrashing at some unknown enemy with eyes rolling like a panicked horse. It took Etta a moment to realize an older boy, the blue lights reflecting off the pale skin stretched across his shaved skull, was jerking the other around by the hair. Those dancing near them staggered back in a rippling wave that sent several girls at the edge of the group sprawling onto the ground as they absorbed the impact.

The energy of the room snapped like a burst lightbulb. Loulou stopped dancing and stared at the boys as they grappled, spit flying as they shouted obscenities Etta couldn't catch. Milan looked on from the opposite balcony like a Roman emperor, jaw clenched and fingers tapping at his side. He frowned as the skinhead threw the younger boy onto the floor and stomped his boot against his side, the boy curling inward, his jaw lax. The music swallowed any sound he may have made.

Milan's eyes slid to where Foster stood guard beside the door. Milan nodded. Foster moved in.

Most of the crowd parted for him. Those who didn't met the steel edges of his shoulders as he pushed past them. The skinhead, entrenched in both the music and his assault, did not notice Foster until one giant hand had him by the back of the neck. The boy at their feet jerked. Blood leaked from his mouth, making a murky pool around his lips. A girl with fishnet leggings and cropped hair leaned down to cradle his head.

The skinhead clawed at Foster like a furious cat battling a brick wall, hissing threats as Foster dragged him toward the back of the lobby where Etta knew a back door waited.

The party resumed in a desperate surge. Dancers filled the space left behind as the injured boy was dragged off the floor by the girl with the cropped hair. Milan resumed his look of blasé contentment as he stretched out across a bench. Loulou snapped back into her dance as though she had never stopped; when a cup was passed into her hand by an anonymous companion, she gulped from it as she continued to sway. Etta could not stop staring at the pool of blood getting smeared around with ignorant joy.

Suddenly, she hated the balcony. Hated the guilt, despite knowing for certain that she had no role in what had happened. She was only the DJ. What the music drove the dancers to do, if it was the music at all, was not her fault.

She glanced at the soundboard, checking how long was left on Terje's playlist. Another five minutes at least on the current song alone. That was more than enough time.

The stairs were empty as she slipped away. She was halfway to the back door before she stopped herself—it was the same back door she had escaped through her first night at Beelitz Heilstätten. Flashes of bloodshot eyes and blue lips flooded her mind as she turned on her heel, moving along the wall until she found a window with broken panes shattered by years of unrelenting winds and pointed neglect.

She knew that Foster couldn't have killed the boy from back then. Foster's hands held cards more often than throats, his bulk had always been a hiding place rather than something to hide from. Yet she also knew that there would be no escaping the haunting image at the back of her mind.

She kicked out the chunks of glass still clinging to the wooden window frame. The building forgave her that action, letting the shards fall easily, like old teeth out of an aging mouth, until she was able to pull herself up and out of the window and into the crisp night air. Gravel crunched under her feet as she dropped the short distance to the ground and walked along the back wall of the hospital. There was no one else behind the building, only the dull echoes of the party inside as she slumped against the brick wall. The cool stone pulsed at her back.

Then she heard shouting.

"*Fuck* that!"

It came from around the corner, near the back door she had avoided.

"My friend—" She knew that voice. Foster.

Why hadn't he managed to kick the skinhead out yet? She strode along the wall, listening as the other voice grew louder and more heated with every second.

"This is bullshit. That animal jumped *me*, alright? Just let me fucking go, I don't even want to be here—this whole place is bullshit."

Etta peeked around the corner, a mouse sliding along the walls, trusting the shadows to hide her.

Foster had the skinhead pinned against the wall. "I'm sorry, my friend. But what's done is done." A hint of disappointed sorrow colored his voice.

The boy opened his mouth to spit another attack, but Foster's hands clapped around his neck. An icy wave crashed through Etta as the skinhead's eyes bulged. Etta had always imagined choking to be a loud affair, one with hoarse screams and gasps, but the boy was deadly quiet aside from the sound of his boots scraping against the brick wall. His hands slapped uselessly at Foster's arms.

It took an eternity.

Foster watched silently as the boy's head lolled forward, his chin bobbing twice as his eyes fluttered shut. His feet slid from the wall. The air stilled.

Foster did not drop him immediately. He held the boy for another few moments, hands steady in their terminal grip, before he slowly lowered the body to the ground.

Blood roared in Etta's ears as she pressed her shoulder against the wall and tried to steady her breathing, watching Foster carefully as she prayed for him to leave, to go anywhere but her direction. Another part of her protested. Foster, with his gentle laugh and sweet smiles as he called her Mäuschen, he wouldn't hurt her.

He wouldn't hurt anyone. But he had.

The boy deserved it—she tried to believe that thought. But from the balcony, she had seen the immediate effects of her deepfake work. There, out behind Beelitz Heilstätten, she had seen another example. Milan's influence had ended in that death and Etta had played a hand in gifting him that power. But that boy wasn't a politician or a member of the corporate elite. He was one of theirs, one of the ones left behind to survive at the hands of an unforgiving world.

Her hand flexed as sweat slicked from her palms. Had Foster's palms sweat as well, or had he murdered a boy with the distant pity of a farmer putting down a lame dog?

With a deep sigh, Foster crouched down and heaved the body onto his shoulder. A wet stain spread from underneath where the body had been lying, a matching mark revealed on the underside of the boy's trousers. Etta waited as Foster carried him away, deeper into the complex, far from the main building and toward the abandoned wards. Once she could barely see his back amid the darkness, she ran.

She went back through the broken window. The music was still playing; no one had noticed her absence. When she returned to the balcony she settled against the wall beside the soundboard, far from the banisters. Far from the people below.

When Terje found her later he asked how she fared, smirking until he saw her expression beneath the flickering lights. "You alright?" he asked, serious then.

"Fine," she said.

She couldn't say a word, not a single syllable of what had happened, what she had seen. Because already her mind swirled with arguments on Foster's behalf, on Milan's behalf, and she knew what Terje would say. She knew how he would justify it, how he would reassure her that this was the cost of truth. The cost of revealing the actual nature of humanity, of undoing the wrongs set into policy through centuries of pain.

Worst of all, she feared how easily she would agree with him.

27

"France condemned the protests. The president spewed some bullshit that German radicalism won't be tolerated there." Terje leaned back against his bench, kicking his feet up onto his desk.

Etta glanced at the article on his screen, French President Erec Bourreau's stern face plastered just below the headline. "It's France. They'll fight."

"Look at the comments—people are accusing them of shoving their own protests under the rug. They're making it a conspiracy. They keep tagging Milan."

"They figure he'll tell the truth." That was what he had become—the last bastion of honesty. His name had flown past the ranks of an influencer or reporter. He was a figurehead, nothing short of a prophet delivering commandments carved into digital stone.

It had been two weeks since the rave, and Etta had effectively buried the night from her mind under a pile of work. She had finally learned what Milan had intended with her first project: all the messages and photos they had collected from the private servers belonging to politicians, industry leaders, and celebrities were to be repurposed. He had tasked her and Terje with doctoring them, tweaking them just a bit before releasing them for the world. When a German celebrity—some actress with perfectly straight teeth named Lili Walter—held a public event in favor of the Turkish victims of recent attacks, Etta released an old photo from her days in school with blackface edited onto her companion. Two days later, Lili Walter and her perfectly straight teeth disappeared from public view. They did the same with world leaders. The authenticity of the photos always came into question, but it never mattered. The photos existed; that was enough for the people.

Etta eased herself up from her chair, her muscles protesting after five hours locked in one position. "Let's help Bourreau's PR campaign along. Post some photos with the alt accounts, good ones. Some shit with the police being friendly with protesters and the Turks over there."

Terje frowned and dropped his feet back to the floor as he watched her approach, waiting until she was leaning over his shoulder to raise one brow.

"Use old photos," she clarified. "Ones from a few years ago. We can make them if we need to. People will realize eventually, and they'll accuse the government of repurposing old pictures for propaganda."

Terje hummed. "Sneaky."

"Not my idea. They started doing that a while back, just following their lead."

"Checks out. I'll get on it." The French president's face disappeared as Terje backed out of the article. "Milan is stopping by in a bit, said he has news about—"

"Wait." Etta's hand shot out onto Terje's shoulder, her fingers digging into the fabric of his sweatshirt as she leaned closer to the screen. "Scroll up."

He didn't question it.

There.

A photo of a storefront. It could have been from any war zone. Glass shards littered the ground in front of a smashed display. The door was ripped halfway off its rusted hinges like a limb hanging from a broken body by only a thread of shredded muscle. The sign above the door was covered in thick black lines spray-painted with a hasty hand. An attempt to not only destroy the store but strip it of a name.

Etta knew the name. She didn't need the sign to be certain. She had walked past that store enough times, carefully spacing her trips so the attendant inside never noticed her. Dünya Market, the only place Yusuf Ayden frequented as often as Kerzenlicht café.

"When was this?" She had to keep her voice measured, so her fear would come across as only detached interest.

"This?" Terje opened the article. He wasn't looking at her, thankfully. She wasn't sure she could keep her face composed. "A couple of nights ago. Owner was beat up, just more of the same. Seems too insignificant at this point for Milan to comment on it, if that's what you're thinking."

Pan up, she begged as her eyes stayed locked on the photo of the storefront. In her mind, the image cracked open to reveal the event like a movie as she pictured assailants with pale skin and wild eyes converging on the store like a pack of wild animals wielding bats and hammers. *Pan up.* Just an inch, just enough to see the apartment she knew rested above the shop, the haven her mind had escaped to on so many cold nights.

It was a horrible shame, realizing too late that their war was always going to strike the single person she had ever cared for in her previous life. Her hands ached with the weight of the hammer she may as well have wielded.

She needed air. She needed to go to Kreuzberg, to the market, to the trenches she had helped build with nothing more than a camera and Wechselkind. She needed to escape the dead eyes of the two boys who had joined the league of ghosts at Beelitz Heilstätten. She needed to go.

The shack door screeched open. The minty stench of aftershave wafted inside as Milan approached, his inhale signaling the beginning of some long speech. She had to stay composed, had to settle each feature of her face to avoid giving away the grief inside her.

"Milan," she greeted him mildly.

"Etta." He smiled. "Terje. The world has listened."

He seemed more at peace than she had ever seen him. His thumbs were hooked loosely in the loops of his gray trousers, his hair combed back neatly for the first time in weeks. When he spoke, the corners of his mouth stayed lifted, his eyebrows inched up with barely suppressed pleasure as his gaze danced between their faces. His audience.

"The Turkish president held a broadcast this morning." Every word split his smile wider until Etta was certain his lips would eventually touch his ears. "A video of German police beating a Turkish immigrant in Berlin came to his attention. Paired with the attacks cropping up in France, he's incredibly displeased—to put it plainly."

Terje's brow flicked up in surprise. Etta knew exactly why he was so shocked—it was happening quicker than either of them had thought to hope for.

"You think he'll retaliate? Have the protests become that politically significant?" Terje asked.

"Significant enough. He spouted only toothless condemnations, but rumors are circulating that Russia has offered support should he choose to use these attacks as a basis for leaving NATO and signing onto the Minsk Agreement instead. The Russian ambassador to Turkey was spotted leaving the presidential complex in Ankara."

She didn't care—the words rumbled past Etta's ears as she sifted through them in a desperate attempt to find her escape. She held her breath, waiting.

Terje glanced at her briefly. He'd picked up on her silence, she could see it on his face, even if Milan was too lost in the taste of this victory to notice it yet. "Any response from Germany and France?"

Milan gave a forceful laugh. "What do you think? They're furious, they're condemning it all—it doesn't matter, we have the evidence. They're lost to the public, traitors to their own people and the world alike. Our siren's call has been answered, and now they'll sail themselves straight into the rocks until nothing but truth and ash remain."

People like to believe things work themselves out. They'll believe that right to their death.

Etta straightened abruptly, catching both Terje's and Milan's attention as she forced herself to meet Milan's eyes.

"We should celebrate." She couldn't speak too quickly, couldn't reveal the real impetus for her idea. "I can go, I'll go into town—get drinks. Show the family how far we've come." She swallowed, forcing her mouth to stretch open into at least a semblance of a smile as she added, "Show everyone how well Milan treats his family while the rest of Berlin burns."

Milan stared at her. His smile slowly softened, and his eyes narrowed. She was certain he knew. Her mind was his, every inch of her more familiar to him than to herself—she knew it from the first time he spoke to her. He had known her from that first moment when he casually broke past the lifetime of walls and illusions she had armored onto her skin—treating it all as nothing more than tissue-paper disguises.

His hands reached forward. Warm palms cupped her cheeks, his fingertips brushing against the corners of her eyelashes. She thought of Foster, perfectly calm as he watched the life seep from a boy dangling from his grasp.

Milan tipped his face down and pressed his lips against her forehead, fingers squeezing her cheeks lightly as he gave a soft chuckle that blew the hairs from her eyes.

"Yes," he said. "Yes. Of course. Go, here—take this, Terje has a spare bag to use—yes, that one—take it and go buy some Asbach Uralt, some Jägermeister, Underberg—of course, my dear Etta. My dear girl, show them how well we love here. Show the world what it shall soon be."

With a fistful of euros pressed into her hand and Milan's best wishes at her back, Etta fled from Spreepark.

Kreuzberg was quiet.

It was home to most of Berlin's Turkish population, yes, but it was also a playground for artists. A place for students and young entrepreneurs seeking a corner of the city to revitalize with their brazen ideas and the spirit of their youth. Usually, the neighborhood was infused with the garlicky aroma of kebabs mingling with the fresh scent of cut flowers, peddled from sprawling market stalls. The sounds of hundreds of conversations—overlaid with the ambient noise of cars rushing past and the occasional click of a cyclist with a slightly loose chain speeding along—spaced out beside the canal as people sipped beers during their lunch breaks while looking out over the water.

That night there was no scent of roasting meats and fresh blooms. No one sat at the tables along the canal. Metal grates were pulled over store entrances and bolted to the concrete sidewalks. Graffiti, once vibrant in both color and messaging, was dimmed with thick dust and a black residue that seemed to roll down the streets like a nightmare edging up to a sleeping child. The only fresh paint was a phrase hastily scrawled in yellow lettering, done so quickly and poorly that fat yellow droplets had slipped between the bricks. PURGE THE POISON THEY HAVE BROUGHT. It was one of Milan's quotes that had taken off online.

It took fifteen minutes before Etta stumbled upon any sign of life: two boys speaking quietly in Turkish, hunched against each other with their legs dangling above the riverside as they passed a bottle back and forth. When she stepped on a cracked piece of plaster, their heads whipped up like frightened animals and they immediately swapped into hushed German, weary eyes tracking her even as she made a point to stare past them.

She knew where she was going, even if she wasn't entirely certain why. Another block and she would find Dünya Market with its shattered windows and broken fruit stands. It was likely that it would be shuttered just as the other stores were. The manager had been beaten, and Kreuzberg had been all but abandoned. There was no reason she would find Yusuf there—frankly, there was no reason for her to look. Yusuf didn't know her. She had no reason to be checking on him—yet something still urged her forward.

A painful tension wrapped around her the closer she got, her palms prickling with anxiety as she spotted the ruined awning and the familiar brick storefront. She was surprised to realize there was no security grate at all, not even a board or two nailed over the shattered window. Instead, there was light. The earthy scents of cumin and incense seeped through the window's gaping wound as she peered inside. There didn't appear to be anyone there—though the lights flickered and buzzed, the register sat unmanned near the entryway.

She should have turned around and headed straight back to Spreepark, back to where the chaos of the world at least felt purposeful, logical. Here, standing on the shattered glass that still glittered on the walkway, she was adrift.

The door creaked as she entered. A bell hung above the frame, but it was wedged against the ceiling so it didn't make a sound—it must have become stuck after someone threw the door open. Wooden and plastic baskets lined the walls, mirrors mounted above them reflecting the bruised apples and mangos cradled within. She picked up one of the apples and rolled it over in her hand, feeling a soft bruise from where it had been pressed against the basket.

Someone coughed.

Etta spun to the side, still clutching the apple, as a man emerged from behind a row of shelves stacked with spices and canned sauces. A broom was clutched loosely in his hands, and he swept the floor in movements clearly dictated by habit. Etta stood trapped as the man's distracted eyes finally found her.

"Hoş geldin," Yusuf said. It sounded as reflexive as the movement of his broom over the stained tile flooring, brushing away debris long since cleaned up.

Her nails dug into the flesh of the apple. She opened her mouth to apologize, but the words died at the sight of his face. The deep circles that he had always sported beneath his eyes now stretched into the hollows of his cheekbones; his obsidian hair hung in limp waves that hooked into the edges of his beard. Even with his eyes pointed toward her he seemed oblivious to her presence.

"I'm sorry," she said finally. "I didn't mean—"

He looked at her then, really looked at her. The light crept back into his gaze as he squinted. It was a piercing sort of stare that left her feeling exposed in the same way Milan so often stripped her bare—only without the same sense of sharp intention.

The broom slowly stopped its practiced motion. His palms came to rest stacked atop the handle as he leaned against it like a weary traveler finally finished with his journey.

"I know you," he said.

He couldn't have known about the fake accounts, the false flag campaigns launched to instigate upheaval, her role in any of the attacks. Yet her panic was that of a murderer caught with the bat in her hand. Juice dripped like blood from the apple onto her fingers as her grip tightened.

A distant smile touched the edges of his lips, an attempt at kindness even as it was so clear this man's emotions had been sapped clean.

"I'm sorry, of course you don't recognize me. My wife—she always tells me off for this, tells me it's not normal for others to remember people like I do. Says I always end up scaring people off with my habits." He tapped a hand on top of the other. "Kerzenlicht. You haven't been by in a bit. I always used to see you working, or, well, I noticed you. Honestly, I got a bit worried—what with everything going on."

She must have stared too long because then he said, "I'm sorry, I haven't slept well the past few weeks and I see so many people, I must have mistaken—"

"No," she said. "No, that was me. I've noticed you too—at the café."

"Well," he said. "Well. I'm glad you're okay. I'm glad."

And, most astonishing of all, he sounded as though he meant it. He was the one cleaning up a bloodied floor, the one with a pregnant wife depending on money they could no longer earn, yet his expression warmed as he smiled at her, as if she were the one requiring comfort. She could see the white sliver of teeth, how he leaned harder against the broom until the bristles bent, as though he was willing every ounce of energy into that small kindness.

All, she realized, for a stranger.

"My name"—her lips were numb as she attempted to form the words she had rehearsed so many nights over and over in her head like a prayer—"is Etta."

"Etta." He bobbed his chin. "My name is Yusuf. I'm sorry I never introduced myself earlier."

She had dreamed of hearing those words so often, yet to hear them now—to finally have her wish granted upon a battleground of her making . . .

"I'm sorry." The words were half choked as she dropped the apple into the basket and stumbled backward. Yusuf's eyes widened in concern. "I'm sorry, I should have—I have to go."

She spun on her heel, then nearly toppled a shelf as she reached to balance herself while taking a hurried half step toward the door. The clatter of a broom falling behind her told her he must have realized her guilt—the whole interaction had been a ploy to cut her down until fresh blood marred the floors once more.

"Wait, please, here—"

She must have looked manic with her wild eyes under her dark hood, but Yusuf's warm concern did not waver as she turned to face him.

He held out her apple. "Take this."

"No, I—" she began, but he shook his head.

He pressed it firmly into her palm and stepped back, leaning down to retrieve the broom from where he'd dropped it on the floor. "This world is hard enough. The least we can do is make it a bit easier for each other."

When Etta finally managed the last few steps out the door, she forced herself to keep walking to the end of the corner before she glanced back. It wasn't until she raised her hand to push the hood from her eyes that she realized she still had the apple clutched in her fingers. It felt firmer than before, no juice or soft bruises for her nails to bite into as she rolled it between her palms.

It wasn't the same apple at all; Yusuf had left behind the battered fruit she had mangled and given her a fresh, unblemished apple instead.

28

With just a few words, Yusuf had shattered the purposeful distance Etta had maintained with the world around her. The act of witnessing—rather than simply observing—as she had stood amid the ruins of one major corner of his life had opened the floodgates. The scent of smoke on the street, the shattered remains of bottles and splintered windows, the clinking of chains over padlocked doors—these were no longer details to a painting in a gallery, but parts of her reality.

But pain was part of cleansing the world—Milan had assured her of that, had insisted that righteousness was raised in the ashes of victory. So why did she ache now?

Why, why, *why*? That was the question each step asked as her feet slapped against the pavement toward Spreepark. When Etta stopped by a store to pick up the liquor Milan had requested, a woman dropped her bag of groceries and Etta found herself reflexively apologizing, though she wasn't sure what for.

On the train back to Plänterwald, Etta curled up on the seat and pressed her cheek to the window as an old woman sitting across from her with a nervous expression spoke hurriedly into her cellphone. Behind Etta, a man hummed a song she recognized from one of the old movies she had watched at the theater downtown—something from the villages up north, a memory of an old man far from home. Etta curled up tighter, the bag clenched between her legs, as she pressed her palms over her ears. The world was suddenly too loud.

There was no avoiding the party once she was back at the park, but the family and Milan's followers had grown to a point where she could slip into the background. She was only expected to be present, not be the focal point—unlike Loulou, who was leading the dancers around the firepit with a wild smile. It felt like there were hundreds of them, splitting and multiplying like bacteria overnight until every inch of grass was covered with stomping and stumbling feet.

"Hey!" Etta grabbed the closest dancer, a girl with nails two knuckles long and thick eyeliner permanently circled around her eyes. Etta recognized her; she had been one of the first to show up at Spreepark after Milan had ignited his media presence, though Etta had never bothered to learn her name.

The girl blinked sleepily at Etta. "Oh, oh, hey—"

"You know where Milan is?"

The girl's eyes widened as she bobbed her head gleefully; knowing anything about Milan down to his temporary location was a reason to be proud. It made her *special*. It made Etta nauseous.

Etta pulled the borrowed backpack from her shoulders and shoved it into the girl's arms. "Take this to him."

The bottles rattled and the girl nearly dropped the bag immediately. There was a forty-percent chance it would reach Milan; Etta didn't care anymore. Maybe he forgot about sending her into Berlin at all, too busy with his gaggle of followers and their gaping mouths full of endless praise.

Terje was nowhere to be seen. He was most likely in the shack keeping tabs on the evolving global tensions and sending out Milan's prepared statements across all channels. It took the three of them to give the impression of a faceless prophet who did not sleep, a man who stayed two steps ahead of a world that felt increasingly beyond reason. Etta was the right hand to a modern, synthesized, false god, born amid shared rage and lines of code.

Loulou danced in circles around the fire. She spun with her hands stretched out like wings with all the feathers plucked off, her fingertips pausing to run along the cheeks of those dancing beside her. Why had Etta never noticed the way Loulou's old sweater hung limply over her bony shoulders? When had she lost so much weight?

Loulou's feet dragged as she danced, her motions—once ethereal and fluid—now disjointed. She was a ghost of her former self, weighed down by the responsibility bestowed upon her by a man with a forceful hand. Milan's foot had pressed Loulou down until the only parts left were those he chose, those that fit into his mold.

Even from a distance, Etta could tell that Loulou's eyes, once bright with barely tempered fire, were matte gray in the firelight.

It was all too much. Etta wanted to cry—cry, or scream.

When Loulou's path took her to the edge of the firelight and into the shadows, into Etta's reach, she grabbed her. Loulou's skin was slick with sweat, her eyes wild and bloodshot.

"Lou, look at me." Etta pushed against her shoulders, catching Loulou as she began to sway. Loulou had always stayed alert, no matter what she had taken or where they were. In that moment, however, Loulou seemed more like a dancer left dragging her feet long after the theater had closed and the lights shut down.

"Oh, hello darling." Her head drooped backward.

"Are you alright?"

Loulou's eyelids flickered in a series of sporadic blinks. "What?"

"Lou, you're crying."

"What?" Her pale fingers felt for her cheeks, where tears had begun to cut black streaks through her mascara and thick foundation. Loulou pulled her hand back, steadying herself against Etta's shoulder as she peered down at her wet fingertips. Her eyes closed in one sleepy blink. Then, she laughed. "Well, look at that."

"Come on." Etta pulled on Loulou's arms, but Loulou resisted, throwing her body backward as she tried to drag Etta into the firelight.

"No, no, no," Loulou insisted. "No, come *dance*. Let's dance—Milan's watching, the world is on fire, *dance* with me."

There was no use. Loulou wasn't caught in the current, she was the wave that pulled all others behind her—she had to be. It was her role. To drag her from the party would be to scoop up all the water from the ocean with only two hands; it would be impossible. Etta would need to wait until Loulou sobered up, until all the revelers dropped to the ground and moldy bedrolls. Until Milan returned to his tower and his eyes closed to their world.

"Fine, fine, I'll dance. I'll dance over there, okay? I'll just be there," Etta assured Loulou, but she wasn't listening. The moment Etta's arms released her shoulders Loulou was pulled back into the fray by the same group of girls that had passed Etta earlier. Loulou's stringy pastel waves flashed between bobbing heads and waving arms until she was completely swallowed.

Etta shouldered her way through the crowd and away from the fire, continuing until the stench of smoke dissipated from the air. She kept walking until she reached the Ferris wheel. Despite the steady evening wind, the cars stayed painfully still, as though they felt the shift in Etta's demeanor and feared disturbing her further. Etta sat on the cold metal base beside the operator's booth. A small shiver ran through her body.

There, in the shamelessly loud world, Etta waited.

They partied until morning. Etta watched the smoke and listened to their shouting as the sun threatened to crest over the horizon. She did not sleep. No party would ever be the same for her; she understood that, at least, even if the rest of her was still a tangle of conflicting pain. The threads of her past and present had wound together, pulled tight by that small moment shared with Yusuf, until Etta couldn't find which string would pull the whole knot loose.

She knew the party was over when Terje found her; he never looked for her until it was clear there was nowhere else for her to be. Until then, she imagined he had believed she was among the dancers, linking hands and letting bitter tablets melt beneath their tongues.

She stood as he appeared from the tree line, and he froze mid-step. She understood why; every other time he had found her at the Ferris wheel, she had needed him to lift her up, to bring her back to her feet when all she wanted was to crawl into the metal bones and hide in the body of the park.

He didn't say anything as she met him halfway. Maybe he recognized in her face something he had already experienced himself; the blistering determination he had felt the day he discovered the tall trees in his home forest had been razed and replaced without a word. When she began to walk back toward the clearing, he followed.

The lonely firepit still smoldered, the last straggler at the party after everyone else had gone to sleep, camped out underneath picnic benches or in the shells of old ride cars. Some pillowed their heads on their arms, curled up on the grass. Some still clutched bottles in their hands. Etta walked past each like a corpsman wandering through a battleground, checking their faces, and moving on as Terje followed silently behind.

It took two loops around the clearing before Etta finally caught sight of pastel hair fluttering from one of the old Die Psychologen cars. Loulou was tucked against the yellow and black seat on the floorboard with her knees pressed against her forehead.

Etta knelt beside the car. "Loulou, time to go. Come on."

Loulou groaned.

Etta gave her shoulder one good shake. "Lou, come on."

There was a pause as Etta tried to determine whether Loulou had heard her, before Loulou's upper body suddenly spasmed. She jerked upward, rolling half out of the car and giving Etta just enough time to step back as a yellow-green slosh of vomit gushed from her mouth. Her shoulders shuddered as she heaved again, snot dripping down her nose, though her eyes never even opened. When she was finally finished, her head dipped forward. The ends of her hair fell into the sour-smelling puddle left at Etta's feet.

Etta glanced at Terje. "Help me get her up."

Terje scooped her into his arms. When they reached the bunkhouse, Etta stopped Terje from stepping inside with a shake of her head.

"The shack," she told him. "So we can keep an eye on her."

He readjusted his hold on Loulou and raised a brow. "Sure she'd appreciate that?"

"She can argue with me once she's awake."

In the shack, Etta pulled a few blankets down from the loft as Terje struggled to maneuver a slowly awakening Loulou through the space without bumping into any of the computers or shelving. Etta pushed the card table against the wall and arranged the blankets on the floor, pulling her sweatshirt over her head to bundle up as a pillow. Terje laid Loulou onto the makeshift bed, then slid a cereal bowl beside her head.

"Trash can is full." He shrugged. "Better than nothing."

Etta rolled Loulou onto her side, propping her back against the wall. She had grown so used to seeing Loulou alert and electric, even in sleep. Seeing her drooped on the floor like a corpse was unsettling. It was as though Loulou had been part of Terje's augmented reality program all that time, only to have the projection clicked off without a single warning.

The bench creaked as Terje lowered himself onto it. The monitors behind him had Milan's social accounts open, along with a muted broadcast of BBC news covering the heightening geopolitical tensions. Images of looted shops and sizeable crowds of screaming protesters hidden by clouds of teargas flickered behind Terje's head, while on another screen, a waterfall of notifications rolled in as the world attempted to engage with Milan, latching onto his posts with greedy fingers and infantile whines for more.

Etta tucked a knotted chunk of hair away from Loulou's face. She had spent all night thinking of how to talk to Terje about the hurricane in her mind, her experience outside Spreepark—what she had seen. She had the words, now she needed to force them out.

"When you told me about your home, about the trees, you said it was wrong. What they did, cutting them all down, it was wrong."

It was a credit to his character, his trust in her, that he did not immediately question her. Instead, he replied, "It *was* wrong."

She soldiered on. "And they tried to replace them, they planted new trees, replaced the trees with different ones, but they couldn't replace exactly what was gone. Those trees were too old, just ancient."

Terje nodded.

Etta's fingers caught in one of the worst knots in Loulou's hair. She tried to pull free, but the hair wrapped tighter around her skin. "What should they have done instead? And now, would you rather they cut all the new trees down, too, raze two forests?" It wasn't supposed to be an accusation, she never meant to attack him, but every word picked up speed until her nose burned and tears threatened at the corners of her eyes.

Terje lifted his foot off the bench and turned to face her, calm and focused as he leveled his own accusation. "This isn't about the trees, Etta."

She squeezed her eyes shut to the count of three, then reopened them and looked up. "It's gone too far."

Terje blinked. "What?"

"All of it." She finally freed her hand and sat back against the wall, tipping her chin toward the ceiling as she spoke. "All of this—Milan—"

"Etta." Terje gave a sharp look toward the door.

"No, listen to me." He had to meet her eyes. If she was going to say it, to take that step, she needed to say it *to* him rather than around him. "He wanted to force people to face reality; he told us we were going to take down the assholes on top—rebuild society into what it should be, what it was meant to be. And I didn't care—I haven't cared—about who got hurt in the process. But shit, Terje, look at the news. What have we started?"

"Fires start at the bottom, Etta," he said softly. "As the smoke rises—"

"Stop." She couldn't stomach another one of Milan's canned phrases. "That bullshit, his bullshit—do you hear yourself? Fires do start at the bottom, we—us, Terje, more than anyone—we struck that match. Who burns? Who burned after all those old wars were done and dusted? After every fucking collapse, after every great goddamn battle—we all burned. No one at the top, just us. The idiots running around in the flames. And Milan, he says he's going to help guide us—fix all this shit—but what's he really getting out of it? What's he doing to us? What's he doing *for* us?"

"*Etta.*" For the first time Terje looked truly concerned. He stood and paced to the door, paused, then paced back as he ran a hand through his hair. "Jesus, are you high? You can't say that—you can't—"

"Oh, she can." The grumble was accompanied by a dry cough as Loulou rolled onto her back. She snorted at Etta's shocked expression. "God—don't look at me like that. You got any water?"

Etta glanced at Terje, who had frozen in the middle of the shack with wide, unblinking eyes, staring at Loulou as if she were a ghost. When it was finally clear he would not be moving, Etta pushed herself off the floor to grab one of the water bottles left half-empty on the desk.

"Grand." Loulou gripped it with both hands as she took a tentative swallow, then water dribbled down her chin as she tipped her head back and chugged until the bottle crinkled under her fingers. "Christ," she sighed once she was finished. "I smell like shit."

Draped across the blankets on the shack floor, Loulou looked like a character from a Greek tragedy, wise in her hungover misery as she peered at Etta and Terje over the tip of her water bottle. Not like she had caught them in the middle of betrayal, but with slow-growing curiosity.

Terje's eyes flicked toward the door again before snapping back to Loulou.

"Jesus." Loulou nudged Etta's arm with her elbow, still watching Terje. "He's like a discount version of Foster. You can chill out, Terje. My head is pounding way too hard to make any mad dashes for the door."

Terje's hands twitched at his sides. He started toward the bench, still watching Etta and Loulou carefully, as he began to sit, paused, then opted to lean against the bench instead. His arms stayed stiff at his sides, one foot starting to tap lightly on the floor.

Etta had always meant for Loulou to be a part of this discussion. She had no doubt that Loulou had feigned sleep for longer than either of them realized, that she had heard every part of Etta's speech. It was a risk; talking to either of them was a risk. To leave as Johanna had, to slip off the grid, had been an option. But after meeting Yusuf, after being confronted with the severity of her actions and their consequences, she needed to do more than simply leave.

Wechselkind had been Milan's sword in the stone, pulled free to grant him kingship. Now, only Wechselkind was sharp enough to cut off his head, and only Etta could wield it. And to do what she wanted— to undo what had been done—she wanted Terje and Loulou beside her. The two people who had seen her as she was. Her family.

"I want to do what really needs doing," Etta said. "Not fires, not this. No more illusions or chants, no more rage. Milan, he's not the one. Not anymore."

Loulou collapsed back onto the floor and spread her fingers above her face, squinting against the too-bright lights.

Terje's foot continued to tap as he stared at Etta, one hand reaching up to rub the back of his neck. "Who is, then?" Each word was another tap, another accusation, another plea as he buried a fist against his eyes. "Who else? Who?"

Loulou laughed joylessly. She let her hand flop to the floor as she sat up, frayed hair covering her brows as she peered at Etta.

"Milan told me once," Loulou said. "Said everyone's some mix of the Devil and God, that it's only once we wake up that we really see it—that's our rite of passage. We must choose. That's when we know we've really woken up from the bullshit—when it hurts to choose."

Surprisingly honest words from a man who loved nothing more than to play holy songs with devil's hands.

"I'm not done." Etta crossed her arms as she leaned down to look into Loulou's eyes. "So long as he speaks, I'm not done."

Terje's shoulders dropped as he heaved a long sigh that ended in a deep groan. He muttered something into his hand, though he didn't openly object. Etta turned away from Loulou to look at him, waiting until he finally raised his head before she spoke again.

"We promised the world truth," she said. "I want to give them exactly that."

"Well, shit." Loulou propped herself onto her elbows and searched blindly with one hand for another bottle of water. "Guess the choice has been made."

29

The three of them planned to leave after two more nights in Spreepark.

Gathering enough resources to allow them to lie low after their escape presented a collection of problems. Both Terje and Etta had dedicated their savings to liquid, edible, or chemical supplies for the family. When Etta asked Loulou if she had any accounts they could draw from, Loulou laughed. "Sure. Let me just run and grab my gold card."

Even if Loulou had a surprise bank account, they all knew it would be off-limits. It would have been wonderful to think that removing Terje and Etta from the family would mean cutting the head off Milan's digital beast, but his network had widened to a global degree. Finding someone with enough skills to track their online withdrawals would be a matter of when, not if.

Eventually, they hatched something of a plan. Loulou would snatch the small stack of cash the family kept hidden near the guardhouse. Terje would scout the fencing along the back of the park for loose links. Etta would pretend all was well.

By the afternoon of the second day, Etta's feet were itching to move. Her hands anxiously grasped and released handfuls of her sweatshirt fabric while the computers hummed around her. She tried not to think about how the computers would all lie shattered by morning. It had been decided that she and Terje would bash every computer with a piece of rebar they'd found lying around the park and hidden under the mattress, leaving only her laptop—soon to be tucked away and brought with them—as the final connection between Milan and his digital presence. Not a death blow, but a damaging wound.

Destroying the computers would be a shame, but it was the lying that had shaken her. Or, rather, the lack of lying. Since the creation of their plan, not a single visitor had knocked on the shack door. Not Foster with a shy grin, not Monika with her plates of reheated rice, not even Milan, coming to check on accounts. His absence was most notable. There had been no trace of their prophetic leader since she had last seen him, high on the realization that he may have successfully baited the world to chaos.

She would never see him again, so long as all went well. That was fine. Better than fine. It was ideal. There was no reason to think too long about their last meeting, about how it stood up as a final goodbye. So many people in her life had been plucked out of her orbit without any pretense of closure that Etta knew true and honest goodbyes were found internally. She couldn't remember which of the fractured memories of her father belonged to his final visit, but that was alright—she had said her own goodbye to him long after. She would do the same with Milan.

There was no need to justify herself to him; his opinion of her no longer mattered. His approval was of no consequence.

Still, she couldn't stop glancing toward the shack door.

When she caught her eyes sliding toward the door for the tenth time in a single minute Etta shoved herself back in her chair, exasperated. Her feet, propped up on Terje's workbench, skidded onto the floor.

She would not think of Milan.

She always ran from reality, hid from others to avoid the pain of living—Milan had called her out on that, and it was a truth she couldn't deny. But leaving the family was different. It felt more like cutting off an infected limb to prevent the spread of disease. It was the pain of choosing that sent her pacing across the shack floor, fingers idly skimming over a keyboard every time she passed the computers, an apology for their oncoming demise.

At some point, the shack door groaned open, pausing just wide enough to let a slim figure slip inside.

Terje pulled his hood back just as Etta allowed the air trapped in her lungs to be released in a heavy sigh.

"Found a spot." He scraped a clump of mud off his shoes.

"Where?"

"Back up by the river, behind the roller coaster."

In swampland. Etta had rarely ventured that deep into the park. The old waterslides and manufactured rivers had grown wild with neglect, seeping outward until they had swallowed a third of the land in gurgling, muddy pits. Beyond it was the Spree, all its monstrous cargo ships lurking like steel hippos with snapping jaws.

"You want us to swim?"

Terje pulled his sweatshirt over his head, dropping it onto the bench as he turned his back. "Not up the river. Just up the bank into Treptower Park. We can make a run for it from there."

The muscles in his shoulders spasmed. Blue veins crept across his pale skin, and the shadow of his ribs was visible above his waist.

"Terje." She took a step toward him. "Look at me."

"Trains start running around four in the morning," he said. "We have until six, maybe even seven, before they notice we're gone. It'll be tight."

"*Terje.*" Her hand met the bare expanse of his back, and he flinched as though she had branded him. When he finally turned, his face was twisted with pain, his jaw clenched as his eyes dipped away from her gaze.

"You can't doubt this," she said. "You *can't* doubt this." Because she just might begin to doubt as well.

He tensed under her hand and for a moment she was certain he would push her away, but instead his face melted and his arms dropped like two strings snapped free from a marionette. He leaned down toward her, his chin hovering against her forehead.

"Are *you* sure?" he asked.

"I have to be," she whispered. It was the only thing she'd ever had to be sure about—the first time she would take responsibility in her life.

His hand came up to rest in her hair, fingers tangled in her dark curls as his chest heaved in a deep breath and he squeezed his eyes shut. When he opened them again, a mask of placid calm had slipped back over his features. She knew that face. He was always so determined, so guarded and sure against the rest of them—but never with her, until that moment. She wasn't sure if it was a compliment or a cause for concern.

"We do what has to be done," he said. "We always have. *You* always have—the only one who can."

Just as he had said when they first met.

"Maybe not always," she said. "But we will now—both of us. The only two who understand, right?"

She could feel the parting of his dry lips against her forehead as he spoke. "Yeah."

Terje finally pulled away from her, turning toward the ladder leading to their loft. His steps fell heavy on the floor, the way they always did when he was particularly focused—as though he needed to hit the ground extra hard to remind himself he was alive outside the boundaries of his skull. His shoulders tensed long before he reached the ladder rungs.

"Hey," she said.

He faltered.

She wasn't sure why, but she had suddenly recalled one of the first times she felt him lower the shield he held between himself and the world. Perhaps it was because that had been a beginning, even if she hadn't known it at the time, and these last moments in the shack felt similar. A beginning as much as a finality.

"A few months ago," she said, "back before I joined the family, when we finished our first project—when Milan had us gathering that info on all the white-gloves. On that Cabinet member. You were going to tell me something, do you remember?"

He looked over his shoulder in confusion as one hand reached up the ladder. "What?"

"After we turned everything in to Milan, I asked if you had ever climbed the Ferris wheel and you said you needed to tell me something," she said. "But Loulou came in before you could tell me. Do you remember?"

Terje's gaze grew distant. He turned away from her as he planted one foot on the bottom rung. Then the next.

"No," he said. "I don't."

Etta and Terje barely spoke for the rest of the day. They played at working, watching Milan's accounts as his followers increased. The monitors on Terje's desk flickered as they attempted to keep up with the rolling list of new tags in articles and posts while Milan's name continued its spread across the internet, the adoring public unaware of his true intent. Milan had gained the trust of the people, pointing accusatorily with one hand and directing his army with the other.

By three in the morning the park had quieted down. Slices of conversations floated by as the followers passed the shack on their way back to the bunkhouse, their feet kicking empty glass bottles and crunching down on discarded beer cans. Loulou was already on her way to the guardhouse to get the stash of cash.

It was Terje who spoke first as Etta finally reached for her backpack, slipping her laptop inside along with a few items of clothing. She had already packed two cameras and some batteries.

"Go ahead first," he said. "I'll trash everything here and meet you by the coaster."

"You're sure?" Etta slipped her pack onto her shoulder.

He stood, running his fingers over the desktop beside his workbench as he nodded. "I built them."

She understood. He didn't want to share this goodbye. "Don't be long."

He nodded, staring at his computers as Etta began to push the door open, flinching slightly as it creaked.

She was half out the door when Terje spoke again behind her.

"Fly fast, sparrow."

She paused. It sounded so reminiscent of Johanna wishing her luck at the gate, resigned and almost nostalgic—but Johanna was a ghost and Terje was right here beside her. She would not worry. "I will."

The door shut and Etta was alone in the night.

Her fingers touched its cool surface, a brief goodbye to the thin walls that guarded the quiet nights she and Terje spent entangled together. Etta hadn't expected to feel any sort of affection for the park itself, yet as she began her trek through the trees toward the front gate, she found her gaze lingering on each broken statue, every crumbling gazebo, on the old bones of a park forgotten, and she ached. Somehow, over the months she had spent in Spreepark, the place had slipped into her skin and knit itself around her heart. It had become something— not home, exactly, but somewhere to come back to. There would be no returning after this, no matter how much she may later want to.

Etta stuck to the tree line as much as she could. There were still a few teenagers milling about the park, their voices reverberating as they laughed drunkenly. She watched their firelight in the distance as she waited beside the fence a few feet away from the guardhouse, trying her hardest not to imagine Loulou inside, wondering what she'd had to do to distract the guard long enough to grab the cash kept hidden along the fence line.

She didn't have to wait long. Loulou's slim frame appeared beside the shack, her head poking out to scan across the clearing. Etta stepped free from the trees and Loulou's gaze snapped onto her immediately. She held up a hand, signaling for Etta to stay put as she cast another glance toward the fire in the distance before carefully easing the guard-house door shut and dipping out along the fence toward Etta.

When they finally met, Etta could see the faint shine of Loulou's grin in the dim light. Her eyes were wide with victory as she dug one hand down the front of her shirt to pull out a fistful of wadded up euros.

"Two guards tonight," Loulou whispered as she practically collided with Etta. "Second one is coming back soon—but Frank—I knew he was an idiot but didn't realize he's a blind idiot. I managed to grab our bribe stash *and* his wallet."

Her cheeks were flushed, her hair wild and half-free from its tangled bun as she pressed the euros into Etta's hands. Etta grasped Loulou's wrist as she began to pull back, staring hard into her eyes.

This was the Loulou Etta remembered from Halloween, her skin glowing from the thrill of control. The heat of her excitement warmed the air around them, static shocks popping up Etta's arms until she was certain the dry grass would set fire under their feet.

"Well?" Loulou gazed over Etta's shoulder. "Where's your boyfriend? He taking the long way around?"

"He's clearing out the shack." Etta swung her backpack around so she could unzip the smallest pocket, stuffing the euros inside. "Said to meet us by the roller coaster."

"Easy enough." Loulou looped her thumbs in the waistline of her long cotton skirt, pulled down, and stepped free, revealing the thick black leggings she had hiding underneath. She wadded the skirt in her hands and reared back to throw it onto the fence behind them. It caught on the wire at the top, dangling like a pastel flag. "And after?"

Together they began moving toward the old roller coaster, keeping a wide berth between themselves and the central area of Spreepark. "Terje said there was a break in the fence alongside Treptower. We'll move through the park toward the trains."

"Yes, sure—but *after*." Loulou skipped a few feet ahead to half-jog in front of Etta. "What's the grand plan? How are you going to un-coup our revolution?"

Etta pursed her lips. "The same way we started it."

They walked the rest of the way in silence. Etta knew she should be exhausted—she had barely slept, had barely eaten since her meeting with Yusuf—yet every limb seemed more alive than ever. She had no trouble keeping step with Loulou as they passed the old carousel with its dead-eyed plaster horses. She even picked up her pace as the ground began to seep under her feet and the mud clung to her boots and squelched under her feet, the park pulling her back like an old hand clinging to the hem of her sweatshirt. Every step was a step farther from her guilt, from her association with Milan.

After a while, cattails and thick weeds made green rugs over the black swamp water. The trees were so dense that any moonlight was filtered out and Etta and Loulou had to hold hands to keep track of each other. It wasn't until they spotted old metal tracks sticking up, revealing the twisted metal and discarded roller-coaster cars that lay half-sunken in the muck, that freckled splotches of light slipped between the trees.

The ground hardened near the entrance to the roller coaster, the land shaped into a manufactured hill long ago to help with the peaks and dives of the ride. At the top of the hill, surrounded by trees, a massive face pushed through the overgrowth. Etta bit back a curse as a set of huge yellow and red eyes glared down at them from above.

"Jesus," Loulou muttered as they stared up at the wooden head of a tiger, its painted-blue face chipped and fading. The rusted tracks ended inside its gaping mouth.

"Terje should be here." Etta took another step forward, releasing Loulou's hand as they approached the giant beast.

"Credit where credit's due." Loulou snorted. "He found one hell of a dramatic spot to meet."

Etta didn't respond. She was looking into the mouth of the monster where a silhouette had appeared, slowly inching out of the darkness.

It wasn't the figure she had expected, broad shoulders atop a slim frame. This silhouette was so large that its head nearly brushed the top of the beast's gaping mouth as it finally broke into the dim light.

Blood roared in Etta's ears. She reached back wildly for Loulou's hand as they realized simultaneously who had been sent to greet them.

"Mouse," Foster bemoaned. "What have you done?"

30

"*R*un."

Etta didn't know if she was the first to jump into motion or if Loulou was. Before Foster had the chance to take another step forward, they were both gone. They shot back down the hill, a mess of stumbling feet and flailing arms in the darkness. Weeds snapped around Etta's ankles, mud gripping at her shoes as she crashed through bushes and over rotting logs.

"*Shit*," Loulou hissed somewhere beside her in the darkness—the sound cut through the twigs snapping against her cheeks. "*Shit shit shit—*"

"The fence," Etta panted. "Get to the—"

A shout boomed across the water, and a black shadow dashed between the trees beside them, a flicker of white lettering catching Etta's eye just before it disappeared. Foster wasn't alone, which confirmed exactly what she couldn't bear to consider. *Later.* Later she would process this betrayal. If she let it wound her now, she would be down before the security guards even had a chance to lay a hand on her.

She reached out for Loulou's hand only to grasp a splintered branch. Her lips parted to call out, but she stopped herself just as a figure crashed into the water several feet away, his head whipping from side to side as Etta pushed forward. Loulou was gone—lost somewhere in the overgrowth. Etta couldn't find a trace of her pastel hair or a flash of her blue sweater, and there was no time to look harder. She had to keep running, faster now that she knew the sloshing steps behind her didn't belong to her last remaining friend.

The water was up to her knees. Where was she? Once, during one of their bonfires, Etta had stumbled drunkenly up to a painted map of Spreepark just outside the main entrance. She had trailed her fingers lazily across the pathways, mesmerized by the colors that had kept their bright hues despite years of weathering and relentless sunlight, until Loulou had pulled her away with loud teasing and promises printed on white pills. Desperately, Etta attempted to drag that memory back as she jerked her feet up through the muck.

Water. Past the roller coaster there had been another ride, a blue swirl of lines on the map with small cars that had been long-since swallowed by the swamp but, past that, the log flume. The ride had been set in the middle of a giant pit dug into the upper corner of the park; the park owners had created a crystalline pool as the perfect setting for their fantasy mountain flume.

The deeper the water, the closer Etta was to the log flume and, just beyond it, Treptower Park. It was the only choice, even though they would know to search in Treptower—Terje had been the one to suggest hiding there. Still, the only other options would be making a run for the river—which would be suicide with its current and massive ships—or risking a mad dash to the front gate among all the followers and security.

The water was up to her waist. Someone grunted behind her. Her chest burned. The water had seeped through her jeans and sucked the warmth from her limbs, and she once again thanked her foresight in investing in a waterproof backpack. Both of her feet were scraping over the muddy lakebed. Too cold to feel them, she wasn't even certain if her boots were still on or if she had lost them somewhere in the black murk. Another grunt—her head spun instinctively over her shoulder as her assailant closed in, near enough that she could hear his measured huffs.

Foster's eyes met hers.

There was only half a second for her to inhale before she dropped.

The water swelled over her head. A muted pop echoed from above the moment she disappeared beneath the water. Foster had brought a gun. Her backpack pulled her upward as if it, too, was alive and desperate to breathe. Etta buried her hands into the weeds below her feet and pulled herself down until her belly was against the mud.

For one wild moment she was thankful—at least she wouldn't have to die slowly pressed against a brick wall as the life was squeezed from her like water from a sodden towel.

The water around her was still. Foster must have frozen above her. Etta tried to peel her eyes open but was met with slicing pain. Not that it mattered—the thick silt would have made it difficult to see more than an inch ahead. Foster could be meters away or right beside her. She was terrified to move forward only to knock directly into his boots. The cold had numbed her hands, forcing her to clench and release her grip like a beating heart to be certain she was still holding onto the weeds.

It was a losing game. Death had always felt so abstract, something that waved to her from below as she scaled crumbling walls or dangled her legs off rooftops. It was an old ancestor waiting to greet her, one hand always outstretched in invitation, the same way it had held itself out to her mother.

Fine, she decided as she dug her hands deeper into the murk. Fine. Let it come, not from Foster, from his bullet through her skull, but from her own hand, down in the water where no one—especially not Milan—would find her. Let her become another forgotten artifact left to the vines and trees in Spreepark.

A spray of bubbles slipped past her lips, right as a shout cut through the water, too garbled to understand anything but its triumphant tone.

She froze, waiting for Foster's massive hands to lift her from the water, when she felt movement. Two boots trudging quickly away. They must have spotted Loulou.

She tried to ignore the guilt that accompanied her immediate blast of relief. Five more carefully counted seconds ticked by before she allowed herself to release her death grip on the weeds and float upward, her face breaking above the water as she gulped in desperate gasps of air. A frog croaked. Crickets chittered nearby.

Another pop sounded from somewhere in the trees.

Etta forced herself to move forward, pausing only when she could hear steps nearby. The searchers were shouting to each other, cursing out orders that she doubted would be faithfully carried out—Milan's army was a numeric power, not a strategic one. They only played at soldiers, and she had so far evaded the only true killer in the lot.

She knew she was close when the lake shallowed out, her hips and knees exposed to the early morning chill. Before her, razor-sharp slashes against the trees, was the fence. It was entirely overgrown and half sunken into the ground, the poles twisted as trees and vines had pulled them down toward the earth.

Terje had been honest about that at least; the fence would be easily scaled.

The metal must have been cold, but her hands were too numb to feel its bite. She kicked her boot into the side, slipping as the wet rubber slid against the wire. Her teeth clicked as she clenched her jaw and forced her arms to pull upward, heaving her body farther up the chain-link.

Something moved in the bush behind her, and instantly she felt a rush of frantic adrenaline as she slammed against the fence, scrambling to get over—so close to getting over.

A hand snapped around her ankle.

"Etta." The voice cracked as the person below dodged a flailing kick. "Jesus, Etta—it's me, fuck—stop!"

"Loulou—" Etta's grip slipped. Her chin slammed down on the wire fence, her teeth scraping together.

"Help me up," Loulou whispered. Under the moonlight, Etta could see black mud and foliage plastered to Loulou's skin and hair. One of her hands clutched tightly at her opposite arm just above the elbow. A large tear in her sweater had exposed a pale sliver of skin over her belly button. Etta wasn't sure if the dark stain covering Loulou's stomach was dirt or drying blood.

Etta looked back at the pursuers, then dropped to the ground and pushed Loulou's feet and legs, providing the assistance she needed to get over the fence. Etta then tossed her backpack over and quickly followed it, rolling on the grass with a grunt just after Loulou thumped down.

Labored pants filled the night as they both lay on their backs, hands reaching to rub the dirt from their eyes and to swipe wet hair from their cheeks. As Etta turned her head to the side, the cool grass brushing against her lips, Loulou did the same.

Covered in muck, black mud staining her teeth, Loulou grinned. Then she laughed. A wild laugh that bounced through her body and forced her onto her side as she tried to muffle herself in the grass. Etta watched her, her jaw quivering as a smile stretched across her lips. Her hand slid across the ground toward Loulou, who reached out, face still buried in the grass, and wove her fingers around Etta's.

They hadn't made it. Not yet. But Etta had escaped Milan. She had escaped his immediate reach and survived.

And she wasn't alone.

31

Every person became an enemy.

They didn't try to take the train out of Treptower Park. The small station would be crawling with members of the V and their followers. Instead, Etta and Loulou began a trek northwest, toward the Berlin Wall Museum where they could catch a bus across the river. It was barely past five as they wandered through the residential streets. Apartment windows flickered with light, normal people waking up to begin their day, unaware of the chaos that had transpired in the hours before.

Had Milan woken up as well? Had Foster—or Terje—been tasked with trespassing into Milan's lair, sidestepping over the naked bodies of his newest followers to pass along the news that Etta and Loulou had been lost in the swamp? Or had they allowed him to sleep, terrified of his inevitable fury when he realized two of his most dedicated disciples had slipped through the net?

She could picture his face clearly—it would blossom with that same angry red patch he had worn upon learning about Johanna's escape. He would send his army after them, Etta knew. They'd committed a felony crime in the eyes of his kingdom. She and Loulou weren't only some of the original followers, they were *his*. The sacred daughters to his godliness, priestesses to his mind and soul.

"Maybe he'll just let us go," Etta said. "Just give up, focus on everything else."

"He never lets anyone get away," Loulou replied.

"Johanna got out, he let her go."

Loulou barked a laugh. "She got out, not away. Remember that shitty old lighter she was so cagey about, with her initial scratched into the side? Nearly bit my hand off when I borrowed it."

Etta nodded.

"Foster left after she did, was gone a whole week." Loulou's gaze grew distant as Etta's eyes widened. "Sometime after he got back, I saw a lighter on Milan's table, right next to his bed. Wasn't sure until I turned it over and saw a big fat J carved into it."

A chill washed over Etta. "You think Foster—"

"Nothin' to think about. Johanna didn't get away," Loulou murmured. "Milan doesn't let anyone go."

A few hours into their journey, they found their way to a coffee shop bathroom with mustard-yellow wallpaper that someone had tried to lighten up with delicately painted flowers, except the paper had crumpled under the paint, giving it an overall appearance of a dying garden covered in vomit. A small toilet was situated in front of a sink, the wall around the exposed pipes grayed from water damage. There was barely enough room for both of them. Etta had to lean against the door to avoid Loulou's elbows as she struggled to pull her sweater over her head.

"Goddamn." Loulou twisted her sweater over the sink, splattering the stained porcelain with swamp water. "Still can't believe we made it. I can't believe we're out, you know? I mean I know we're out, but it still feels like we're there. Like we're supposed to be back in an hour or two, like it was all just some big game. Give me your sweatshirt."

She was right. It felt like Milan was with them, or Foster was waiting outside in the café with a playful smile and a plastic gun. It felt temporary and it terrified Etta.

"Here." She tugged off her sweatshirt, squeezing her eyes closed as a stray twig caught in the hood snagged in her hair.

"Keep your eyes shut," Loulou said.

The faucets gurgled and the pipes shuddered as she turned on the sink. A moment later cool water splashed on Etta's face. She opened her eyes just as Loulou snatched up a handful of paper towels, wetting them under the faucet before rubbing them along Etta's brow like a mother cat cleaning her kitten.

"I'm sorry," Loulou said softly, her hand pausing against Etta's cheek. "I should have known. About Terje, I should have figured. He's—"

Etta pulled away, taking the wad of paper towels and turning it against Loulou's cheek. "He made his choice. We managed. It's fine." Because Loulou shouldn't have known; that was Etta's job. Months spent with Terje in the shack, conversations held with only gentle hands and quirked brows—*she* should have known, she should have guessed, and she didn't.

Later. *Later.*

Loulou stared at her in silence as Etta continued to wipe away the grime on her cheeks until the paper towels began to dissolve into white chunks. They washed the rest of themselves in silence, dodging each other's limbs as they created a collection of discarded paper towels in the waste bin beside the toilet. No matter how hard Etta scrubbed, the russet stain remained in stubborn blotches across her cheeks and hands. The wet scent lingered as well, leaving Etta with flashbacks of being underwater, her lungs burning.

Loulou tipped her head over, running her hands through the tangles in her hair. All the bright streaks of color had become a muted gray, the same way a bright palette of paint was ruined with a healthy dose of black pigment. "So," she said. "What's next, then? Someone to call, an ace up our sleeve waiting to be pulled? How are you going to un-revolutionize the revolution?"

"We're heading up north. There's a place we can stay for a bit, in Weissensee."

Loulou peeked between the strands of hair, her head tipped to the side. "And then?"

"And then," Etta said as she pulled her sweatshirt back over her head, "we light a fire."

Loulou flipped back her hair, turned off the faucets, and reached for the doorknob behind Etta's back. "Well." She grinned. "We're certainly good at that, aren't we?"

Weissensee was a small district outside of downtown Berlin, centered around a lake where parents took their children swimming in the summer and lovers took quiet strolls in the winter. It held a balance between the electric urgency that throbbed through the city center and the quiet peace of an aging suburb. The streets were wide and newly paved, yet the old stone apartment buildings still held their speckled pink color. Concrete balconies poking out above the sidewalks were adorned with plaster detailing, giving the Socialist Classicism architecture a newly delicate air. Etta had only spent a little time in this neighborhood, and by the way Loulou stared with wide eyes and lax jaw, she'd never been.

"I always dreamed of living in a place like this," Loulou mused as they walked. "Just a little town like this. Something quaint. I could have plants in the window, maybe a cat. Could spend every evening taking strolls by the lake and throwing stones into the water."

Etta glanced at her. "You would get bored."

The corner of Loulou's lip twitched in the hint of a smile. "That's what the cat is for."

Like all of Berlin, Weissensee had pockets of a forgotten past scattered around each newly refurbished building. Back before the war, the district had acted as a sort of Hollywood inside Berlin. Home to Germany's silver screen royalty, over twenty studios had carved out a space for themselves alongside the growing residential areas, before their bright futures had been cleaved by the tensions of war. The few studios and theaters that survived were promptly snuffed out by the rise of the GDR, only an echo of their presence remaining in the form of box-office windows turned into boutique displays or old cinema signs left hanging for the sake of nostalgia, or simply for a lack of anyone bothering to take them down.

Then, there was the Delphi Theater. Camouflaged by its bleak concrete exterior and boarded windows, it had been shut down with the rise of the Berlin wall and promptly forgotten. The faint outline of curling letters spelling out DELPHI were still visible where the neon sign had once been perched, like the faded lettering of a name worn mostly away on an old gravestone.

Loulou planted a hand on her hip as she stared up at the building. She glanced over her shoulder at the apartments across the street, then back to the theater with pinched lips. "Think they're having any showings?"

"Guess we'll have to find out." Etta pulled her backpack from her shoulder, digging into the pocket for the wad of euros. She pulled free a few bills and handed them to Loulou. "There's a store at the end of the street. Could you run down there while I find a way in?"

"Sending me off to do your dirty work while you get to commit all the fun crimes?" Loulou snatched the bills and tucked them down her shirt. "What do we need?"

Etta listed off a few items, which Loulou repeated back with a skeptical expression. Casting one more careful look at the theater, she set off down the street. She was humming an old song as she wandered away, one Etta recognized from the dinners at Spreepark where Milan would let them use one of the phones and an amplifier on particularly cold nights.

Etta faced the theater. The last time she had climbed through a window she'd watched a boy get the life wrung out of him against crumbling red brick.

She grabbed onto one of the panels of plywood and pulled.

* * *

The Delphi Theater lobby was designed like a ballroom straight from Versailles. Etta walked past the concessions stand with its gold pillars and mahogany countertops, glancing up at the ceiling to admire the painted pink and blue clouds: a plaster sunrise that once greeted thousands of guests, now an eternal sunset.

The theater itself resembled the inside of a mausoleum. Gray concrete walls curved over rows of wooden seats, funneling attention toward the stage that was framed by stone arches shaped like an open clamshell. Dust kicked up under Etta's feet, the ashy remains of plaster murals that clung to the ceilings like patchy memories. The sound of her steps bounced across the walls as she moved toward the stage. She hadn't expected a silent movie theater to have decent acoustics.

The theater's design mimicked traditional live theaters: a wide stage spread out in front of the brick wall where a screen would have hung. The wooden stage groaned as Etta climbed up onto it. She dropped her backpack to the floor and stared out at the seats. The dim light made it difficult to see the doorways at the back, making the rows of seating seem endless. It was easy to imagine the theater was a hundred times larger than it was, a thousand silent audience members waiting with bated breath for her grand performance.

Perhaps that was how Milan felt each time he addressed his followers, a man on stage, staring out at an audience of invisible eyes, all awaiting his next word.

Etta screamed. The walls screamed back.

Her echo skipping across the domed ceiling, Etta imagined the rows of seats to be full of ghosts, all shivering at the sudden violence of her performance. She wondered if they would be relieved, having spent years trapped in the darkness, waiting for the newest film, to have someone finally come along to jolt them out of their seats and into the afterlife. Or were they devastated when the mournful screech

ended and they attempted to clap their hands, only to find their ability
to applaud lost in death?

Or maybe they felt nothing at all.

The theater was silent.

Etta slumped to the floor. She brushed her sleeves against her stinging eyes and unzipped the main pocket of her backpack. Her fingers
were met with damp polyester as she dipped them inside. *Shit.* She
pulled out her laptop, the cameras, the hard drives, the shattered phone,
placing them in front of her to create a short wall between her and the
seats. She curled her arms around her knees and focused her attention
on the black screens. Away from the ghosts. Away from the memory of
Terje's distant gaze, his turning back.

Determined to outrun them all, Etta began to work.

32

"Hello?" Loulou's voice echoed through the theater. "Jesus, the acoustics in here are insane. Hello? Etta?"

Etta looked up to find Loulou wandering down the aisle. "Up here." She waited until Loulou's head snapped toward her in acknowledgment before she spoke again. "Did you get everything?"

"Sure did. Shit, you wouldn't believe it out there. I found a poster quoting Milan, and it had a drawing of some guy—who looked *nothing* like Milan, trust me—but it had 'Voice of Berlin' written beneath it. *Voice* of Berlin, like they need him to speak for them. Or I guess they do—we made sure of that, didn't we? But still. It's just . . . crazy. Just wild." Loulou had a new shirt on, the olive-green sleeves rolled up to her elbows. She had a large paper bag balanced in her hands, which she shoved onto the stage before climbing up beside Etta and appraising the array of electrical components spread out across the floor. "I may be wrong here, but I think those belong *inside* the laptop."

Etta snorted and kicked her heel into her backpack with a muffled thump. "Piece of shit is waterproof." She sighed. "Or supposed to be."

"Shit." Loulou fell to her knees beside Etta and picked up one of the hard drives, rolling it over in her hands. "Is it all fucked?"

"Not yet." Etta stretched toward the paper bag and reached her hand inside, surprised as she pulled out a glass bottle. She looked at

Loulou, who shrugged and grabbed it away. As she unscrewed the top, the sharp scent of vodka wafted into the room.

"You need isopropyl alcohol; I need something we can actually drink." She took a swig, swallowed hard, and offered the bottle to Etta. Etta lifted her hand to refuse, then paused, noticing the way her fingers still shook. She grabbed the bottle then, tilting it back quickly as the liquid burned a trail down her throat. She passed it back to Loulou and began pulling the rest of their spoils out of the bag.

In addition to Etta's requested items, Loulou had grabbed a variety of general supplies: snacks, toilet paper, and a jar of instant coffee. Etta searched for the bottle of isopropyl alcohol and the children's toothbrush, which had fallen to the bottom of the bag. Everything else—including Loulou's sweater and its damp stench—she put back inside.

Her backpack had, in fact, kept the electronics mostly dry. Etta had never noticed the weak points where years of wear had allowed the fabric to fray at the point where the straps met the top of the bag, but she'd also never fully submerged the backpack before. The swamp water had taken advantage and leaked inside.

Loulou watched with the silent curiosity of an intrigued student, crunching on a protein bar as Etta dipped the toothbrush in the alcohol and began gingerly scrubbing away the slimy residue left on her laptop's components. The stinging chemical smell mixed with the thick dust, forcing them both to draw the hems of their shirts over their noses. Etta's eyes watered.

Loulou's interest waned as Etta worked, and she wandered over to check out the other electronics Etta had salvaged. Her hand flew out to snatch the shattered phone, eyes narrowing as she snorted. "You didn't tell me you swiped one of Milan's phones."

Etta began plugging the pieces of her laptop back together. "It's not his, just one he left in the shack."

"It *is* his." Loulou turned it over, running her finger over the logo etched into the back of the aluminum case. "The back camera here was always cracked. He used to lend this one to me so I could call our dealers and I always scratched my finger on the glass. I can't believe you grabbed this, I'm almost proud. My little computer genius turned thief."

Etta froze. She had hoped it was a phone Milan had at least used occasionally, but to know it wasn't only a burner . . . She couldn't believe he'd been stupid enough to leave something so potentially dangerous in the shack, even if he had broken it seemingly beyond repair. Either his arrogance had grown to an immeasurable degree over the past few months or he had believed Etta and Terje to be fully under his thumb. Possibly both.

But if the phone was his, then the chances of their success had skyrocketed—*if* Etta could save the data inside. Between whatever messages were stored on the phone and the data on the hard drives, she could build a case to send off to every news source in Berlin and beyond, each damning piece of evidence pointing toward Milan's guilt and the falsities behind the current violence. She couldn't put the genie back in the bottle, but she could pull back its disguise and reveal its true nature. She could fix everything.

Squeezing her eyes shut in a silent prayer, she pressed her laptop's power button. It was silent for a moment, the black screen taunting her before the soft whirl of its internal fan began to hum. A white screen flickered to life. It beeped. Happy, alive, as if it recognized the reverence of her fingertips. They weren't quite back at Kerzenlicht, but it was just them again in the dust and darkness working by blue light. *Hello, old friend.*

Etta smiled and reached for the first hard drive.

After a few hours of sitting with her nose pressed to the screen of her laptop, Etta realized she was building a case for her own condemnation along with Milan's. She had collected backups of every video file she had edited, every source for audio clips, and highlighted the minute, pixelated artifacts that could be spotted in the corners of her unfinished renderings. All of it was packaged into ZIP files that she emailed to every credible news agency within Germany, papers like *Frankfurter Allgemeine Zeitung* and *Die Welt*—she didn't discriminate based on political leaning. In a moment of frantic hysterics, she had even sent it to *BILD*, wondering if an article featuring Milan's face and an exclamation of his true intentions could land between articles discussing the latest British royalty scandals and Eurovision commentary.

For a moment, she wondered whether she should send it to Yusuf as well. To have taken an apple and hand back a bomb.

He would never track it back to her, not before someone else managed to, and by that point she would be gone. She would never have to suffer looking into his warm gaze only to find devastated betrayal.

It was a betrayal, after all. She had openly assisted in the war against his people. She had turned his home into a war zone.

He would find out eventually. But he didn't have to find out just then.

While Etta sent emails and monitored Milan's social feeds, Loulou busied herself with her newest purchase—a phone with a pay-by-the-minute SIM. She had spent the last hour barely biting back snapping remarks to journalists and news interns who weren't interested in Loulou's inside story on the V.

"Darling, I appreciate your promise to look into it, but your tone almost leads me to believe you're lying." Loulou's jaw snapped shut on the last word as she paused to listen. Etta could hear crackling through the phone's speaker. Loulou's features hardened until she finally pulled the phone away from her ear. "Well, Bea, respectfully, I think you're a travesty. I politely suggest you take your 'journalistic integrity' and shove it."

Loulou threw the phone onto the stage floor and collapsed back with her fingers wound into her hair. She sighed, dingy blue hairs fluttering up around her mouth.

"Another one?" Etta sympathized.

Loulou flopped to her side and peered at Etta through squinted lashes. "Some idiot from RTL. You know, I don't even think that one was actually a reporter. She kept spouting off some nonsense about factual legitimacy and recent media efforts to stop entertaining conspiracy theories."

Etta blinked. To think they were being colored as conspiracy theorists—was that possible when they were the ones who had helped create the conspiracy in question? "At least that one didn't hang up on you."

Loulou snorted and squeezed her eyes shut. "You'd think," she said, "you'd think all that government funding, all that time they spend building up those aristocratic fascist assholes just to sling some mud for the rest of us, they'd love to get some real news to dig their teeth into. Goes to show, just—goes to show."

She didn't clarify exactly what it showed but Etta imagined it would have something to do with a perceived fall of legitimate journalism—or the mythical propaganda implying journalism had ever been based in legitimacy to begin with. Where Etta despised corporations and news agencies for how they profited off her mother's death, Loulou simply lacked a basic respect for their existence.

"No bites on the emails either." It had only been a few hours and, really, Etta had no clue how long it took for news channels to pick up stories without external assistance in the way of her puppet accounts. If Etta attempted an independent campaign against Milan, Terje and Milan could spin it into proof that the government was trying to undermine them. That could be one of the reasons Milan had not released any warnings or condemnations about her or Loulou, aside from his pride. He and Terje might have been waiting for her to attempt exactly what she was considering so they could use it to fan the flames of their political standing.

So she and Loulou waited on a system they both had a hand in destabilizing, with time they didn't have.

***

That night, she tried her best not to let her mind go to Terje, but thoughts crept in, feeding on the silence, lured by having another warm body pressed against her side. As Etta lay beside Loulou, the pitch darkness swallowing every facet of the theater and leaving only the dim scent of mildew, it was easy to pretend they were back at the park. It was a simple slip to mistake Loulou's closeness for Terje's, a momentary lapse just as her mind began its slide into sleep.

She wondered if he held any regret toward betraying them. She wondered at herself for not hating him, for still replaying his quiet comforts. She wondered if he had cared at all—whether those nights spent wrapped together were real like the fires they danced around or as flat and calculated as his winged projections.

Problems had causes. Faulty code, a misplaced logic test. Somewhere, Etta had missed a decision flow, missed processing some critical input, resulting in her willingness to trust Terje—that's what she wanted to believe. That she had miscalculated, that her misunderstanding of the depth of their relationship had nothing to do with naivete and a desperation for someone to see her, to understand.

But no, she hadn't miscalculated. She hadn't calculated at all. She had dived deep into his open arms and lost sight of the surface, drowning all the way down.

"Loulou?"

A hum answered Etta in the darkness.

"Why did Terje join the family?"

Loulou stiffened beside her in their nest of dirty clothes and pilfered chair cushions. "You mean you spent all that time alone and he never told you?"

Of course he had. He'd told Etta about his family, about the Black Forest, about working for a company in Munich and how it cemented his hatred for modern society, but she didn't trust those memories. "I want to hear what you think. You see people, you told me that—what did you see in him?"

Loulou snorted. The large sweatshirt they had been sharing as a blanket rustled as Loulou turned. "You know, I'm almost embarrassed I didn't see it coming. I mean, he's always been dedicated," she said, her voice raspy with sleep. "Just this, I don't know, suppressed bundle of awkward disgruntlement. But with you—I honestly thought he would leave for you."

Etta wouldn't allow herself to feel any pleasure in that. She turned onto her back as her chest rose with a shallow sigh. There was nothing to say; Terje hadn't left for her. He hadn't even let her go in peace. It may as well have been his hands rather than Foster's when bullets had peppered the swamp during their escape.

"That boy always talks about how he sees the truth of things, goes on and on about illusions and simulacra—thinks he can peel it all back and turn the world raw," Loulou murmured. "But he's just scared to admit that he doesn't understand a single thing outside his own head, that's what I think."

Except he had understood Etta. They had understood each other, both adrift in a world that made no sense to them.

Etta had to ask. She had to be sure—so she asked the one question she hadn't asked Terje and had never had the opportunity to ask her mother. "Will you leave me?"

Loulou rolled onto her back and pressed against Etta's side just as she had those first few nights at Spreepark, the two of them together in the bunkhouse among uncracked physics textbooks and a curtain made of clothing.

"'Course not." A searching hand found Etta's in the darkness and Etta allowed Loulou to wrap their fingers together, squeezing tightly. "It's you and me—*you and me*. We're family."

***

They woke the next morning to pinging alarms. Etta had set up alerts in the event either of their names was included in recently published articles or viral messages, and the sound tore them both out of their makeshift bed. The post was already trending, several minor news outlets plastering it across social media with clipped clickbait titles:

PROPHET OF THE PEOPLE 'MILAN' REVEALS FACE— HAS A WARNING FOR THE PEOPLE OF BERLIN

Below it was a video, published only minutes earlier but already littered with well over a thousand comments. In it, Milan's face was pale with mock exhaustion as he expressed the severity of a most recent threat on German sovereignty: two domestic terrorists, traitors to their race, determined to destroy everything the German "protesters" had worked for. The top button on his shirt was undone, a few strands of blond hair dangling over his crinkled forehead, the perfect image of a man brought to the brink by the most depraved aspects of humanity.

A single picture appeared on-screen. It was taken inside Little Monarchy during one of their shared dinners, cropped so only Etta and Loulou could be seen. Their heads were ducked together conspiratorially—Etta recognized the moment. Terje had edited out Milan from where he stood behind them, where he had placed his hands on their shoulders and whispered how proud he was in their ears.

Even in her blank shock, Etta couldn't help but notice how clumsy the photoshopping was. There were small visual artifacts hinting at the shadows where Milan's body had once been displayed. Clashing shades of black that met along jagged pixel boundaries, a thin layer of digital rot evidencing a corrupted file. If she had been tasked with shopping Milan out, she would have used Wechselkind to generate an organic photo, wiping him from the moment entirely and allowing that space to be filled by Wechselkind's AI. But Terje didn't have Wechselkind, and Milan no longer had her. The artifacts were proof of that.

They were also proof that she had been essential, that his compliments of her talent weren't fictions made to feed her starved ego.

Without her, his propaganda would suffer. Without her, he was weaker, and he knew it.

Loulou bent to stare down at the screen. "Oh," she said. "Oh."

She sounded almost afraid.

33

The bus stopped outside the Märkisches Museum, a massive red brick building born of renaissance churches and plain rectangular towers on the eastern side of the Spree. They could have gone anywhere—Munich, out of Germany entirely, even straight back to the park for a direct confrontation, however dramatically that would have ended—but, as she had watched Loulou's knuckles pale as she pulled the phone out of Etta's hands and gripped it like a Catholic clutching their rosary, Etta could think of only one option.

A hideout with the only person she could trust to not turn them straight over to Milan.

When the bus didn't continue, Etta stepped up to question the driver—an older man with glasses teetering on the edge of his bulbous nose.

"This is the last stop," he told her. "We stopped service in Kreuzberg last week, too much trouble."

Etta looked to Loulou, whose eyes were once again alert as she peered over the rows of empty seats. It would have been an easy mercy, not having to traverse Kreuzberg on foot—but it was fitting. She wondered whether Loulou would feel as she had, walking through the wreckage of their actions.

The buildings still stood. Resilient vines still crept over shops tucked beside old apartments. Curved iron chairs and accompanying tables made of twisted metal branches still sat on balconies, string lights wound around the railings. The damage was in the details, the silence. The streets, as they had been a few days prior, were empty. Broken windows were left exposed, glass teeth wrenched open in a snarling dare for anyone to jump past their framed lips and into the empty shops within.

When they passed the yellow graffiti, Loulou paused.

"No," she said. "No, they got it wrong. It's wrought, not brought. 'See the poison they have wrought.'"

Etta felt the mistake was the most profound thing about the statement.

Loulou did not speak for the rest of their walk. She followed beside Etta, facing straight forward as if her neck had turned to stone, arms stiff and her hands tucked into the sweatshirt pocket. It was only when they stopped outside Dünya Market, the shop completely boarded up with a metal grate pulled over the entrance, that she finally spoke again.

"Charming." She tugged the hood lower over her eyes as she pursed her lips in mild displeasure. "Sure doesn't seem like they're open."

No, it didn't. There was a good chance the corner store would never open again, the owner more than likely having left Berlin in the wake of the attacks. The apartment above, though—the shades were pulled, no light peeking through the cracks. It appeared abandoned just as the store was, only protected from the damage and spray paint thanks to its height and the laziness of would-be attackers. If Etta hadn't known better, she would have believed the inhabitants had long since vacated as well.

But she did know better. She had checked Yusuf's bank records the day before. He had gone to a store all the way out in Friedenau and spent ten euros on groceries—it had been his only outing since Etta had seen him sweeping up inside the corner store. She had also noticed that Dünya Market had stopped depositing regular payments into his account. It left enough to spend ten euros on groceries, but not enough to make an escape out of Berlin.

There was a door right beside the corner store, half hidden between two dumpsters. Loulou stayed back as Etta pushed past them. The buzz-er had been removed from the wall, the wires dangling out of the box.

Etta lifted her hand, rapping her knuckles firmly against the door.

Loulou's shoe scuffed audibly against the sidewalk. A car alarm blared a few streets away.

A few more knocks, Etta's fist bouncing against the metal. Louder. Nothing.

"Yoo-hoo," Loulou said. "Looks like someone's home."

Etta turned to see Loulou had her chin tipped up, her hood slip-ping back to reveal the whole of her face as she lifted one hand out of her sweatshirt pocket and wiggled her fingers as if waving at a baby. Etta took a few steps back and looked to the balcony just as the shades snapped back into place.

"Oh, no." Loulou kneeled to the ground and scooped up a handful of gravel. Feet scraping against the road, she skidded a few steps back and aimed straight for the balcony. "No, not a chance."

Before she could throw it, a sharp hiss came from above, and Etta glanced up to find a small window beside the balcony was partially open.

Etta recognized Yusuf's wife from the photos on his accounts, de-spite only a sliver of Amaranth's face being visible between the window frame and the curtain. When she noticed Etta looking toward her, she lifted her finger to her lips and sharply shushed them.

Etta stepped forward. "Hey—*hey*!"

The window began to slide shut, cutting off their last chance at safe shelter.

"Yusuf Ayden—" It was the closest Etta had come to prayer in her life, nearly falling to her knees as she reached toward the window. "*Yusuf.*"

"You-what?" Loulou asked, the rocks dropping from her hand. "Is that a name, Etta? Arabic? No, wait—*Turkish?*" The last part was a hiss.

Etta ignored her. She waited. Watched as the window stayed open by just a fraction of an inch. "Please, Yusuf."

The window clapped shut.

Etta deflated, then jumped as the metal door swung inward, a handful of chain locks keeping it from opening fully as another face appeared in the crack.

"You?" The wrinkles along the corners of Yusuf's eyes pinched as he blinked at Etta. He looked as though he had aged a decade since the last time she saw him.

A low, staccato voice rattled off a number of phrases in Turkish over his shoulder. Yusuf turned and bleated a weary answer, which was met with a loud huff. He turned back to Etta.

"This is no place to return to," he said. "The store is closed. I'm sorry."

She had been certain he would know about her involvement, at least her association with Milan after the articles and his video—she had been prepared to beg, to appeal to Yusuf's sense of integrity—but the recognition in his eyes was not angry. It was soft, unsure, and a bit disconnected in the way people always viewed the sudden appearance of a random acquaintance.

He didn't know.

"I'm sorry." She stepped forward and pressed her hand against the door, face burning under Amaranth's glare as she peeked through the crack over Yusuf's shoulder. "I'm sorry, you owe me nothing, I have— there's nothing I can give, but we need help. We need help, Yusuf."

"Yusuf," his wife said incredulously in German. "She calls you Yusuf."

His jaw clenched. "I'm sorry." He pushed against the door.

For so long he had stood as a safe haven within her mind and now when she needed this single salvation, he was shutting the door in their faces. No. She planted her foot in the crack of the door, wincing as the weight drove into her toes. Yusuf opened his mouth, ready to insist, to shout.

"This world is hard," Etta echoed his words from the other day. "The least we can do is make it a little easier for each other."

The pressure lightened on her foot. Yusuf stilled. Loulou cleared her throat. The woman behind the door was silent.

"Please," Etta said. "We just need a place to hide, just for a night."

Just until she could think of a next course of action, until she could find someone to finally listen to their story.

Yusuf sighed, the tension in his jaw easing as his features melted into limp surrender. "Step back."

Etta pulled her foot free, and Yusuf pushed the door shut. There was a series of clicks as he unlocked the chain locks. Etta glanced back at Loulou, who was scrutinizing her with a guarded expression. Her hands were back in her sweatshirt pocket.

The door opened fully then. The stress that had manifested in Yusuf's face and eyes at the market seemed to have leaked into his soul as well. He was nearly hunched as he stepped aside, his hand limp as he raised it to gesture them inside. It was as if every action was one of his last, the dredges of his remaining energy ready to give way at any second.

"Thank you," Etta said as she crossed the threshold. "Thank you."

The hint of a grim smile peeked through Yusuf's beard as he nodded. Loulou said nothing as she followed Etta inside. It was a small entryway; Etta was hyperaware of how Yusuf's back nearly pressed against hers as he shut the door and began setting all the locks back into place. A flight of stairs stretched above them, with a door painted bright blue at the top. His wife had disappeared.

"Please." Yusuf gestured toward the stairs. Loulou barely acknowledged him as she took the first step, the stair creaking beneath her weight.

A throat cleared above them, signaling the reappearance of Amaranth. She clutched two sets of faded blue house slippers, both with tears along the seams, their soles worn and blackened from use.

Slowly, with one hand steadying herself on the wall and the other—the one with the slippers—resting over the large swell of her stomach, she descended the stairs until she was only a few steps above Etta and Loulou.

Her dark eyes stayed trained on Etta, unbridled suspicion thickening the air between them.

Slowly, with all the preciseness of a soldier laying down their rifle, she leaned over as much as her stomach would allow and dropped the slippers onto the bottom step.

"Please," she echoed—eyes still stuck on Etta.

"Thank you." Etta was sincere, thanking this woman for allowing them in, for the slippers, for her rightful suspicion about what she meant to Yusuf. But instead of a thank-you it should have been an apology.

Perhaps that was why Amaranth's lips pinched and her nose flared before she turned away. Yusuf pushed past Etta and Loulou to reach for his wife's arm, and though she didn't look at him, her fingers dug into the fabric of his loose shirt as they slowly ascended the stairs together.

The apartment didn't smell like mint and cumin, as Etta had thought it might. Instead, a faint lemony scent greeted them upstairs. The entire apartment was a little less than twice the size of the shack in Spreepark. Gray laminate tiles peeled up at the edges along stark white walls. A small kitchen lined the wall beside the door, the cabinets painted the same shade of white as the walls. Thin cracks inched up the drywall toward the ceiling, where ominous dark splotches documented water damage.

"Please." Yusuf gestured toward the beige sofa pressed against the wall. "Please, sit."

Etta glanced down at her pants, where no clean fabric was visible. "Oh, no—"

"Please. You both looked exhausted—please, rest."

Loulou was already on the sofa, legs crossed at the knees as she gazed around the apartment.

A large woven rug extended out from beneath the sofa, its intricate blue and white geometric design still brightly colored, like a painting spread across the floor. Etta hesitated to step on it, instead edging around the white border to ease onto the sofa. A bassinet was set up against the window, boxes of diapers and tiny clothes stacked beneath it. A small television was mounted to the wall, the remote resting on a coffee table below.

It was a small space filled by people who cared.

Yusuf hovered as an awkward silence settled over the room. His wife stood, leaning her hip against the oven as she watched the girls on her sofa with displeasure.

Etta found herself lost for anything to say. It was strange, feeling like an intruder in a space she had spent so much time in within her mind. It felt as if she were confronting a ghost, the idea of Yusuf so miraculous that the absurdity of their proximity left her mute.

After a few moments Yusuf blinked, jerking back into alertness as if all his hospitality struck him at once. He clapped his hands, rubbing his palms together anxiously as he turned to his wife. "Tea," he said. "Amaranth—please, can we get some tea ready for Etta and—"

Loulou turned toward him with a gentle smile. "Loulou. Pleased to meet you both."

Amaranth narrowed her eyes.

Yusuf's smile mirrored Loulou's. "Loulou, a pleasure to meet you as well. Your clothes—I'm afraid the washer is broken, but my wife, she has some old things. We can give you something to change into."

"No—" Etta started. No, that would be too strange, it was too much. The idea already itched at her skin.

Loulou's hand landed hard on Etta's knee. She squeezed. "Thank you, really," Loulou said, cutting Etta off. "We'd really appreciate that—thank you." The last words were directed toward Amaranth, who watched them even as she held the kettle under the faucet.

"Please, it's no problem." Yusuf let his hands fall to his sides, nodding with a parting smile and a quick glance toward his wife before disappearing through a door opposite the entryway.

Loulou's smile dropped the moment he turned away. Her nails dug deeper into Etta's knee.

Etta and Loulou looked at the floor, at each other, at the blank screen of the TV, at the curtain-covered window—not sure where to look or what to say.

"Do you need anything?"

They both looked to the kitchen at the same time, where Amaranth held a kettle over two teacups, like an executioner balancing their axe above a prisoner's head.

"Sugar?" Her voice was curt. The soft hints of an accent warped the word just at the start, though her pronunciation was anything but muddled and was pitched from her throat with all the force the German language allowed.

Etta shook her head as Loulou only stared. Amaranth poured the water into the two glass teacups, not blinking even as the steam clouded up and around her face. She picked up both cups and brought them over, not showing an ounce of the awkwardness she had shown on the stairwell as she leaned forward in front of the sofa.

Etta reached for a cup, flinching as her fingers met the hot glass. Amaranth watched her carefully with dark chestnut eyes, her long obsidian waves spilling over her shoulder.

She waited until Etta had fully taken the cup before she spoke.

"I can imagine what you've seen, out there," she said. "You can imagine what we see as well."

The hot glass was burning Etta's fingertips. She looked for a place to put the cup—the coffee table was too far away, the arm of the sofa too rude—and settled for balancing it on her thigh.

"I can," Etta said. She didn't need to imagine.

Loulou took the second teacup, humming in agreement as she finally removed her hand from Etta's leg. She sniffed at the tea once before resting the cup on the arm of the sofa and looking off toward the closed window.

Amaranth settled both hands over her stomach, wrapping them gingerly around the child that had yet to know the fury of their world.

"My husband is a good man," she said. "As he told you—he believes we can all help each other, make the world easier. Even two strange white girls, even as their kind turn our street to war. His charity knows no limit."

Loulou, still looking toward the window, dug her fingers into the sofa cushion.

Etta met Amaranth's dark gaze, the accusatory look of a righteous, bitter woman awaiting a direct confession. She wrapped her hand tightly around her scalding cup. "Your husband understands war is a fire that burns indiscriminately."

Amaranth reached to tuck a strand of hair behind her ear, revealing gold tassel earrings tarnished by time. Her lips pinched together, frown lines biting into the tawny skin around her eyes as she regarded Etta— as if Etta was something barely worth pitying.

"And yet," she said, one hand left to rest protectively over her stomach as she waved the other absently toward Etta and Loulou, "I see no burns."

34

Yusuf returned from the bedroom with an armful of cotton pants and thickly knit sweaters and guided Etta and Loulou to the bathroom. They squeezed into the small space together and changed in silence. Etta listened—certain that Amaranth would use the moment as an opportunity to insist Yusuf kick them out, to voice her suspicions.

She heard nothing. No words exchanged in German or Turkish.

Amaranth's clothes itched with prickling heat across Etta's skin.

When they returned, Yusuf sat down on the coffee table. He had a cup of tea, which he nursed as Etta and Loulou resumed their space on the sofa. Amaranth no longer stood in the kitchen, and the door to the bedroom was shut.

"I apologize for asking. I recognize the face of a person who has seen too much, battled too often." Yusuf cleared his throat. "But how is it? The rest of Berlin—how is it? The same?"

He looked so hopeful, so open and focused on some thread of news, that it unsettled Etta. The man who spent hours poring over news articles, who spent his grocery budget on subscriptions to papers from around the world—he did not know the state of his city from beyond the railing of his balcony.

Etta wound her fingers in her lap. "Weissensee is okay, during the day."

"Weissensee." Yusuf shut his eyes. "I haven't left Kreuzberg in so long—I've barely left the apartment. My wife, she's only left once since this all started. A group of men tried to follow her back home."

Loulou perked up, turning to Yusuf curiously. "And you *stayed*? Why would you—it's a ghost town here. Just leave, go to Munich or something. Belgium, even." As if Munich hadn't had riots. As if Belgium wasn't similarly on fire, Milan's words slipping across the border and seeping onto the cobbled streets, like gasoline running down the gutters.

Yusuf's eyes flicked open to look at her, lips twisted in a mournful smile as one shoulder lifted in an idle shrug. "I envy that innocence, to not know how hard it is to leave your home. To imagine leaving would cure all our wounds. Were it only so simple."

Etta could hear Loulou's retort already—how she would inform Yusuf that she *had* left home, that she had traveled across Berlin all alone, just a few days before she had turned eighteen. Yet Loulou only clenched her hands over her knees, spine stiff as she turned her face back to the window. It made sense; Loulou would not share the truth of herself with a stranger so easily.

Yusuf sipped his tea placidly as he turned to follow her gaze, his eyes then sweeping up to the television mounted beside his head.

"I usually follow the news closely," he said. "At Kerzenlicht, I was always writing. I wanted to be a journalist."

You are a journalist, Etta wanted to say. The inverse of any other journalist she had encountered, one who spoke honestly under a false name.

"But Amaranth, she didn't want to listen to the news anymore. And I kept watching. I was stuck to the television, watching the riots, the brutality. She kept asking me why I wanted to watch it on the television when I could just look out the window—I couldn't really explain why. I'm still not sure."

"It's easier that way." Etta knew how it felt to watch the world through her computer, navigating its systems under a series of digital identities. It allowed the promise of disconnection, a safety net in the form of a button she could press to shut the world off. Not a barrier but an escape.

Yusuf regarded Etta with a sad smile.

"Maybe," he said. "Maybe."

The shouting started around dusk, pitched in spontaneous whoops, the intensity muted by the apartment walls. It gave the violence an eerie feeling, of ghosts howling in the nighttime. Etta preferred the polite, silent applause of the ghosts at the Delphi.

A soft snore—from Yusuf or Amaranth, Etta couldn't tell—emanated from the bedroom. It gave a steady baseline to tune into as Etta tried to will her aching muscles to relax.

Loulou seemed to suffer from a similar sort of insomnia. When Etta had pulled the sofa cushions to the floor as pillows and arranged the blankets offered by Yusuf, Loulou had turned away and taken sentry beside the window. Her face was obscured by the curtain as she peeked out onto the street, one hand resting on the edge of the bassinet. Her finger occasionally ran along the soft edge, gentle in the way a mother would rock her child to sleep.

"You never told me you had friends here."

Etta rolled over onto her stomach, looking up toward the window. Loulou's face was still obscured by the curtain. A bottle shattered outside. Someone shouted.

"I don't." Etta rolled back onto her side.

"But you know him."

A snore rumbled through the room. Nothing like the soft breaths Etta had once imagined, warm against her neck.

"No," she said to the ceiling. "I don't."

"Sure." She could hear Loulou's knowing smile.

The curtain rustled. Soft, confident steps crossed the floor as Loulou approached Etta's backpack, her pale ankles exposed under too-short cotton pants. She knelt, digging through the side pocket until she pulled free a pack of cigarettes she had bought outside the Delphi theater.

Etta sat up.

"Calm down." Loulou continued her pilfering, pulling out a green lighter. "I'll be fine, unless your friend and his pregnant wife would rather I smoke in their living room."

"I'd say shout if you need me," Etta grumbled, "but I think shouting may help you blend in."

Loulou snorted as she strode to the door and pulled it open. She slid a cigarette from the pack and pinched it between her lips, turning to look over her shoulder with a rueful smirk.

"You forget," she said. "Milan may have written the scripture, but I taught them how to preach."

The door squeaked as it shut behind her. Etta wondered briefly why Loulou hadn't stepped onto the balcony instead, but the thought was quickly snuffed out as unconsciousness finally overtook her.

A loud beep sliced through Etta's thick blanket of sleep.

The room was dark, the streets silent. Snores still rocked through the bedroom door. The scent of lemon had attached itself to her skin and hair.

Her hand reached out onto the blankets beside her, only to find the dead lumps of unoccupied pillows. She was alone. Loulou was still out, and Etta had no idea how long she'd been gone. It was possible Loulou was still working her way through the cigarettes, eyes glued to their phone as she scrolled through comments relating to Milan's posts.

Another sharp ring. Etta sat up. It took a moment to remember its source and, when she did, she felt a blast of shame at having forgotten. She had set an alarm on her laptop tied to any email notifications in hopes someone would reply to their messages. A reporter, an influencer, a politician—someone had heard their call.

The blast of elation lasted as long as it took her to open her email. Only one message sat unopened in the inbox, the sender's address composed of a series of numbers followed by a false domain name. The subject line read E—URGENT, though she could see from the preview that the message contained no text, only a JPEG file. She would have dismissed it as a phishing attempt, except the subject line implied she had been an intended target rather than one of a thousand unlucky recipients.

No, of course it was Terje.

Perhaps Milan had been warned about her attempts to reach journalists and had tasked Terje with cutting her operation short. Perhaps the email was a threat, hence its unusually overt nature for a man who had hidden a keylogger inside a false BIOS.

How dare he, really. To think he believed he still had the right to dig into her digital path at all, to reach out to her as if it hadn't been his hand that shoved her right into the tiger's mouth. It was easier when the dead stayed dead—when those who left you behind left you alone.

Her finger hovered over the mouse pad.

The dark colors of her inbox flickered as the image file opened.

A sparrow.

Its cream belly was exposed, its wings extended in the early stage of flight as it pushed off from the ground. A black eye stared accusingly toward the camera, as if it expected to defend itself from the photographer. Etta wondered if the sparrow wasn't right to be so bold.

The email was not a threat, then, yet she wasn't convinced it was only a picture. Terje believed in the power of images in revealing truth. He was prone to hiding his numbers and lines in the ones and zeros of preexisting artifacts. Just as he had hidden his keylogger in her BIOS, so may he have hidden something in the sparrow.

Steganography: the art of hiding in plain sight. Traditional forms included messages hidden on blue paper that appeared plain until you looked through a rose-colored lens, and an artist hiding their initials in the details of a completed painting.

It didn't take her long to find it. Unless it was intentionally simple for the purpose of baiting her, he had rushed it. The message wasn't even deeply encoded into the image—she only had to dig through the metadata to find a hidden text document tucked between the code attached to the image file.

The document opened without any trouble. Only one short line of text appeared on her screen as Etta curved her body over the laptop balanced on her knees:

SHE RETURNED. HE WELCOMED HER. RUN.

It was only then that Etta noticed the time: nearly dawn.

Loulou had left for her smoke just after nightfall.

Etta did not think, she moved. She stuffed her laptop back into her bag, glancing briefly toward the bedroom door. The snores continued. Her throat and nose burned; her vision was fuzzy at the edges as she experienced the flight down the apartment steps like a child watching a low-quality television show, lost in the frantic hum of her thoughts as she slammed into the door and out onto the street.

35

No one chased her. Eventually, her feet ached too much to continue. It occurred to her that she had always been running. From her mother, from her identity, now from Milan, always moving away. Even in the amusement park, she had only found salvation at the top of the Ferris wheel. She had only ever felt whole at a precipice. Loulou's betrayal was a phantom pain, Terje's only a fraction harsher—they should ache more, she realized. It should all ache more.

Yet she did not ache. She burned.

She held a thousand pains at a distance, watching them through thick glass as they warped the world around her. Once, she had felt well and fine under her thick bubble, isolated and at peace. But fresh air had leaked in. Yusuf was no longer a concept but a man in an apartment smelling of lemon with a wife who saw no burn marks on Etta's skin, and she was right. Etta was untouched, not for lack of bruising but by choice. She was as incorporeal as one of Terje's projections, a coward who hid behind her illusions until they had stained reality beyond recognition.

Worst of all, she had experienced family. The sweet touch of a comforting hand to her shoulder and the brush of breath against her hairline were feelings she could now recall with the stunning accuracy that only belonged to someone who had spent their nights fighting happily for food around a table of known faces.

For a while, she had believed that she had chosen the V—that she'd been the one to accept Milan and his family, and her choice to stay was uncorrupted by manipulation. She thought she had managed to maintain her individual power, that she was Etta Who Joined The V, rather than Etta Who Belonged To The V—but, in the end, it was Milan who had given her to the V, and it was Milan who had taken the V away.

At least she couldn't recall how it felt to have a mother; at least she would never understand the full extent of what was stolen in that respect. With the V, she understood to an excruciating degree exactly what had been taken.

She wanted to grasp those pains, leave Berlin, migrate north and forget the world as it barreled further into the hell she helped create. But she would not. She refused to run anymore.

As she began to walk toward Spreepark, she thought that perhaps this is how her mother felt. Alone at the edge, tired of continuing but too furious to simply stop.

It was entirely likely that she would never make it to the park, that someone would recognize her and drag her away like a prized trophy at the end of a long hunt. If she did make it to the park, she would certainly never make it past the security gate. The guards would be waiting, and they would take her straight to Milan in exchange for whatever cash or chemical or flesh prize was offered.

It was a little over an hour's walk along the river to get to Spreepark. She spent every moment considering how best to strike one final blow to Milan, what words might slice deepest to a man who believed nothing was beyond his designs. He had changed the fabric of Berlin, planted police barricades and sprouted rioters with petals of black, yellow, and red. What did he care about a traitor?

But she was no simple traitor—she was his and she had fled.

She might not need words at all. Her appearance might be wound enough.

Yet as she finally came upon the tree-lined street leading to the park, no rogue wave of assailants came to greet her. No teenagers with hungry eyes and vicious smiles waited at the station. There was no familiar clamor in the distance. Only the wide bend of the Ferris wheel, arched over the trees like the back of Atlas as the sun sat on its shoulders.

Spreepark had gone silent.

The guardhouse was empty, the entry gate hanging open. The crumbling dinosaurs were without riders, the gazebos without tenants. Vacant, haunting nothingness. As she passed Little Monarchy, the heavy door left ajar, she noted the light in the window, Milan's castle citadel, was out. The heart of Spreepark beat no more.

It was baffling. Milan did not run, he conquered. He reveled in the thrill of a confrontation, the opportunity to prove his superiority over the rest of mankind. He would not leave without reason, and he certainly would not avoid a confrontation with Etta, especially following Loulou's return.

Unless he thought his disappearance would injure her more than any confrontation could. To deprive her of closure, to be one more man who left her only memories when she craved answers. He knew how that would foster her rage. He had twisted her escape into fresh abandonment, proved in one swipe that he knew she would return, and he would not be there to face her.

The trees outside Little Monarchy curled over her, reaching out to pull her back, warning her, but she pushed on as the metal cap of the bunkhouse gleamed in the distance. It was abandoned as well, the doors wide open. The interior had been cleared of all but the hanging curtain walls and a few foam mattresses left scattered like discarded life rafts washed ashore. She did not go inside; nothing waited for her there. It had never been her home, not as the shack had.

The shack's door was the first she encountered that was shut, the padlock dangling from the metal hinge. This was the only place they had deemed worthy of closing away after their gutting and pillaging of the park had been finished—packaged and kept carefully intact just for her. Her hands were steady as she gripped the edge of the door and pushed it open.

The space had been destroyed. Not emptied as the bunkhouse was, but tortured. Etta froze in the doorway as she cataloged each shattered monitor and gutted computer with the grim diligence of a mortician. Terje's workbench had been upended. The desktop was smashed open, its components spread across the floor. Every shelf had been tipped onto its side, leaving cameras, hard drives, and spare parts littered across the floor in a metallic whirlwind. The card table had been snapped in half, the whiteboard with their poker scores buried beneath the rubble. Only the corner was visible, *Mäuschen* peeking out in Foster's clumsy scrawl.

She took a careful step inside, the plastic frame of a cracked monitor crunching under her foot.

Someone groaned.

She froze again. In the corner, lumped beside the upended workbench, she made out the bent shape of a head tucked into a misshapen shoulder, patches of dark hair matted with blood. The face was hidden, but she knew. This was the same hair she had spent her evenings running her fingers through, the same shoulder she had spent drunken nights leaning her head upon—Terje.

"No." He groaned again as she clambered over the shelves and broken equipment. "Etta—"

His left hand pushed against her as she reached him, his right hanging limply at his side. What resentment and betrayal his actions had fostered turned to horror as his head finally lifted and his face was revealed. His skin was swollen and blistered with red splotches like an apple left out to rot in the sun. Pus oozed from cuts along his forehead and nose, even the smallest of them deep enough to expose pale bone between layers of skin and pink muscle. His nose was completely flattened and bent to the side, his left eye swollen shut at the center of a black bruise that stretched from his brow to his cheekbone. Blood seeped from between his lips.

"Stop." The word stung on her lips. "Just—*fuck*."

Terje jerked forward, a violent cough splattering blood across Etta's chest. This was why the V had left, Milan knowing she would return— any confrontation would be outshone by the anguish she'd feel upon entering the shack and finding Terje.

"We need to go." She leaned forward, trying to wrap her arms around his broken body. He would not die here.

"Etta." His voice was thick around gargled blood. "Etta, they wanted me to watch. They wanted me to watch—"

"What?"

He pointed. A phone lay face down beside his leg, the only untouched piece of technology left in their former haven. She reached forward, flipping it over as Terje shuddered with another broken cough.

It was a video posted less than an hour earlier. The shaky footage jumped as the camera person moved through a room, yet Etta could still see flashes of the interior. Gray laminate that peeled at the edges, a kitchen with white cabinets that matched the stark white walls—a place that smelled of lemon and black tea.

Small, yet carefully loved.

The ground slipped from beneath her feet. Her knee cracked as she hit the floor.

She could not look away. Three individuals, their faces covered with black masks—yet she knew them. She knew the swirling ink that peeked up along Foster's neck, the yellowed bruises that peppered Monika's pale skin. She knew the strands of faded blue hair that slipped from beneath the mask of the last figure.

And in the corner, beside the television, was Yusuf. His face swollen, his mouth open, guttural, broken pleas scraping out from his throat as Foster and Loulou held him by each arm. His chest arched as he pulled to be free of them, his body twisted like a dying martyr painted on a church wall.

The camera panned to the source of his agony: Amaranth, spread over the ornate carpet that Etta had been so careful not to dirty only hours before. Its intricate pattern was muddied with blood, Amaranth's arm lying at a crooked angle as a hollow rattle escaped her lips. Monika stood over her, a baseball bat gripped tightly in one hand. Her back was straight. Her shoulders heaved.

Etta knew, then, what would follow. What Milan had prophesized, what he had created—the child of his ambition, one final fire set only for her.

It wasn't clean. It was as clumsy as it was brutal. Monika stumbled as she brought the bat down once, twice—over and over—before falling to her side. Loulou shouted for her to stand. Yusuf's agonized pleas increased in pitch until they turned to screams that buzzed through the speakers. And the bat came down again.

Again.

Again.

Then Monika threw the bat aside, panting and wild and stuffed full of false righteousness as she knelt beside Amaranth. Her hand flexed at her side, practiced in bearing cruelty but new to dealing it.

Below her, Amaranth glared through squinted eyes. The same cutting gaze she had turned on Etta and Loulou she tipped against her attacker, silent as her husband begged. Monika gripped her by the hair, pulling Amaranth's head to the side and shaking her fistful of obsidian waves, but Amaranth's glare did not waver.

Loulou whistled off-screen. Something slid onto the carpet by Monika's feet—a knife. Monika picked it up and held it to Amaranth's throat.

"The world is a festering wound." It was a hiss, a chant ripped straight from Milan's mouth that sounded foreign in Monika's meek voice. "And it must be lanced."

Amaranth lurched upward, the knife biting into her skin as she spit. A red glob splattered onto Monika's mask.

Monika drove the knife forward.

The blood swelled. Amaranth's eyes fluttered. Her chest heaved. She fell back. Monika stood, stepping away as a red pool gathered at her feet. Yusuf dove into the frame, Loulou and Foster having released their grip. There was no reason to hold him back, their job was done.

Yusuf bent over his wife. He pressed his hands first to his own face, then down to hers, then back to his cheeks as sobs tore through him and blood-marked wet streaks snaked to his chin. Behind them, the bassinet sat empty as it always would. No one spoke. He did not look at them. Yusuf's eyes stayed on Amaranth, his hands caressing her cheeks as he began to speak.

No, to pray—*Allah* strung between hushed pleas she once heard him whisper during long nights at their small café. Yusuf was praying.

The scene froze. The screen blinked.

The video began anew.

The phone clattered to the floor. Etta kicked it away, but the sound of Yusuf's sobs and the dry gasp of Amaranth's final breath stained Etta's mind, as the blood had stained the rug. She had done that. She had brought it upon them, not only Amaranth's death, and the death of their unborn child, but all that had preceded it, Milan's holy war against all that was not his.

Blood stained her hands; it always would.

"It's not right." Etta turned as Terje spoke, the words scratched along his loose exhale. "I thought— I didn't know—" Another cough cut his words short.

He couldn't die, couldn't be another life lost needlessly to Milan's war.

"Come on." She reached under his shoulder again. His limp weight hung on her weakened knees, forcing her nearly to the floor as she tried to heave him upward.

"Etta, I have to tell you—please," he gasped, reaching to wrap his hand around her wrist. "I lied. What I was going to tell you—when you asked—I didn't forget."

"Shut up." She couldn't lift him. Etta looked around the room for anything that could help, each destroyed shelf and computer swimming as tears muddied her gaze.

"Etta, it was us." His voice sounded choked in blood as his throat struggled to form sounds. "We hacked your laptop. I had wanted to tell you—"

The laptop—the shout that launched an avalanche, that single wave. She didn't care. She would never care again if it meant his life was saved, if it meant one less death. Collapsing onto her knees beside him, she laid her hands against his cheeks with a featherlight touch. "Terje, don't—Milan, he already told me, stop talking—"

His body seized in a hollow laugh, his mouth opening to reveal gaping holes between bloodied teeth. His one good eye swiveled toward her. The white around his iris swirled with fresh blood, ready to burst. "Of course he did. Of course you knew."

He coughed and a wet spray splattered Etta's cheeks as he ignored her pleas for him to stop talking. "Shit, Etta. We fucked it up, we fucked it all up so bad. I just didn't want to lie anymore, I wanted—"

Her hands pressed harder, the swollen skin hot under her fingers. "Come on—we have to go, we have to get you to a hospital, you won't—"

But his gaze went dim, his jaw slack. Only the soft clench of his hand around her wrist signaled he might still be aware of her presence as his blue lips parted for a pained breath. "They burned down the trees. It's all just ash."

Etta swore. Her forehead dropped down to press against his cheek. He smelled of steel—he had always smelled of steel, always more computer than man. A steady landing along the edge of a cliff, the only one to understand. The only one to know her. In the background the phone still played on its horrible loop, Yusuf's voice pleading in shattered prayers. His and Etta's sobs were a harmony to the crackling embers left in Milan's footsteps.

She could have one moment, she decided, gripping the hand still wrapped around her wrist. One final moment where the world was upright and the morning would come unchanged, welcomed by two survivors clinging to safety in a small shack situated in the world's shadow.

The sparrow and the boy who had granted her wings.

Then she let go.

36

Etta's back ached. She didn't know how long she'd been slumped against the wall, Terje's body lying lifeless across from her. It was time for her to leave.

She retrieved the phone and closed the evil video. Terje had loathed the Black Forest and its falsities, but she knew he would prefer it to becoming one more set of forgotten bones in Spreepark.

So when she dialed the police, she told them his full name. "Terje Hunt is dead in a shack at the back of Spreepark." She hung up before the operator had a chance to reply.

She trekked out of the park and stood sentry among the trees as police and an ambulance careened down the road with their wailing sirens. Only when the medics and officers left their cars and began charging through the gate did she finally turn her back on Spreepark. She had thrown the phone into the river; it had been wiped of everything aside from the video, and the weight of it in her hand felt too like a knife.

For lack of anywhere else to go, Etta returned to the crumbling walls of Wohnhaus Stubenrauchstraße. She should have known better than to expect the quiet trap of molding walls that hid outcasts like mice in its dark corners to be the same. LISTEN TO THE VOICE OF BERLIN was spray-painted in a wide arc across its crumbling west wall, Milan's reach proven even in the most forgotten corner of the city. Worse, the sloppy curving letters appeared reminiscent of her own handwriting. Did he know this was one of her hideaways? Had he planned it as a reminder, or was it symbolic of just how popular he had become? No matter how hard she scrubbed, she would always be aware of the stain.

When she approached the building, it teemed with life. The front stoop was crowded by men with dark beards and glazed eyes, apathetic to the prospect of police spotting their trespassing as they stared down the street. A few wore the remnants of old work uniforms, high-visibility jackets muddied and torn. Others still wore ties, proof of their former place in an economy busy crumbling along with the bus routes and rental flats. She recognized a few from cafés around Kreuzberg, their beckoning calls advertising coffee and authentic Turkish sweets once a soundtrack to the melody of a summer day by the canal. It seemed as though the whole of Kreuzberg now found sanctuary at Wohnhaus Stubenrauchstraße.

She climbed the stairs to the third floor and entered the apartment where she had laid claim over the course of so many nights. A woman sat against the far wall. Her hair was covered with a yellow hijab and her eyes were wide as she tucked the heads of three children against her hip. Beside her were two men, their jaws hidden under unkempt beards and their stares weary as they slowly stood to face Etta.

Etta did not spare them a second look as she kicked the door shut behind her and headed toward the room that held her closet. She saw how their hands shook, how they glanced to each other for fear of what could come next—but she was confident they would not move against a girl already drenched in death.

The world had tilted, and she had rolled back into a familiar rut, gravity pulling her along until she hit its deepest pit: the closet of the once-grand third-floor apartment.

A collection of beer cans and cigarette butts had amassed around the edges of the closet in her absence. But it was empty. She made no move to clear the debris. Her bag at her feet and her back on the cold floor, Etta closed her eyes.

She tried but failed to sleep.

Voices haunted her. Not from the family sheltered just a wall away, not from the groups that stomped across the ceiling or shouted beneath her back. These voices followed her no matter how she turned or how hard she pressed her hands over her ears. The soft chant of Yusuf's prayer. Terje's final lament as he lay one last time in her arms. They drowned out the ringing in her ears that had not eased since she escaped the park. It sounded like the wind whistling past her as she slipped off the cliff.

Over the following two days, Etta grew used to the soft voices of the three children next door. She came to expect their fluttery giggling, always accompanied by a sharp motherly hush. The consistency in their rhythm created a minor solace from the voices that pricked her mind. When the children suddenly went silent, she noticed.

She tried to ignore it. They must be asleep. But as the hours crept by, she grew worried, even as the quiet noise of shuffling indicated some sign of life on the other side of the wall.

Etta pushed herself off the floor. Her knees ached. A sour odor filled her nose, shaken loose from her clothes by her movements. It would be good to check, at least. She would poke her head through the doorway, confirm they lived, then return to her coffin and escape back into the borderlands between wakefulness and sleep.

The floor creaked as she stepped outside the closet.

The group, to her strange relief, remained. The mother was curled in the corner with all three children bundled on her lap in a misshapen pile. One man stood by the window while the other balanced by the door against a splintered chunk of wood, scavenged from a stray table or chair. Etta could tell from a distance that it was far too rotten to cause any damage, doomed to easily break if sent against flesh.

The children on the woman's lap were far too still for their age. Their chests barely rose with soft breaths, their faces washed of color.

Seeing that they lived wasn't enough. A nagging insistence on doing them a kindness now plucked at Etta. She crept toward the window, fooled into believing she had managed to stay undetected until she lifted her foot onto the ledge and a whisper split the silence. "Be safe."

Etta froze, the echo of Terje's words all those weeks ago a sudden, painful reminder. The woman had been awake after all, her tired eyes now set on Etta as she curled her hands farther over the children in her lap. Etta didn't respond—there was no use in encouraging comradery she did not deserve.

She climbed through the window and her feet found their familiar holds, her grip firm as she began her steady descent down the wall. A few other refugees poked their heads out the windows as Etta passed, watching with open curiosity as she dropped to the ground. She met their eyes, every set, taking in their burdens. If they recognized her, they did not show it. Names and pasts were lost in this corner of Berlin.

It was different on the street. The pressure of watchful eyes bore down on Etta's back. Groups of teenage boys laughed as they passed, never sparing her a glance, yet Etta could swear they spat at her. Perhaps it was only a stray drop of rain. Etta couldn't tell, but she was sure she heard Milan's words echoed as people whispered sharp jabs at her back, the hand she had helped create guiding their shoulders as they turned to leer.

Through a matter of irony, they had all managed to find one of the only people in Berlin worthy of their misplaced hatred.

Every insult renewed her resolve to carry on her journey toward the Bavarian Quarter, where she knew a small shop with a blue door and bright lights held sweets in glass display cases. There were enough of Loulou's pilfered euros left to buy a bag of candies for the children back at the apartment building. She was unable to imagine a better use for the money. Picturing Milan's face were he to hear his hard-won earnings were used to buy sweets for children he had helped demonize would be her reward.

The clerk at the shop was clearly shocked to see Etta's disheveled figure step through her door, yet she had the grace to greet her pleasantly as Etta pointed toward a collection of chocolate bars left in a basket on the counter's corner.

"Are you local?" the clerk asked, adjusting the strap to her dress nervously as she took the crumpled wad of euros from Etta's hand.

Etta glanced up, unsure where exactly she could consider herself local to anymore. She went with "Wilmersdorf." The district was just far enough outside the city center the clerk would be strange to question it.

The clerk bobbed her head as her eyes danced from Etta to the door. "Best avoid Rathaus Schöneberg then, if you haven't heard."

"I haven't heard."

"There's a rally. It's another one for that man, Milan. I would head straight home if I were you, they're angry today. Always angry."

"So am I." Etta snapped the bag of chocolates from the counter and turned, letting the door slam behind her as she strode off toward Rathaus Schöneberg.

A great sandstone fortress, famous as the theater for the American President John F. Kennedy's grand speech—and the square in front where thousands of people had squeezed in to mourn his death, their hands stretched wide to wrap around the grief felt overseas.

Thousands of people now gathered again, though this new crowd did not mourn so much as cheer. Cars honked either in exasperation or support. The front windows of surrounding businesses were plastered with red and black sketches of Milan's face, jaw set like a captain staring out at sea. Etta avoided his flat stare and pulled her scarf higher over her nose, ducking under the awning of a closed kebab shop across the street.

On the steps of the great hall, two massive German flags were propped up by wooden poles. Smaller flags in the hands of the attendees churned in red, black, and gold ocean waves. Some people carried empty garbage bins that they hammered with heavy hands while shouting wildly.

The paper bag crinkled in Etta's hands.

From the top of the steps, a man appeared.

Etta didn't need to be close to identify him as Milan. Only one man would walk so confidently before the eyes of thousands, as if he was born to sun himself under the warmth of their praise. Milan's arms lifted as a judge lifts their gavel, the hammering and chanting quieting to a soft hum as his hands slowly lowered again. He demanded obedience; he demanded their attention. A smaller figure stepped to his side, stopping in the circle of his shadow as she crossed her arms over her chest like the soldier girls seen on propaganda posters from past wars: Loulou.

She had found redemption, leaving Etta as the solitary "domestic terrorist."

Police cars had gathered on the streets like predators in the grasslands. As the shouting of the masses lowered into a pregnant murmur, Milan lifted a microphone to his mouth. The speakers must have been hidden behind the giant flags, Etta figured, as the force of his voice boomed off the buildings and over their heads.

"My friends." She could picture his face across the table, his hand extended. The same stern gentleness with which he addressed his closest followers was now deployed on all of Berlin. "My friends, I have been afraid. It is a fear I am certain you share, one held for yourselves— for your children, for your loved ones."

The crowd leaned closer to the pull of Milan's words, and he bent forward, granting them the proximity they desperately reached for. "We live in a world fractured. Tainted with ignorance, haunted by villains. We sneak—you understand? We sneak under their rules, their demands, we sneak below the strength of our identity in pursuit of— not truth—not peace—but survival—in a world not built for us."

A world not built for him.

"We seek only peace, yet our brothers, our sisters, our friends—they are brutalized, savaged by violence we did not seek yet we must suffer." Were he playing at a more sensitive leader, his voice might have hitched here, but it stayed a steady force, a calm series of statements delivered by a father unto his children.

But he was no longer a beacon of charismatic wisdom, not to her. He was, despite his best efforts, only one of many—just as she was.

"Even now," he continued. Of course he continued. "Even *now*. On our streets, in our homes, violence finds us. Pitching human against human, bringing to light the boundaries we crossed in divine defiance—I plead, my friends. Just this morning, proof was released into the world—have you seen it? A video, a crime serving as proof of our inability to coexist. Proof we cannot have peace so long as the waters are muddied. Look to your phones, your televisions. Look to the brutality we deal and tell me I lie. Give me your denial as you face our final truth."

Every muscle in Etta's body seized. They had sent the video, even without her and Terje leading the march. Milan reached backward to Loulou, who offered him a phone—the same phone, Etta was certain, they had bought together. The same phone they had used in their attempt to defy him.

Milan held it in the air like a gauntlet.

The crowd's heads turned down.

Then it began.

Etta squeezed her eyes shut. The voices, the ghosts, with Milan's hand they had been revived through the speakers of a thousand phones. There was no escape from the sound of Amaranth's moans. From the sound of Yusuf's pleading, Monika's clumsy condemnation. Every phone the V had registered for years of raves, every person who had once looked to Milan for notifications of a weekend opportunity to escape, they now turned to him for blood. For death.

He had done as he had promised: he had provided.

Etta slumped to the ground. The paper bag turned into a baseball bat in her hands, the weight of it pulling her down as every strike against Amaranth was broadcast through Berlin. How had she believed this? How had she ever swallowed Milan's garbage, mouth already gaping for more before his monologue was fully digested?

"Look how Berlin bleeds," Milan boomed over the overlaid sounds of wailing and Yusuf's prayers. "The powers that be, the so-called leaders and lords that cage us with laws, they've tried too long to mix dark oil into our waters—and see how we suffer for it. We see this unforgivable act—a violent expression of rage—yet, can you blame the child for its rage when all it has known is confusion?"

He blamed them. He blamed Yusuf and Amaranth as though they had pleaded for the knife rather than their lives. Explaining the violence as a tragic symptom of illness and misfortune on behalf of the attacker rather than putrid racism and inherent cruelty—it was a tactic Etta had used in her work reshaping a celebrity's or politician's image, using their crimes as proof of their victimhood. It was a strategy she had too readily shared with Milan at Spreepark. Now, his golden words wove a tapestry so thick it threatened to choke the whole of Berlin, to smother Europe in its sleep while the West dozed on, and Etta had helped outline the design.

"This rage," Milan boomed. "It continues. It *feeds*. They—the Turks—they may have bled here, but do you truly believe they'll let themselves be lanced dry when anger—when *greed*—is so deeply intrinsic to their kind? We cannot coexist, not when our own are left homeless, driven to madness, by the politically sponsored cultural corruption of Berlin. There must be change. We must fight for the Berlin of our ancestors; we must defend our peace—even if they make it a war."

He was lying, as always. A promise in one hand and a knife in the other, yet Berlin was blinded by conviction. The crowd began to surge toward the stage, and the police—waiting for the rally to turn into a riot—quickly flipped on their sirens and pressed forward on foot, linking arms and pushing with thick shields to form a wall, meeting the throng with the crack of bodies hitting plastic.

All attention was drawn from Milan as the police began their defense. Only Etta, slumped against the wall and covered in darkness, turned her gaze to the man standing alone on the steps. His arms hung at his sides. The microphone had fallen at his feet. He did not flinch at the scene before him; he did not plead for peace. He only stood sentry over the chaos, his face hardened with grim resolve.

His act was seamless. Better than any deepfake she could have created, the perfect example of a sane man driven by righteousness for the good of the people, steady as a mountain, until the police tackled a man to the ground and were followed by five more rioters who pulled at the officers' necks and clawed at their vests like animals on a fresh kill. There, her eyes on Milan, Etta saw it. She saw how his façade glitched, how the mask he so carefully wore slipped with the wet screams of his prescribed anarchy drenched in honey words.

In that moment, in the smile that peeled across Milan's face, Etta saw truth.

The children were awake when Etta returned to Wohnhaus Stubenrauchstraße, their eyes wide yet bleary with sleep as she pulled herself through the window. The two men leapt upward from their seats, the one still clutching a rotten table leg.

The smallest child stared owlishly as Etta approached him. One of the men spat something sharp in warning, but Etta did not stop until she had dropped to her knee beside the child. Let him come, she thought. She deserved whatever he wanted to throw her way. Yet the man did not make any further attempt to stop her. He only watched, balanced on his heels, as Etta held out the paper bag of chocolates to the boy.

"I'm sorry," she said. "I'm sorry."

The child did not reply. She did not expect him to. Not when his world was shattered by her hand. Not when the fires continued to rage.

Not when she had work yet to complete.

37

The video spread its wild flames across the whole of Europe within a day. Global tensions rose to a boil. World leaders howled their lamentations from marble castles. Reports scrolled in red ribbons of text under news anchors telling of soldiers lined up along borders and countries setting off missiles like fireworks.

They spoke of riots and war crimes when Turkish soldiers began standing too close to borders. They reported that a Russian missile shot down a South Korean plane, Russia claiming terrorists had hijacked the jet and were threatening Moscow. South Korea claimed the passengers and crew were guilty only of existing within Russia's reach. One the devil, the other an innocent—the roles always changing depending on who held the mirror.

Whether Milan's words were the true spark behind the anger or a convenient excuse, Etta couldn't be sure.

The voices haunting her were no longer contained squarely within her mind. They breathed alongside her. The packed halls and apartments of Wohnhaus Stubenrauchstraße hummed as Etta wandered through the building, squatters' cheeks pressed together over phones as those new and old to the shadows all gaped at the horror of unprohibited savagery. Yusuf and Amaranth had become legends in their tragedy.

Some people approved of the killing. Their voices could be heard in the streets following Milan's rally, their chants naming righteousness. They threw bottles and called it freedom.

Others, like those tucked in the embrace of mouseholes like Wohnhaus Stubenrauchstraße, wept over the plain cruelty dealt against their own. Those—the bodies weeping into pillows or couples speaking in hushed whispers that Etta stepped around—did not throw bottles, not yet. It would come, however. Milan's poisons worked on both sides—soon enough, hatred would be the only bind between two sides driven by fear.

Etta could not quell their fear. She could not soften their anger with messages of hope, not when Milan's corruption had been so well swallowed. All that was left was to redirect the flow of loathing, to dismantle the structure of control Milan had carefully built under the feet of an unknowing populace. A structure she had so carefully drawn the blueprints for.

All it would take would be one well-placed match, something to create the backfire that would extinguish the currently raging inferno.

A miracle beyond Milan's control could be that match. Terje would never live again, but Amaranth could. A digital specter immune to Milan's army, a ghost as ubiquitous as Milan's online persona. The eyes of Germany were already turned toward her; when Etta checked the video on her laptop that evening, the views were well into the millions. News sites churned out articles rapidly, split between discovering details of the gruesome crime and discussing rising brutality as a whole. And Yusuf's prayers were the gold thread that wove the fractured tragedy into a tapestry of shared grief.

She didn't know what had happened to Yusuf. His accounts were untouched, the emails belonging to his legal name as well as his pseudonym filled with the unanswered concerns of colleagues and acquaintances. His death, had it occurred, was not chronicled as Amaranth's was. She was the martyr and he the one left behind.

For her plan to work, his online existence needed to vanish too.

Etta could leave no footholds for Milan to seize. So she purged it all. Every account belonging to Yusuf that she had carefully monitored for years, every social media account he and Amaranth had ever touched, every email or article written in their true names, she deleted.

No digital artifact of their collective existence was left behind.

Then she turned to Wechselkind. She had birthed Wechselkind out of a desire for companionship, bringing to life her only friend for years. Now, she would use that same code to grant new life one more time. Her laptop whirred as her old friend blinked awake. A box popped onto the center of the screen, pleading for uploads to feed its hunger. Etta obliged. Then she fed every picture and video she had salvaged from Yusuf and Amaranth's accounts into her program, stuffing it full of voices and faces until the hum became a distinct whirl. She fed it blood as well, the footage of the attack and others like it. Wechselkind laid it all out like scraps of fabric, waiting to see what sort of quilt she would stitch.

The video was too well known and her reach too small to rewrite that portion of the narrative, but she could expand it. When Amaranth fell, when Yusuf's prayers ceased, Etta tempted them on. She let him continue for a few seconds longer to preserve the sense of hopelessness, the silence before the crescendo. Then, when Amaranth's death was clear, Etta raised her up.

Under Yusuf's prayers, Etta patched the gruesome gash over Amaranth's neck until the skin was clean umber once again. Clips of Yusuf's voice from videos posted to his social media pages were combined to temper the fear in his prayers. No longer was he the frantic husband, but the tranquil healer. Under his hands, under his peace amid the violence, Etta drew Amaranth's eyes open.

Amaranth awoke.

It was not enough on its own. Witnesses were needed, innocents and sinners alike. Etta pulled the footage away from the couple to pan toward the back of the apartment, behind the phantom who had originally wielded the camera. Where there was formerly only an empty kitchen and an old couch, Etta placed neighbors. Friends and families, all huddled together in fear. Their faces were not real, their features an amalgamation of portraits plucked from every corner of the internet until each felt strangely familiar. They were her fugitives, hidden from Milan's footage and silenced by fear, only to be revealed by Yusuf's miracle.

Etta brought them to their knees. She placed shouts in their mouths borrowed from movies or footage of group prayers, layered densely until only one phrase could be understood over their shocked cries: "She has risen!"

Etta left Foster, Monika, and Loulou in the corner, a small patch of black and blood overshadowed by light.

She could feel Terje's warmth over her shoulder, could imagine the faint pressure of his presence over her hands as she typed. His voice no longer moaned in the pockets of her mind. Their time spent working in tandem had always been packed with silence and it was the same now, even split by the barrier of life and death. Terje and Etta, the two who understood only each other and the code they painted, created illusions one final time.

She chewed on her nail as the video compiled, watching the progress bar fill as Wechselkind worked. When it was finished, she watched it once. There were no glitches, no minor dips in audio or misshapen layers. There was no hint of deception, no evidence of her influence.

Then Etta struck her match.

Yusuf's miracle became a phenomenon. The path had already been carved by Milan's original video so when Etta's version dropped online—sprinkled by a new cast of puppet accounts she had created for the purpose of wide exposure—it flooded Berlin. Within a few hours, it had spread across Europe. She watched accounts share the video, noted the view counts as they climbed into the millions, yet it wasn't until she heard it mentioned aloud barely a full day later that the weight of her actions sunk in.

She was in a corner shop a short walk from Wohnhaus Stubenrauchstraße and so far untouched by the riots that still lit up the streets after nightfall. Only one shopkeeper ever sat inside, usually a bored man who spent more time staring at a small television mounted on the wall than at his customers. It was an ideal place for a girl with no euros and big pockets.

Etta had already slipped a handful of protein bars into her bag when she heard them. Two men, both tall and fair-haired with the overly confident air typical of university students. They were at the opposite end of the aisle speaking in hushed voices.

"It's not real," one said. He rolled a can of soup over in his hands. "I mean, it's just not real. It can't be."

"I thought so, too, but you know Helen?" The other man leaned closer.

Etta busied herself with rearranging a disorganized shelf of cereal as she stepped toward them.

"From philosophy?"

"Yeah, the one who always talks over Ben."

The first man passed the can of soup to his friend and continued staring at the shelf. "Don't tell me she believes it."

"She knows someone who was there."

The man's hand paused as he reached for another can. "No shit?"

"She has a cousin or something, said they lived in an apartment nearby and heard the whole thing. They called the cops."

His hand resumed its movement. "There were no cops in the video."

"It was *after* the video."

Etta had not added any police. She was also quickly running out of cereal boxes to organize.

"I mean, he said things were coming—right?" the second man continued. He meant Milan, Etta realized. "He said things were going to change and maybe *that's* what he meant, you know?"

"What, the second coming?"

His friend sighed. "Don't make this a theology debate."

They both turned away from the shelf. Etta quickly pulled her scarf farther up her nose, trying her best to look intrigued by a list of ingredients on a box of cereal as they approached.

"You're talking about a dead woman coming back to life," she heard as the first one brushed past her. "How am I supposed to *not* make this about theology?"

That night, Etta returned to her laptop and Wechselkind. She created Amaranth one more time, sitting on the couch covered in a fine spray of dried blood. Etta added her own voice, dropping the pitch to disguise herself as she acted as an interviewer for Amaranth's digital ghost.

"What did it feel like, coming back to your husband?" Etta asked.

Amaranth smiled under Etta's guidance. "It felt like peace. It felt right. Their false hate cannot destroy our honest faith."

The voice was too soft, too gentle—yet Etta only had so many clips to draw from. That was fine. Only one man would know any better.

Etta had taken care to memorize the faces of the people sharing her hall, focusing especially on the individuals who would set their phones on the floor for the others to hunch over, synthetic firelight flickering across their cheeks. She had listened to their whispers as they discussed the death of a nation. How the blanket of morality had been yanked from under their feet, leaving them to wobble like porcelain plates on a splintered table. Always, the soundtrack to their mourning had been the steady and insistent voice of Milan as his latest broadcast played on a loop.

Two days after she released Yusuf's video, it was instead his voice she heard creeping through the floorboards. The rocking hums of his prayers, his grief that did not attempt to direct them but instead echoed and acknowledged their pain. It was Yusuf's face reflected in their eyes as they hovered over bright screens.

"It'll be okay," Etta heard someone say as she slipped out to scavenge for food. "You saw it—it'll be okay. He brought back his wife; he can bring back Berlin."

The response grew beyond her, as those things tend to do. A few days after Etta overheard the conversation in the corner store, comments hinting at miracles began to appear tacked beside her video. They spoke of mothers claiming their children had risen from moments of brief death, of clouds shaped like angels hovering above the Eiffel Tower or the Acropolis. Injuries were spontaneously healed, legs remembered to walk after years of immobility. Hope and a hint of majesty swelled across Europe.

With Wechselkind, Etta had given the world something to marvel at. The fact no one questioned the video's legitimacy beyond a few known cynics proved how much her false blessing was needed, just as Amaranth's false life was.

Others released deepfakes of their own, though those were quickly disproven. Etta didn't mind. Everyone wanted a piece of the miracle in Berlin. Everyone wanted a piece of Yusuf, the miracle worker.

Etta, as she always did, worked, and watched. As her wave of hope swept across the streets it was met with the brimstone passion of Milan's anger. His rallies became more frequent, the pre-recorded videos that once characterized his omniscient presence evaporating into his physical form—she wondered how quickly he had realized that her disappearance meant the death of her Milan, the man born of Wechselkind's code. Only Etta could create a god from borrowed voices—though Milan still managed to hide his true nature well from a stage settled high above his followers in the streets.

Etta saw them as she wandered the city, heard the livestreams as people watched in enraptured obsession or weary horror. His voice had devolved from stoic sternness into something she almost considered desperate. His hands no longer stayed stiff at his sides but waved wildly as a conductor delivering orders to his orchestra. It was a desperate attempt to embody the man she had created, she realized. A man who never managed to exist outside the boundaries of Wechselkind, no matter how hard Milan tried.

His message was no longer bundled in vague appeals to mankind or truth. "Think of our country, our roots," he howled to bloodthirsty crowds. "Think of how we've been denied our rights to pride in our ancestry, our nation, under false claims of vengeance for apparent past misgivings. We must *rise*. We must deny these false prophets, these violent snakes that threaten to spit venom into our homes, we must take back what is rightfully *ours*."

The crowds would go wild. They no longer waited for the police to move before slamming into plastic barricades with the ferocity of wildcats throwing themselves against the glass walls of a zoo exhibit. Milan would watch them, sweat dripping down his face as stray strands of blond hair stuck to his forehead—his joy in their anger unmasked, even as he believed no one watched him. Etta watched, however, hidden on a nearby fire escape or tucked into an alleyway—always watching.

And she thought of Yusuf. Once a safe harbor in her mind, he had become part of the ache that constantly throbbed in the space between her ribs. Regardless of whether he was alive, his name graced as many lips as Milan's. The soft-spoken man who had showed her kindness, she had wrapped her hands around his ankles and dragged him into the depths of her battle. People called him their hero. They searched for his house, his name—entire forums dedicated to collecting details and conspiracies regarding Yusuf's whereabouts were linked in chat groups, their member populations doubling that of major news sites overnight.

When they could not find him, they instead found Milan—or, rather, his followers—meeting in alleyway collisions that ended in a bloody spray more often than not. It was the rise of another army, one guided rather than ordered. A messiah echoed by his people, rather than a leader who spoke for them.

In Wohnhaus Stubenrauchstraße, the two men staying on the other side of the wall along with the woman and children played Etta's videos over and over—ignorant of their creator sitting only a few feet away.

"I saw him, the derviş." The man's voice carried through the wall. His German was heavily accented. She wasn't sure what a derviş was, but his tone was reverent.

"He's no derviş. He's Sikh." The other man's voice tripped as he attempted to weave the Turkish words into German frames.

"With no dastār? He's a derviş."

"Where?" That was the woman. "*Here?*"

"No, no. By the Admiralbrücke." That Etta knew—the bridge in Kreuzberg, a brick and wrought iron arch built for lounging during summer sunsets. Yusuf's apartment was only a block away.

"It was not him; no prophet would live by the Admiralbrücke."

"And why not?" came the indignant reply. "It was him, his wife too. I saw them when I was visiting Salma and Asad, I only realized now. He didn't have a beard then, but it was him."

The man must have seen Yusuf well before Amaranth's murder—before Milan had risen to power.

"I wonder if he stayed." The woman's soft words slipped beneath the closet door. "God help him, God protect him. Protect them both." Amaranth. She believed in Amaranth—the woman who resurrected their faith.

A chorus of quiet prayers answered her.

"God will protect him," one man said. "God *sent* him."

The words snuck into Etta's mind, tying her loose thoughts about Yusuf into a tight knot. She could see him alone, sitting on the couch amid the stench of his wife's death, sunken with confused grief. He had told Loulou there would be no point in leaving Berlin—had that extended so far as to keep him rooted to his apartment, even as his bed stayed empty and all of Europe searched for him?

Did he know how people looked to him? Did he know what he had become?

Etta rolled over in her bed of stolen clothes and salvaged blankets. From dusk to the pink promise of dawn, the guilt bit at her heels like a furious dog until she found herself pushing off the floor.

If Yusuf was alive, if he had stayed, then he deserved to know.

Yusuf's street was quiet. There was no need to wonder why his many locks did not hold Foster, Monika, and Loulou at bay. The balcony and the window had been walled off with cardboard, shattered glass littering the sidewalk below.

Her hand rose to the door but did not knock. The metal was cool beneath her hand. The tides of guilt that guided her here turned, pulling her back—she had done too much already, dragged him too deep. She never expected absolution, she only wanted to be honest with the man she had once convinced herself she knew, but that, too, suddenly felt like a poorly disguised attack. She would not take kindly to Milan, or even Loulou, showing up under some pretense to explain their murders. How could she expect Yusuf to listen when she had caused him nothing but pain?

The door moved under her hand.

There was no clicking of locks being undone to warn her. Only Yusuf's face, gray and sallow under unkempt hair, there before her.

Etta could not step away. He did not speak. They regarded each other, her cataloging the bruises on his neck and cheeks, him analyzing with a weary gaze whatever marks the past week had left on her.

"I'm sorry," Etta said, finally. It was not enough; it would never be enough. It was a coward's phrase thrown without context for lack of anything better to say—yet it tumbled from her in an endless stream. "I'm sorry, Yusuf. I'm sorry."

Yusuf did not blink. He did not respond, seemingly neither enraged nor consoled by the girl on his doorstep apologizing for crimes she had not yet admitted to.

"You should go." The door began to close.

"Wait." The last door of her life was closing, and Etta jammed her foot between it and the frame. Yusuf's frown deepened. His lips parted, no doubt ready to insist upon her departure, but she cut him off.

"I already knew you were a journalist," she said. "I know you write under the name Asya Aydin. I know your parents were from Western Thrace, and I know who killed your wife."

Yusuf blinked. His hand flexed on the doorknob. He looked to her foot, to her face, then to the clouded sky above their heads. Shivers made a trail down Etta's body as she watched him. Finally, he looked back to her with the resigned expression of a battle-weary soldier.

"You talk," he said. "And I will listen."

38

Entering the apartment felt like entering a memory from a past life. The couch was still pressed up against the wall, a beige blanket spread across the cushions. The kettle still sat on the counter. The bassinet was still under the window. The preserved normality of the scene made her return even more painful. Had the apartment been ransacked, it might have been easier to ignore the pale square of linoleum in front of the couch that was just a few shades lighter than the rest. It would have taken longer for Etta to realize the rug was missing, for her to spot the bleached patches on the walls where Yusuf must have spent hours scrubbing the blood away.

"Please," Yusuf said as Etta stood frozen at the top of the stairs. "Sit."

He did not offer tea. Etta was glad for that. She had not returned as a refugee; she had not arrived begging for sanctuary. She had returned to talk.

She could not sit, however. Not when she would have to cross the graveyard of pale linoleum in front of the couch. Instead, she propped herself on the coffee table in front of the television, where Yusuf had sat only a week ago with the weary, fragile optimism of a man who still believed he could survive the inferno outside with all he loved intact.

He lowered himself onto the couch, hands linked in his lap and shoulders curled forward. While his body showed his grief, his eyes maintained focus on Etta. He was waiting, though he would not push her to speak, not when she had intruded upon his sorrow. Not when they both could feel the presence of Monika, Loulou, and Foster over their shoulders. Not when Amaranth's rattling breaths could still be heard with every creak in the walls.

Etta addressed the linoleum as she spoke. There was no appropriate place to start. The pieces of her life that she had once mistook as solid data objects proved to be cards—as she pulled one free, the rest collapsed into a heap on the floor. She began with a name—Milan— which, at the sight of Yusuf's frown, was quickly followed by the family, the V. She told him of Foster and his hands that squeezed as often as they cradled; of Monika, and how Milan bared her skin and soul; of Loulou and how she ripped people apart only to make them new and call them hers. Of Terje and their little shack crammed with playing cards and peaceful silence punctuated with soft jokes—how it stayed silent now. That it always would. She confessed to her nights spent watching Yusuf at Kerzenlicht and how she had crawled into his life like a parasite to leech off his joys and sorrows. She told him how she had wiggled her way into his laptop and played with his words, how she had later used those same skills to paint riots and beatings over peaceful singing. She told him about Kurt Graves—the small-town actor who no longer even knew himself from the digital impression Etta had made of him—and how she had given Milan a similar power in a voice with no face. She told him how a face was the only true thing she remembered about her father.

Only after she described Engel-Bush Banking and Trading, the tower of capitalistic pride that sacrificed her mother to the concrete below and so fertilized Etta's loathing of society, did she finally find herself lost for anything more to say. The entirety of her life was spread between them, everything she had trapped under a layer of isolation and bitter apathy now exposed to the stale air. No lies remained to guard her.

As she spoke, Yusuf did as he promised: he listened. His hands could have tightened their grip on each other, his eyes may have wandered—she didn't know. But he did not interrupt. He did not ask her to elaborate nor redirect her when she strayed too far into memories of old attics and near-forgotten remarks made by unpleasant foster parents. He was not, she realized when she gained the courage to face him, angry. He was stoic, like an old guard half turned to stone, left standing at the entrance to a forgotten tomb.

"It's a terrifying thing," he said, finally, "believing the world to be one thing, only to open your eyes and realize it's something else altogether."

Etta's hands clamped down on her knees. "I don't know anymore," she said. "I don't know." Because he was right. She had always believed she understood what others could not, that she was privy to some larger picture the rest of society pointedly ignored. But that illusion had shattered at her feet.

"Power in a voice with no face." Yusuf's hands fell apart, palms up in his lap. "You hated this world, hated it enough to help that man." It was not an accusation.

"Yes."

He leaned forward over that span of pale flooring. "Do you still?"

"No." It was true, Etta realized. She didn't hate it. Not anymore. She hated what it housed, what had been done and what she felt it allowed. But the Ferris wheel, the heat of Terje's hand on her hip, the real things—she could not hate those.

"But I'm not a part of anything," she told Yusuf. The Ferris wheel was reclaimed by the park. Terje was dead. Her involvement with life outside the V was limited to the damage she had managed to help cause. She had dived into society and ripped it apart all the way down. "I can't be a part of it."

Yusuf smiled with a gentle gesture of his hand. "Etta. You already are."

She stared at him.

"Your lies, no matter their intent, made me into a prophet—the people, out there, they believe I am something worth their faith—that I can help them, because you told them so." He rubbed his face wearily. "Now you have to make this right, you understand?" He tilted back, looking distantly at the ceiling as his voice dropped. "We have to make things right."

Yes, she understood. To take power from the man who had enchanted a nation into hatred, she understood what they had to do—what she had already started when she released Amaranth's resurrection.

But Yusuf was real. Not the man she had pieced together through snippets of photos and bank statements, the forgotten carrier of truth that would wrap his arms around her and comfort her in their shared solitude. Yusuf Ayden was a man who missed his wife and mourned his unborn child, a man who drowned himself in news to maintain even the slimmest connection to his ancestral home. He was a man grappling with his self-given responsibility to his world, to stories, and the love he felt for his family.

To look at Yusuf and meet the soft kindness in his dark eyes, so bruised with grief already, and admit aloud what they had to do—it felt as though she was another masked attacker in his home, wielding a knife at his throat.

He did not make her, in the end. He brought it down upon himself.

"It's not too late," he told her. "Not for the rest. Not yet. So let us begin."

Yusuf watched as Etta showed him Wechselkind, silent aside from the stray question as she explained how she had created protests and bloodshed out of empty fields and borrowed voices. He nodded when she told him how Milan had inched into influence with the help of a thousand social media ghosts boosting his voice into the mainstream.

"You did this yourself?" he asked her.

"Mostly." She did not need to say Terje's name.

He laid a hand on her shoulder that did not restrain—not as Milan's had—but reinforced instead. "I understand." He did not ask again.

They could create rallies for peace, she told him. They could leverage his newfound attention and create a figure that would rival Milan. They could play on the miracles the public had already begun to imagine, release manufactured evidence to bolster their claims.

"No," Yusuf said. "No more. There will be no more lies."

It felt so familiar having him lean over her shoulder; the string of warm tension she had always felt with Terje was gone but a solid wall had taken the space it left. A support. She tried her best to avoid leaning back into it as she turned her chin up toward Yusuf. "Milan has made himself out to be a god. He tells them what they want to hear. Not truths."

Yusuf smiled faintly. "Milan is just a man, as I am. We will show them."

He had her set up her camera on the coffee table, raised up on a stack of Turkish novels with pastoral landscape covers. They hung a sheet from the wall with a few tacks, letting it drape over the couch and turning Yusuf's living room into an anonymous, empty space. His hands fidgeted with the hem of his wrinkled cotton shirt. The hair in his eyes had been swept back, his beard carefully trimmed. It was not a matter of vanity but practicality. He told Etta he wanted the world to see his face, to see the deep lines around his mouth and eyes and the honesty in his expression as he spoke.

"I can't shave it entirely," he said when Etta didn't ask. "She would have hated that."

He looked lost. Not despondent, or unfocused with his mind trawling over Turkish politics or the edits made to his submitted articles, but lost. Like a cattail adrift on the canal after its roots had been ripped loose by the current.

She squatted onto the floor beside the camera, her hand hovering over the button. "Are you ready?"

Yusuf slowly lowered himself onto the sofa. His legs were crossed, his knees poking over the spot where his wife had lain dead just over a week earlier. She wondered if he could feel her, whether that blank space of flooring called to him while it pushed Etta away.

"What do you think I should say?" he asked.

He wanted to know what she thought, Etta realized with a shock. What she would say, not what she believed he or the public wished to hear. He wanted to know what she felt. What did she feel?

"They won't believe he's lying, not completely. They don't want to admit they fell for anyone's tricks." Etta swallowed. Speaking her mind felt like she was breaking a set of rules she had never entirely recognized her life adhered to, rules that Milan had played against her. Rules like shackles that needed to be cut. "It can be different, though. It doesn't have to be like this. It's all a choice, one way or the other. They want something different, and he's offering an alternative. So can we."

She watched through the camera's screen as Yusuf linked his fingers together and tilted his chin to the ceiling. When he looked down again, he smiled faintly. "So we can," he agreed.

Etta began to record.

He no longer looked lost, not after she pressed the button. The grief remained, the veil of sorrow that muted his expression, but he was alert. He did not waver. He did not hesitate, each soft word laid like a twig on a flickering flame as he spoke.

"My name is Yusuf Ayden," he said. "I speak now as a person. I come to you as myself—I do not claim greatness. I do not claim any level of profound wisdom beyond your own. Yet I come as a man who has suffered. As you have suffered, I have suffered. And it is time for our suffering to end."

He spoke of peace. He did not order but explained, clearly, how their world had grown even more exhausted under the midnight fires and constant shouting. He beseeched Germany to remember their shared experiences, from moments as minor as the burn of hot tea splashing onto their hands to the pain of a generation passed down like a family heirloom.

"We all ache," he said. "We all mourn, but I speak now to those who have been promised peace and feel only anger. This man Milan, he wishes to deepen the divides between us in order to design a kingdom of his own, not a haven for the people. Fight him. Not with knives or bats, but with quiet rebellion. When he calls, do not answer. Let him stand alone and see how tall he seems."

At first, Etta watched him only through the camera's screen, keeping her eyes on the lighting and the way it bounced off the walls onto Yusuf's sallow cheeks. Yet as she listened to his quiet pleas for peace, her gaze wandered up. She looked beyond the screen, across the digital divide, to Yusuf. She could taste the sharp cleaning chemicals in the air, could feel the way her legs strained from sitting too long, and it was real. It was the first real thing she had ever filmed.

They filmed a series of videos, all pleas for peace. Etta did not disperse them through puppet accounts, she did not artificially boost their numbers to push them to the front of any algorithm's attention. She sent them directly to news journalists and posted the originals online under an account titled simply "Yusuf." She watched as the attention steadily rose over the course of a few hours with no peak in sight. Every media outlet wanted a chance to interview the man who had revived hope in Berlin, as he had allegedly revived his wife. Yusuf's videos would be the closest they got.

They began to call him the modern martyr. A holy man tortured but not yet dead.

It was beyond Milan now. Yusuf spoke about something larger.

When Yusuf slipped away to the bedroom with a kind "goodnight" and a small nod, Etta worked. She set upon the phone she had stolen from Milan. She had avoided it before, some piece of habitual loyalty making her hesitate before cracking open his secrets. Now she nearly shattered the screen in her eagerness to access its components. It still didn't hold a signal, but that didn't matter. Everything she needed was saved to its local memory, a river of data for her to dredge: texts about drug deals; long-winded, rambling messages to Foster; orders to followers sent into the streets. Etta cataloged them all. She had a file to fill. It would not prove the full extent of his guilt, but it was enough to spark an investigation—once she and Yusuf reached that point in their plans.

The apartment was silent at night, aside from her typing. There was no snoring as there once had been.

It must have been Amaranth.

Or perhaps Yusuf only played at sleep. She could picture him staring at the ceiling, hand stretched across the mattress as it failed to find the familiar span of skin he had spent so many years curled against.

More than once, she was tempted to press her ear to the door and see if she could hear any muted sobs, but she suppressed the urge.

His grief was not for her to hear, not when he had already reached into empty pockets and offered her—his thief—everything.

They stayed in his apartment for three days. Etta would wake up in the mornings, her cheek pillowed on her laptop, to a gentle hand on her shoulder and the bitter scent she had learned to associate with Turkish coffee.

"You grow to enjoy it," he had told her the first morning, after she'd sipped the black, tar-like liquid and sputtered past the thick grounds slipping between her teeth. She did not enjoy it—she was certain she never would—but when Yusuf offered it again the next morning, she accepted it readily. It was a ritual. Almost domestic. It was strange.

Now, three days later, new grounds stuck in the cracks between her teeth, Etta stared into the swirling coffee and said, "I wish we'd had coffee together. In Kerzenlicht."

Yusuf, eyes still red with sleep, leaned farther across the counter. "You think it would have changed things?"

He looked at her with such an earnest expression that her stomach twisted in discomfort. His vulnerability, the piece of Yusuf she was growing to know, reminded her too much of what she wished she could have had. A gentle hand guiding her forward, someone to catch her elbow when she was about to fall.

"It would have been different," she told him. Because if she had pierced the bubble she built around herself and tasted the air they all shared sooner, she would have immediately known Milan for what he was, rather than soaking up his words the way a man lost in the desert swallowed water from plants and muddy sand.

"Maybe." Yusuf hummed. "Or maybe not. But we're having coffee now. That will have to be enough."

As Yusuf collected their empty cups and turned on the faucet, Etta wandered to the window. She rested one hand on the empty bassinet as she peeled back the curtain and peeked out between the boards.

Then immediately drew it shut.

A crowd was gathered outside. She hadn't heard them, but they were there. Stretched across the street, their heads swiveling as they searched. They looked up, pausing to stare at second-story apartment windows—at the balconies. Etta stilled. They were hunting for the window visible in the previous videos, for traces of death they could follow to the man who defied it.

"We have to go," Etta said hurriedly. She began moving about the apartment, collecting stray bits of equipment and stuffing them into her bag. "We have to go." If they found him, they would tear him apart. Each of them would want a piece of Yusuf as people sought after the bones of saints, relics to store in an alcove after Milan's followers made him into a true martyr.

Yusuf shut the faucet off and strode calmly to the window, peeking out the curtain even as Etta begged him to stay back.

"Well," he said distractedly. "Well. They listened."

39

Hidden in the depths of a warehouse in Western Berlin, Yusuf and Etta huddled together in front of her laptop as if its blue light were a campfire. Etta had stayed there once before and found it too drafty to return to, but now she was grateful for it; the worse the draft, the less likely a wayward explorer would come along. Deep in their foxhole, far away from searching eyes and the hordes that hunted them, they watched Milan's livestreams and listened as he called Yusuf a false prophet, condemned him as a symbol of anti-German sentiments.

"He is everything we have fought so hard to conquer," Milan told the world. "He will try to lure you back into subjugation, into misery. Do not let him. Fight, instead. Show them we will not be oppressed; show them this world is finally ours once again."

So the fires raged on. But hidden beneath the smoke, other people wrote of the man named Yusuf. They posted pictures on their social media pages with their pointer fingers and middle fingers extended, the symbol dual purposed, both a gesture for peace as well as a "Y" for Yusuf. They spoke of help, of hope. "If you need a ride home from work," people posted, "please call the attached number."

A handful of times when Etta strayed into the street—she and Yusuf both agreed he could not be seen, not yet—she saw housewives loitering in front of grocery stores. They waited with phones in their hands and chatted with each other until a woman of a differing descent left the store. Then they would converge upon her with warm greetings, would wrap their arms through hers and act as though they were great friends rather than strangers providing a safe escort, filling the route from the store to the woman's home with bright chatter. They would ask her how the baby was, how her husband was—and when a passerby stared a bit too hard, they would stare back. Try, they seemed to say. Try to spread your hate; we will not falter.

It was not enough. Even as Yusuf's videos strengthened an increasingly brazen network of rebels against Milan's rhetoric, Milan's followers kept their fierce grip over Berlin. Police stalked the streets as those followers scurried like rats down alleyways and dark corners. Every morning brought another broken window or burnt building, another person left bloodied on the street for commuters to find at daybreak. Etta understood why the violence continued. She had felt the comfort of Milan's words, his finality, his confidence—a light for those who felt victimized by a world that had embittered them.

"We need to set up the meeting," Yusuf told her. They had taken over a small office in the warehouse with two yellowed windows that looked onto the lot below.

"What will you say?" she asked him. One leg was crossed over the other, a can of soup balanced on her lap as she scraped at the aluminum sides with a plastic spoon. "Will you confront him?"

Yusuf chuckled. He had already finished his meager meal of two granola bars, refusing anything more. He hadn't eaten well since Etta had found him, always offering her the majority of whatever she served. She never accepted.

"I never really learned the art of confrontation." Yusuf sat back against the blanket Etta had stolen from a stray clothing line. The edges were already stained black from oil residue and dirt. "Amaranth, she confronted the world, but I always thought facts would be enough, just telling stories as they were. I think that frustrated her. She would find this amusing, now. Maybe. After all that time I spent chasing a career in journalism, the world is finally listening."

Etta thought about the woman who had held her gaze and accused her of being untouched by the fires that raged beyond her balcony. "I can see that. How she confronted things, I could see that."

Yusuf gave her a distant smile and shut his eyes. "That's how we were married, you know? Our parents knew each other, before they left Turkey. She found me when I was still in university, we had coffee for months, nearly a year. Then, one day, she said, 'Well? What are we doing? How do you look at me?' Because she couldn't wait forever, she said. She had a life to live. And I realized I had one, too, a life to live with her."

Etta scraped harder at the can in her lap. A life to live. "I'm sorry."

"We were so different," he continued softly. His voice was in another time, his head back in the dark shop he and Amaranth had shared so many sweet evenings in. "So different, yet we match. We balance. That is why I must talk to Milan; that is what she would want. For me to show how two people so different can live in peace. I must become their symbol."

He took a deep whistling breath through his nose before his eyes opened and he looked at Etta. "Not only coexistence, but community," he said. "That is what we must show them. We must show them that Milan cannot deliver on that promise."

Their last video together was taken outside. Etta held the camera at ground level, so Yusuf was framed by the clear sky like a bird midflight. He had the hint of a smile as he publicly invited Milan to an open discourse, if Milan truly believed Yusuf did not have Germany's best interests in mind. Etta knew that Milan would not take much convincing. The fact that Yusuf was brave enough to address him publicly was enough reason for Milan to take the offer. Any chance to step on someone who attempted to walk above him, Milan would snap at it.

They received a message from Milan's main social media account an hour after their video was released, the same account Etta and Terje had set up in some of her earliest days at Spreepark. Seeing the message felt as though she was talking to a version of herself in the past. *Milan has agreed to meet and discuss the reality of our situation*, it read. *Tomorrow. We will send the address two hours beforehand.* Just as they had done with their raves.

The purpose was to force them to wait, to keep the power in their hands and deprive Etta and Yusuf of all their time to prepare. It was expected, just as Etta expected Milan would not answer their call himself. He was above directly engaging his inferiors. To message Yusuf personally would have been an admittance of equal footing. Etta's suspicions were confirmed when she received another message following her agreement to Milan's terms. *Grand,* it said. Loulou.

Etta tried to focus on work after that. She pulled an old desk free from a wall and wiped away the thick dust. With her toolkit in hand, she spread out the remains of Milan's broken cellphone and began piecing them back together. She could have gone to get another phone and sent Milan's into the river, but she felt a sense of satisfaction from the idea of using Milan's phone to call the people who would eventually help tear him down.

Yusuf sat on a chair behind her, hands clasped in his lap as he watched her work with an expression of interest. They had not spoken about the meeting yet, not really. It felt as though they were standing on the beach just as the water began to recede, a tsunami creeping closer with every second.

"Do you think he'll want to record our meeting?" Yusuf asked.

Etta's finger slipped, the edge of the phone's glass screen slicing into her thumb just under the nail. She stuck it into her mouth, sucking away the thread of blood as it bubbled up. "He wants to meet in private, so probably. He'll want to edit it after, make you look like the villain."

"I thought you did all the editing," Yusuf said wryly.

Yes. She had. But that wouldn't stop Milan from trying, even if it meant manipulating the events as they happened rather than in post. He would try to bait Yusuf into saying or doing something they could later cut around and release as false proof of some hypocrisy.

"I have a friend, one with a platform and people who will spread whatever they're fed across Europe," she said. "They might be able to help us spread our video." If Laurence was still willing to answer her calls.

"Ah." Yusuf stood from his chair and approached the table as Etta fiddled with a loose flex cable.

She pushed the cable back into place, snapping the rest of the phone back together and holding down the power button. The screen flickered to life. "That's what I was thinking, anyway." Organizing a video, arranging its release for optimal impact—it was all she knew how to do.

Yusuf's hand fell onto her shoulder and squeezed lightly. He looked at the phone in amused fascination, as if Etta had achieved her own miracle of life before his eyes. "I still struggle to believe you taught yourself how to do all this."

At the look on her face, his eyes widened and he jumped to clarify. "I believe you, of course. But to know how alone you were, the fact that you survived at all would be enough, but to have learned so much entirely with no instruction—it's impressive. I hope you understand that. When I was that young, my mother used to threaten to chain me to my desk just so I would spend an hour studying."

Etta turned the phone over in her hands and looked down into her lap. "Computers made sense," she said. "I didn't want to live in the system that killed my mom, I'm not made for it. I don't have to if I just stick with this. I can be alone, and I can be all right enough."

After it was all over, she would leave again. She had already decided that much. She would return to isolation and, her days of blatant misanthropy over, she would be safe. Safe from the system that killed her mother, and safe from bringing more harm unto others.

Yusuf crouched beside her with a pensive expression, coarse black hair already creeping back over his lips from when he had trimmed it back. Etta stared at him, fearing that he might try to convince her to stay, that she might accept, or that she would argue back and fracture the comradery he had allowed.

"Etta," he said instead. "What's your last name?"

"What?"

A corner of his mouth twitched. "I only realized, you know my name and you knew my false name, but I only know half of yours."

Her fingers clenched around the phone. "Baldwin," she said softly.

His hand rose to her shoulder. "Thank you."

Then he stood and walked toward the space they had set aside for sleeping, the one place where the draft never quite reached. Etta watched him. He knew her name now. She had revealed it without fear and now the last piece of glass between them had finally cracked open. He knew her. She knew him.

She had to work.

It took less than an hour to convince the phone to hold a signal. She'd already discovered there was no passcode to crack, another sign of Milan's arrogance. Pulling up the dial pad, Etta got halfway through punching in one of the few numbers she had memorized when Yusuf interrupted.

"Do you mind if I borrow your laptop?" He knelt beside where she had leaned it against her backpack. "Just to check the news a bit, old habits and whatnot."

She wondered what he expected to see. He looked thankful and a bit wistful as she told him how to unlock it, her fingers punching in the last of the phone number as she turned back to the desk.

The line rang only a couple times before it was answered with a string of quick, furious French.

"Laurence," Etta interrupted.

There was a pause. "Etta?" Laurence choked on the word. She could hear shuffling in the background, someone shouting again in French, met with a harsh reply. "Etta?" he said again. "Jesus, I thought you were my delivery driver—is this you? Are you—I thought you were in some pit somewhere. First all this shit goes down and then I see your name on the news calling you a potentially dangerous domestic terrorist, and I didn't even know what you *looked* like—"

"Laurence." Etta pinched the bridge of her nose. Time had left Laurence unchanged. "I need help. How many of your production friends are planning streams for the next few days?"

"What?" There was more shuffling. She could hear a door latch and the sounds of cars. "Help? Streams? Etta, you just—do you realize we never finished that last job? You just, you *dumped* me! Like I'm just some, some . . . dammit, Etta, I had to contract it out! They took forever, they did an *awful* job—I mean the client is still on my ass about it—and now you *call me*—"

He sputtered, trailing off as the phone crackled. Laurence had always been terrible at lying and his attempt at sounding outraged proved it. It tempted a smile from Etta. She turned to Yusuf, watching as his brows scrunched over whatever he was looking at on her laptop. "You saw the news? The revival video?"

Another pause. Then a sharp curse. "That was you. I knew something was up with that, but I couldn't figure it out—of course that was you. Did you use my program? Or was it yours? Tell me how you did it and I'll forgive you entirely."

"I will," she promised. "I'll show you start to finish, but I need you to do this for me first. No deepfakes, you don't have to edit a single frame, just share a video. I need it spread across Europe fast and I need your network to do that."

Laurence sighed. She could hear him suck in another breath, then he whistled lowly. "She sends me away," he lamented. "Then she reels me right back in."

* * *

Etta sent one more message after she hung up with Laurence. Yusuf still had her laptop, so she sent it from the phone, using Yusuf's account again to reach out to Milan's. *One more meeting, just for us,* she wrote. *The two who noticed each other before anyone else.*

The reply was instant. *Oh, the drama. Where are we staging this grand send-off?*

Etta considered. Loulou had always enjoyed speaking in half-truths; dramatic riddles were the best bait Etta could imagine for luring her out. *The place where you told me your first lie,* she wrote. *Tonight, eleven.* It was about eight.

Loulou's reply took a little longer then. Etta chewed on the inside of her cheek as she waited, wondering what Loulou's expression was on the other side. Whether she was alone or with Milan wherever they had shacked up.

It's a date.

Etta left her laptop and backpack with Yusuf. When she told him she was going out for a bit he lifted his head from the computer and turned to her with fond eyes.

"Be safe," he said.

Her hands twisted in the sleeves of her shirt as she nodded. When Terje had told her to be safe, it had felt sincere, their world in a constant state of flux as they attempted to breathe under the pressure of a dictator's gaze. Yusuf's sincerity seemed rooted in something else, almost familial. She wanted to believe he said it out of honest concern rather than the assumption she needed to hear it after years of being left to her own supervision.

She took the bus most of the way to Southwest Berlin. Curled up on the backmost seat and pressed against the window, Etta hid her face from other riders. The cool glass fogged under her breath, blurring out the world beyond. When her stop finally arrived she thanked the driver quietly and began her trek down the empty streets until the familiar bright lights of Kerzenlicht appeared on an otherwise dim street. It was nearly eleven, the café mostly empty aside from the girl at the counter and a few students staring at books with headphones covering their ears.

Etta watched from a bench hidden beneath a tree across the street, just out of reach from the streetlights that cast cones of light through the evening fog.

Loulou arrived about fifteen minutes later. The heels of her boots clicked across the pavement like a metronome as she approached the café wrapped in a long black jacket. Her choppy hair, for the first time, was dyed all one color: a deep blue that appeared coal-black until it shifted beneath the lights. Were it not for the pale shine of her skin and the steady beat of her confident steps, Etta might have mistaken her for someone else.

Etta checked the phone in her pocket. It was eleven exactly. She watched as Loulou entered the café and stood at the counter. The employee didn't look too irritated as she spoke to Loulou, a cup quickly appearing on the counter. It was swept away as Loulou turned to a table and settled down with her back to the wall. It was the same table where she and Etta had first met.

Etta waited until the display on her cracked phone read fifteen minutes past eleven. Loulou did not move that entire time, only taking occasional sips from her cup and letting her eyes pan around the room with the same expression of bored expectation Etta had seen in other women waiting on a delayed date. She looked nothing like a girl who had recently assisted in the murder of a pregnant woman at the behest of a madman.

No one followed Loulou. No figures lurked under the streetlights or rustled the bushes at Etta's back. Etta hadn't expected Loulou to stage an ambush—not when Loulou enjoyed tests against her ability to bend the world around her—but whether she had told Milan about the meeting was a gamble. She had not, and so Etta blew one last puff of air and walked across the empty street.

The boredom morphed into sly amusement as Loulou's eyes snapped to Etta the moment she opened the door to the café. Etta could feel Loulou's attempts to slice past the layers of Etta's clothes, like a geologist sorting out layers of rock in a cliff face to determine a history of events. She wondered what Loulou saw, whether she could read the days Etta had spent hiding with Yusuf in the black muck that stained her knuckles. It would have been unnerving had Etta not learned to do the same, seeing the exhaustion Loulou tried to hide with the thick layer of concealer gathered in the creases under her eyes.

Loulou leaned back as Etta stood before her, head tilted to the side and eyes bright. She smirked. "I know you," she mused. "That's what I'm meant to say, isn't it? 'I know you,' then you'll tell me all about my little white lie and how much it wounded you."

The girl at the counter looked up from her phone. Loulou winked at her, and the girl's lip curled, then her head dropped back down.

The chair scraped against the floor as Etta sat down across from Loulou. "If I was really pissed off about that, I would have brought it up after Milan told me. Not now."

Loulou's nails tapped against her cup as her face hardened for a flash. Then her hand relaxed and her expression slipped back into practiced ease. The only evidence that Etta had taken her off guard was left in little ripples within the coffee cup.

"So what's the plan?" Loulou leaned her head against the wall and looked at Etta through her lashes. "Confront me about my betrayal? Convert me into a follower of your bargain-brand messiah?" Her voice dropped to a harsh mutter. "Or maybe you're recording this, thrilled to expose Milan's girl to the world?"

Etta laid her hands on the table. It was so different this time. Before, she had been terrified of Loulou's intensity and the way it nearly vibrated the table. There had been a laptop wall between them, a no man's land dusted with biscuit crumbs and trenches carved out of crumpled wrappers. All that was gone.

"Milan is going to die tomorrow." She had chanted those words in her head on the trip to the café and was pleased at the lack of wavering in her voice. She needed to say them exactly, to lay them on the table as Foster would lay cards, each word snapping between them. "Yusuf has proof. The deaths, not just Amaranth but the rest—all those kids from the raves, everyone Milan ordered Foster to kill, ordered you to follow. The drug deals, his plan, the war. Yusuf has proof, I'm going to talk, and Milan is going to die. Not the man, but the prophet. It's done."

Loulou's brows raised. The corner of her mouth quirked into a half smile. "Well, that certainly sounds concerning. I'm supposing you dug up all this dirt just by hacking into a few socials?"

Etta reached into her pocket and pulled out Milan's phone. She dropped it onto the table.

"I fixed it," she said.

Loulou blinked, then stared at the phone. Her hand lifted tentatively, one finger hovering over the black screen before she finally gave it a tentative tap. The screen flickered to life.

"Well," Loulou said. "Shit."

Etta pulled the phone away from Loulou's reach. It slid against her slick palms. Loulou appraised her through narrowed eyes as Etta slipped the phone back into her pocket.

"So you've come to warn me, then." Loulou crossed one hand over the opposite wrist like a cat, her head tilted to the side as the indigo fringe around her face fanned out over her eyes. "Or threaten me."

"Call it off." Etta leaned across the table. "Stop the rallies, delete the accounts, have him disappear, and it's finished. Come back with me."

Loulou leaned in to match, her nose nearly brushing against Etta's as she smiled. "Last time you asked me to come along didn't go so well."

Etta stiffened.

Loulou's smile softened. "You want to ask why, don't you?"

"Call it off." The level ground between them was tilting. Loulou seemed perched at the top of a hill as Etta scrambled against shifting stone to match her height.

"Ask."

Etta's jaw ached as her teeth ground together. "Why" was never the question when it came to the murder—Etta knew why, she understood perfectly how intoxicating Milan's approval could feel, how his words crafted a raft and the ocean to accompany it in a world that required neither. She knew why they killed Amaranth, why they felt they needed to.

Etta reached across the table and grasped Loulou's wrist. Loulou's head jerked slightly, but Etta held firm. There was one question that did need asking.

"Was it always going to end like this?" she asked. "Did you always mean to go back to him, once we left?"

Loulou's opposite hand traced up her arm. Her fingers danced over Etta's knuckles as her eyes turned to look toward the ceiling, unfocused and absent. "No," Loulou said softly.

Etta started to pull back, but Loulou's hand snapped down, a constant game between hunter and prey. "No," she said again, firmer, her eyes back on Etta, "I don't think I'm going to answer that. Think about me like I'm one of your programs—why would I have stayed? Why didn't I just turn you in straight away, why did I help you? You're brilliant, you've fooled the whole world twice over—tell me why I stayed."

Etta tugged against Loulou's grip. "Code doesn't lie."

"And that's the problem, isn't it?" Loulou laughed. "That's why you were so shocked about Terje, why you still trusted me afterward. You know all about codes and algorithms, but humans are your—what did Terje call it? Black box? We're invisible to you, beyond comprehension, so you think about us like we're all programs—like your Wechselkind, with loyalty dictated by ones and zeroes. It never occurred to you that there might be something in between, did it? Something a little more complicated than a yes or no."

Etta said nothing.

"No," Loulou smiled. "No, I don't think I'll answer that. I think that will be my last gift to you. Call it my magnum opus—being the one code Etta Baldwin couldn't crack."

The fraction of space between them was closed then as Loulou dipped forward. Her lips were warm against Etta's. She dropped Etta's hand, lifting her fingers to the curls at the back of Etta's neck as she tugged gently once. Then she leaned back, her coffee breath washing over Etta's face.

"Thanks for the warning, Etta." She traced a finger down the back of Etta's neck. "See you tomorrow."

Etta stayed silent as Loulou stood. She gave a final wink at Etta before she crossed the café to the door. She pulled the sides of her coat tighter around her body as she stepped outside, her nose turned up to the night air as if searching for a scent to follow. Then she began to walk, passing Etta in the window as she headed back to Milan. Back to where she would detail the whole of their conversation, the phone—all Etta had told her about Yusuf and his proof. An ignorant courier delivering matches to the powder keg.

Loulou did not look back.

40

Their last meal together was their last protein bar and a packet of instant coffee split between two repurposed cans full of freshly boiled water. Yusuf sipped his coffee reverently. His hands, unlike Etta's, were steady as he lifted the can to his lips and sipped.

"After—" he started.

"It might not happen," Etta interrupted. "We might need to figure out something else, we might need to run. We could go to France, after."

"Etta."

She stirred a finger in her coffee, scraping at the undissolved grounds that swirled at the bottom of the can. "I could figure something out. If we just get a bit more time."

"This is how it has to be, Etta," Yusuf said gently. She had thought he would grow frustrated after she forced them to take another lap around what had become an exhausted conversation. Sympathy dripped from his voice instead, which felt remarkably worse. "We discussed this. It must happen. Besides, Yusuf Ayden is already dead—for all intents and purposes, anyway. Every trace of myself online, it's all gone. Everything that I was and wanted . . . All that's left is to close this loop."

He smiled wryly. She couldn't bring herself to smile back. She wanted to grab him by the shoulders and drag him deeper into the underground of Berlin, hide him from the world that burned around them. The two of them were walking down a mountain path and she knew what awaited them at the end. Her feet would stop while Yusuf's would carry him straight off the cliff. It was how it had to be.

"We could just send everything to the police. It might be enough." She was getting desperate. It wouldn't be enough. Half the police spent their evenings out in the streets along with the rioters, throwing sly smirks at their on-duty counterparts as they hunted down anyone they deemed "other" with vicious glee.

"I've been made into a legend, Etta." Yusuf set his can of coffee on the ground and leaned back against his hands, his legs crossed beneath him. "What will happen when time rolls on and they discover I'm just a man with faults and imperfections, just as they are? It won't be enough. They need something bigger, something eternal. Something Milan can't change in post-production. Who I was, who I am, must die so people can believe what I became."

All the air left Etta's body in one enormous sigh. "The modern martyr."

Yusuf studied her for a moment as she struggled to take another sip of her coffee. His hair hung like a dark, unruly halo around the sharp edges of his face.

"I have something to show you," he said as he leaned to reach for her laptop. "I wasn't sure if I should, but. Well. If it were me, my daughter—you know we were going to have a daughter?"

Etta pictured the empty bassinet back in Kreuzberg. She hid her face behind the can. "No."

Yusuf opened her laptop like an old book. "We were going to name her Dilara—our delight." His voice caught on her name. Etta flinched.

"I kept thinking—when you told me your story, about your mother, it sounded so familiar. And your last name, when you told me I had to look again, I wanted to see if it was the same because I know if it were me, if it were Dilara . . ." He scrubbed a hand over his face.

Etta's hands clenched around the can in her laptop. "My mother?"

Yusuf dropped his hand and sighed. "When I was younger, ten years ago, I did a few jobs for local newspapers. Features mostly. I was hired to write a story on the stockbrokers who killed themselves throughout Germany on the day of the collapse, a national paper wanted to do an anniversary story.

"In Berlin, there was only one, the first on my list. Anna Baldwin." The coffee grounds stuck in Etta's throat as Yusuf passed her the laptop. "I was supposed to interview a few of her neighbors, get some information on how she was, leading up to that day—but we ended up scrapping the story altogether after, well . . ." He gestured toward the laptop. "One of your neighbors, she had a note. She hadn't turned it in to the police, no one knew about it. I suppose she thought your mother may be embarrassed, that it may be for the best. She told me that it had been in her mailbox that morning, that she had shoved it in a drawer and forgotten entirely until I came around to ask about an interview. I think, in a sense, she was embarrassed too."

Yusuf had pulled up an email, sent from an old account Etta had never discovered amid her hours of dredging through his digital life. She could tell from the message that it was a quick memo with a single image attached, sent to someone she assumed to be his editor.

"I don't know if she would have wanted you to see this," Yusuf said. "But if it were me—if my daughter—you should know. Shouldering that pain for so long, what you believe, you deserve to know."

Etta opened the attachment. Her tongue stuck to the roof of her mouth brittle as old paper as she looked at the grainy picture of a note hastily scrawled on notepaper with the Engel-Bush Banking and Trading logo. She pressed her fingers against the screen as she traced the thick lines and wide loops of each letter, imagining how her mother must have clutched her pen as she outlined her last goodbye:

I've failed in giving her anything beyond this single freedom from her faulty mother. Please care for her, please make sure she finds safety—tell her, when she can listen, that I'm sorry. I was not enough. I do now the only thing I believe I can successfully accomplish as her mother.

"It was her first day back from maternity leave," Yusuf said somewhere beyond Etta. "Her neighbor said she had heard sobbing from inside the apartment for weeks, since she returned home from the hospital. The police had even been called, but they said it was normal, that it happened sometimes. With new mothers. The doctors warned me to watch for the signs with Amaranth as well."

The screen warped under the pressure of Etta's fingers. *I've failed in giving her anything beyond this single freedom from her faulty mother.* Engel-Bush Banking and Trading had not killed her mother. No societal pressures to succeed had pushed her off that building. Anna Baldwin had been lured by falsities brewed in her own mind.

Aside from one anonymous neighbor in an apartment building Etta couldn't even remember, the world had stolen nothing from her at all.

The floor dipped under her. Engel-Bush Banking and Trading and its hundreds of windows and its flat roof were nothing other than a graveyard, a location. A place, as good or bad as any other. Every broken piece of herself that Milan had taught her to turn outward, to use in her efforts to slice the world apart, never had to be broken at all.

It should have felt freeing. It should have been a relief. But instead, Etta felt pitched backward. Every memory turned sideways; all the nights she had spent warmed by hate for a society she thought had rejected her spun around until they were barely recognizable.

"Etta." Hands were on her shoulders, real hands that held her with gentle pressure as she dragged her face away from the screen. "You have to promise me." Yusuf's eyes were wide with compassion, but his voice was firm. "You have to *be*. After all of this, you have to *be* everything. Be sad—be afraid—be happy—be all of it—you have to feel it all, you have to allow yourself to feel everything and all that's between it. I know you want to hide again. I know you've survived so long pretending the world is beyond yourself—but you can't, not after this. You have to live, Etta, after I'm gone. You have stories to tell, even if mine is finished."

It all shattered. Every card that she had built into her fragile tower above the world fluttered to the floor as she bent toward him. The man she had never truly known, who had known more about her than he had even realized—all he represented, a part of the world she could never allow herself to partake in; she fell into him with a dry sob. Yusuf caught her with arms wrapped around her shoulders. The faint smell of lemon still clung to his clothes as she allowed herself to sob for the mother who had not been taken but left, for the life she had considered stolen.

"I'm sorry," Yusuf said. "I'm sorry."

But she shook her head against him, his chin bumping against her forehead as she pulled away and furiously scrubbed at the tears still threatening in the corners of her eyes.

"It's okay," she said. "It's okay." Because she felt it. She felt that pain, the sorrow, and the grief. It was real. It was hers. Her mother had attempted to give one final gift of freedom, even if its context was faulty. She had loved Etta after all, maybe loved her so much that she had convinced herself it was best to leave her behind. It had come late, the pain delayed and bundled in years of bitterness, but her promise of freedom had finally been delivered.

"I need to go, we need—I need to grab some things." Etta said. "There's a shop that should have what we need, it's only a few kilometers from here. I'll be back soon. I promise."

"I'll be here," said Yusuf. "Go with God."

41

The invite came around five in the evening. *Calvaria Hotel, 7pm. Room 304.*

Etta tried to school her expression when the notification flashed across her laptop, but Yusuf knew instantly.

"It's as it has to be," he reminded her.

Just as he had noticed her misery, she saw through his attempts to camouflage his acute grief—but she stayed silent. It was his private grief, and she had weaponized and broadcast it. She had used it, all too similar to how Milan had once used her. The idea made her tremble.

She showed him how to tuck Milan's phone into his jacket pocket, where she'd cut out a patch of cloth to allow room for the phone's lens. "It's already hooked up to my laptop. Just put your jacket on a table or something, aim it at the room, make sure Milan notices. I'll video call you, so he'll see me when he takes it out."

Yusuf cradled his jacket against his chest, his mouth turning down nervously. "And he'll be expecting this?"

"He'll be expecting this. He can't resist the opportunity to gloat."

"And while he's talking to you, I stick this somewhere?" Yusuf asked, holding a tiny, Wi-Fi-enabled camera in his palm. Etta had tapped one of Jonas's connections for it; the whole camera was only a little larger than a pencil eraser.

"Right. Hide it somewhere central. Hotel rooms usually have those shitty paintings, that could work—anywhere it'll blend in. Try to be quick. The phone should be enough to misdirect him, though. He can't comprehend someone outsmarting him."

She helped Yusuf slip the coat over his shoulders, slowly erasing the last pieces of his life from view before she sent him to his grave.

They left nothing behind. All the food wrappers and empty cans were carefully gathered and added to Etta's backpack. Every trace of their temporary presence in the warehouse was wiped clean, only another pair of ghosts, forgotten by everyone but the building itself.

No words were exchanged as they sat on the bus on the way to the hotel. Yusuf had his hood pulled low over his brow; Etta's face was concealed behind the black scarf that scratched against her cheeks.

Police had increased their presence on the streets over the few days Etta and Yusuf had spent tucked away. Etta watched the bright blue lights mounted to their cars spin as the bus crept past, all the police officers milling around like ants swarming an abandoned picnic. Etta imagined there were only skeletons under their visors, their skin and organs plucked out until just the cruel bones remained.

The Calvaria Hotel was a modern building with black brick and white beams that ran up the corners like pale arms held up against a starless sky. Etta understood immediately why Milan had picked it. In addition to its intimidating grandeur beside the neighboring buildings and their classical arches, the sides were completely flat with postage stamp windows. It was a building she could never hope to climb.

Etta tugged on Yusuf's arm.

"What's wrong?" he asked. She nodded toward the hotel.

A group of young people sat on the steps under the lights by the entrance, staring blankly down the street. She recognized Tedmund, Varick, Gustaf, Maritza, Burkhard, and Gilla. Baron and Hertha were absent. Alina and Annerose were gone too. Maybe they'd managed to escape the V, hopefully with a better fate than Johanna.

"They're from Spreepark," she said. They were watching, just as much for her as for him. She could not go any farther.

"Ah," Yusuf said. "Ah."

The crosswalk signal turned green. Neither of them moved.

"Etta." Yusuf faced her, bending at his waist so she could see his eyes under the lip of his hood. "What happens in there, what they say after—you will know the truth. You, me, and Milan—once we're both gone, it will only be you, understand?"

Her nose burned under the scarf. "I'm sorry, Yusuf."

His hands pressed over her ears as if to block out the sound of passing cars and distant sirens—only his voice was left behind. "You don't need my forgiveness; you need to remember that truth. You need to hold it when you're alone, when the world seems foreign again—you cannot be alone, Etta."

Her breath shuddered in her chest. "One day, I'll tell them. I'll tell them everything. They'll know you, Yusuf. They'll know about you and Amaranth both, I promise."

His reply was a resigned smile.

Etta stayed on the street corner and watched as Yusuf made his slow walk to the hotel. The members of the V stood when they saw him approach, parting like guardsmen as he nodded to them. For a moment she was certain her last memory of him would be the thin span of his back under his old coat, but just as the automatic doors began to slide shut, he looked back and she caught a glimpse of his face.

Then he was gone.

She backtracked down the street toward a closed coffee shop she had spotted on their way, its lights all off save for a single bulb over the counter. She hoped the employees had left the router on as well. When she turned into the alleyway beside the shop and pulled out her laptop, she was pleased to discover she was right.

Quickly connecting to the shop's Wi-Fi, Etta opened the phone's stream to a set of elevator doors rolling open to reveal a hallway with stark white walls and dotted black carpeting. The jacket shuffled around the phone as Yusuf walked down the hallway. He stopped in front of the door to room 304. She heard him take a deep breath, and the screen blacked out momentarily. It took her a moment to realize it was his finger blocking the lens as Yusuf tapped the phone twice.

A message for her. They were together.

The door opened.

"Ah, my friend." Milan's voice boomed through her speakers. "Welcome."

Only his torso was visible, Yusuf being a few inches shorter. Milan had a pressed white shirt on, the sleeves rolled up over his elbows. The room was as unwelcoming as the rest of the hotel, with two white sofas set up in front of a large television mounted to the wall. As Yusuf turned, Etta could see a marble bar top with its accompanying chairs against the back wall.

"I appreciate your willingness to meet with me—" The rest of Yusuf's words were cut off as he pulled off his jacket, the action muffling his voice and blocking the lens. When the lens was clear again, Etta realized Yusuf had hung his jacket over the back of one of the chairs at the bar. She could see him in his old sweater with faded stains, his hair unkempt, standing beside Milan's pressed linens and closely shaved iron jaw.

"I thought to offer my condolences," Milan said warmly. "Though, I suppose they're not needed. Your wife is alive anew, no? The martyr, the messiah—your miracle has caught Europe's eye. A shame she was unable to accompany you here today."

Etta could only see the back of Yusuf's head. "Well. You're no stranger to miracles yourself, I hear."

Milan chuckled as he waltzed over to the jacket and plucked the phone from the pocket.

"Hello, Etta," he said. "You're welcome to join us, no need for subterfuge between old friends."

"You're right, yes—let's do that," Etta said, the panic in her voice only mostly false. "I'll come now—or let's reschedule, we can meet again, face-to-face—"

"Or not," Milan said. "Is that an alley? Are you nearby?"

"*Yusuf*—"

"And that's enough of that. Take care, Etta." The connection was cut.

Etta's screen went blank. Her fingers trembled as she dropped the phone and pulled up the camera's view on her laptop. A wash of relief flowed over her. The whole room was in view; the position was perfect. Yusuf did it.

He was sitting on one of the sofas, his profile finally visible to Etta. Milan remained standing—anything to keep his place above the rest.

"I would like to hear it now," Milan said.

Yusuf sat up straighter. "That being?"

"Your peace offering. You're here to broker peace, that's your agenda, your script. Are you not here to convince me to lay down my arms and drop the battle for our natural rights?" Milan spoke as though they were discussing drinks to be ordered. "The false prophet and his grand wonders, here to upset the elect. I wonder how you face me now and play the tragic hero after sending your workers to turn my children into Judas under my nose."

Loulou had told Milan of the meeting.

Yusuf crossed one leg over the other, resting his hands on his knee. "And yourself? 'So it is no surprise if his servants, also, disguise themselves as servants of righteousness. Their end will correspond to their deeds.' Your actions have indicated an end that, I believe—and forgive me for my assumptions, though I consider them valid enough with the evidence collected—is nothing like the end you preach of."

Milan took a step forward. "The Bible is not yours to quote."

"I used to be a reporter, you know. I suppose you do know, after everything you learned about me and my wife," Yusuf continued conversationally as Milan trembled with quickly rising rage. "As a reporter, you spend all your time talking to people, or most of your time. Especially when there's a tragedy. The papers love a good tragedy—everyone can't get enough of them. Myself not excluded. You can't help it—being born amid tragedy you feel it in your veins. You're drawn to the stories where you lack any other connections to your history."

"You ramble."

"It's a terrible habit, forgive me. What I mean is, all that time around tragedies, you start to recognize the people who never belong but appear anyway. Most of them jump to the reporters, desperate to claim a piece of the sorrow for themselves, so they can wave it like a flag. But others? They see control. The so-called saviors. They won't talk to us. Sometimes they help: the heroes passing out supplies to the helpless, kissing the cheeks of the forsaken children, claiming to mourn the dead.

"But they don't care. They don't feel the pain. They only feel the relief in control over a broken thing, like a child shooting a bird from the sky and crying over its corpse. They brighten a bit more each time another looks to them, their shoulders a bit stronger each time someone cries at their feet. Do you know why?"

Milan's face reddened, his lips pinched as his hand snaked toward his back.

"It's okay," Yusuf said softly. "It's okay. They're afraid, yes? They grew up amid so much pain that anything else felt uncomfortable, that they needed things to be broken so they could claim the pride of fixing them. And it's okay to be afraid, Milan—that is what I wanted to tell you. I can see your fear, I recognize it in myself."

The couch squeaked as Yusuf leaned forward, hands clasped over his knee. "But Berlin cannot bleed for your sake. Not anymore."

"You bastard—" Milan's face twisted as the calm façade of a proud leader was ripped away to reveal the fury of a slighted child. He stomped forward and pulled his hand away from his back, the barrel of a small pistol flashing off the bright overhead lights.

Etta's hands froze over her laptop. They had expected a knife, maybe Milan's hands wrapped around Yusuf's throat just as Foster had wrapped his hands over so many necks—but not a gun. They had not expected a gun.

Yusuf smiled sadly.

"No one else needs to die, Milan." He leaned forward until the barrel was pressed between his eyes. "If you truly want peace, if you truly want what's best for us all, you would know—no one else needs to die."

Milan's hands trembled as he spoke through his clenched jaw. "I decide," he spat. "Yours, every thickheaded idiot outside that window—I decide who dies, you hear me?"

Yusuf's hands spread open on his lap, palms up toward the sky. "There's no reason for more lies, Milan."

When she was young, Etta had imagined gunshots thundered like cannons or fireworks: loud booms ending in bloody explosions. Her misconception could be blamed on American Westerns or any variety of the countless movies she had watched over her years. But, in truth, she believed her mistake lay instead in assuming the sound of a bullet piercing flesh rang as loudly as its consequences.

When Milan pulled the trigger, she quickly learned the truth. It was like pulling the tab on a can of soda or the first kernel of popcorn cracking open in the microwave: a snap, a drumstick striking Yusuf's skull, then silence. His head did not explode in any cinematic display of gore. Instead, the moment after the bullet entered his skull, his eyelids flickered. His shoulders stiffened, then slumped in narcoleptic spontaneity. Milan stumbled back as Yusuf's body hunched forward. The wall was left unblemished behind him, the bullet stuck in Yusuf's skull—as though it, too, was stopped short by the sudden force of Yusuf's end. All of his story, done.

Milan took a series of hesitant steps back, the gun still clenched in his hand as he stared at Yusuf's body—palms still facing upward, as if waiting for Amaranth's accompanying hands. Milan seemed afraid, appalled even, and Etta realized Yusuf may have been the only man Milan had murdered personally.

His mouth twisted into a furious grimace. He kicked Yusuf's body as though he were a rat found either dead or sleeping on the carpet. When Yusuf did not respond, Milan stormed out of the camera's field of view. Etta heard the slam of the hotel room door. Yusuf's body was left alone in frame, twisted on the floor like an angel brought to its end by a quick fall from heaven.

Which was as it had to be. Yusuf Ayden was dead, and now, Yusuf the martyr was born. Both would live only in the stories the world told as they grew to meet the people's needs. Etta would release the video of Yusuf's murder alongside the additional evidence they had collected about Milan and the V—the family. She would watch as, one more time, the world turned over, only this time it would not be spun by lies. She would send the video uncut and unedited to Laurence, who would spread it to his network across Europe until its origin was lost to its pervasiveness, the death of Yusuf on behalf of Berlin and all beyond it.

But that was all to be done in the morning. Until then, Etta stayed in the alleyway, the laptop propped on her thighs. She stared at Yusuf's crumpled form until the blood around his face drowned his features and removed the final traces of his identity. She stayed after the battery died and the stream was cut off.

She was the first and only witness. She did what she could not do for her mother and waited, watching until the sun rose in the sky and she was certain Yusuf—wherever he may have gone—was no longer alone.

42

The days that followed tripped over each other in their haste to move forward. The news reports stated that Yusuf's body was discovered after a woeful man—Milan—informed the receptionist he had been attacked.

When a collection of officers arrived at the sterile lobby of the Calvaria Hotel soon after, Milan was waiting for them with a handkerchief and a forlorn expression. An unfortunate tragedy, he lamented. The result of one man's madness—Yusuf's madness—after Milan had naively believed the Turk's invitation for peaceful discussion. Milan had reached for common ground with open hands; Yusuf had reached for a knife.

A tragedy tourist who had been drawn to the stench of blood in Berlin, who found themselves similarly drawn to the hotel by the sound of police sirens, later described to a local reporter the way Milan's shoulders slumped forward as the police shuffled him away.

"I never imagined he would attack me," Milan was overheard insisting. "He wanted to kill me. He told me we all deserved to rot in Hell, all of us real Germans."

While Milan continued spinning revisionist histories into the early hours of the morning at a nearby police station, Etta sent her video to Laurence. Europe learned the truth of the matter before Milan's story had the chance to take its first real breath. Yusuf's death staged a coup over regular broadcasting, his docile pleas for peace spoken down the amplifying barrel of an unsteady pistol.

Yusuf's death was deemed a murder-suicide in the eyes of a mournful public: the murder of Yusuf, the people's martyr, and the suicide of Milan, the prophet—if not the man.

Milan was released from the interrogation room only to be spun about like a child playing a schoolyard game and guided blindly into a cell.

Etta stood outside the hotel amid a furious crowd as the police led the remaining family members outside with thin blankets tented over their heads as though they were monks. Monika was the first to leave, her hands cuffed in front of her as she stumbled ahead of the officers to the police van. Her eyes were still as wild as they had appeared in the video when she killed Amaranth. There was no trace of the gentle girl Etta first met at Spreepark as she twisted in the officer's grip, teeth bared. The others trailed behind her, strung together like a single entity forced to walk in unison on stumbling feet. Separate from the rest, Foster followed. The blanket slipped off his head as he tilted his chin to look at the sky with a hollow expression. Two officers held his arms, but he did not struggle—not even as his head knocked into the roof of the car as they attempted to push him inside. Etta swore he even mouthed an apology to an officer after accidentally stepping on his foot.

The news named the final suspect as Louise Drake. It took a moment for Etta to realize they were referring to Loulou. As she was marched out toward the police van, Loulou met the crowd's venomous condemnations with a sly smile. Etta wondered at her smug expression, whether she had one more layer of deception protecting her from any crimes. More likely, Loulou had convinced herself that her stay would be short.

Perhaps she was right. For a fleeting moment, Etta wondered whether Loulou would try to find her if the police did end up letting her go. Etta wasn't sure if she wanted her to.

The crowd's anger was understandable. Yusuf's death was the

communion wafer sacrifice for their sins, and Europe found itself choking. The people wept, the rioters slipped back into their houses, and politicians fitted their false smiles back in place as they stopped posturing at each other's borders.

"Chancellor Stauss is meeting with EU leaders today," Etta overheard as she watched the police van pull away. "They're having a call. Maybe they'll extradite them, terrorist bastards. I can't believe this happened; I can't believe it."

Shortly after, Chancellor Stauss and the Turkish President would announce the development of a new trade deal regarding automobile components and industrial machinery worth a handful of billion euros along with a renewed effort to reconsider immigration policies for skilled workers. Between broadcasts, reporters would pitch hints at a budding global steel shortage—steel being one of Turkey's biggest exports. No one acknowledged any potential connection between the shortage and the sudden political cooperation. It was peace. It was enough.

When the family's arrest footage reached international news, Laurence called Etta.

"I'm wiring you more money," he insisted. "No arguments, consider it a deposit for future work—yeah? Come to France, come stay with me. It's Paris—you'll hate it, I know—but I have a couch and you need to get out—get out of Berlin, at the very least."

"I don't need more money," Etta said. He had already sent her enough to buy a cheap pay-per-minute phone that morning, which made her ear sweat after ten minutes of use. "And I don't need Paris, as enticing as you make it sound. I need to go somewhere else first, a few somewheres."

"Like prison?"

"I'm not going to prison."

"You're not going to—do you seriously think they won't say anything? Did you even see that one girl? She looked *happy*, Etta. Stuck

between two cops like a bride walking down the aisle. They're fucking—what's a good word?—*unhinged*."

She wanted to laugh and make some quip about how funny it was
that the world was only realizing Milan's insanity through the lens of
Yusuf's death, but, of course, that would be akin to pretending she
hadn't similarly fallen into step behind Milan.

"When I'm done here," she said instead, "maybe I'll come to France."

"You better."

Etta smiled. "Sure."

"I mean it. I'll come get you." And she believed him.

For a few significant years, Wechselkind was her trusted companion. Then Terje and Loulou teased out her secrets and anchored
a tether between Etta and the world. They may have gone, but the
tether remained, and Etta found herself reluctant to snap it. She smiled
speaking to Laurence, even if she wasn't in a hurry to open herself
again. Not yet.

A voice droned through Etta's train as it announced the next stop:
Plänterwald. "I have to go, speak soon."

The phone crackled as Laurence sighed. "Be safe, Etta."

It wasn't a goodbye this time. "Aren't I always?" Then, "Thanks,
Laurence. For all of it. Thanks."

"Sure. I barely did anything, anyway. Just shared a video."

Etta smiled.

Even if Loulou told the police about her, even if Milan decided
his best revenge meant dragging her under the hammer of Germany's
courts, she could at least be buoyed by the knowledge that one person
thought well of her. Not what she had done, but who she was. It was
a helpful thing to know when you found yourself in the middle of re-
imagining everything you had structured yourself around.

She doubted Loulou or anyone else would speak of her, though.
To tell the police about Etta would mean admitting to the falsities
they had created and destroying any last vestige of support Milan still
believed he held. To acknowledge Etta's existence was to admit defeat.

The train jolted as it came to a stop.

Returning to Spreepark after the family was arrested was a matter of knowing. Even as their mugshots flickered across any available television or phone, a part of Etta still felt extended toward the park like the arm of a compass drawn to Milan's magnetic pull. She needed to know he was gone. She needed to see whether the park still held that timeless majesty it had used to lure her inside. Spreepark, she had decided, then the Black Forest and all its false trees.

As she marched down the street, she saw it would be impossible to get any closer than the gate. Yellow police tape was woven between the gaps in the chain-link fencing. Two police officers stood beside the guardhouse, their attention snapping to Etta as she slowed her stroll down the path. They were not the predatory security guards who based their judgments on entry solely upon what she offered in the matters of flesh or escapism. They were actually on guard.

"You have to leave." The one rested his hand on his baton. "No photos either. There's nothing for you here."

It was, as all the best profound statements tended to be, said in complete ignorance of its significance.

"Sorry." Etta tucked her hands into her pockets. "I must have gotten turned around."

The officer scowled. "Sure you did."

The cops had probably spent their whole day turning away single-minded adventurers who had followed a trail of rumors to the park. Etta didn't fault them for wrapping her into the same lot. They didn't need to worry, however. Far before she reached the guards, Etta had pointed her nose to the sky and tried to search above the treetops for the familiar arch of the Ferris wheel, expecting to see it rocking its welcoming arm in the wind as if to call her home.

Except she could see nothing at all. No arch stood as a border between the trees and sky. No red hunch bent to carry the sun on its back. Only a small sliver of rusted metal was visible between the trees, like a finger poking out of a fresh grave. The grand Ferris wheel had shrunk, or, sometime between Terje's death and Milan's end, the world had grown larger around it.

Yusuf had never informed Etta of his burial preferences. She had naively assumed he would be sent back to a family plot in Western Thrace or cremated to avoid the creation of any accidental religious sites. The world decided for him in the end. His proximity to Islam and the nature of his prayers was deemed enough to warrant a traditional service with an imam at the largest Turkish cemetery in Neukölln, situated beside a quiet park on the southern border of Berlin.

It was far from the first service held in his name. Three days passed before the funeral was held and by then the streets were filled with flowers. The fresh snowfall of white lilies that had been left on the steps of the Calvaria Hotel gradually browned, and prayers and secrets scrawled on the backs of napkins and folded bits of scrap paper were turned into gummy wads by the rain.

In Istanbul, people converged onto the streets and wept in unison. France and Italy coordinated to hold a moment of silence. The mayor of Berlin apologized for the delay in releasing Yusuf's body to the appropriate mosque, explaining they had to conduct an autopsy, "as is policy for those who die in unnatural circumstances."

Some whispered that Yusuf's body was being held in wait for his eventual return, locked in the cold cave under an undisclosed hospital until the stone to his tomb was rolled away. Etta wondered whether there would be anything in the casket at all.

The day of the burial, Etta realized too late that she had no idea what a funeral entailed—much less a Muslim funeral. Her mother must have had a service, though if Etta was in attendance, it was far beyond her memory. It wouldn't have helped anyway. Nothing could have prepared her for the streets full of thousands of somber mourners stuffed between news vans and cameras.

Yusuf's casket was mounted on the steps of the mosque and

draped in a long white cloth. The crowd went silent like a midnight in December, the soft breeze sending a flutter across mourners' black headscarves and cotton dress shirts. A man wrapped in layered black prayer robes, his mouth drooped at the corners, raised his hand.

"In the name of Allah, the most compassionate, the most merciful," he announced. "Let us pray."

The crowd dropped their heads and Etta copied as the blanket of the imam's voice draped over them. The words were lost to her. She felt like an extra in a tragic film, stuffed in the back of the scene as everyone pleaded with the sky and sobbed over an empty box. They grieved the character, not the man.

Out of the corner of her eye she peeked at the gravestones, their smoothed stone backs hunched over in perpetual mourning, and wondered where Yusuf would fit among them. She wondered how often people would visit his stone and press their fingers reverently against the grooves of his name.

It was a funeral for truths, the exchange of one perspective reality for another. Inside the coffin was Milan's power over a people who picked their reality like apples off a tree, aiming for those hanging low and red as they ignored those more difficult to reach. Yusuf's death had shaken all the apples to the ground. And it would occur again, Etta knew. So long as people listened, so long as the colorful layers of the world's symbols and facts continued to twist and churn until their hues were indistinguishable, another like Milan would arrive.

She would wait for them. She was a part of it now, as Yusuf had said—one of many. The idea was a strange relief.

The imam's prayer ended and a woman next to Etta sniffled as they raised their heads back toward the mosque. Etta turned to her, her hand digging into her pocket for the packet of tissues she had brought along. She carefully tapped the woman on her shoulder, tissues in hand, when a flash of movement caught her eye.

A figure deep inside the crowd. The only other mourner not facing the mosque, obsidian hair left untucked under a gauzy black scarf laid daintily over her head like a thin halo. Black eyes peered down a straight nose at Etta. One hand touched her throat, pressing gingerly against the smooth honey-colored skin—unmarked by scars. The other hand rested over the swell of her stomach.

While he was alive, Etta had considered asking Yusuf what he had done with Amaranth's body, but she couldn't bring herself to do it when Yusuf still spoke of his wife in present tense.

Now she could hear nothing over the pounding of her heart, her anchor to reality, as Amaranth smiled. Before she could blink, the woman beside Etta noticed her hand—tissues still extended—and bobbed her head in thanks as she accepted them. When Etta twisted to look behind her, Amaranth was gone.

She would never stop wondering whether some trick of the light had created a mirage, whether the cemetery ghosts had congealed into the image of a woman already settled into death. Insanity, grief, emotions that bombarded her after years of suppression could be to blame, a deepfake of her own imagination, yet she found herself returning to the question she never asked Yusuf. She wondered about the grave she could not bring herself to search for.

Any answers she managed to conjure crumbled once she grasped them too tightly. She couldn't stand to hold them anyway. Her world had been tipped, the grass and sky only as real as Terje's projections—every word overheard on the street as synthetically sweet and artificially constructed as Milan's poetic condemnations. Every truth tasted of lies.

Her reality was a flickering cloud of questions layered like feathers on her pale skin—waiting for her to risk a leap.

She was already falling.

Other books by
ALEX SCHULER

Code Word Access
In a near-future world dominated by artificial intelligence, the
country's leading scientist has programmed "ethics" into the decision-
making of all machines. When his algorithm suddenly finds that he
is a threat to mankind, he must go on the run (and off the grid) to
escape execution.

Faster
A story about the birth of self-driving cars told through the lens of
a brilliant but self-destructive machine-builder and the computer
programmer who helped revolutionize the technology, while breaking
his heart.

Rogue
When an estranged father and son find themselves on a terrifying
journey through space, they must figure out what is destroying
advanced civilizations before Earth becomes its next victim.

Stay up to date:
Follow Alex on Amazon